# THE
# DISSECTION
# MURDERS

# THE
# DISSECTION
# MURDERS

A
DS MADDOX
NOVEL

## STEVE PACKWOOD

LEVEL
BEST BOOKS

*First edition*

*ISBN: 978-1-68512-631-5*

*Cover art by Level Best Designs*

*This book was professionally typeset on Reedsy.*
*Find out more at reedsy.com*

*"I am constant as the Northern Star,*
*of whose true, fixed and resting quality*
*there is no fellow in the firmament."*

—*From Julius Caesar by William Shakespeare*

*For my wife, Sue.*
*You are my 'Northern Star',*
*a constant, fixed, and guiding light, giving*
*support, encouragement, and love.*

# Praise for The Dissection Murders

"I was immediately caught up in this intriguing debut novel. I felt like an observing rookie cop watching in awe the way the investigation was handled. I loved the cop humor too. And the end? I thought I saw it coming, but no, I was so surprised! I loved this book, I have put it on my 'Best of the Year' list. Rating A."—**Maggie Mason**, reviewer for *Deadly Pleasures Mystery Magazine*, recipient of the Don Sandstrom Lifetime Achievement for Mystery Fandom Award, and contributing author to "*20th Century Crime and Mystery Writers*"

"I'm a sucker for a good British police detective novel and Steve Packwood's *The Dissection Murders* certainly proved to be an exceptional one. Artful dialogue, engaging characters and a puzzling mystery hit the spot for me."—**George Easter**, editor of *Deadly Pleasures Mystery Magazine*

"*The Dissection Murders* is the debut novel by Steve Packwood, an ex-police officer and a writer with talent, whose book I admired for its authenticity and its wry style and tone."—**Geoffrey Wansell**, book reviewer at *The Daily Mail*.

"A complex plot full of unexpected twists, laughs and horrors. A police procedural with a difference!"—**Anne Cater**, book reviewer at *The Daily Express* and Judge for the Crime Writers Association Daggers Awards

"With 30 years as a London police officer, Steve Packwood is authoritative on the humour, language and relationships in a major investigation team. I thoroughly enjoyed this book and had not anticipated the final shocking twist. Excellent!"—**Des Flanders QPM** (Queen's Police Medal), Retired Metropolitan Police Assistant Commissioner.

"Written by a 30-year veteran, this exciting story differs from many other offerings in this genre by giving a refreshingly authentic glimpse of the dark 'other world' the police step into and out of to perform their demanding duty. This gripping narrative takes you on a journey of jaw-dropping twists and staggering revelations until its shocking and unpredictable denouement. Compelling!"—**Alison Versluys**, Retired Metropolitan Police Inspector

"Packwood deftly combines a deeply disturbing and dark thriller with hilarious banter and irreverent verbal exchanges unique to police officers the world over. The author's voice comes through loud and clear, telling you this guy is the real deal, he's been there. Gripping and unsettling, you'll want more as soon as possible."—**Ken Favaro**, author of *The Three Tensions* and *Real Strategy;* frequent contributor to *Harvard Business Review, Forbes.com,* and *Strategy and Business.*

"A fast-paced, dark, and gritty novel. The reader hears the authentic bantering voices of the British Police, profane, sharp, and comical, whilst being kept guessing as the plot twists and turns to its unpredictable climax. Thrilling and hugely enjoyable. Highly recommended."—**Dr. Alison Satchithanantham**

"Look out for a unique serial killer, but stay for the mentor and protégé relationship between DS Maddox and rookie DC Bennett. This is that rare puzzle piece where I didn't figure out the killer's identity until the end. Bravo! A thriller that starts off as a kettle on a low simmer and builds to a screaming boil. I look forward to the next installment of Maddox and Bennett."—**Gabriel Valjan**, Agatha, Anthony, and Shamus-nominated author of the Shane Cleary series

# POLICE RANKS and GLOSSARY of TERMS

## POLICE RANKS

| Uniform Branch | Criminal Investigation Department (CID) |
|---|---|
| Police Constable (PC) | Detective Constable (DC) |
| Police Sergeant (PS) | Detective Sergeant (DS) |
| Inspector | Detective Inspector (DI) |
| Chief Inspector | Detective Chief Inspector (DCI) |
| Superintendent | Detective Superintendent |
| Chief Superintendent | Detective Chief Superintendent |

# GLOSSARY OF TERMS AND EXPRESSIONS

| | |
|---|---|
| Area Car | Emergency Response Vehicle |
| The Big House | New Scotland Yard, Met Police HQ |
| Brummy | Slang, relating to or from Birmingham |
| Bogey | Nasal debris/or disgusting object |
| The Bums Rush | Slang, to be fobbed off and mis-directed |
| Cab-Office | London taxi's operations office |
| Chummy | Slang, suspect or wanted person |
| Dabs | Slang, fingerprints |
| Full English | Cooked breakfast of sausage, bacon and eggs |
| Geordie | Person from N.E. England |
| Hammer Horror/Christopher Lee | Horror film studio/actor |
| HRT | Hormone Replacement Therapy |
| The Job | The Police Service |
| Like a dog with two dicks | Slang, a state of great happiness |
| MDMA | Hallucinatory drug, Ecstasy or 'E' |
| The Mob | Slang, British armed services |
| The Nick | Slang, a Police Station |
| Old Bill/The Bill | Slang, The Metropolitan Police |
| Old sweat | A person with great experience |
| Oppo | A colleague, friend or partner |
| Played away from home | Slang, having an affair |
| Plod | Slang, the Police/a Police Officer |
| Red Brick | A prestigious university |
| Rugby Sevens | Seven-a-side version of Rugby football |

| | |
|---|---|
| A Shout | An emergency call for the police |
| Skip/Skipper | Informal term for a police sergeant |
| Slot/Slotted | Slang, shoot someone |
| SLR | British Army, Self-Loading Rifle |
| Territorial Support Group/TSG | Police public order unit |
| Tits up | Slang, a situation gone wrong |
| Tyres pumped up | Slang, sexual intercourse |
| A wet | A drink, usually a cup of tea. |
| Wrap | Slang, a small packet of drugs |

# Chapter One

As the door was pulled shut by the pretty flight attendant and the pilot wound the engines up to full power, five of the aircraft's passengers were blissfully unaware that their imminent and untimely demise had merely pre-empted the inevitable. They had already been marked down for death. They just didn't know it.

\* \* \*

The sudden sensation of acceleration from a standing start to the chest-crushing rate of climb was amplified by the smallness of the jet. The young men, so wild and raucous a few moments earlier, found their bodies thrust rearwards into their seats, their heads pressed firmly back, strong hands gripping armrests, and the recent laughter and banter temporarily ceased.

The executive jet hurtled along the runway, lifted its nose, and tore skywards with none of the ponderousness of its larger, passenger-crammed, commercial cousins. The aircraft with its ten occupants had barely cleared the furthermost environs of the small airport when its pilot, wishing he were still throwing an RAF Tornado around the skies, banked hard to port, standing the jet on its wingtip to the great joy and excitement of the young passengers, as he pointed the aircraft eastwards towards the continent.

\* \* \*

Thompson took aim and hefted the rugby ball, missile-like, along the length of the cabin with deadly accuracy, striking the back of Vaughan-Hughes's head.

"*Pow!* He shoots, he scores!" Garson Thompson, captain of the rugby sevens team, en route to Milan to compete with the best of the Italian private school system, punched the air. Osian Vaughan-Hughes rubbed the back of his skull vigorously, scrambled for the ball near his feet, and spun around to search for his attacker, knowing full well that his friend Garson was responsible.

The cabin was filled with hoots and howls as the ball was flung back and forth with increasing force and rowdiness until the gigantic frame of Lynton Fiennes stood as the ball was about to pass over him. With an impressive degree of nonchalance, he caught it with one hand and nodded towards the attractive woman cowering with a fixed, false smile on her face at the front of the aircraft.

"I'm sorry, miss. My friends here are on day release from the kindergarten; they'll calm down now and let you do your job." The hostess's smile changed from grim tolerance to gratitude. Lynton resumed his seat, keeping the rugby ball on his lap, gently digging his best friend Chase Bingley in the ribs. "You'd think these boys had never flown in a private jet before."

Lynton Fiennes's observation was correct. The members of Frankton Abbey School's rugby sevens team, like the rest of the boarders, were from an extremely narrow strata of society: *very* wealthy families. Although many of the school's students were from a socially upper class, the landed gentry or possessors of ennobled bloodlines, it was also a fact that class was neither an obstacle nor a guarantee for attending Franks as the school was universally known. There was but a single constraint on being chauffeured through the archway of the imposing, centuries-old gatehouse, to halt in the gravelled courtyard beyond, to ascend the worn steps which led to the Tudor Hall reception. There was only one barrier to prevent shoes clicking on the five-hundred-year-old flagstones of the former Great Hall, as a lackey carried Bottega luggage or a Louis Vuitton trunk behind, and that curb was a paucity of great wealth.

Amongst Franks' students were the sons of City financiers, rock and pop stars, actors, bankers, crime lords, foreign Heads of State, some tainted with corruption and fewer without. The progeny of industry captains and entrepreneurs sat comfortably alongside the male offspring of best-seller writers or television game-show presenters. As long as it was possible to pay the eye-watering fees, you were in. Even the son of the biggest National Lottery winner ever, a simple man from the grubbier end of Birmingham, was allowed within its ancient, hallowed walls.

The owner of the executive jet the players were presently enjoying was that self-same lottery winner, Vernon Whittcock. His son, Gary, sat alone at the front of the aircraft. Whittcock senior had hit the headlines, as with a bewildered expression and a universally mocked broad Brummy accent, he'd declared, '*Oi just guessed moi numbers, didn't oi.*' The media loved it; '*Didn't oi*' became a national catchphrase, an expression of dumb luck leading to profound success.

The benign mockery by the press of Whittcock senior mutated into sadistic ridicule on the lips of his son's classmates. Gary's father had collected over one hundred and twenty million pounds in winnings, catapulting him instantly into the ranks of the super-rich. With the best intentions but woeful naivety, he cast his son into the privileged bearpit that was Frankton Abbey School.

The hostess held her hand to her mouth and coughed gently to attract attention.

"Gentlemen, Gentlemen, it is my pleasure on behalf of your benefactor, Mr Vernon Whittcock, to now pass amongst you and take orders for drinks." She paused, recalling the words she had been directed to say. "Mr Whittcock assured me even if you are underage, as soon as we leave UK airspace, you've escaped the long arm of the law and may order whatever you wish." The announcement was met with whoops of delight. Gary Whittcock squirmed with embarrassment at the unedifying spectacle of the young hostess's requirement to mention the largesse they were enjoying was meted out by his father.

The truth was every other member of the team, whether aged seventeen or eighteen, was an experienced partaker of alcohol in all its forms, from beer to wine, from spirits to cocktails, and, of course, the best champagne. The reality was they were also frequent users of cocaine and cannabis. The declaration that it was okay to have a drink on the aircraft was recognised for what it was, an embarrassing attempt by Whittcock senior to promote his child's non-existent popularity.

The chance to put the son of their benefactor in his place was not to be missed, and Garson Thompson grasped the opportunity for sarcastic mockery. "Oi, White-Cock! Big wow and *huge* thanks to your father for a glass of vino. *Huge* grats and *huge* respect."

In response to his team captain, Gary twisted in his seat, swallowed his irritation, smiled warmly, gave a thumbs up, and called back, "You're welcome, Cap. Just a start, I'm sure." His eyes fell to Japhet, one of the Gold twins, who sat next to each other on the opposite side of the aisle. Japhet and Jacob Gold were *nearly* stereotypical twins, they looked alike, sounded alike and shared mannerisms and physical traits. Japhet, noting he was being observed, half smiled and nodded to Gary, raising a warning eyebrow as he did so, before turning away to continue speaking with his twin. He completely missed Gary's returned warm, affectionate smile.

The hostess, moving amongst the passengers taking orders, reserved a special smile for the muscular hulk that was Lynton Fiennes, the owner of the only voice that had called out to calm the rowdy, spoiled young men. Her feelings were mis-placed. As she passed him by, Lynton, feeling he'd earned some gratitude, ran his hand up the back of her leg, only a swift step forward prevented his incursion travelling further beneath her skirt. She carried on with her job, her loathing for the hideous passengers suppressed beneath her professional smile.

\* \* \*

The damage to the rear pressure bulkhead, which secured the integrity of the pressurised passenger cabin, had been minor. It had occurred several years earlier as a result of yet another former RAF jet-jockey giving the aircraft the beans on take-off. Holding the jet down longer than required to rotate and achieve flight, the pilot had intended to thrill his passengers with a Space Shuttle-style lift-off. What he achieved instead was too steep a climb angle at the moment he left Earth. The tail section hit the runway with a momentous thud and the rear pressure bulkhead popped from its housing. The contrite aviator aborted the flight, and whilst the aircraft was sent for repair, the pilot was sent to collect his cards and seek new employment.

The airframe engineer making the repair acted in good faith. Outwardly, his fix seemed more than enough for the inspector to declare the mend satisfactory and re-issue the airworthiness certificate. The engineer had made a mistake, the inspector an even greater one.

Over the following years, as the aircraft repeatedly pressurised and de-pressurised, the bolts which secured the umbrella-like bulkhead moved and flexed microscopically. A crack appeared in the fixture at the repair point, a symptom caused by an issue as old as pressurised flight itself, metal fatigue.

\* \* \*

The executive jet carrying the Franks School rugby sevens was cruising at 41,000 feet, as most execs usually did, about 10,000 feet higher than commercial jets, out of the way of the busy and congested skies far below but consequently subjected to more physical stresses. The expanding crack in the rear pressure bulkhead finally ended its three-year journey from one bolt hole to its nearest neighbour. It was enough; the resultant domino effect of failure, bolt-to-bolt, was sudden and dramatic.

The circular bulkhead, subject to colossal pressures, shattered in a detonation of instant, catastrophic decompression. Dozens of jagged metal fragments exploded, radiating outwards, smashing and slicing everything in their path. Critically, all the control cables and tubing carrying hydraulic fluid to the rear of the aircraft were severed. The crucial control of the rudder and tail elevators was irretrievably and fatally lost.

Mercifully, the young men of Frankton Abbey School and the pretty air hostess were unconscious within two minutes of the decompression, so knew nothing of the final minutes of their lives. The pilot and co-pilot were less lucky, strapping oxygen masks to their faces, they struggled manfully with controls which wouldn't control, trying to fly an aircraft which wouldn't fly. For twenty-six excruciating minutes, the aircraft plunged, twisted, rolled, and banked before its inevitable vertical dive into the countryside of France. The pilot's final terrified screams and exhortations to God were taped and later re-played to horrified accident investigators on the black box flight recorder.

* * *

Of the ten atomised bodies in the smouldering crater, Fate robbed only five of long and happy lives.

# Chapter Two

## Eighteen Years Later

**M**artine walked stiffly into the expansive kitchen, dropped the pre-prepared selection of vegetables and fruits into the juicer and hit the button. As the machine squealed and vibrated on the pink Italian marble counter, she stretched out, arching her spine, arms straining above her, fingers intertwined, head back, eyes looking upwards to the high arched ceiling. With a gasp, she let her body relax. Sweat stains darkened the armpits of her grey top, the towelling headband which held her long blonde hair out of her reddened face was heavy with perspiration.

"Oh my God!" she exclaimed out loud. "This must be *so* good for me… because it hurts *so* much!" Martine poured the contents of the juicer into a glass and gulped at it, pulling a face at the disagreeable taste, not a scrap on a good quality, chilled, white wine, which was what she could really do with. Sticking to the fitness regime, half an hour in the gym each morning, a freshly made, healthy juice, and avoiding fat, grease, carbs, and all the other good stuff was actually starting to show results: her tummy was flatter, her hips less broad.

The gym in the annex to her sprawling house was as well-equipped as any commercial venture and, until a few months ago, had existed more for show than use. Her personal trainer, Alexander Cristanou, arrived three afternoons a week and 'beasted' her mercilessly for an hour. Martine was biding her time, keen to develop the relationship further than the professional physicality in the gym and the sexual gymnastics in the bedroom into which she had finally cornered him a mere four weeks ago. Alexander, good-looking and thirty years her junior, was just the sort of trophy she regularly wanted on her arm at the various high-profile functions and public events her status and notoriety demanded. Alexander had needed more than an encouraging nudge to perform his duty in the bedroom and was already pushing back at any form of public relationship. Martine would see about that.

The glass wall slid back at the touch of a button, allowing her to access the wide terrace beyond. Martine placed her juice on a table slumped into the sun-warmed chair, and contemplated the extensive grounds that spread out before her. It was a bright Saturday morning. The sky was a crisp blue and dotted with cotton candy clouds. Birdsong emanated from the line of high poplars which bordered the right-hand side of the vista. The trees were a treasured green barrier between Martine and her detested neighbour, who lurked malevolently on the other side.

In Martine's opinion, that neighbour, Bernard Campion, was a low-born thug, plain and simple. A man who'd made his money supplying sportswear and equipment from a network of warehouses, probably manned by workers of ambiguous immigration status and almost certainly labouring beyond permitted hours on less than minimum wage. His on-line businesses were obscenely ubiquitous, it seemed a search for *anything* provoked an unwanted and habitually crude 'pop-up' to appear on the screen, requiring a hunt for a miniscule 'x' to close down the offensiveness from view. To Martine Walsingham's discerning eye, Bernard Campion exemplified that most unforgivable of human sins; he was common.

When he first purchased the adjoining property, Bernard had behaved as required, keeping to himself, out of Martine's way. The peace and quiet was only a Phoney War; the tranquillity enjoyed in the district began to be regularly shattered by Campion's parties. '*Parties!*' Martine had spat the word. Campion was clearly on a mission to outdo the excesses of Hugh Hefner's infamous Playboy Mansion orgies.

Martine limited her reaction to a polite and restrained letter to Campion from her solicitor. The document expressed *'dismay'* at her new neighbour's *'Bacchanalian Revelries'* and *'concerns'* for the *'tone'* of the neighbourhood in which she *'resided'* and into which Campion had *'imposed'* and *'inflicted'* himself, becoming a *'blot'* on the community.

Campion's reaction should have been wholly predictable when one considered the sort of man he was. He commenced a noisy and disruptive building project on the other side of the poplars. Martine was convinced the required planning permissions had been circumvented by greasing the right palms and knowing the right people. Campion was well known as a generous donor to the political party of Government and a frequent television pundit espousing his more extreme views and policies. Alongside the incessant noise and dust of building works, was the continuance of his wild and scurrilous gatherings.

In response, Martine hired a company, *AirTight Private Investigations*, apparently skilled in such delicate matters, to infiltrate one such event and obtain filmed and photographic evidence of the debauchery. Her intention was to release the results to the gutter press and finish Campion, illuminated in the spotlight of negative publicity.

Martine, recklessly risking her coffin-tipped, shellac nails, excitedly tore open the bulging manila envelope containing the report produced for her by *AirTight*. She was expecting lurid, salacious photographs, in-depth, descriptions of drink and drug-fuelled depravity, preferably with a naked Bernard Campion centre stage, captured for posterity in an improper and humiliating sexual tryst. Instead, the envelope surrendered image after image of what could only be described as a sophisticated and very civilised tea party. Conspicuously well-clothed ladies and gentlemen were pictured seated on armchairs and sofas in the drawing room or conservatory. The dissolute revellers sipped at infusions poured from solid silver Georgian teapots into fine porcelain teacups. They nibbled on crust-trimmed triangular sandwiches or pecked daintily at little cakes served by liveried footmen. The final photograph was of Bernard Campion himself. Disappointingly for Martine, he was not captured enjoying the intimate company of an inappropriately young girl, or boy for that matter.

Instead, he was sitting in a high-backed leather chair holding a very old copy of Vogue magazine before him. Martine recognised the face which adorned its cover, her own, from her 'it girl', modelling prime. Campion's face was peering around from behind the magazine, grinning smugly to the photographer. Martine's humiliation and degradation were made complete by the exaggerated Cockney wide-boy wink that Campion was directing straight at her, through the lens. It was a belittling indignity beyond her experience.

As if proof of the capricious nature of Fate was required, it turned out that of all the private eyes she could have engaged, *AirTight Private Investigations* was a company set up by Campion himself and managed by his younger brother, Clifford. At the behest of the elder Campion, *AirTight* had the amusing audacity to enclose their invoice in the report. When Martine refused to pay, they threatened her with court. She paid. *Every* dealing with her monstrous neighbour brought a new weeping sore into her life. It was intolerable.

\* \* \*

Martine found the adage about vengeance and consuming chilled food to be accurate beyond measure. Through a friend, an associate of her now-deceased first husband, she was informed of the availability of a tract of land. This so-called 'Ransom-Strip' was a mere twelve feet wide but ran for a distance of over a half of a mile on the southern border of Campion's property before turning at ninety degrees to enclose his gardens alongside the wooded area that bordered his land. It then turned a highly satisfactory ninety degrees to cross the access road to his house.

Ransom strips were a device employed by land and property developers to either maintain control in a given area or force the purchase of a small amount of real estate at an eye-wateringly exorbitant price. Campion's people had let him down badly as to the existence of this particular strip and, more importantly, its availability. In a clandestine operation of which MI6 or the CIA would have been proud, Martine acquired the tract and, when the ink on the registry was just about dry, instructed her solicitor to send Bernard Campion a letter informing him of the fact.

The twist of the knife was a now disputed right of access to Campion's property *across* land owned by Martine. It went very quiet for a week until a delivery of flowers, which wouldn't have been out of place at a Chicago mobster's funeral, turned up. The accompanying card was an apology, an offer of a truce, the proffering of the hand of friendship in reconciliation. Knowing that one of the hands in question, the whip hand, was hers, Martine graciously accepted the flowers. Campion was as good as his word; the parties stopped, and peace descended. Martine, however, still detested her common neighbour and instructed lawyers to examine how she could prevent him from crossing *her* land to get to *his* house. For her, the war wasn't over. Martine was fundamentally a kind-hearted woman but once crossed, another, less charitable side to her character came charging to the fore.

# Chapter Three

As Martine sipped at the juice and listened to the birds, she felt at peace with the world. She had endured several heartaches and one very real tragedy in her time on earth but now, right now, was a good time. The ending of her second marriage three years earlier had been a relief if the truth were known and had ultimately cemented her financial situation as an appropriately wealthy woman. Her first husband had left her for a younger model who'd eventually induced a fatal heart attack in him. Their separation was no surprise, the heartbreak taking them to a very dark place, from which they'd clawed out at different paces and in different ways. Their parting was inevitable.

Her second marriage had ended with a financial settlement to add to her first. This ex had been generous, and the separation without rancor. To Martine it was merely her just reward and guaranteed a continuation of the lifestyle to which she'd become accustomed. Martine smiled to herself and took another sip of the juice, not so bad. Perhaps she was getting used to it.

The chimes rang throughout the house. *'Really?'* she gasped irritably. She placed the glass on the table and, using the arms of the chair, pulled herself stiffly from it. On weekdays, her housekeeper dealt with the mundanities of preparing vegetables and fruit, of pressing the button on the juicer and answering the door. At the weekend, her housekeeper was off duty, so it fell to Martine to endure blending her own juice and opening her own door.

One of the numerous control panels set in the walls throughout the house indicated a caller at the main gate, two hundred yards from the residence at the end of the drive. Martine pressed a button, and the screen sprang to life, projecting the image of the caller.

"Oh! Well, hello." She failed to conceal the surprise in her voice, this was not expected. "What can I do for you?" As the visitor answered, Martine was scanning the complex panel, looking for the button that would open the gates, allowing vehicular access. The highly unlikely named housekeeper, Mary-Mary Murphy was proficient at its operation, Martine was not.

So good her father named her twice, Mary-Mary went by the day-to-day epithet of just the single Mary. During her interview, Martine had examined the C.V. and passport, which bore the full-named dreadfulness. Mary sat impassively opposite her. Martine was honour bound to ask. 'Er... Mary-Mary?' The interviewee raised a single eyebrow on her broad, slightly flat face and answered in a soft Waterford Irish accent. 'Me poor, dead father had a deep and abiding love and affection for The Holy Mother', Martine nodded with no understanding before Mary-Mary continued. 'He also had a terrible stutter'. 'I see' was all Martine could manage. Mary-Mary leant forward and smiled, 'and a liking for the Guinness. You can pick any one or more of those as a reason, Madam'. Martine had laughed heartily, deeply attracted to this gentle featured, sixty-year-old. She hired her on the spot.

Mary didn't work weekends; those two days were devoted to her sister and the worship of God. Mary would return at 7am on Monday, unpack a small bag in her bedroom, and be available from 8am each weekday. Martine habitually freed Mary from her duties mid-afternoon on Fridays, to facilitate her journey by taxi the sixty miles to her sister's house. Martine gladly paid for the taxi each way, and Mary-Mary accepted, just as gladly.

Juicing and door answering aside, Mary's weekend absences left Martine with space which she cherished. Interruptions were unexpected, and visitors normally unwelcome, but this one intrigued her. Her only regret was she looked like shit. What the hell! Beneath the sweaty outfit, she knew she looked good, and for her age, *very* good. Apart from just a teeny little bit of Botox, a very socially acceptable set of porcelain dental veneers, a bit of a bum lift, and a pair of extremely discrete breast implants, Martine was just as Mother Nature had made her.

Identifying the button, she pressed it, and two hundred yards away, the ornate gates rolled back to allow the vehicle entry. The cameras overlooking the gate didn't record the car's registration number nor the facial features of the driver. The closed-circuit system for the house likewise failed to record the details of the visitor or imprint any visual trace. The advanced and exorbitantly expensive security systems had been bypassed and subverted. Only Martine's eyes were watching, only her brain making a recording.

Martine waited at the open front door as the car curved around the low-walled island, coming to a stop next to the steps of the entrance. Wishing she'd taken a shower as soon as she'd finished her work-out, she was conscious of her red cheeks and multiple sweat stains, nevertheless she gave her best polite smile to her visitor. "You've caught me looking my best!" She flicked her hair from side to side, a parody of a hundred shampoo advertisements.

"Everyone has the right to let it all hang out in their own home." The visitor reassured.

Martine shrugged. "Come in, I'll make coffee, and then you can tell me what I've done to deserve your presence." The visitor laughed, bounded up the steps, and followed Martine into her house.

The coffee maker was proving its worth and Martine was delighted she'd invested some time with Mary to understand its workings. Conversation was light, easy and humourous but Martine was waiting for the punchline, she speculated on what it would be, excited at the possibilities but retaining a degree of reserve until she knew for sure what was happening here.

"Shall we sit on the terrace? It's so nice outside, so *peaceful*." Martine invited, the last word was barbed, the recent history of dispute and unpleasantness still rankled. Martine had trouble letting it go.

"Why not? It really *is* such a lovely day."

Martine didn't reach the threshold. She felt a pressure on the right side of her neck, a hand gripping her ponytail, and within a moment, the world started to change. It was difficult to describe but the universe felt thick somehow, the air around her had acquired a density, light seemed weighted and then it all folded inwards and the floor charged towards her.

"You've just received an injection of Ketamine." The voice sounded deep as it oscillated back and forth from the far distance to close by. Martine was aware she was lying on the marble tiled floor, the slabs were cold, the ceiling seemed to be as far away as distant space.

"I've calculated and measured the dosage for you very carefully; you've slipped into what the urban dictionary calls a 'K-Hole.' Your body and mind should feel as if they've separated. Can you feel that?" Martine heard the voice and understood the words, but the otherworldly sensations she was experiencing prevented her from properly processing their meaning. She tried to answer, only a gurgle fell from her lips, but she knew she'd asked 'why?'

"Your body is paralysed but you'll remain conscious, I want you conscious, I need you to be able to hear me, understand what I'm saying and most of all understand what I'm doing to you." Martine's world was a mental landscape of shuddering, undulating shapes, sounds, and feelings, but she could hear, she could understand, and she was stricken with fear and dread. Again, she tried to speak, the result the same as before, but the visitor knew, understood instinctively.

"You're asking 'why' aren't you? I know that's what you're asking. Well, I'm going to tell you, I *want* you to know why." Martine felt hands tugging at her clothing, the freezing sensation of the cold floor intensified, she knew she'd been stripped and her flesh was bare and vulnerable. Naked, bewildered, and terrified, she waited. The visitor held the scalpel, flourished it in Martine's eyeline.

"Can you see this?" The blade swept slowly back and forth across Martine's field of vision, metronome-like, counting seconds. Counting down. "It's time to get started." Martine tried to move; she sent messages to every part of her body. Move! Escape! Do something! Her body remained inert.

"I'll talk as I work. Here it comes, ready or not!"

Martine felt the blade enter her abdomen, and the cutting and slicing began. The horror wasn't the pain, there was no pain, just a tugging sensation and a coldness. The horror was she knew she was being dissected, dissected whilst alive.

# Chapter Four

**M**ary-Mary Murphy smiled at the waiting taxi driver and turned to face the control panel on the tall brick pillar next to the wrought iron gates. It was exactly 6.45am on Monday morning. She methodically pressed a series of numbers and letters, and the gates rolled back. Mary-Mary resumed her seat for the short ride to the front door of the house, exited, and waved the driver farewell. Her day was going to be like any other Monday, she would go to her room, unpack her small suitcase, prepare and consume a light breakfast for herself and then begin her duties for Miss Martine at 8am.

Lately the mistress of the house was indulging in one of her periodic fitness fads, this one involved stalking back and forth in her gym for twenty minutes, mentally preparing herself for exercise, before actually doing something for ten minutes. This sometimes involved a degree of effort that resulted in perspiration and sometimes didn't. What definitely did involve a lot of perspiration was Miss Martine's thrice weekly rutting session with her personal trainer, Alexander. Poor lad! Several times, Mary had caught sight of his fleeting expression of self-pity mixed with gritty resolve as he was dragged to the bedroom to perform with a woman a decade older than his mother. The mistress wasn't an unattractive woman, not for her age anyway, but Mary's view of Martine Walsingham was that, as with her life, her body's best bits were now behind her.

Mary viewed the dalliance with the good-looking fitness instructor as the mistress's desperate attempt to cling to her youth and preserve her desirability. Realistically, she hit one out of two, but not for the reasons she imagined. Her youth and beauty may have waned, even with the help of Botox, silicone, and the surgeon's knife, but the desirability of the multi-millionairess Martine Walsingham still had legs. After all, she was a reasonably well-known socialite, sometime television pundit, and long-time darling of the illuminati of chic. Although faded, there was still something to be gained from Martine. Mary's opinion was young Alexanders' sexual performances could only be part of a long-term plan, a door to be opened by Martine onto a new world as a celebrity trainer to the stars. Why else, she reasoned, would he put himself through the grunting, groaning, screaming, and thrashing about each Monday, Wednesday, and Friday afternoon? Mary tutted to herself; she'd need to put the sheets in for a wash after today's matinee performance.

Mary slid her pass card down the slot next to the front door and heard the click of the locks rolling back. Crossing the entrance hall she was aware of a draft, a soft breeze on her face, she shrugged mentally and walked the corridor to the right, which led to her private quarters. Martine had her faults, Holy Mary, Mother of God, she really *did* have her faults but meanness and lack of consideration for her housekeeper did not number amongst them. Mary had a large bedroom with a walk-in wardrobe, an en-suite bathroom, and a sitting room equipped with a state-of-the-art television with access to more channels than she had years on this planet, few of which were worth watching.

Her life was comfortable and lucrative. Mary received a generous salary, paid nothing for food and board, and the cost of her weekly taxi to her sister's was also met by Miss Martine. The mistress was not unknown to provide gifts on the spur of the moment, for no better reason than, *'Oh I saw this and thought you'd like it'*. Mary-Mary Murphy was convinced that Mistress Martine was doomed to spend eternity in the fires of hell for her lack of Faith, the debaucheries of the flesh, and flagrant breaches of the Seven Sins, but she took no pleasure in this knowledge, especially when contrarily she could show such kindness. Consequently, Mary committed some of her devotions each weekend to praying for the soul of Martine Walsingham, praying that she would mend her sinful ways, praying that

Hell didn't await her, perhaps just a few millennia in Purgatory to reflect would be fair, before taking her place in Paradise, after all, there was a great deal of good in her.

Fifteen minutes later, Mary was dressed in her housekeeper's garb, an immaculately starched and ironed white apron over a dark blue dress and hair tied up in a neat bun. She headed toward the kitchen; the draught was there again, stronger as she got nearer. It crossed her mind that the mistress may have already risen and opened the high, wide, sliding glass doors to the terrace; it would explain the breeze. Mary moved through the open-plan hall to the rear of the house; the first thing she noted confirmed her suspicions. The glass wall was open wide, she saw a tumbler half full of the atrocious mix of juiced fruit and vegetables which were part of the current regime, resting outside on the terrace table.

"Miss Martine? Miss Martine?" She called, not too loudly, if she were mistaken and the mistress was still asleep she wouldn't take kindly to her housekeeper shouting out like a docker. Mary smiled, everyone who raised their voice, for any reason, was described as a docker by the mistress, she was such a snob.

Mary saw the bare feet first. The breakfast table and chairs obscured the full view. Two feet, far apart, toes angled upwards. Mary rushed forward to help. The sight revealed itself in its totality. Miss Martine was naked. Lying on her back. Her arms spread wide, crucifix-like. The dark red pool of dried blood lay beneath her body like a rug. So much blood. But all Mary could see was the gaping hole that was her abdomen. The flesh was cut and peeled back, folded out to display the hollow horror within. Mary's hands rushed to her face, her fingers splayed out, trying and *not* trying simultaneously to hide the vision before her. She saw through the gaps with wide eyes, unable to tear her gaze away. It *was* Miss Martine; that much was obvious. It *must* be Miss Martine; who else could it be? Even though her features were hidden. Hidden beneath some abomination lying across her face but it *was* her, it *had* to be her.

Mary screamed and screamed and screamed.

# Chapter Five

Detective Sergeant Grant Maddox knew all about tiredness. He'd learned to accept fatigue throughout his Royal Marines service, fighting a war in the far-flung Falklands in what the press kept calling a 'conflict' and during two deployments in Northern Ireland in what the same people euphemistically called 'The Troubles.' Grant had discovered what exhaustion was and how to carry on and work through it, but back then, he had youth and physical fitness on his side. That was thirty years ago.

The tall, balding, slightly overweight figure he now was, with great effort, heaved itself out of the car and staggered to his front door, key in hand, thinking only of bed. It was dark, and he'd been awake for over twenty-three hours. How he'd completed the forty-minute drive home without crashing his car, he'd no idea. Extreme tiredness manifested itself in the guise of drunkenness, and he felt as if he'd had a heavy night out on the town.

Although long, the day had been successful. If you could glibly apply that word to the domestic tragedy of Grace and Melvin O'Hara. Grace's body bore the signs of her torment, great clumps of hair and scalp torn from her head, shattered teeth, crushed eye sockets, imprints on her face from the boots which had stamped, kicked and deformed her skull. It was a sight he'd seen many times in various forms, his reaction was as consistent as the conveyor belt of domestic killings, one of revulsion, fury, and sorrow.

Melvin had been traced to an address in the early evening. A covert observation had been mounted whilst Grant obtained an entry warrant, organized the specialist team to pry open the reinforced door, and several firearm officers to make the initial entry, a rare necessity in England, but Melvin O'Hara reportedly had access to a shotgun. He arranged for Territorial Support Group Officers to initiate and hold a cordon, dog handlers to deal with the ubiquitous pit bull terrier, which was within, and sundry other resources needed to ensure a safe and successful arrest.

The hours of preparation had rolled into the night and, thence, the early morning. Grant had given his briefing for the operation before 4am, smiling broadly when he saw an old friend from his time as a Sergeant on the armed response unit was in charge of the firearms team. Babatunde Okafor, of Nigerian heritage, was born and raised in Paddington and joined the firearms department as a constable three years after Grant. Grant was immediately drawn to the huge new recruit who was funny, intelligent, enthusiastic, willing to listen and learn, and who promised to be a good bloke to have around or at least hide behind. Six feet, six inches tall, and with a chest so wide it reputedly spanned two time zones, Babs presented a formidable sight. When Grant left firearms to join the CID, the newly promoted Sergeant Okafor naturally took Grant's place and was in charge of his team.

Grant knew that with Babs on scene, at least the armed side of the operation would be dealt with professionally and efficiently. If only this were true of the officer ostensibly in charge, Detective Inspector Brian 'Doddy' Dodds. "I'm sorry, Granty," his old friend and boss, Detective Chief Inspector Paul Winter, had uttered with genuine regret. "I know he's useless but he *is* a Detective Inspector, he *has* to be nominally in charge of the op, even if it's you doing everything. In fact, I insist you do everything, let him prance around like an idiot feeling in control, but for God's sake, don't let him make any decisions. Remember the dying declaration incident?"

Grant did indeed remember the case Paul Winter was referring to. Doddy's most famous cock-up to date concerned a stabbing victim, critically injured but still capable of providing a statement naming his attacker; he was left alone in his hospital bed overnight. 'It's late, everyone's tired, he can give a statement in the morning', Doddy had announced. 'Are you *sure*, Guv?' a lowly Detective Constable had asked. 'His condition is critical;

shouldn't we get a 'dying declaration' down on paper, just in case? It'll be admissible in court.' Doddy, faced with what he considered a mutiny had snapped brusquely, 'I said in the *morning!*' Of course, the stabbing victim died overnight, and *all* his evidence with him.

Grant had smiled reassuringly at the DCI, "don't worry Guv, thankfully he's content to fluster and bluster and let everyone else do the work, I'll let him feel he's in command, I won't let him rock the boat."

"You're a good man, Granty. I'll never understand why you stopped at sergeant, having idiots like Doddy and me senior to you! How do you cope?" Paul laughed and slapped his DS's shoulder.

"You know as well as I do every promotion takes you one step away from the job you joined to do. I'd go crazy having to juggle personalities and petty jealousies, the press, senior officers, budgets, and God knows what else like you do. Leave me to a nice, respectable murderer any day of the week."

The arrest of Melvin O'Hara had been made with relatively little trouble, the only casualty being a dog handler who'd exited the target house with a pit bull terrier hanging off the arm of his padded protective suit, shaking its head and snarling ferociously, to be deposited harmlessly in a confinement cage. Despite the armour the power of the dog's jaws had caused bruising to the officer who'd raised a laugh with his sincere exhortation, "fuckin' 'orrible things Pit Bulls, hairy sharks, that's all they are."

\* \* \*

Grant unlocked his front door and entered the hallway, dropping the car keys in a dish, kicking his shoes into the corner, and immediately ascending the stairs. Light seeped from under the door of the back bedroom, and he heard a soft female voice talking gently from within. He tapped the door with his fingernails, the slightest of sounds to show he was there.

"S'okay, come in." A soft, hushed feminine voice. Grant pushed the door and took in the sight of his eldest daughter Constance seated in a high-backed chair in the corner. Connie held Grants granddaughter, Saffron, at her shoulder, alternating between patting her back and rubbing it in small circles, he saw the empty baby-bottle on the table beside her. "Just waiting for a little bit of wind, then we're back down," Connie whispered, her face a smile. Just at that moment, a belch of incongruous depth and volume escaped baby Saffy's lips. Grandfather and daughter stifled their laughter, not wishing to stir the child as she drifted back to sleep.

"Good grief! Where did she park her lorry?" Grant murmured softly, causing Connie to stifle more laughter. Grant couldn't help himself, he took the short steps to the corner and placed his large hand ever so carefully on his granddaughter's head, encircling it. He felt the softest, finest blonde hair and the warmth of the skin in his palm and, not for the first time, wondered in awe that everything this child would ever think of, hope for, or feel was held, encompassed within his single hand. For a moment, the unwelcome image of Grace O'Hara's despoiled head intruded into his thoughts, the knowledge that once upon a time, she too had been like this baby, her whole life before her, not knowing how terrible the last line of that story would be. Grant forced the image away into the recesses of his mind to join the multitude of other horrors filed away there, where the reality of his other world dwelt. The exhaustion of the day melted as his powerful love for this baby overwhelmed him for a moment, and he felt his eyes well up.

"Daddy, you look terrible. Are you alright?" Connie reached out and placed her hand on her father's arm.

"Just tired. Everything's fine; I need to sleep, that's all."

Grant smiled weakly, bent slightly, and kissed the top of Connie's head. He never burdened either of his daughters with the other world in which he lived part of the time. He viewed his family life as an impermeable space, somewhere separate and unconnected with the dark, sometimes evil place his job took him to. In the past, he'd talked to his wife of some experiences, the war he fought on the opposite side of the planet as an eighteen-year-old boy, but he never told of the full horrors he'd seen, and certainly not of the horror he'd committed, which still haunted him. In the early police years, he'd sometimes unburdened himself to her, but she couldn't truly understand; it was unfairly saddling her with issues he should face alone.

The watershed moment was the shooting in the shopping mall and feeling the need to unload, for his own sake, about that day. He should have kept it to himself. It was the final straw for his wife. She came close to a breakdown. He resigned from the firearms department within a week. Now, he strictly limited himself to telling the stories that were funny, interesting, or absurd. As for his youngest daughter, so recently enrolled in the ranks of The Met, well, she would experience the other world herself soon enough, in all its grimness, and she too would learn to leave it outside the front door as he had.

Grant Maddox was imbued with an overwhelming duty to protect. To safeguard his family first and the weak and vulnerable of his city and country next. The drive to protect had driven him to sprint across the Falls Road in West Belfast to render first aid to a fallen comrade, knowing the sniper who'd shot him was still out there. It was the duty which made him use his own body as a shield, to protect a wounded comrade as bullets whistled past on the slopes of Mount Harriet in the South Atlantic. Grant Maddox was as likely to shed his duty to protect others as he was to shed his own skin. It would never happen.

Grant had many qualities, but it was his intrinsic need to protect that made him truly stand out from others. Lydia, his wife of nearly thirty years, recognised this along with other virtues and on occasion, to his utter embarrassment, would tap his forehead with an extended finger, parodying a scene from Spielberg's E.T. and declare that Grant was 'Goooooooood'. It almost always brought a tear to his eye; that's why she did it.

The welfare of his family was paramount and always would be. He was fifty-one years old, he *could* retire in two years' time, take his pension and bow out gracefully. But the break-up of Connie's marriage, deserted by her scum-bag husband only weeks before Saffy's birth, and the burden of financially supporting them both had kicked the prospect of retirement into the long grass. He wouldn't be walking away any time soon.

Grant didn't mind on two counts. He would work until his last day on earth if his family needed it, no question and furthermore, no resentment. Secondly, he enjoyed his work, even the horror of some aspects. He thought he could make a difference, that he could do something well that was difficult, something many others couldn't do at all. During his promotion interview, he'd been asked what his hobbies and interests were, and his one-word answer had raised a smile. 'Family', he'd said.

In the peaceful shadows of Connie's bedroom, when his daughter pressed the point, she squeezed his arm and asked again. *"Really,* Daddy, are you sure you're okay?"* There was never any question that Grant Maddox would say anything other than,

"Just tired, sweetie. Thanks for asking. I'm off to bed. Love you."

# Chapter Six

Paula Bingley was a mess. She knew it. She also knew and took comfort from the knowledge that she was a *nearly* functioning mess. The 'nearly' was very important to her. It meant that although every day her condition was degenerating and spiralling, her fall was slow and gradual. In her mind, she pictured her life as a steep mountainside slope upon which she clung precariously. Looking up, she could see the gradient stretching higher, towards a clear blue sky, the happy place that had once been her life. A glance down the slope, dropping away, plummeting into darkness, revealed only a black void far below. Paula was perched on that incline, hanging on by her fingertips, sliding down, slipping but ever so slowly.

Her descent into the murky abyss had started many years before. All *had* been well in Paula Bingley's world. Then it happened.

People have different ways of dealing with things. Her husband threw himself into his work, excessively long hours, endless meetings, scrutinising details, examining the big picture, making decisions. He deliberately crammed his mind, packed it with the policies that could make or break an international company that employed thousands, and crowded it with the intricate minutiae he should have been delegating. It was his way. It was how *he* coped. It worked for him. For Paula, there was the empty house. There was the empty room. There were the memories, the self-recriminations, the if only's, the wishing, wishing, wishing for a way to relive and so re-order *that* day.

She'd started to slip down the mountainside slope, leaving the happy place far above, now out of reach. Because she started so high, because the slope down to the bottom was so long, she knew it would take a great deal of time to arrive there. That's what she meant when she judged herself as nearly functioning. Paula Bingley hadn't tumbled, falling uncontrollably headlong into a pit of helpless drug abuse, nor of destitution, homelessness, physical decay, and death. That would come, she was intelligent enough to know she would arrive at that destination eventually, but not yet.

*  *  *

Paula's ex-husband was gone from her day-to-day life, he'd found a younger model, blonde haired, trout-pouted, air-headed, supplied and fitted with pneumatic tits. Crucially for her ex-husband, Paula's replacement didn't cry all day, *every* day. She didn't smash her head into mirrors, she didn't tear her hair out, she didn't curl up in a ball on the floor and scream until her throat bled, she didn't guzzle pills, washed down with copious quantities of wine, her super-flat, toned and tanned stomach hadn't been pumped out, time after time.

However, her ex-husband, Damian, *was* still a presence in her life, though a distant, disembodied one. The third-floor apartment in the chic, West London Art-Deco block was hers. Damian had bought it for her. He paid the staggering monthly management charges; he paid all the utility bills, and he put a monthly allowance into a bank account for her. His duty done to the woman he'd once loved, he cut actual contact with her out of his life.

*  *  *

It was the first of the month. She tapped the numbers on the ATM, and a glowing screen appeared, showing that her allowance had been deposited; she sighed with relief. Each month she feared the green 'enter' button would cause the display to coalesce into Damian's face, emotionless, implacable, his lips forming into a disapproving snarl and pronouncing, *'No more, that's it.'*

Paula was at the lower end of the previous night's high. It made her paranoid; she knew that about herself, too. Paula Bingley was full to the brim with self-knowledge. Knowing she'd withdraw £120 cash from the ATM, knowing she'd head straight to the trendy coffee bar not two hundred yards away. Knowing she would nurse an over-priced, and pretentiously titled, cup of coffee and wait until Anil turned up. She knew she'd hand over £100 cash to her smiling supplier for the wraps of heroin and then scamper eagerly back to her apartment to slip another few feet down the slope of her mountainside. Paula Bingley knew it all.

\* \* \*

Paula was feeling especially unwell today, even prompting a question about her health from Anil as he passed the drugs under the table to her eager fingers. The short return journey from the coffee bar took her longer than usual. She stopped at the foot of the steps to her apartment block entrance, taking a deep breath before beginning the ascent, which appeared particularly challenging today. After only two steps of the ten, which led to the doors of the plush, carpeted lobby, she heard a voice from behind her.

"Paula. Paula Bingley?" Paula froze, a shudder passed like a wave through her body and she began to shake, her paranoia attaching a police officer to the voice. She turned slowly to face the consequences.

"*Paula Bingley. I have grounds to suspect you are in possession of a controlled drug. Namely heroin. You are under arrest.*" The shaking became uncontrollable. It wasn't the arrest, it wasn't the personal shame, it wasn't the disgrace she'd bring on the high-profile name of her industrialist ex-husband. Her dread was her detention would prevent her from taking the drugs hidden deep in the inside pocket of her jacket.

"*Paula!* Are you alright?" Paula shook her head focussing on the enquirer. The police officer dissolved, returning to the haunted depths of her addled imagination.

"Are you feeling alright? You look shaken up."

"I'm fine. Thank you." Paula looked more intently at the face before her.

"Oh. Sorry, I didn't recognise you. Hello. I'm fine, really. I was a hundred miles away and not expecting my name to be called out."

"I think it's more than that. You're as pale as a ghost, and you're shivering. You live here now?" Paula nodded her reply. "Let's get you to your apartment and rustle you up a hot, sugary cup of tea. That'll help."

Paula protested, she needed something other than sweet tea coursing through her body and this interruption was preventing that need materialising. "No. Really, I'm fine. You must be very busy. Please don't let me delay you."

Paula felt a strong hand on her shoulder, guiding her up the final few steps and onwards into the lobby. "I insist. I do have a meeting later but I was only going to wander around, getting the air for the next hour. Let me help you, and you can bring me up to date on your life. How's that sound?"

Paula was unable to resist and steeled herself to survive the next hour of desperate need, made infinitely worse by the knowledge that the means to ease that agony was nestled in her pocket.

* * *

Paula Bingley was more than used to the feeling of dis-embodiment induced by the presence of drugs hurtling through her veins to invade her brain and overwhelm the senses. The thud to the side of her neck was unexpected, although the cold wave through her blood stream was familiar, the sight of the carpeted floor rushing up towards her not unknown. The Ketamine, fusing with the remnants of heroin in her system, was producing a totally unfamiliar sensation. There was a voice, a voice calling her name. The voice was on the other side of the valley, and the wind that swept between the slopes sometimes carried the voice away and sometimes magnified it. Her name. The voice was calling her name.

* * *

Time had passed. How much time was beyond understanding. Everything, including time, had turned into plasticine and was stretched, re-modelled, distorted, re-coloured, and unreal. Paula didn't know she was lying naked on the floor of her drawing room. She didn't comprehend the fury of her visitor who was trying to explain something to her, something she didn't understand, something she couldn't acknowledge.

Paula Bingley was a mess. She knew it. She began to laugh, for no reason but she laughed. Paralysed on the floor, staring at the swirling, undulating ceiling, the light fitting above her morphing into a hundred faces each joined in with her hilarity. Paula was aware of a pulling and tugging sensation somewhere low down on her body. There was no pain, but the intensity of the wrenching and yanking was increasing. She heard the visitor's voice once more. Closer this time, angry, full of rage. The familiar face suddenly loomed above her own, twisted with wrath and loathing.

*"Want to see it? Do you? Do you want to see it?"* Paula stopped her silent laughing; it had all been silent. The hatred was so intense it forced its way into her understanding. *"Here! Here it is. Have it!"* A bloody, fleshy shape seemed to hover over her face, tendrils hung and swung from the central mass, making it seem to be a living, hideous, alien being. The alien receded, it was high above her now, dollops of blood fell from it onto her face, into her open mouth.

*"HAVE IT!"* The object hit her face with such force Paula had to gasp for breath.

\* \* \*

Paula Bingley was unaware of the catastrophe which had been visited upon her body. She was unaware of the blood streaming out of her being sucked up by the soiled, once-luxurious carpet upon which she lay. She was unaware she was dying. She didn't hear the sound of the shower running in her bathroom a short distance away. She was unaware of her breaths getting faster, the inhalations hindered by the object lying across her nose and mouth, her body trying to fill blood-starved lungs with oxygen. She never understood her heart's final efforts, beating many times its normal rate, desperate to utilise so little blood to do the job of so much more. Paula Bingley *was* aware that she had finally slipped down the full length of the mountainside, the darkness of the void, once so far away, was now everywhere, it was her whole world. She didn't understand any of it, but instinctively, she looked around, desperate to see if he was there, longing to see his face, willing it to happen. Suddenly, from the gloom, floating gently towards her, she saw him. It *was* him. It was him.

For the first time in eighteen years all was well in Paula Bingley's world once more. Beneath the abomination which lay across her face, Paula Bingley smiled.

# Chapter Seven

Since Melvin O'Hara's arrest, Grant Maddox had juggled the never-ending stream of casework that dropped onto his desk with the ongoing preparation for the trial. That wasn't strictly true; very little actually *landed* on his desk anymore. It popped up on a computer screen, which stared at him with its single malevolent eye, daring him to log in and accept the assigned workload. It was a very different world to the one he had joined nearly thirty years previously.

"Hi, Skip." Grant's memories were disturbed by the recently qualified DC Amber Bennett, in her mid-twenties, tall, slim, dark-haired, and pretty. When she'd arrived in the CID main office there was so much drool dripping appreciatively from the mouths of the menfolk of the department the floor became a slip-hazard. Amber was about the same age as Grant's youngest daughter, Monza, who, as a probationary constable, was just starting out on her police career. Grants mind connected the two girls, he couldn't think of them as adult women. Instead, by their tender years and chosen profession, his protective instincts were fully activated, and consequently, he had tucked Amber under a shielding, fatherly wing.

"Hi Amber, how you doing?" Grant rubbed his eyes, so many hours staring at the glowing screen could not be good for him.

"It's the O'Hara job, Skipper. Would you go through the exhibit list and the statement links with me to make sure I've got everything in order and it makes sense? When the trial dates come out, I want to be ready to go." Amber planted a helpless expression on her face and grinned at her sergeant, who laughed at the display.

"We both know that it'll be spot on…. don't we?" Amber replaced her expression with a Stan Laurel look of confusion. Grant laughed out loud. "Yes…alright, alright." He was helpless in the face of such exhortations, and Amber knew it. In four months, she'd come to trust and care for the big man who always seemed to be looking out for her. Whether it was the unwanted attention of men who should know better or whether it was with some item or point of procedure, he'd kept a weather eye out for her. He'd judged her well, and in time, when she'd found her feet and become more confident in her abilities and her place, he'd backed off, letting her assert herself and be her own person. His protection was never undermining nor overwhelming, and for that, she was thankful.

\* \* \*

Amber, fresh out of Detective Training School, had been at her desk only a few days, feeling out of her depth and wondering if she'd made the right decision to specialise. She'd thought the swear word had been uttered under her breath as she pressed the keys and tried for the umpteenth time to update a vulnerable missing person report with a folio number and circulate it to adjoining divisions. The long legs and firm buttocks of DC Don Chamberlain draped themselves over the corner of her desk.

"Language, language, young lady!" He teased her, flashing perfect teeth in a polished smile. "Are you struggling, Sweetie?" Don leant forward to examine the computer screen, placing an arm around Amber's shoulder to steady himself. "Maybe I could help?" Amber *did* need help but was more than a little uncomfortable at the over-familiarity being displayed by this good-looking-and-knew-it officer. Of course, she'd been in similar situations before; she had spent three years in The Job and had batted off countless approaches, some clumsy, some subtle, some hilarious, and some, very few, intimidating. This situation needed handling correctly, she was the new girl, in a new job, fitting in was important, she would definitely need the help and goodwill of her colleagues to get on, but at what price? She knew she had to draw a line in the sand, but where? As a stuck-up, distant, women's libber, who knew her rights and wasn't afraid to institute complaints procedure for any infringements was one thing, acquiring a reputation as a doormat was quite another. Don was now rubbing her shoulder, words falling like honey from his lips.

"The system wasn't designed for coppers, it's user-unfriendly, and it took me ages to master it, but let's see if we can navigate the problem together. What is it you're trying to do?"

Amber's quandary was solved for her as a shadow crossed the screen, cast by a figure standing behind her from which direction a voice issued, loud and clear for the whole office to hear.

"Put it away, Don. Save all that bollocks for Grab-a-Granny night at the Locarno, or better still, for when you get home to the wife and kids." There was a general round of hilarity from the desks scattered through the office. "And for the record I spend half my life correcting the cock-ups *you* put on the system, now fuck off back to your desk." Don Chamberlain smiled broadly; what else could he do? He put his hands up in a pose of surrender to show he wasn't up to no good, like a footballer who commits a grievous foul, pleading, *'Not me, ref.'*

Amber, embarrassed and struggling to know how to react to the intrusion, span her chair to see who had dismissed the office Lothario so harshly. She was greeted by the smiling face of Detective Sergeant Grant Maddox and immediately realised that his admonishment hadn't been so cruel after all, delivered as it was with a knowing grin that formed part of the brutal banter which was the lifeblood of the Police Service.

The DS pulled a chair from an adjoining desk, placed it next to Amber, and slumped down into it. "Dirty Don Chamberlain is right about one thing, this system was *never* designed with coppers in mind, but it's what we're stuck with. I'll happily go through it with you if you like, as your swearing was louder than you thought and telegraphed your distress!"

Amber laughed and replied. "If you would please, Sarge. Show me once and I'll get it, I'm a quick learner."

Grant nodded. "That's what I'd heard. You've come with a first-rate report, it's a good office here, good blokes and girls, a bit of a bear-pit at times, but there's no real harm in anyone, not even Dirty Don." Grant turned to look at DC Chamberlain, now seated at his desk on the other side of the room and called out to him. "Hands out from under the desk Don, you filthy self-abusing animal, put 'em where we can see them." The office burst into laughter once more as Dirty Don, laughing too, lifted his hands theatrically into view with great exaggeration, putting them on his desktop.

Grant spent ten minutes explaining the system to Amber, concluding with a friendly and reassuring, 'Got it now?' Amber adored her skipper from that moment on.

* * *

Grant was walking with Amber to review the exhibits list as requested when a grim-faced DCI Winter opened the door to his glass-walled office, held onto the side of it, and with his head peeking around, called. "Granty, got a minute?" Winter disappeared from sight; the door left half open.

Grant patted Amber on the shoulder. "Start going through it. I'll join you in a minute, okay?"

* * *

Grant Maddox had a great deal of time and respect for his old friend Detective Chief Inspector Paul Winter, who managed to walk the tightrope between being the unquestionable boss who gave the orders and expected them to be carried out and a man who was liked and respected by the rank and file for his professionalism and integrity. The CID office took its lead from the top man, and this one knew his stuff, worked at least as hard as anyone else and harder than most, listened to all voices with patience and respect, and glued the whole edifice together with a sense of humour which was dry, witty and very often self-deprecating.

Winter was just slumping back into his chair, his face still grimly set, as Grant entered the office. "Close the door, please, Granty, park your bum." Winter nodded towards the chair on the other side of his desk.

DS Maddox sat opposite his boss and for the next ten minutes listened in silence and with mounting revulsion as DCI Winter described what he'd just been told by the early turn, uniform Duty Officer, and what his officers had found when they responded to a call at the apartment block of Charleroi Mansions, not thirty minutes earlier.

# Chapter Eight

Grant progressed along the tastefully decorated corridor, absorbing the art deco wall lamps and half-moon onyx console tables heavily laden with fresh-cut flowers. Shining, striped wallpaper adorned with elaborately framed artwork hung on the walls. Charleroi Mansions thought Grant, his steps springing slightly in the deep shag-pile of the carpet, was a residence way above his pay grade.

He spied the figure of uniform sergeant Lance Bilton ahead of him, standing next to a shiny new probationary officer. She was holding the Incident Log and staring with wide eyes at the approach of DS Maddox and DC Bennett. Grant could almost see and hear the cogs turning as she tried to remember their names and ran through what was required of her in the record, for which one day she may be required to give evidence.

The high, wide, varnished teak door gaped open behind the two uniforms, and the indiscernible gabble of numerous people inside the apartment could be heard escaping through the opening. There was a sudden flash of light from within, which shone briefly, reflecting off the polished brass number and letter affixed to the door, evidence of the photographer at work out of sight. Grant saw Bilton lean towards the junior officer, and he lip-read his own and Amber's name being relayed to her. A degree of relief that one thing less was pressuring her was immediately apparent on her face.

"Hiya Lance." Maddox offered.

"Sarge." Amber smiled a grim smile as she, too, acknowledged the early-turn section sergeant.

"Granty, Amber." Lance Bilton replied, tilting his head to the probationer.

"Names there, times there. You can say 'Known to me', that's okay." The guidance given to the log-book keeper, a finger dabbed onto a point on a page. Lance turned his full attention back to the detectives. "It's not good, Granty" he said, his tone evidence of the understatement.

Grant nodded. "Old man Winter told me the basics he got from your guvnor; sounds bloody awful."

"*Bloody* is right. I haven't seen anything like it outside a morgue. Thank God the first bloke on the scene was an old sweat who's seen it all, done it all, with a strong stomach, or I suspect your crime scene would be decorated with a full English breakfast."

Grant nodded, thankful for that mercy. "Who was that?" asked Grant.

"Alex Surtees, our area car driver. A good lad, ex-para." Lance seemed to feel these few small words were more than enough, to sum up, the quality and capabilities of one of his officers. Grant agreed, knowing of the short, stocky, no-nonsense Geordie.

"Why was he here? What was the original call?" Grant looked across at Amber, who'd asked the question. He was glad, what he didn't want, or need, was an oppo who stayed silent and floated around without interest or involvement.

Lance Bilton directed his answer to the young DC. "The concierge was at his desk in the lobby at 10.30am, when he sees a South Asian or Arabic looking male hanging around outside, looking in occasionally, he said he looked edgy and nervous. He wanders off, but about ten minutes later, he's back and peeking into the lobby all over again. So our bloke, thinking he's up to no good and planning to creep in when the coast is clear, goes out and confronts him."

"Good for him!" Grant enthused. "Shows some dedication, especially as I bet he's on minimum wage. We still have this bloke do we? The concierge, what's his name?"

Grant saw Lance's face drop. "I knew you were going to ask that." The woman officer, pre-empting her sergeant, turned the log-book pages back and held it up for him to read, Grant noticed her smile slightly. The sergeant took a deep breath, "errr... his name is Przemyslaw...Grzeszczyk. It's the usual spelling, one of the Royal Tunbridge Wells Grzeszczyk's, I'm presuming." Grant and Amber had to remember where they were and stifled an audible laugh.

Grant couldn't miss the chance for a comment. "Strangled with your bare tongue. Well done, Lance."

The section sergeant gave a sarcastic wince and returned to the matter at hand. "Yes, we have him; he's in the building manager's office with a PC, giving an initial statement, I thought it might help to get it in early and fresh."

"It will. It *really* will; the more contemporaneous it is, the more weight it'll carry in court. Thanks Lance, good work. So what happened outside?"

"Well, our Asian/Arab chummy says to the concierge, he has a friend who lives here, says he sees her regularly he may even have said *every* day, it'll be in his statement, but she hasn't been around for four or five days and he was worried about her." Grant and Amber turned their heads to face each other. Here was the first lead forming already, who was this man?

"Our Polish bloke asks what his friend's name is, and he says 'Paula.' Well, the concierge knows there's a Paula in Apartment 3F, right here," Lance jerked his head to the entrance behind him. "Full name Paula Bingley. He also knows, 'cos he ain't stupid, that Paula has a bit of a drug habit, and this Asian/Arab guy looks the sort of bloke who's been supplying it."

"Description?" Amber again.

Lance consulted a notebook he pulled from a back pocket. "The full description will be in the statement, but hang on, where is it? Here we go. Male, South Asian or Arabic, aged about twenty-five, short and slim, black oiled hair, tied in a ponytail, dressed smartly, whatever that means, but best of all, he has a lazy eye, you know, one crossed eye."

"I *know* what a lazy eye is, Lance," Grant sighed.

"Er, yeh, obviously. The statement will tell more. The Polish guy was pretty shaken by what he found upstairs, he did really well to give us this much."

"Well, it *is* something to be going on with." Grant agreed. "Crime Squad may have some info and descriptions of local dealers, if that's what he is, which'll give us a name. He sounds pretty distinctive; if he's in the system, they'll find him."

"So, either he's genuinely concerned for this Paula's welfare," Amber observed, "or, more likely, he wants to know what's happened to a regular and reliable customer."

"*Or* he's owned money," added Grant.

"Exactly!" Lance Bilton confirmed. "Anyway, chummy scampers off, and the concierge phones up to Paula Bingley's apartment and gets no reply. He goes to her mailbox and sees it's packed with uncollected junk mail. So he's left with going and seeing if she's in. He takes the spare key from the manager's office and knocks her door repeatedly, no reply, so he opens up and…finds her. Calls 999 and enter stage left, Old Bill."

"CCTV?" Amber enquired. "There's a camera here." She pointed to the end of the corridor, "and I saw cameras outside the front door and in the lobby."

"Ah!" answered the sergeant. "Good point. I asked er… Mr Grez… whatever it is. Apparently the block only has a concierge weekdays, 8am to 8pm. There's no coverage at all on the weekends. He came in at 7.45am on Monday and the whole CCTV surveillance system had gone down at some point over the weekend. It *was* working properly at 8pm on Friday when he was last on duty. It went tits up at some point after that. He called an engineer Monday morning, and he's due here tomorrow."

Grant shook his head in disappointment. "Shit! Today's Thursday, so we've a big black hole for near-as-damn-it a week. Bugger!" It *had* seemed so hopeful a few minutes ago. A filmed record of the suspicious 'dealer' and even an image of whoever had entered the apartment would have been too much to ask.

"Okay, Lance. Keep doing the stuff you're doing. It's appreciated. And you…" Grant spoke to the probationer, "…that incident log is the foundation block of this crime scene and its processing. What you're doing is important; do it well. We're all a cog in the machine with a job to do." Then he winked at her. The girl beamed at the encouragement from the Detective Sergeant. "Lance, will you give me a shout when the scene is released?" Grant held up his personal radio and shook it.

"Will do."

* * *

Grant and Amber turned and made their way down to the lobby, taking the stairs, Grant talking as they walked. "I know, I know, the temptation is to just take a peek, we were right there, at the door, there'd be no harm done having a look, and I can guarantee that DI Dodds would charge in and tramp all over it, but *we* won't. The place is full of people trying to do their job. Photographers, fingerprints, forensics, and so on. They'll be dusting for prints, swabbing for blood, dabbing for body fluids, semen, saliva, snot, hairs, fibres, and obviously looking for DNA. Searching for *anything* which is foreign to the scene and if we go in, even if we tiptoe, ever so carefully, well firstly it's seriously disrespectful to our colleagues who are trying to do their job without Plod banging about and secondly you never know, we may take something in which shouldn't be there, or *much* worse, take something out which may be vital and not even know it."

"Locard's Principle of Exchange." Amber offered.

"Exactly," agreed Grant. "Every contact leaves a trace; that's the principle. There're plenty of useful things to do until the scene is released to us. Let's have a mooch around the place, get the lie of the land, and then look in on the concierge and see if *we* can pronounce his name.

# Chapter Nine

He placed the tray on the table and slid himself into a seat opposite Amber. Only two pence change out of fourteen quid for two cups of coffee! Grant was staggered. The Migliorè Coffee House was not an establishment he'd frequented before and, at these prices, was unlikely to ever visit again. He considered mentioning the daylight robbery to which he had just been subjected to Amber, who was staring blankly down at the tabletop and decided against it. She was shaken. *Really* shaken. If the truth were known, so was he, he was just controlling it better. Seeking refuge in the nearby trendy café to calm down and process the last half hour was a good idea. Away from the nick, away from their colleagues, away from questions. All would be faced and dealt with, but not yet. First, he needed to help Amber.

"Do you know that they have something chalked on the board called *'il fantastico capo del magro frappuccino al cioccolato moka.'* I made myself remember it. I'll be able to say it at will for the rest of my life. *'Il fantastico capo del magro frappuccino al cioccolato moka'*. I might ask for one in our canteen, just to see what Doreen's reaction is."

Grant took the cups from the tray and continued with his story. "I said to the girl at the counter, the one with the badge that says, 'Barista Supremo Numero Uno,' you can see her there, the one with the bolt through her nose; I said, what's that in English then? She looked at me utterly lost, managing to speak and not pass out with the mental effort, and said, 'dunno, you want one?' Then, the bloke there, with the hole-ring in his ear, I could stick my head through, and the tattooed neck leaned in. I see his badge says, 'Capo

42

del Barista Supremo.' Now I remember my Mafia movies and 'Capo' means the boss, so I'm expecting something good, he looks me up and down like I was an insect which had just crawled out from a cave, which is a bloody liberty considering he looks like he lives in one. 'That Sir', he said, 'is the fantastic boss of the skinny choca mocha frappuccino'. Is that what you want?' I said, 'I just want two coffees, please.' He tuts at me and tells bolt through the nose girl, 'two Americanos and wanders off. I *still* don't know what an *il fantastico capo del magro frappuccino al cioccolato moka'* is!" Grant pulled his best confused face; Amber laughed. It was exactly what he'd been trying to do, provide a momentary distraction.

"Two cups of coffee, you'd have thought I'd made an indecent proposal. Honestly, Amber, the world has caught up, overtaken me, and scampered off into the far distance."

Amber smiled, and there was silence between them for a few seconds. "I'm okay." Amber brought them both back. "You're being very kind; I know what you're doing, I appreciate it, and it's working." Amber raised her face and looked directly at her sergeant. "I *was* shocked... dammit, I'm *still* shocked, but I'm okay." She paused for a few moments; Grant waited for her to speak. When she did, there was a tremble in her voice. "This is the job we picked, isn't it?"

Grant reached across the table and placed his hand gently on top of hers for just a moment and squeezed. It was a fleeting, intimate, physical contact from a senior male colleague to a junior female one and the most kind, fatherly, and appropriate gesture she'd ever experienced in the workplace.

"Don't be so nice," she said; her words were choked with emotion and disguised with a laugh. "You'll make me cry."

"Do you want to hear the platitudes? 'We're only human', or 'we're ordinary people dealing with extraordinary circumstances', or 'you shouldn't have joined if you can't take a joke.' There's plenty of them. But we need to factor in our humanity, or frailty, if you like. You're right, we *did* pick this job, no one made us, so you have to ask, why did we make that choice?" Grant raised an eyebrow. "Why did *you* make that choice?"

"Why?" She echoed. "Well, I wanted to make a difference, to help people, to serve. There're the standard altruistic reasons but there's other stuff, it's interesting, challenging, reasonably well-paid and secure."

Grant smiled and nodded in agreement and then spoke with earnestness. "*And* then there's the calling, the vocation. There's an element to a copper's psyche, it's the bit that stops you walking away when you should keep going. It's the bit which makes you run towards danger when you should be running away from it, it's the call of duty if you like. The part of you when the appeal goes out, '*Somebody! Somebody! Why doesn't **somebody** do something!*' hears the reply, shouting from inside your head, 'that's a call to *me*, personally'. Grant jabbed the middle of his chest with a finger in emphasis. Amber listened intently, this was the pep-talk she'd never had before.

Grant leant forward, his expression serious, these words meant something to him and he wanted them to mean something to Amber. "The good copper is the person who steps up to the plate, who, for better or worse, *tries* to do the right thing rather than do nothing." Grant took a sip of his coffee. "So it follows that we want to go where angels fear to tread, we need to look at the horror straight in the eye, need to face the evil, and I think there's an arrogance about us that wants to be tested and not recoil. Don't you want to show the doubters of this world and the rest of those doing the sneering you're as good or better than them?" Grant answered his own question. "Of course you do. But there's a cost, so it's back to the platitudes. We *deal* with it, whatever it is, professionally and humanely, we deal with it. When we're with friends and colleagues, we make jokes and laugh with our famous black humour, and when we get home, when we're either alone or with loved ones whom we trust...then we cry."

"Do you cry, Sarge?" she asked.

Grant leant back in his chair. "*Me!* God no! I'm far too hard!" They both laughed. Amber sipped her extortionately expensive coffee and reflected that she wouldn't have thought it possible to laugh, not so soon after seeing *that*.

# Chapter Ten

It had been little more than an hour earlier that they'd both slipped blue plastic covers over their shoes and rammed hands into pockets, an old trick to prevent that most human of instincts: to unconsciously touch things they were examining closely. Amber had followed Grant through the wide entrance and along the hallway into apartment 3F Charleroi Mansions, placing each foot carefully on the forensic stepping plates that paved the way. It was another world from the tidy opulence of the environment outside the front door. Obviously, once upon a time, this was a wonderful living space. The ceilings were lofty, light flooded in, penetrating even to this corridor, the most distant point from the wide and high windows. It was a space Amber could only dream about living in one day, but not like this, not in this condition.

The carpet, once bright and luxuriant, was faded and stained. Rubbish was littered everywhere: newspapers, empty fast-food wrappings, pizza boxes, empty wine, beer, and cider bottles. Crushed extra strong export lager cans were scattered about, along with screwed-up items of clothing, thrown willy-nilly. Grant stopped and nodded towards a scorched piece of foil secreted under a table close to the wall. "They missed that one."

Amber smiled. The brief precis from the forensics team had spoken of numerous articles indicating drug use in the apartment, each item had been noted, bagged and numbered, ready for analysis. The first and obvious conclusion, re-enforced by the statement from the Polish concierge who thankfully asked to be simply called 'Pete', and the findings in the flat, were that the murder was drug-related. 'Might be,' was the laconic observation from DS Maddox.

Grant stopped. Amber, at that moment, looking to her side, almost walked into him, her foot slipping and nearly going over the edge of the shiny metal plate protecting the floor from her steps. Her vision ahead was blocked by her sergeant's broad back. She waited, knowing what she was about to see, they'd both been told, but the words and the reality were oceans apart.

"Oh, my God!" Grant uttered the words slowly. He tore his eyes away from Paula Bingley, making himself examine and assess the crime scene. The windows opposite were dirty, the curtains, also filthy, drawn back. The room's electric lights were switched on, several bulbs blown and not working. He made a mental note to ask if the forensic examiners had opened the blinds or turned the lights on, had the crime scene been found exactly like this?

The windows looked out onto the inner quad of Charleroi Mansions, he could see into numerous apartments opposite, equally each would have a view into this one. Could the killer have been at work in full view of an observing neighbour? Much depended upon the time of day the offence was committed and the position of the curtains. His eyes were pulled, magnetically, back down to the body. He wanted to resist the urge to gawp, desperate to be a professional but the shock was overpowering, to stare felt disrespectful and a breach of the victims dignity. He made a decision.

"Alright, Amber," he said, "let's have a damn good look, let's get it over with, and then we can do our job with that moment behind us." Amber stared straight ahead as Grant took a sideways step to the adjacent plate; the movement, on later reflection, appeared to be like a painter revealing a work of art to an admiring crowd.

Grant had said, 'Oh my God!'

As Amber stared down, her legs wobbled, and her mouth opened and closed involuntarily. 'Oh my God!' was utterly inadequate.

\* \* \*

Paula Bingley's violated body lay spread-eagled on its back. Her nakedness revealed the ravages drug abuse had wreaked upon her small body, and it *was* a pitifully small body. Her skin was pallid, the red line of lividity plain to see on her lower back, thighs, and legs, the gravitational settling of the blood and a clear indication that the body had been in situ from the time of death or very shortly thereafter. Many, many bruises and sores covered her arms and legs, the soles of her feet were filthy. Personal, physical neglect was writ large, but all, *everything*, was overwhelmingly eclipsed by the horror that had been visited upon her abdomen and the thing which lay across her face.

Grant tried to observe objectively, attempted to view the damage systematically and through the eyes of the offender. Obviously, a very sharp blade had been used to slice into the lower portion of Paula's torso. The first cut was probably the vertical one, from below her ribcage, through her navel, to her vagina. Several lateral cuts had been made, slicing across the width of the body, the flesh pulled and folded back, exposing the bright yellow layer of fat below the skin. Grant stepped forward, bending slightly, trying to view the detail amongst the dark, dried blood and viscera. He saw the answer to his question. Incredibly, the pulled-back flesh had been stapled-gunned down to hold it in place so the monster who committed this crime could work unimpeded. This was a prepared and organised killer. The cold practicality of remembering to bring a staple gun added even more horror to the murder of Paula Bingley, as if it needed it.

The hole in the body's abdomen was a gaping maw that dragged the eyes to it, but as catastrophic as that damage was, a special horror competed for attention. Paula's face was hidden beneath a lump of bloodied tissue the size of a man's clenched hand. If this chunk of gore *had* been a fist, the grasping fingers appeared to be clutching at dangling pieces of flesh, sagging out of each side, hanging over Paula's face, forming a 'T' shape of bloody muscular material.

"It's a guess, but do you know what I think that is?" Grant's voice was little more than a whisper.

"I think it's her womb, Sarge."

"I think you're right."

# Chapter Eleven

The Migliorè Coffee House was crowded despite the close-to-criminal cost of their coffee, which begrudgingly Grant had to confess was very good. Clearly, the trendy café attracted a certain crowd, hipsters and the selfie generation. Grant's attention had naturally fixed on his shaken young colleague and pulling her back from the dark place that 3F, Charleroi Mansions, had taken her. He'd been gripped in a similar horror once, only he'd been there at a much younger age and in very different circumstances, far away on a small cluster of disputed islands set in a chilled, far off sea. *His* baptism had been the shock of losing friends, facing his own mortality, seeing first-hand the bloody, stomach-turning effect of weaponry on the human body, and the lifelong self-questioning and self-doubts that come with the taking of another man's life.

The conversation between the two detectives flowed, both clawing back to normalcy, a deliberate act of kindness and experience on the detective sergeant's part. As time passed Grant looked around at his surroundings with eyes that observed properly for the first time since leaving the crime scene.

As Amber sipped the last of her coffee, Grant twisted in his seat to examine the other side of the café and noticed a short South Asian man stand up from the table at which he'd been sitting alone. His mobile phone was pressed to his ear, Grant only caught the words, 'Same as usual', fall from his lips. The man turned to leave, distinguished by a pronounced lazy eye and sporting a pony-tail, tied from his back-combed and oiled hair, he navigated the short distance from his table to the door and left the café.

"Well, bugger me! Look!" he hissed to Amber. "It couldn't be, could it?" Grant was out of his seat and beginning to cross the floor towards the exit before Amber's coffee cup hit its saucer. The object of Grant's interest had already exited, Amber fumbled in her handbag for her personal radio and at the same time rushed to catch-up with her sergeant, who was trying to extricate himself through the hindering maze of tables, chairs and customers, each of whom was unaware of his urgent need to pass.

* * *

Anil Butt was heading home from the Migliorè, or more accurately, his parent's home, a brisk twenty-five minute walk away. The center of his drug-dealing empire was the back bedroom of a modest three-bedroom, semi-detached house in a pleasant, tree-lined street in West London suburbia. He had to acknowledge that it wasn't much of an empire, and when he finally passed his accountancy studies, he would drop his illegal activities like a hot yam.

Anil was twenty-three years old and, to his parent's open annoyance, was making heavy weather of his studies at the local university, which his highly critical father never tired of pointing out wasn't a real university but a polytechnic with a name change masquerading as the genuine article.

"Why can't you be more like your brother Birbal? He went to a real University, Birmingham; that's a Red Brick!"

It was like a stuck record, each evening his father would examine his younger son, possessor of a faulty eye, greasy ponytail and unsuitably trendy Western clothes and begin his list of criticisms. 'What do you think you look like? Why do you wear an earring, are you a lover of young boys? Is that what my son is? A Nancy-boy? Can't you see how you're looked at when we're at prayers, with that Western girly hairstyle tied behind your head?' His father, a proud Indian, saved the word 'Western' as a description for anything of which he strongly disapproved. 'Did Birbal ever have earrings or Nancy-boy hair like that? No! We named him Birbal, meaning Braveheart, and he's lived up to that name. He'll be a huge success and bring pride to our name. You? You only bring embarrassment.'

It was a damning and much-repeated indictment from which Anil longed to escape. He resented *everything* about his parents, even their choice of his name. Whereas brother Birbal's was a very respectable and acceptable 'Braveheart,' his own appellation, Anil, meant 'Great Wind.' How inappropriate was that when your family name was Butt? If he didn't want to scream, he'd laugh, 'Great Wind Butt!'

Anil Butt would describe his drug-dealing activity as linear, inasmuch as he had only one contact, a fellow student at University from whom he purchased his supply. He could acquire mainstream products, heroin, MDMA, and cocaine in small amounts and had built up a tiny list of clientele by adopting a particular look and dress. He found, to his surprise, that if you looked sleazy enough, projected a certain underworldliness, you ended up being approached and asked for drugs. He was amazed at how easy it was, and once he'd satisfactorily supplied a few customers, others appeared, and the money rolled in. What he'd do if his supplier moved on, whether to pastures new or to a small room with a heavy metal door, unsanitary toilet arrangements, and bars on the windows, he knew not. The truth was Anil was a nervous drug dealer, neither menacing nor cold-hearted. He was terrified of being arrested and even more terrified of the prospect that one day he may acquire his own small room, with his own heavy metal door, unsanitary toilet arrangements, and bars on the windows.

Anil's best customer by far was Paula Bingley. He liked her, and he felt sorry for her. She paid enormously over the odds for his product and always paid cash, neither asking for nor expecting credit as some of his customers did. As soon as they reached *that* point, he cut all contact, assuming they'd reached a moment of desperation where *his* safety or freedom could be compromised or threatened. He was, therefore, very protective of Paula; she was his Golden Goose.

He had a pattern of rounds that he liked to keep. It was a routine circuit of trendy coffee houses, of which there were many. It wasn't an obvious place to deal with his product. He stayed away from pubs, from clubs, from dark alleys. He never sold at university, or at youth clubs or at gigs, he never went out to sell at night or in a place he didn't know. He had fewer than twenty customers, and he preferred it that way. Anil was both savvy and cautious and had chosen his business as a means to an end with an exit strategy in mind. He intended to enjoy a degree of material comfort during his studies whilst saving enough from his dealings to buy his own little flat to which he could escape as soon as possible. Anil wasn't greedy, selling drugs had presented itself accidentally and he reasoned, if it wasn't him taking advantage it would be someone else.

# Chapter Twelve

Anil was a worried man. Worried for his principal customer, Paula, and far, far more concerned for himself. He'd made a serious mistake. Several months previously whilst sitting with Paula at the Migliorè Coffee House, a member of staff had been taking an age to clear and clean an adjoining table, making it unsafe to make the usual exchange immediately. They had talked a little longer than they usually did to appear as normal customers. She had talked of her life and revealed its tragedy and loss, spoken of heartache and loneliness, Anil had been deeply moved. She was a woman older than his mother, a woman whom he naturally and culturally respected and esteemed, but a woman life had mistreated and who now, in turn, was mistreating life. He recognised his part in her fall but also saw her downward spiral, which had begun long before his arrival on the scene and would continue with another supplier if he was not there. He felt absolved, but common humanity demanded a degree of compassion.

"I feel a little ill," she'd said at that meeting months before. Anil had looked at her closely. She did look ill. Her face, pale at the best of times, was white; her hands, clutching the sides of an oversized coffee cup, were shaking, the milky brown contents sloshing about.

"Can I help?" he'd asked. "Do you live near here?"

Paula had nodded.

Anil had walked with Paula the short distance to Charleroi Mansions. When they'd arrived at the steps leading to the entrance Paula extended her arm, an unspoken request for help, Anil had taken it, and they ascended together. It was a weekend, and as the lobby and its desk were empty Anil

52

was unaware of the weekday presence of a concierge. He let a low whistle escape his lips as he took in the sumptuous surroundings.

"You live *here?*" he'd asked.

Paula hadn't answered.

"Are you okay from here then?" Anil had been uncomfortable and wanted to get away.

"Please," was all she'd said.

Anil had taken her to the front door of her apartment, number 3F. He saw the disorder inside through the opened door and was saddened.

"I hope you feel better soon. I'll see you again, usual place, yeh?" Paula had forced a smile and closed the door without a further word, reaching into her pocket, clutching a wrap with shaking fingers.

* * *

Anil had made another mistake. It had been five days since Paula had appeared at the Migliorè. The last time he'd seen her, on Saturday, she'd looked ill, displaying similar symptoms to those of several months previously. He'd made his sale as usual; she'd paid as usual, making her departure a little sooner than was prudent. It made sense to take time at the coffee house to look like proper customers and not act in a suspicious manner. On this occasion, as an act of self-interested kindness, he'd decided to follow her at a distance just to make sure she got home in one piece. He was relieved when he saw her safely reach the steps that led up to the doors of Charleroi Mansions and even more relieved when he saw that she had bumped into someone she apparently knew. He watched the two figures ascend the stairs together and turned away, reassured all was well.

He'd never been more wrong.

That was Saturday, and he'd seen no sign of Paula since. He was concerned on two counts: for her welfare and for the state of his business. He needed Paula's revenue. He'd just cut two customers off his list in as many days.

'Hey, Anil, just a couple of tabs, you know I'm good for it, I'll pay next time, I'll pay double the rate, treble! You know I'm good for it.'

It was a line he'd heard before and, as far as he was concerned, were the last words he'd ever hear on the matter. Consequently, his cash flow had taken a hit, and with no-shows from Paula day after day, it was starting to hurt.

That's when he made his mistake.

It was Thursday, he walked by the entrance to the apartments and saw with surprise a neatly dressed man in the lobby, in a dark jacket, white shirt and tie. Anil looked into the murk of the vestibule, trying to discern what he was doing there. Obviously, Anil couldn't enter with this man present. He walked away, circumnavigating the block, pondering his course of action. He knew Paula's apartment, he would just ring the doorbell, check she was okay and offer her the three wraps he had in his pocket, she would have the cash, he was sure.

The man was *still* in the lobby, Anil made a decision, turned and walked away. He jumped as the hand descended upon his shoulder.

"Can I help you?" a voice with a heavy accent.

Anil turned to face the tall, stocky Polish concierge of Charleroi Mansions.

\* \* \*

By the time Grant had traversed the closely packed tables, chairs, and obstructive customers of the coffee house and reached the door, the man with the ponytail had crossed the busy road outside and was looking up at the darkening sky. The clouds looked threatening, heavy with the prospect of rain. The target of Grant's attention, his decision made regarding the weather, raised a hand, and within seconds, a black cab pulled up, blocking him from sight. Grant looked left and right, desperate for a gap in the traffic, needing to get to the suspect before the cab pulled away. Amber appeared at his side with her radio in hand as the cab drove off.

"*There!* In the cab." Grant pointed across the roadway. "Get its number and circulate it." Capricious Fate decided that Grant had been rewarded enough with the sight of his quarry, the witness confronted by Polish Pete, the Concierge, only hours earlier. Having dangled the prize before him,

Fate decided it was time to yank it away. Any view of the cab was lost as a double-decker bus slowed and halted in front of the two officers. Grant ran to his right, past the stationary vehicle, and Amber ran to the left to cross in front of it. Neither tactic worked. Anil Butt, fearing a downpour, had at the last minute decided to treat himself to a taxi-ride home, totally unaware of his pursuers.

Grant looked heavenward and swore copiously as the cab, swamped by other identical black vehicles, disappeared into the busy traffic. If he'd known the taxi contained the man who'd watched Paula Bingley walk up the steps into Charleroi Mansions, side by side with her killer, he'd have sworn even longer and harder.

# Chapter Thirteen

As Amber, urgently but forlornly, called for units in the vicinity to search for a black Hackney cab, probably heading east, containing a cross-eyed Asian with a pony-tail, a furious Grant Maddox stormed back into the Migliorè Coffee House, walked straight to the front of the queue and directed his frustration at the Capo Del Barista Supremo.

"*You!* Who was that Asian man with the dodgy eye and pony-tail who just left? Who was he?" The Capo Del Barista Supremo, although named Derek Trubshaw at birth, now insisted upon being called Del'roi, flared his nostrils, and hoisted his eyebrows at this rock ape's breach of protocol. He remembered him as the man who had displayed his Philistine ignorance and ordered 'two cups of coffee.'

"Sir, there is a queue, and you are jumping it." Del'roi smirked and looked to those at the counter waiting for service with smug, superior satisfaction. He felt no compunction in offending and insulting this man on two counts. Firstly, his was not the sort of custom that The Migliorè Coffee House sought, and secondly, it was as plain as the large nose on the ape's face that he wouldn't be bringing any return business any time soon. Del'roi recalled seeing the horror on Grant's face when the price of his 'two coffees' was rung up.

With the confidence born of this knowledge, Del'roi went for it. "So, if Sir would display some good manners and take his place at the back of the queue like a civilised gentleman, he will be served *when* it is his turn." Del'roi was already on thin ice, but when he held up a finger in front of Grant's face and wagged it slowly back and forth as if admonishing a naughty boy, he fell right through into the freezing waters below.

Grant Maddox was a quiet and gentle soul at heart. He was intelligent, kind, considerate, and tolerant, but he was a man who also possessed a fuse of limited length. He was, after all, an ex-Royal Marine with combat experience in The Falklands Campaign, two tours of Northern Ireland, eight years as a Firearms Response Officer, and a total of twenty-eight years as a police officer under his belt. Occasionally, when someone managed to press *all* his buttons, there was an uncharacteristic reaction. On the day he'd seen contempt and horror visited on a pathetic drug-addicted lady, the day he'd just missed what he suspected was a vital witness by seconds, the Capo Del Barista Supremo had pressed one button too many.

Derek 'Del'roi' Trubshaw was more than a little surprised to suddenly find that his face was over the customer side of the counter, his torso hovering a foot or more above its surface, his hips taking his weight on the counter's edge, while his legs dangled in fresh air on the staff side. He was also more than a little alarmed at the hostility and fury written on the twisted, snarling face, which was six inches in front of his own. A black shape with a silver motif was held an inch from his right eye, far too close to focus on and recognise as a Police Warrant Card.

"I am a Police Officer investigating a murder; that man was a suspect. Now smart-arse Capo Barista...*who was he?*" Grant, who had gripped Derek by the front of his shirt, lifting him from the ground and dragging him to his present position, now reinforced the importance of his enquiry by shaking the barista up and down and side to side vigorously.

"*I don't know, I don't know.*" Derek squealed, his voice pitched high enough to alarm nearby dogs. "He comes in most days, has a triple venti, half sweet, skinny caramel macchiato, talks to an old lady, and leaves." Grant, unsatisfied and finding the pretentiousness of The Migliorè's available coffee choices insufferably irritating, shook Derek some more.

"What do you mean you don't know him? Don't you write names on the cups?"

"*That's not us! That's not us!*" The squealing continued. Derek's fear and desperation was transmitted in every frantic syllable. "Please, please, put me down; I'm sorry, I'm sorry, *I'm **so** sorry!*" Derek wasn't sure what he was sorry for, but it seemed like a reasonable start to his plea for mercy.

"How's the interview going then, Sarge?" Amber's calm voice at Grant's shoulder poured oil onto troubled waters. Grant lowered the hand that was holding his warrant card at Derek's eye and released his grip on the Capo Barista, who fell across the counter with a satisfying thud. Still angry, he answered Amber by snarling at the fearful coffee maker,

"I'm considering making an arrest for obstruction in a case of *murder.*" Grant emphasised the last word, loud and clear across the whole café. Derek Trubshaw had only been making coffee for three weeks, which was two weeks longer than the Barista Supremo Numero Uno, Britney Cooper, who sported the bolt through her nose. Derek needed this job, whatever the circumstances, whatever the rights or wrongs, tangling with a policeman investigating a murder would not be seen as a good career move by his manager, Signore Bonetti.

*\* \* \**

Grant sipped at his complimentary *il fantastico capo del magro frappuccino al cioccolato moka,* nodding with approval. Amber was scribbling in her notebook at his side as Capo Del Barista Supremo Derek Trubshaw told all he knew about the comings and goings of the pony-tailed man. Although he pleaded ignorance, it was apparent that he was fully aware of Anil Butt's activities, while it had to be conceded he knew nothing of his identity or address, likewise the sad, pale faced woman with whom the possible witness/suspect sat and spoke.

The encounter with the Capo Barista, Del'roi, had yielded some useful information. The pony-tailed South Asian man, whom the staff impolitely referred to amongst themselves as 'Cock-eye', was in almost daily contact with Paula Bingley. He was, without doubt, the supplier of her drugs and was if Polish Pete was to be believed, not a suspect for murder but could quite possibly hold an important clue as to who was. From the Capo Barista's description, cock-eyed, pony-tail boy appeared to be a friend of Paula's, his presence at The Migliorè a regular event, which went back how long? Del'roi knew not; his employment stretched back less than a month.

The interview concluded with a promise from Del'roi to instantly call should 'Cock-eye' return to the café and for enquiries to be made to trace previous employees who may have more to tell about the relationship between Paula and her dealer.

Grant and Amber closed the coffee house door behind them and began the journey back to the station. They would need to report to DCI Winter and put in motion the wheels of a murder investigation. There was much to do.

"You're stronger than you look, Skip. You shook him around like a rag doll." Amber observed, the amusement plain in her voice.

"Yeh, well," was all he managed in reply. Grant was displeased with his loss of temper.

"Interesting interview technique," she pushed, "I must have been off that day at Detective School."

"He pressed my buttons," Grant's voice was a growl, "and I was more than annoyed at letting chummy slip through our fingers."

"Hmmm. I'll have to try it, though. So it's a 'Grab-Pull-Shake-Question.' Is that the right order?" Grant reluctantly began to smile. It was Amber's turn to pull him back from somewhere he didn't want to be.

"Yeh. You've got it. 'Grab-Pull-Shake-Question.' Follow that with 'Shake-Question, Shake-Question'. Repeat until satisfied."

Amber laughed.

Grant shrugged. "He pissed me off." It was as much of an explanation as he was going to give.

"You *will* warn me if I start to piss you off, won't you?"

They both laughed.

# Chapter Fourteen

It is a fact that successful major crime investigations usually have their breakthroughs early on. The so-called 'Golden Hour' was misnamed, being in actuality a short-hand reference to an unspecified but critically short time period early in an investigation. *The 'Golden 24 Hours'* would be more accurate but not as catchy. The first twenty-four hours should reveal vital witnesses, crucial exhibits, and damning forensic evidence, and in an ideal world, suspicion would inexorably come to point, like a fickle finger of fate, at a prime suspect.

According to the television and movies, this prime suspect would invariably agree to be interviewed without legal representation. A very good-looking officer, always with perfect teeth, would then present a carefully constructed catalogue of evidence, delivered with the quivering emotion of deep personal involvement. The suspect would crack and admit all. This fanciful process to a confession, as old as *Perry Mason*, as ancient as *Dragnet*, as archaic as *Kojak* and *Columbo*, was parodied by all real coppers with the line, delivered in a mock East-London drawl, *'You're too good for me, copper, I put me 'ands up.'* It was a sad joke. The only people who ever said, *'You're too good for me, copper...'* were frustrated cops making the joke. Real criminals habitually said, 'no comment.'

\* \* \*

Grant sat at his desk and scanned the reports from the various investigative actions completed so far in the Paula Bingley case. He noted that the scene *was* found with the curtains closed and the lights turned on. Logically, that *had* to have been the case. House to house, or more accurately apartment to apartment, enquiries had been made. Nothing of importance was discovered other than neighbours were not impressed with Ms. Bingley, nor her lifestyle. Apparently, she brought the tone of the place down. 'Imagine trying to sell one's property and a prospective purchaser saw *that thing*'. One near neighbour had offered in what she thought was a reasonable tone to a door-knocking Detective Constable. Grant couldn't help but conjure the undignified and brutalised image of Paula Bingley into his mind. Slaughtered like an animal in an abattoir by someone else who considered her only as a 'that thing' and not as a fellow human being.

The statement from Polish Pete had been the start of the investigative timeline and opened the door on an associate of the victim, the lazy-eyed, pony-tailed man from the coffee house. Grant groaned inwardly at the loss of this witness, at the warped collusion of circumstances ganging up on him. The tables, chairs, and customers blocked his swift movement to the door, the suspect's obvious last-second decision to take a taxi after looking up to assess the weather, the bus pulling up in front of Amber and himself to block the view of the cab's number. He had done what he could with this information. Grant was satisfied that should his quarry return to the Migliorè he would be called. A circulation to cab drivers had been made via Cab-Office to find the driver concerned. Grant also surmised that his suspect's next destination, whether it be home or not, was within a mile or two of the café; after all, he'd been considering walking. That may be important one day.

Other officers were looking into Paula's private life, her family, her ex-husband, and any friends who'd managed to stay with her during her decline. Those enquiries were on-going but from what he'd heard, didn't offer much hope of helping with the investigation. Paula's life choices had shut down her world, populated with no one of note and with a living space shrunken to a litter-bin apartment.

\* \* \*

Grant, Amber, and DCI Winter attended the post-mortem examination, which had taken place the day after Paula's body was discovered. The West London morgue was a familiar venue for Grant and the DCI, less so for Amber. The three officers had donned gowns and plastic shoe covers and exited the locker space into the examination room. The sight was always one that demanded a few seconds to assimilate, even after numerous visits. Stainless steel tables, more like large shallow trays if the truth be known, bore the bodies of the subjects awaiting examination. On the day of Paula Bingley's post-mortem the mortuary was half full. A teenage victim of an asthma attack lay next to an eighty-year-old pedestrian who'd thought it was safe to cross; he was wrong. Next was an alcoholic rough sleeper in his forties looking twenty years older, while opposite lay an old lady who had lived alone; no one had known she had passed away until the smell crept out of the letterbox. Here was the reality of human tragedy made flesh.

All the bodies had been prepared by mortuary technicians, ready for close attention and scrutiny by the pathologist. Each body had been opened in the familiar 'Y' cut from the shoulders to the pelvic bone. The most disturbing sight was always the manner in which the face of the subjects was folded, pulled down to the chin to allow access to the cranium and so the brain. The first time Grant had seen the incision made around the back of the head and watched as a very pretty and diminutive twenty-something girl rip the scalp away from the skull, he had stood open-mouthed. Only by a power of will had he kept that morning's Full-English in place. He'd seen horrors before, on the battlefields in the South Atlantic and in the aftermath of car-bombs on the streets of Ulster, however, the casual, detached sterility of that act of face-removal seemed worse than all those hot-blooded mutilations. Grant shook his head at the image. What sort of a world was this that his job, his way of making a living and providing for his family, should involve getting used to a sight like this? Grant Maddox recalled the sad but profoundly true words spoken by Amber Bennett so recently as they had sat, stunned and shocked in the Migliorè Coffee House, 'This is the job we picked, isn't it?' It was.

Paula Bingley's wasted little body had endured further mutilation and indignity, but this time in the pursuit of the person whose actions had brought her to this place. Grant's next thought was answered by the examining pathologist as if he had spoken it out loud.

"I suspect that this lady would have been lying here in the not-too-distant future if this misfortune hadn't befallen her. She was well on the way to a premature death, I'm afraid."

The observing officers, in the presence of an expert figure of authority, naturally spoke little and listened intently as the pathologist conducted his examination. Speaking into a recording device, he reported his findings and related observations and listed the size, weight, and condition of internal organs as an assistant took numerous photographs. Grant looked to his left at Amber; she saw his movement and returned his glance. He raised an enquiring eyebrow and said, 'You okay?' She nodded in the affirmative and both returned their attention to the examination.

"You'll want the cause of death first, I expect?" It was a rhetorical question, of course they did. "Until tox comes back to confirm one way or the other, I'll say this lady died of simple, straightforward exsanguination. She bled to death. There are no other signs of violence on her person and no marks about the neck to indicate strangulation. No bursting of capillaries in her eyes, which may hint at asphyxiation. No blunt trauma, no wounds to her body other than the rather obvious one. As far as I can tell, the mutilation she suffered doesn't hide any other wound from us, whether accidentally or by intent. So, it looks like catastrophic blood loss. This lady was obviously dependent on drugs, what sort or what cocktail toxicology will tell us, and whether they were contributary or not. It's a wait-and-see, people!"

"Thank you, Doctor. What can you tell me about the removal of the organ, which I'm presuming was her womb?" DCI Winter asked. "Was this done with any skill, for example?" The pathologist looked up, his hands disturbingly resting *inside* the abdomen of Paula Bingley.

"Certainly." The doctor almost sounded cheerful. "I hope you won't be offended if I put this in layman-speak. I'll obviously put all the medical jargon in my report."

DCI Winter smiled, "layman-speak will be wonderful, make it as simple as you like and I promise we won't be offended."

The pathologist took a deep breath. "This lady has been the subject of a total hysterectomy; the womb has been removed at the cervix with the fallopian tubes and ovaries still attached and intact. The surgery, I'll call it that, lacking any other word, was, in my opinion, performed by someone without medical training. The abdominal incisions to gain access were apparently made with a scalpel or a similar very sharp instrument. The first incision appears to have been a vertical cut from the sternum to the pubis. All the cuts were much larger than were necessary to gain access to the presumed objective. There are two lateral cuts, one high, at the upper end of the vertical incision, the other one low, at its base, here and here, forming a giant capital letter 'I' if you like."

The doctor pointed to the slices across Paula's stomach. "The effect of these cuts is to open the abdomen like a parcel; only one of these incisions was necessary; the other was made for ease of access; the use of a staple gun as a form of retractor is a practical solution, but clumsy. An attacker with medical knowledge would make the incisions here and here."

The doctor directed the officer's attention once more to the gaping hole in Paula Bingley. "Retraction would occur naturally, no need for staples. Additionally, I have examined the extracted organ and noted that it has several lacerations, which indicate either a very clumsy process of removal, a hurried procedure, or both. The extraction may have been hindered by environmental conditions, of course, lighting, for example. The answer to your question detective is no, the removal does not indicate medical knowledge. Having said that, he's not done a bad job of it. Frankly, there is so much you can find online nowadays, never mind from books."

* * *

The investigating officers had to wait two days for the results, which shone a whole new light on the murder.

"Ketamine!" Grant had exclaimed as he read the initial report in the DCI's office.

64

DI Dodds had managed to inveigle himself into this review and nodded sagely as he studied his copy of the pathologist's report. "Hmmm, yes, Ketamine. It makes sense, and I always thought it might be something like that."

The DCI raised an eyebrow. "Really, Doddy, how so? You never mentioned anything."

"Well, who would lie there and let someone cut their bits out unless incapacitated? I *always* suspected Ketamine."

"Thank God you're here." Doddy missed the DCI's sarcasm totally. Grant Maddox didn't.

# Chapter Fifteen

Grant opened his front door with care, entering and holding the Yale lock until the door was properly shut so it would make no sound. Tip-toeing, he flicked his shoes off into a corner of the hall and crept towards the kitchen; as he passed the open door to the sitting room, a voice called out from the inky darkness.

"Grant?"

"Lyddy. Lyddy my love, what are you doing up this late? It's nearly 1 o'clock." Grant's heart sank.

"I'm glad you're home; I've missed you." Lydia hesitated. "It's been a bad day."

Grant already knew that sitting alone in the dark this late was a sure sign of his wife's suffering.

"Well, I'm here now, gorgeous. How about coming into the kitchen and keeping me company while I have tea and toast? I'm famished."

Lydia emerged from the shadow into the hallway, lit through the glass front door by the streetlamp over the road. She wasn't tall; Grant had always joked when they hugged how her face fit snugly into the crease between his broad chest and shoulder. 'You were made to fit me,' he'd said from their earliest days together. The words always made her glow.

He smiled and held his arms out to his wife to offer comfort and reassurance. She weakly returned his smile. Her face was still very pretty, even though it was showing the signs of her age, she was now fifty. However old she may be, in Grant's eyes she would always be 'my lovely' or 'my gorgeous' or 'my beautiful', or on occasion when he was feeling particularly

*East-Enders*, she would be his 'treacle'. Whichever affectionate epithet he chose, his manner with his wife always dripped with a deep warmth, an overriding need to care for and to protect, but most of all, with a profound and heart-bursting love.

Lydia lay her head on her husband's chest, and he enfolded her in his arms, her face naturally slotting into place in the dip of his shoulder, as it always had, from their first embrace to this.

"Hello, Titch," he whispered. "See how well you fit, made for me you were!"

He felt a shaking as his wife laughed at his oft-used expression. She wrapped her arms around his waist and pulled him tight as if to pull him inside her, where she could keep him forever, so he couldn't get away. Lydia needed Grant. Her life was a constant battle to overcome the demons that fought to take control of her, threatening to make her collapse into a physical and mental car crash.

She smiled as she extricated herself from his arms. "You sit down; you've been working all day; I'll make your tea and toast. Come on."

She padded in bare feet to the kitchen and flipped the light switch. Grant looked at Lydia in the bright light, and a wave of desire swept over him. His wife wore a baggy T-shirt and pyjama bottoms, but there was no disguising the swing of her large breasts, bra-less under her shirt. No hiding the curve of her shapely backside in the unflattering tartan bottoms. She was as pretty as a picture, with dark hair cut in a bob that just reached her shoulders and big brown eyes that shone when she smiled. Grant sighed inwardly, guilt, shame, fury, and frustration churning inside him. All emotions directed at himself, none, not for one moment, at his wife. What had happened to her had been his fault. Her forgiveness would never be enough because he could never forgive himself.

"One slice or two and choose marmalade, jam, or Marmite?" she asked.

It was a scene of domestic normality. It hid so much.

\* \* \*

Grant dabbed the side of his mouth with the napkin, took a last, long gulp of tea, and slumped back in the chair.

"How was your day?" Lydia asked the question.

After divulging the details of the shopping mall shooting so many years ago, Grant had learned to never fully, or honestly, answer that question again. From their earliest days, Lydia had been what his mother described as 'delicate'. His father gave a different description, 'she's a cracker son, look at the size of her knockers'. His father was right, she was a 'cracker' and her 'knockers' were very lovely indeed but Grant saw far more than that. His mother had been right, Lydia was delicate, but that made her even more attractive to his protective instinct.

He never wanted anyone else as a wife, not even close. It was simple to explain: he loved her. They married, they had two daughters, and they were happy, especially once Grant left the firearms unit and moved to the CID. Their marriage had been wonderful until…

Grant smiled and batted away her question, "Oh, busy, wall-to-wall paperwork, you know how it is." He said no more.

# Chapter Sixteen

D etective Chief Inspector Paul Winter was slumped in his chair. It was gone midnight. The CID main office was brightly lit but empty. The investigation's pace had slowed to a grind remarkably quickly; the main piece of evidence was the abused body of Paula Bingley herself and the pages of forensic reports relating to her.

Paula Bingley's toxicology reports listed copious amounts of heroin in her system, although apparently no new additional dose on the day of her demise. Paula was also awash with the residue of extra strong export lager, the addled alcoholic's beverage of choice. Then, of course, there was the Ketamine. A precise dosage, the report specified, enough to render the victim helpless but remain conscious. This left a huge question unanswered: what was the motive for this attack? The DCI was impressed that pathology had estimated the time of death as sometime on Saturday, probably in the second half of that day. Facts from the investigation supported this hypothesis.

Enquiries had found Paula's cash withdrawal of £120.00 at the ATM nearest her home on Saturday morning at 10:51am. Five twenty pound notes and two tenner's had been dispensed. The ATM camera had chronicled Paula Bingley's tense and anxious face when pressing the buttons, but she was alone. It appeared that duress hadn't reared its head, nor was the presence of the pony-tailed dealer visible in the recording. Subsequently, thirteen pounds and a penny were found in a pocket of Paula's discarded clothing at the crime scene, the serial number of the ten-pound note linking it to the ATM issue, the remaining three pounds and a penny matching the exact change from a ten-pound note for coffee at the Migliorè. It wasn't a great leap to assume that the missing £100.00 had paid for the wraps of heroin found in the same pocket, leaving the found amount, which Paula hadn't had the opportunity to spend. It all pointed to Paula's death taking place sometime near or after noon on Saturday. More sinister was the revelation that the CCTV system at Charleroi Mansions had been deliberately and expertly sabotaged. An act that pointed straight as an arrow to premeditation.

\* \* \*

DCI Winter jumped slightly as the door to his office was knocked on and opened almost simultaneously, and Grant Maddox's face peeked around the corner.

"Fuck me, Granty. I nearly soiled myself; I thought I was the last man standing tonight."

"Sorry, Guv. I'm nearly done. I've just got something on the last action you gave me."

The DCI leant forward, leaning wearily on his desktop. "Remind me."

Grant smiled. His boss did have a lot on his plate, from supervising the large team of detectives and civilian staff to fending off the press one minute and engaging their support the next, and reporting progress to senior officers who wanted results yesterday. All this whilst also guiding the enquiry and issuing investigative actions. Paul Winter was a master at juggling and earned the trust and respect of his officers by bearing those burdens and leaving his team free to get on with the job unencumbered.

"Paula's ex-husband, Damian Bingley?" Grant reminded.

A look of recognition spread over the DCI's face. "Oh, yes, yes. What have you got?" Winter opened a desk drawer, removed a bottle of *Famous Grouse* from within, followed by two white Styrofoam cups. "I take it you'll have one with me, Granty?"

Grant smiled, when the '*Grouse*' was out it was informal time. "Thanks Paul, just a small one, I've got to drive home."

Winter sloshed a couple of drams of the golden liquid into each of the cups and handed one to his DS. "Cheers."

"Cheers."

"So, the ex-husband, tell me what we have?"

Grant sipped at the Scotch, deciding that was as much as he was going to consume, took a deep breath, and answered. "The problem is that the ex-husband, Damian Bingley, is in Australia at the moment, Sydney, to be precise. He has business interests and homes all around the world. It must be hell for him." Grant couldn't disguise his envy. "There's no possibility he's directly involved in his ex-wife's murder; he's been out there over a month. So the question is, is he involved indirectly?"

Grant looked down at the liquid in his cup, shrugged, and took another sip. "Damian Bingley is a very, *very* rich man, now in his late fifties. He made his millions in the mobile phone boom, sold out his interests and re-invested in computer games just in time for a huge boom in demand for that. He's never been shy of publicity, courted it actually, he appeared in several 'beg me for an investment in your crack-pot scheme' television programmes and was a regular go-to pundit on news channels whenever anything financial was a lead story. He married Paula Castle, as she was, in 1980, when he was an up-and-comer, so she was there for the ride to riches. Now all this personal stuff about Damian is on the public record, on the Internet, in Companies House, etc. When I contacted Damian's British P.A., I was referred to Australia. I fought my way through to his *Australian* P.A., who, to be fair, wanted to help but was constrained by her boss's schedule."

"Fuck his schedule, this is a murder investigation, and the victim is this bloke's wife!" The DCI's temper flared at the tiniest hint of *any* obstruction to *his* investigation.

"Quite so." Grant sympathised. "But I figured, softly, softly, catchee monkey. If this guy is uninvolved he can only either help or hinder, better he helps, besides which, why wind up a very rich guy with media access?"

"Good point. Carry on." Winter conceded, smacking his lips after draining his cup and reaching for the bottle.

"New South Wales Police have been very helpful; there's a DC out there

I've been liaising with; not easy with the time difference, hence why I'm still here."

"On time and a half, though." Winter raised his re-filled cup in salute; the enhanced pay rate for overtime was the compensation for the energy-sapping hours being worked.

Grant laughed. "That's a good point from *you* this time." Grant decided to take just *one* more sip and mirrored Winter's toast to overtime. "Well, my bloke in Sydney has tracked down Bingley's Aussie P.A. and managed to get some info. He hasn't been able to tie him down to obtain a formal statement yet, but he will. He stresses there's no objection forthcoming, they're willing to help, it's just a matter of time management, finding a few hours in his schedule. However the P.A. did provide some personal stuff which may help until we get Damian Bingley committed to a statement on paper, the Aussie DC has just sent it to me, it's mid-morning out there."

"What did we get?"

"Well, here's the interesting thing: when Bingley married Paula, she was very pregnant. They had a son, Chase Bingley." Winter raised an eyebrow.

"A son? So where's he? There's been no suggestion of next of kin?"

Grant hesitated, knowing what memories the next words would evoke. "Apparently, he died." Grant paused. "That was the start of Paula's slide, it's what ended the marriage."

The two officers sat in silence, Grant avoiding Paul's eyes. Whilst both his daughters lived, had grown and flourished, his friend's only child, Melanie, aged only seventeen, had been taken by leukemia four years earlier, a personal heartbreak the knowledge of which was shared with very few colleagues. Whatever judgment they'd previously levelled at Paula Bingley for the lifestyle she'd chosen, it was now tempered by the impact of the dreadful loss of a child. Paula Bingley's tragedy now made even worse.

"Good work, Granty." Winter broke the silence. "Obviously we need more information, try and press your Aussie to get the statement ASAP. Do we think this has any bearing on the case? Do we know when or the circumstances of..." Winter waved his hand in the air, struggling for a name.

"Chase, Chase Bingley."

"Right! Chase Bingley. Do we know when or how he died?"

Grant shook his head. "I'm just telling you what the P.A. told the DC, who told me. It's a bit of a convoluted communication chain, I'm not even sure if that degree of personal information had been authorised by Damian Bingley, but I've sent back a request to get all they can as soon as they can."

"Okay. Well done." Winter held up the bottle, waggling it from side to side. "Another drop?"

Grant laughed and stood. "Thanks, Paul, but I need to get home. Lydia hasn't been doing so well recently." He hesitated, deliberating for a few moments, making a decision. "It's coming up to the anniversary."

Paul Winter's face grimaced in understanding. "Oh. Yes, yes, of course it is. Go home, Granty, look after your wife."

"Cheers, Paul." Grant Maddox opened the office door to leave but was halted as his boss called out.

"Don't be in a rush to get here in the morning. The world won't end without you for a few hours." Grant smiled and nodded. He and Paul went back a long way.

# Chapter Seventeen

As instructed by DCI Winter, Detective Sergeant Grant Maddox sauntered into the main office mid-morning, feeling all the better for a solid eight-hour sleep. He immediately sensed that there was a different atmosphere; something had happened. Groups of officers were in huddles, talking excitedly.

"Morning Skip. Nice of you to turn up."

"Didn't realise that you'd gone part-time."

"You look familiar, but I can't put a name to your face."

Grant smiled and batted off the good-natured banter from each officer he passed with the traditional Met Police repost of, "Fuck off."

A hand waved from a desk; it was attached to DC Amber Bennett. "Skipper! Skipper! The guvnor wants you in his office ASAP." Grant smiled, nodded, and made an exaggerated cartoon-character rotation on the spot, turning towards Winter's office.

"He's in a good mood, must have had his tyres pumped up last night." A Detective Constable offered to his colleague on the other side of his desk. Grant *was* in a good mood; sleep, not laughter, was definitely the best medicine. As far as having his 'tyres pumped', that was something he'd put to the back of his mind for a long while now.

\* \* \*

Grant knocked and entered DCI Paul Winter's office in one fluid movement. The guvnor was stretched back in his chair over which his suit jacket was draped, his shirt top button undone, his tie loosened, hands behind his head, facing up at the ceiling, eyes closed. He was a picture of a man deep in thought. At the sound of the door, Paul opened his eyes and nodded towards a figure sitting opposite him. "Detective Sergeant Grant Maddox, meet Detective Inspector Heidi Yorke of Surrey Police."

The stranger, who was a smartly dressed woman in her forties, stood and offered her hand. She looked Grant, who was six foot two, straight in the eye. He couldn't help himself, in a reflex action he looked down at her feet.

Heidi laughed, obviously used to such a reaction. "Flats I'm afraid, no heels, it's all me." Captured and embarrassed, Grant lifted his gaze to look the County Force DI face to face. As he felt his cheeks colouring up, a most unusual sensation, he managed to blurt out the required, "pleased to meet you," and shook the proffered hand.

"Fuck me! He's blushing." The DCI laughed out loud. "Right, I've heard this already and I need to speak with those upstairs." He raised his eyes, looking up towards the ceiling, his meaning clear: he had information to impart to his seniors whose offices were one floor above. "Stay here. I'll speak with you later."

"Look, erm, I'm sorry about that, I…" Grant's voice trailed off.

Heidi resumed her seat, smiled, and held up both hands in a don't worry gesture. "Grant, please don't worry. I've had it all from the day I joined The Job, and it won't stop. I'm very tall. I've embraced it. Just don't call me Lurch or Brienne."

Maddox sighed internally with relief that he'd been let off so easily. He had to ask. "Lurch, I know, Addams Family, right? But Brienne?"

Heidi smiled. "*Game of Thrones*, Lady Brienne, the really tall lady knight, you know the one? She's a bit blokey. I'm tall, but I'm *not* blokey."

"Ah, *Game of Thrones,* aware of it, but it passed me by." Content that the required niceties had been exchanged Grant was keen to get down to business, curious as to why a Surrey Police Detective Inspector was in his boss's office.

"So, the Guvnor said you have something to tell me, ma'am."

"I do, Granty, I do."

Grant had immediately warmed to this woman, smiling inwardly at her self-deprecation *and* the easy use of his nickname. He didn't know it, but he'd just met a friend for life.

\* \* \*

An hour later, Grant lifted the tray from the station canteen counter and weaved through the tables, packed with lunching officers and civilian staff, towards the waiting DI Yorke, his mind awhirl with the story she'd just recounted in DCI Winter's office. Although he'd never heard of her prior to her demise, he *was* aware of the murder of Martine Walsingham three weeks previously; it was a story splashed all over the media in consequence of the victim being a one-time it-girl and sometime B-List celebrity, but Heidi Yorke's information was totally unexpected.

Martine was an extremely wealthy divorcee, a member of the social circle who went places, did things, and said stuff that seemed to be of interest to wide swathes of the population. Why? Grant had no idea. She *knew* people apparently and was, in her time, something of a beauty, a woman designers wanted to hang their clothes on, magazines wanted to print features about, and who attracted all sorts who wanted to use her for their own ends. Sadly, her wealth, status, and numerous rich and famous friends did her no good. She'd still ended up dead. As far as Grant was aware, uncomplicatedly stabbed to death in her kitchen. How the investigation was progressing, he had no idea. That was a Surrey Police problem; he had enough on his plate.

"Obviously we kept the specifics of the murder confidential," Heidi had said in Winter's office. "Apart from the sensationalism the details would elicit, we had the family's feelings to consider and wanted the worst of it in our back pocket...to sift the wheat from the chaff, you understand?"

Grant understood exactly what Heidi was saying. This sort of prominent case would attract any number of publicity-seeking wannabees claiming to have killed a person of note, desperate for the attention associated with the act. A significant detail known only to investigators could be used to eliminate them from the enquiry. "I *do* understand," Grant answered.

* * *

The story imparted, the two detectives headed off for refreshments. "Coffee, white without, and a ham sandwich. Met Police cuisine at its finest," Grant announced. Having successfully navigated the canteen assault course, he placed the loaded tray on the table and sat down opposite Heidi Yorke, removing his order of tea and a Cornish pasty.

"Thank you, Grant. The pasty looks good, but I mustn't. They're about a thousand calories each."

"Well, thanks for that, pile the guilt on," Grant replied with mock offence.

Heidi shrugged. "You're welcome."

Grant looked the DI in the eye, "So this is what we've got," he counted off extended fingers. "Women, in their fifties, wealthy or wealthy once, injected with Ketamine, dissected whilst conscious, and their wombs removed. The latter being dropped or, more likely, thrown in their faces. Cause of death: blood loss. No sign of sexual assault, no sign of theft, no forced entry, no prints or DNA from forensics, in both cases all surveillance and CCTV skillfully bypassed." Grant took a breath. "Is that it?"

Heidi Yorke picked up the baton. "The dissection of the women in both cases wasn't thought to be by a trained person; however, with the second victim, your Paula Bingley, a staple gun was used to hold open the abdominal cavity, and the removal was less clumsy, neater."

Grant shook his head slowly from side to side. "Having attended the scene, *neat* is not the word I'd have immediately picked as a description. However, it does seem our killer is becoming more proficient. The staples act as retractors and improve dexterity, which points to a process and an advance in technique."

Heidi Yorke nodded her agreement, sipping her coffee before making her observation. "If we have a serial killer on our hands, a pattern is often followed. The frequency of the attacks tends to increase the skill of the attacker. Then it can go one of two ways: our murderer surrenders to the overwhelming desire to kill, the process takes on the form of a frenzy, out of control, and significantly, it changes from an organised event to a disorganised one in criminological terms. Or..."

Grant finished the sentence. "...or he gets better, smarter, more elusive or...stops. And we have nothing."

"Nothing." Heidi echoed. "But we do have something for now. The similarity of the victims, what's the connection, what drives the killer's choice of victim? What does the manner of their deaths mean, and what is the fixation with the womb? Then there's the necessary knowledge and risky exposure to tamper with the surveillance kit. And something else we must consider: both women appear to have felt safe and secure enough to allow their killers access to them."

"They knew their killer?" Grant hoisted it up there. The two detectives sat in silence for a while until Heidi broke the silence.

"Right! This has been good. I've a lot to look into at my end. There are lines of enquiry to follow and clear away. There's a nasty land dispute with none other than Martine's next-door neighbour, Bernard Campion, and a personal trainer who was getting far too personal, to look into. Never mind researching Martine's convoluted background, it's amazing how many people an 'It-girl' knows, even one who's past her prime. It makes my head spin."

Picking up on Heidi's reference to the neighbour, Grand queried, "Bernard Campion! *The* Bernard Campion? The Digital Home Warehouse man?"

Heidi nodded. "And don't forget generous political donor. He's *not* a nice man and a guy with lots of connections, if you know what I mean. Martine did something to him which made him *very* angry."

"But the Paula Bingley murder, the manner of the attack, it must point away from Campion?"

Heidi rose from the table. "You'd think so, but until we find a connection between the women or a reason the killer chose his victims *outside* of a connection between them, well, I'm not excluding anything. And from what your DCI said, neither will you...will you?"

Grant laughed at his assessment by a fellow professional. "No. I won't. Good to meet you, ma'am. We'll keep in touch."

Heidi offered her hand, which he gladly took. "Definitely. Good to meet you too, thanks for lunch and…please, call me Heidi, we *are* grown-ups."

"Heidi, it is."

# Chapter Eighteen

The discovery of an earlier, near identical murder had electrified the officers investigating the Paula Bingley killing. New priority lines of investigation had been opened, chief amongst these was digging deep into the lives of the victims, examining their habits, movements, associates, interests, friends, and friends of friends. Scrutinising two lives, apparently on different tracks, looking for a reason that someone would wish to drug, dissect and murder the two women.

Grant Maddox was re-reading the Surrey Police crime-scene report for the Martine Walsingham murder for the umpteenth time. The corresponding Met report for Paula Bingley lay on his desk. When he'd finished one, he swapped them over in his hand and read them again, searching for some small point that would provide a link between the victims other than the horrific manner of their deaths.

The tall, gangly figure of DCI Paul Winter entered the main office. A few heads turned to look at him as he examined the whiteboard, which listed the actions being undertaken and their progress. When he clapped his hands, all heads turned toward him.

"Ladies, Gents, listen in, please, listen in. I have some…er, interesting news."

Grant raised an eyebrow, his curiosity roused.

"This is from the Big House, as part of the ongoing policy of transparency and openness, as a continuance of The Met's desire to embrace and befriend the media rather than alienate what we should consider an allied resource, it's been decided that we'll be entertaining a couple of visitors." Heads swivelled from one to another as the gathered officers tried to second guess the meaning of the announcement, there was a hubbub of conversation at the news.

Winter waved his hands to still the commotion. "I'm sure you're aware of the work of Isla Baxter, the journalist and TV reporter. She's been producing the '*Isla Investigates*' documentaries for many years, Ladies and Gents, we… this investigation…is the subject of her next documentary."

There were gasps from around the room. From some there was obvious excitement and delight, a young, enthusiastic voice called out, 'We're going to be on the tele? Cool!' The racket and clamor built up, an obvious split in opinion forming between those that saw excitement and celebrity come calling while others saw inevitable interference and constraints on how they conducted themselves and their work.

Winter clapped his hands once more, and the room quietened. "Really, guys? *Really?*" The DCI's exasperation was obvious. "Can we calm down and maintain some professionalism please? My understanding is that Miss Baxter and one other, a camera operator/soundman, will constitute the whole operation. Both persons are security cleared, and we're ordered to allow *full* access. Miss Baxter has contractually undertaken to produce and release no film or recording until the case is completed *successfully*. That means unless this investigation is solved and an offender is convicted, *everything* stays in the can. The premise of Miss Baxter's piece is the start-to-finish record of a major investigation. If the result of this case is open-ended, there is no documentary. I have an assurance of that." Winter looked over to the table, which held a young DC. "So if you want your granny to see you on the tele, you better get your finger out." There was irritation in his voice. To anyone who knew Winter it seemed apparent that the idea of embracing the reporters was not one he approved.

A wall of sound hit the DCI as questions and comments flew at him from every corner, Winter strode, grim faced, to his office door and addressed his team before disappearing inside. "When you've all calmed down, we'll talk again. For now, let the news sink in."

"Isla Baxter! Fuck me!" Grant turned to see the expression of delight on Amber Bennett's face as she expressed her astonishment. "I mean Skip, she's big, really big. Wait 'til I tell my mum, she'll be thrilled. Do you think we can get autographs?" Her face lit up with a thought, "Or a photo, a selfie with Isla Baxter, wow!"

Grant was wide-eyed. "Bloody hell, Amber, I didn't think you'd be so star-struck. I reckon you should wait until the Terms of Reference are clearly and properly defined before you tell *anyone* about this, even your mum."

Amber's face was a picture of contrition. "Sorry Skip, yeh, you're right, but I mean, have you seen any *Isla Investigates* programmes? She's been everywhere, seen and done everything. From interviewing drug barons in the South American jungle, exposing people traffickers, to really upsetting that Russian Oligarch, Vasily-whats-is-name-'ovitch, she had to escape out the back of a hotel when a dozen of his heavies came looking for her. She's been shot at, assaulted, nearly blown up, she's an award-winning legend and she's coming here! You *must* be excited."

Grant looked down at the crime scene report in his hand and the one on the desktop. How could having Isla Baxter hanging around asking questions and wanting explanations while her mate rammed his camera up their noses be anything but a distraction from the work at hand? He'd discerned that Winter wasn't delighted at the turn of events either. Grant looked at the beaming face of his young DC and couldn't disappoint.

"You're right, it *will* be exciting."

He turned his attention back to the reports.

# Chapter Nineteen

I sla Baxter, with Paul Winter, was making her way around the office, shaking hands, smiling freely. She was in her mid-thirties, small in stature, with a firm, fit body, solid looking, Grant thought. She was pretty in a girl-next-door way; her face was unlikely to turn heads if she wasn't famous, but when she smiled, her blue eyes lit up in a pleasing manner. Her hair was light brown and styled in a modern, no-nonsense short cut; it was still feminine, but, like the rest of her demeanour, exuded strength and practicality. Isla Baxter wouldn't be fussing with her hair in a war zone any time soon.

Grant could see from the tilt of her head and her expression that she was trying to remember the names and roles of those to whom Paul Winter was introducing. Her assistant followed in her wake. He was also in his mid-thirties, of medium build, medium height, also sporting short, light brown hair which sat atop a face with unremarkable, even features. He also smiled but less enthusiastically, spending more time looking around the room, absorbing the atmosphere, and studying the wall charts which were plastered with notes, photos, and writing. Grant made the assessment, Isla was all about people, the assistant was all about the environment. Isla was all about style and presentation; the assistant was all about practicalities and content. It looked like a perfect coupling of skills and characters.

DCI Winter smiled and made the introductions. "This is Detective Sergeant Grant Maddox, Granty to his mates, Isla Baxter and her assistant, Robert Pagett." Hands were shaken, and more smiles were exchanged.

"Detective Sergeant. I'm pleased to meet you. May I call you Granty? I'm hoping to be friends with the *whole* team."

"Of course. Welcome to our lair." The small cluster laughed uncomfort-ably. "This is Amber Bennett, a DC and my sidekick, we all need one." Grant nodded towards Pagett.

Isla smiled at the joke. "If the truth be known Granty, Rob here," Isla flicked her head sideways, "is far from being a sidekick, he's more *'Isla Investigates'* than I am. We're a two-man team, with one doing most of the work. I bet it's the same with you, eh Amber?" Isla smiled broadly in a girl-to-girl conspiracy. Grant decided that Isla was a clever woman, skilled at winning people over, and on closer inspection, was rather attractive after all.

Amber blushed, her face reddening in an instant. "I'd never claim that Miss Baxter, I'm very new and learning all I can from the skipper here. He won't say so, but he's about the best there is." Grant looked at Amber, wondering what he'd done to elicit such praise.

"Please call me, Isla. We all need to be comfortable together. This project can only work if we get on. If we trust each other, there will be no more Miss Baxter. Okay?"

DCI Winter placed a guiding hand on Isla's shoulder, eager to move her on, to get the introductions over, keen to get back to his office, keen to get back to work. As they moved away, Rob Pagett looked back and nodded. He hadn't spoken a word, deferring to Isla Baxter. Grant returned the nod.

Grant Maddox had been a copper long enough to recognise the expression on Pagett's face, it was a look all police officers got to recognise eventually. The look on Rob Pagett's face said to Grant, loud and clear, 'I don't like coppers.'

* * *

"I want to thank all of you in advance for your friendship, co-operation, and commitment to this project." Isla Baxter stood in front of the gathered officers, with Rob Pagett lurking behind. "Rob and I have been all around the world, we've found ourselves in all sorts of situations, many of them very unpleasant, many of them frightening. For those reasons, I want to express a sincere feeling of gratitude to you and all your comrades all over the United Kingdom. When we're in *this* country we know, *absolutely know*, that when a victim calls for help, it *will* come. When a crime is committed a dedicated group of men and women *will* investigate and will do so without fear or favour, malice or ill-will. We know the cancer of corruption will not tinge the actions and motivations of *our* police. These simple facts are something we take for granted here. For Rob and me, with our experiences from around the world, I can assure you that we *do not* take you for granted at all. We want to engage with you, as you complete this project, because we have such high regard for you, your skill and dedication and we want to showcase that in our documentary." Isla paused for effect, looking around the room, locking eyes with several of the team before continuing.

"I don't want anyone here to believe that we're here to trick you, show you up, or put you in a bad light." Isla pointed a finger and swept it around the room. "We are fans of our British Police, the best in the world; just show us what you've got, honest, straightforward, warts and all. Now, I understand that this is something of a tradition." Isla waved towards several carrier bags leaning against the wall, which Pagett picked up and began to unpack. "Apparently I need to say, 'Cream cakes for the lads.' Help yourself guys. Thank you."

A cheer went up in the office. Isla Baxter certainly knew how to make a speech, knew what buttons to press to get a smile from the team and get them all onside, and cream cakes was a nice touch. Grant laughed to a smiling Amber Bennett.

"Go and get me a good one, loadsa jam, loadsa cream, a coronary bun."

"Will do, Skip. She spoke well, didn't she? In the long run, this sort of exposure may well help us get the public on board, more willing to help or come forward, more willing to see the problems we face, have a more realistic understanding of what we can and can't do. Don't you think?"

"Yeh, yeh, what you said. Now get my cake before they all disappear."

85

# Chapter Twenty

The following morning the DCI executed a masterstroke by appointing DI Brian Dodds as the liaison between the Investigation Team and the two documentary makers. In one fell-swoop he'd gifted Isla Baxter a senior detective officer to guide and advise her, his rank an obvious compliment and a symbol of his commitment to the project sanctioned by 'The Big House.' At the same time, he'd shifted a fucking idiot from under everyone else's feet, helping to lubricate the smooth running of the investigation. As Grant watched Doddy schmooze his way around the office, never more than six inches from Isla Baxter, a sycophantic grin plastered to his face, his admiration for Winter soared to new heights.

Rob Pagett was floating about the office, pad in hand, recording names, ranks, and responsibilities, getting a handle on the investigation into the brutal murder of two women. So far, there'd been no filming. In a corner, on a desk reserved for Isla and himself, lay Rob Pagett's camera. During this settling-in-phase, Isla was working her way into the scenery, becoming part of the backdrop, and the presence of the unused camera was a process, getting the officers familiar with its existence in their lives. When the camera was eventually lifted to Pagett's shoulder, it would be less of an intrusion, and maybe people would act naturally. Time would tell.

\* \* \*

Grant Maddox had never been one to dodge a challenge or a threat, but that didn't mean he had met issues head-on. As an ex-Royal Marine, 'the thinking soldiers', he knew sometimes to come at a threat from an unexpected angle was best. An old Job expression for accepting an inevitable unpleasantness popped into his mind. 'It's a shit sandwich and you're going to have to take a bite'. Grant's assessment was Rob Pagett was definitely the shit in this sandwich. He resolved to find out more about that young man.

Grant strolled the short distance to the *Isla Investigates* desk and looked down at the camera. About a foot and a half of black metal and plastic, its surface covered in numerous controls and buttons. Grant lifted the device by its integral handle.

"Light, isn't it?"

Grant turned to see the owner of the refined and educated voice and found the face of Rob Pagett. "Two and a half kilo's. If you need to move fast, get in, or get out of somewhere in a hurry, especially if bullets are flying, you don't want to be lugging a heavy weight with you."

Grant smiled. "Two and a half kilo's, what's that in old money?" He raised and lowered the camera in assessment. "Six pounds, maybe? It looks complicated." Pagett reached over and took the camera out of the DS's hand, putting it down, carefully, on the desktop.

"It is. Over six thousand pounds worth of complicated." Pagett looked for Grant to be suitably impressed, Grant decided to reward him with a low whistle as the cameraman continued with his pitch. "The Canon XF 305 high definition camcorder, with eighteen times magnification wide-angle L-series lens, auto *or* manual focus, zoom and iris, HD capture to compact flash with two slots, and HD embedded audio and timecode. Anything else I can help you with?" The disrespect and aversion in his upmarket voice was undisguised.

Grant smiled inwardly, refusing to bite. Instead, he pointed to the extensive tattoos which adorned Rob Pagett's exposed arms. "Nice sleeve, that's the expression, isn't it? A sleeve? What's all that mean?" He waved a finger up and down Pagett's right arm.

The cameraman looked down and traced the images with his fingertip. "They represent where we've been, what we've done."

"You and Isla?"

"Obviously. Each image is a place, a country, or a city, but with a bite taken out."

Grant stared more closely, seeing the specific shapes amongst the swirling colours and patterns. He pointed to one. "What's that?"

"That's Mali. It's in West Africa."

Grant raised a sarcastic eyebrow, "Really?"

"We did a piece there that pissed off the U.N., the French, and what they laughingly referred to as their Government."

"And that one?" Grant pointed to another tattoo.

"Mexico. We exposed the struggle between The Police and The Government to partner with the drug cartels. All of them, rotten to the core."

"That one?" Grant pointed again.

"The Congo."

"Africa again, right?"

Pagett ignored the sarcasm. "After slaughtering over a million Tutsis in Rwanda, nearly two million Hutus bolted to the Congo to escape the U.N. forces who were sent in. They formed militia groups and fought *everyone*, as many as three million were killed. No one cared, just ignorant black folk killing other ignorant black folk." His voice dripped sarcasm. "We did a piece on child soldiers and Western arms suppliers."

"That one? Last one, promise."

Pagett shrugged. "The Bahamas. It's a tax haven for the rich and well-to-do, corrupt, and criminal are better descriptions. We found the cream of English society and exposed them for what they are, fucking parasites."

Grant looked at the numerous images adorning the flesh of Rob Pagett's arm, each outline *did* indeed have a serrated bite-mark, as if a shark had taken a mouthful. "And now your next piece is us, the Met Police. Do you intend to take a bite out of us as well, Robert? Are you hoping for a tattooed Met Police badge on your arm, maybe just nibbled at or maybe with a dirty, great big chunk taken out of it?" Grant's voice was calm but he injected an edge, an accusation, he wanted to see the reaction if this man's life's work and a role he clearly relished, was challenged.

Pagett was rattled. "I just do the filming Mr Policeman, if it isn't there I can't capture it, if it is, I do. That's my job. We were promised transparency; if you aren't ashamed or hiding something, why would I bite you?"

Grant let Pagett's question hang unanswered, instead he changed the subject pointing at a series of elaborate, artistic tattoos on Pagett's left arm, quite unlike the harsh and business-like representations on the right. "These are different, what are they about?" Along the length of the left forearm was depicted an angel, wings part-folded back, a beautiful, serene but deeply sad female face. Robes were loosely coiled around her body as if blown there by a gust of wind. The rippling curves of fabric formed the shape of parchment, similar to that bearing a motto under a coat of arms, elaborately notated thereon were two names, 'Robbie' and 'Cassandra'.

"You ask a lot of questions, don't you?"

Grant shrugged. "We've all got jobs, Robbie, asking questions, well, it's *my* job." Grant echoed Pagett's earlier words. To the cameraman's immense irritation, Grant patted the camera like a good dog before turning and walking away.

# Chapter Twenty-One

H is e-mail inbox list was headed with a message from New South Wales Police, Australia.

> *"For the attention of DS GRANT MADDOX...please find attached a statement from Damian Bingley as requested. Apologies for the delay mate, the bloke was a bit of a bugger to tie down. Hope it helps and please ask if you need more info or anything clarifying. Australia, as you know, is practically a crime-free country so I have nothing else to do but chase around running errands for you.*
> *Cheers Pom.*
> *Stay safe.*
> *DC Bruce O'Leary. (And yes! My name really IS Bruce!)"*

Grant laughed out loud at the e-mail, not just at the comedy of an Aussie called Bruce, he supposed some of them had to be, but at the helpful but purposefully grumpy informality. It was the sort of attitude he liked. He clicked for the attachment and read the statement from the ex-husband of his victim, Paula Bingley.

\* \* \*

"Yes, Granty?" enquired Winter. "What can I do for you?"

Maddox slumped in the seat opposite his guvnor, the print-out of the e-mail in his hand. "Our statement from the colonies, Guv." Grant waved the sheets of paper.

"Summarise it for me."

Grant scanned the papers. "Well, the background is Damian Bingley knocked up our girl, Paula Castle, as she was then. He did the decent thing, and they married. Actually, I think they were in love, he certainly says so, and his later actions support that. Damian was a whiz-kid entrepreneur who went from success to success and made millions and millions. The baby was a boy called Chase. Born in…" Grant scanned the statement, "…1980. Apparently it was a difficult birth, some complications with medical names that this Damian can't pronounce or remember. The bottom line is that Chase ended up being an only child. Paula doted on the boy, spoiled him rotten, *really* rotten. Mr Bingley says that there was a lot of friction between Paula and him about how young Chase was turning out." Grant waved the statement some more. "He goes on about how *he* made it through hard work and he thought Chase should do the same, I think there's a lot of guilt regarding what happened later."

"What happened later?" Paul Winter leant forward, resting his arms on the desktop.

"Tragedy. A double tragedy actually. The Bingley's sent young Chase to Frankton Abbey School."

"Whoa! Chase Bingley went to Franks?" The DCI couldn't stop himself. "That's the top, the best, the most…"

"… expensive school in the world?" interrupted Grant.

"Exactly. Keep going, what tragedy?"

"Like I said, a *double* tragedy," answered Maddox. "You must remember the *Frankton Abbey Rugby Seven Crash*? It was all over the papers."

A look of realisation spread on Winter's face. "Of course, bloody awful. About fifteen years ago?"

"Eighteen years ago. The '*super-privileged sons of the super-rich and super-famous killed in jet-crash horror*', the headlines went something like that." Grant remembered clearly; the story held the front pages for days.

"And Chase Bingley was on board?" DCI Winter's voice was hushed.

"Seventeen years old, a winner in life's lottery, splattered all over a field in France, along with the rest of them. An utter waste."

Grant waved the statement again. "So, they lost their boy, and the marriage went tits up…as can happen sometimes." Grant chose his words with care. "Mr Bingley admits to neglecting Paula, throwing himself into his work, trying to erase the pain of his loss. Paula went another way. She had a breakdown, never stopped crying, turned Chase's room into a shrine, lost it completely, attempted suicide, and of course, as we know, she started taking drugs."

Winter nodded with solemn empathy, not needing to be told the pressures the loss of a child induced.

"Inevitably," Grant continued, "there was a split. Damian found a new love and expanded his business empire, while Paula spiralled downwards. In fairness, Damian tried to get her help, the best detox centers, the best rehab, the best counselors, but you've got to want to be saved, haven't you?"

Winter nodded once more.

"So, Bingley did the best he could; he purchased a very nice property for her, the apartment in Charleroi Mansions, worth millions; it was set up with all running costs covered forever. He put money in place to cover any and all private medical expenses for the rest of her life, and there was money to cover all costs should she ever seek rehabilitation. He bought her another house on the south coast with the same setup should she wish to live there and provided an eye-watering monthly allowance for life as well. Considering how wealthy he was, she could have had much more, and he would have given it, he says,"

Grant scanned the final page of the statement. "Here it is; I'll read it. *'Paula was the mother to my son; I loved her once but our tragic loss drove us apart. The memory of what Paula once was, and for the sake of the memory of our son, I gladly and willingly agreed to provide for her. However that wish was tempered by the obvious manner in which Paula would spend any monies granted her. Ultimately, when we separated, she asked for nothing, nothing at all. Not a penny. I fear she was intent upon self-destruction. The provisions I made for her, were forced on her by my legal representatives. I wish I could have done more for Paula. I wish I could have saved her. I was unable to do so. I lament her loss, the terrible sadness of her later life and the manner she left it will always haunt me. I can only hope she is now re-united with our son and she has found peace and happiness at his side in an afterlife.'*

I don't think that he had anything to do with her death boss."

Grant lay the papers on the desk.

"I can't see that either. What did he have to gain?"

"But," Grant raised a finger, Winter raised an eyebrow in response, "Bingley does make an interesting reference early in his statement, almost in passing. When he's talking about his empire building, he gives some details, showing off a bit, I thought, but he mentions an early business partner. Guess who?"

"Tell me."

"Bernard Campion."

"No shit! Mr Digital Home Warehouse, Martine Walsingham's neighbour?"

"The one and the same. The man she was in a nasty dispute with, the man who we both know has questionable associations and a questionable history."

DCI Winter rubbed his chin. "Now *that* is interesting. It's a connection between our victims."

Grant smiled broadly. "It is guv. It really is."

# Chapter Twenty-Two

D I Yorke waited patiently as Grant read and re-read the statement she'd taken from Bernard Campion the previous day. It could have been e-mailed, but she wanted to speak to Grant in person about a mad idea she had. Although not the lead officer on the case, Heidi recognised that DCI Winter had deputed Grant to take a lead in all but name, over and above the other ranking officer, DI Dodds.

\* \* \*

Heidi had encountered DI Dodds briefly and wasn't impressed. Doddy looked the part of a detective, strong featured, broad shouldered and barrel chested, a no-nonsense shaved head, a sharp suit, an easy smile and a look of confident competence. He'd immediately shot himself in the foot on their first meeting when he'd glided over to the tall, striking Surrey Police Detective Inspector and introduced himself and his role.

"Hi, I'm Detective Inspector Brian Dodds; call me Doddy; everyone does; I'm the lead on the Pauline Binley case; anything at all, ask, and ye shall receive." He'd beamed a whitened, even-toothed smile.

Heidi had responded, "Isn't that *Paula Bingley?*"

Doddy had shrugged, unconcerned, his dazzling and winning smile fixed as ever. "Whatever, what's in a name? Can I buy you a coffee?" The hit on her was obvious and cringeworthy.

As all the good newspaper reporters used to say, DI Yorke made her excuses and left.

\* \* \*

As she'd sought out DS Maddox, armed with the statement, she'd noted with surprise that Detective Inspector Dodds was in the corner of the main office, seated with none other than internationally famous reporter Isla Baxter, while a man pointed a camera above her shoulder, focussed on his face. Doddy looked right at home; an easy smile played across his face as he answered questions and proffered theories and solutions.

"Wanker" thought Heidi.

\* \* \*

Grant skimmed through the bulk of Campion's statement, reading out loud pertinent sections for his own and Amber Bennett's benefit. He dropped the papers on his desktop and tapped them with his fingertips.

"Well?" asked Heidi, "what do you think?"

Grant frowned for a few moments, non-committal.

Heidi pushed, looking across to Amber for support. "The only link we've found between the two victims is the business association between the ex-husband of one victim and the neighbour of the other. A neighbour with whom there was an acrimonious series of disputes. In the statement, he's quite open about it. He says that Martine Walsingham was the bane of his life, 'rude, arrogant, litigious, unreasonable, unbalanced.' *All* those words are in his statement."

Grant nodded; she was right, but his face betrayed an uneasiness. "Yes, okay, Campion didn't have a substantiated alibi for the whole weekend of the murder. Part of the time, he was at home, next door, and unaccompanied, but that doesn't make him a killer. Even if he *was* involved, I can't imagine him doing it personally anyway."

The Surrey DI conceded the point. "Alright, so he's not the sort of man who would dirty his hands personally, and let's face it, the hands would be very dirty, wet, and sticky, along with everything else. He'd pay someone. He could afford it, and he's got the dodgy contacts." Heidi sighed. "Is he a viable suspect?"

Grant was aware of the background facts, the noise complaints, the new buildings adjacent to Martine's house, and the acrimonious and unfinished dispute regarding the ransom strip of land. Heidi's team had done well digging out this history, and undoubtedly, Campion's life would be easier without Martine Walsingham being in it.

"Campion *is* a shifty character," Grant conceded, "no question. From what I understand, he's a man with dodgy connections who holds a grudge, and I could understand he'd want Martine gone. But even with a motive, it seems a giant leap to dissect his neighbor on her kitchen floor, and why would Paula Bingley end up the same way?"

Heidi took a deep breath. "Okay, this is far-fetched, and I accept that, but we only have this one link between our victims at the moment." She took another deep breath and plunged in. "I read of a case in the USA where a guy wanted his wife dead. I can't remember why, but he had loads of reasons that everyone knew about. If he killed her or even *had* her killed, he would be the prime suspect, plain and simple. First rule of crime detection, if it wasn't the butler, it was the husband, right?"

Grant laughed and agreed, "Right!"

"Well, this guy murdered *another* woman, totally randomly and in a manner which was brutally distinctive, a modus operandi all his own. Then, when this 'killer's' M.O. had been established, he murdered his wife in the *same* way. The investigators were looking for a double murderer, not a domestic killer. He screwed up and was caught, but he *could* have got away with it, you understand?"

"A proxy-killing!" Amber Bennett interjected excitedly. "Like 'Strangers on a Train,' you know, the Hitchcock film. Two strangers agree to kill the obstacle to the other person's plans. It leaves them with an alibi and a false trail for the police to follow. What if someone kills Martine for Campion and Campion kills, or has someone else kill Paula for whatever reason, and everyone is happy? It's a possibility, I think."

Outnumbered by women, Grant felt pressured to overrule his gut feeling. "I do understand; I *do* get it."

Heidi pressed her case, "And we *have* considered, *have* thought that both victims knew the attacker or felt secure enough to allow him access. *Both* victims knew Campion; if he turned up at Martine's door, would she have refused him? If he bumped into Paula would she feel safe with an old business associate of her ex? It's probably yes in both cases." Heidi sat back.

Amber took up Heidi's processing, "And maybe Campion wouldn't have the stomach to do the actual slicing and dicing, but he could've administered the disabling drug and left the victim for someone else to finish off."

Grant rubbed his chin. "It seems a long shot but obviously it's a line of enquiry we need to follow, but…" Grant felt something else was going on. "…well, do you propose to bring him in? Take DNA, seize his phone to track his movements? If, as we both suspect, this is something he'd have hired someone to do, what does that prove?"

Heidi Yorke visibly slumped in her seat. "It's fantastical, I know, but it just popped in there." Heidi tapped the side of her head. "Lateral thinking," she looked apologetic, "born of desperation for a break." She sighed. "I've had this for weeks longer than you; I'll be candid: I'm struggling, clutching at straws. My investigation needs help."

Grant's liking and respect for Heidi Yorke grew. It took both strength of character and professional maturity to make such an admission to a colleague. Sometimes the bravest words a person could utter were 'help me.'

"You're right, forgive me, let's follow it up," Grant answered, "see if he's made any unaccounted-for payments to anyone. Two murders, especially like ours, don't come cheap. Maybe do some snooping around his associates. It's worth looking at. Besides, what else do we have at the moment? 'Proxy-killing', eh? Listen to you!" Grant smiled at the young detective who was re-reading the statement.

# Chapter Twenty-Three

Someone, somewhere, evidently on a much higher pay grade than anyone in the office, thought it was a good idea. Discourteously, without reference to the DCI, an academic had been engaged to produce an offender profile, now as they say on TV shows, the 'results were in'. Grant clicked his inbox icon and opened the document.

*A Report by Professor Rufus Cassilis PhD, FAcSS, Hon FBPsS, FRSM,*
*FAPA, C.Psychol*
*A Psychological Assessment of the Offender in the Cases of*
*Walsingham and Bingley.*

Grant scanned through the introduction; there were plenty of 'possibilities' and 'likelihoods,' lots of 'maybes' and 'feasibly' scattered throughout the text. The Professor was covering the bases in the event he was way off the mark when the truth finally came out. Grant sympathised, it took a certain courage to hang a theory out for all to see and shoot at. On the second page, Grant began to read with earnest concentration.

*"The subject is classified as an organised offender. He, the subject is most certainly male, prepares carefully before the attacks. The venue of each incident has clearly been reconnoitered, and all forms of surveillance have been disabled. This speaks of skill and knowledge of electronics, CCTV, telephone, cable, and alarm systems. To have been able to attack these security systems so successfully indicates not only knowledge but*

*a long period of preparation and planning.*

*The victims are white females in their fifties and are linked by a degree of wealth outside the parameters of normal experience. These women were highly privileged, even Paula Bingley, who, despite being trapped in a spiral of drug abuse, living in near squalor, was residing in an apartment of substantial worth in a building of considerable prestige and status. Additionally, she was provided with a monthly allowance by her ex-husband, of which most could only dream.*

*The victims were injected in the neck, directly into the common carotid artery. The drug chosen, Ketamine, would surge through the body, and the effects would be near instantaneous.*

*The choice of drug is significant, especially considering how the attacks would have developed. Ketamine is a sedative analgesic which precipitates disassociation in the subject. Unlike many drugs its toxic effect is minimal, blood pressure is barely affected, nor is the airway. The subject, although rendered helpless, unable to move or resist, is unharmed. Ketamine is a drug of conscious sedation. It will induce stupor, confusion and disorientation, medically called narcosis, it will also negate pain, medically called analgesia. In all other respects, vital signs are preserved. It means that despite the horrific injuries visited upon these women, while awake and aware, they felt no pain. These attacks were not motivated by sadism, nor were they sexually assaulted.*

*Regarding the focus of the offender's attack, the victims were subjected to a total hysterectomy with bilateral salpingo-oophorectomy, namely removal of the womb to the cervix, encompassing both fallopian tubes and both ovaries. This is a surgery that, properly undertaken, can take at the very least one and up to two hours in an operating theatre. Examination of the victims' bodies indicates that the subject displayed no obvious surgical knowledge or skill. The rudimentary instructions necessary to conduct the removal can be obtained through medical books or online. Removal during the first murder was clumsy and hurried, probably taking as little as fifteen to twenty minutes. The womb, with attached fallopian tubes and ovaries, showed signs of being cut and* damaged during the process. The second removal was much improved, perhaps took a little longer, was neater and the removed organs showed fewer signs of damage.

The subject is a man with formidable misogynistic tendencies, a man with enough anger, indeed fury, to want to kill a particular type of woman, or a **specific** woman. It seems the focus of his rage is directed to that which a woman has, but of which he is deficient, namely the womb.

We must consider his choice of the womb. What does it signify? The womb is a most powerful symbol of womanhood, of feminine fertility; it's the source of a woman's ability to create another human being. So why has our killer chosen wealthy, late middle-aged ladies to sedate and dissect, removing the organ of reproduction from women who are past reproductive age? The blood spatter on the hard kitchen floor of the first victim shows a pattern consistent with the womb either being dropped from a height into the victim's face or far more likely, as I believe was the case, it was thrown with force. The carpet under the body of the second victim disguised any blood spatter evidence, but we can safely assume the same action on the killer's part.

I believe his misogynistic tendencies were fostered by his relationship with the aforementioned 'specific' woman, his **mother**. In some manner, which I cannot specify, this relationship was outside what we would consider the normal bounds. There may have been a form of physical or sexual abuse. There may have been neglect or a conditional or unconditional removal of love and affection, I suspect a controlling and overwhelming dominance of him during his formative years and probably continuing on past them. Whatever the form his relationship with his mother took, it was warped, and consequently, his world view of women was warped. Whilst his mother lived, this view was one which he held but which he was unable to act upon. I believe the trigger that precipitated this series of horrific attacks was the death of his mother.

I believe the mother of our killer was wealthy and powerful, either in reality or at least in his eyes. I believe she died in the last six to eighteen *months. I believe she was aged between fifty and sixty. I believe the killer is attacking his own mother, transposing her onto the victims. Twice, to our knowledge so far, but I don't believe he's ready to stop yet. He is removing the power she had over him, the power of giving life to him. He's cutting out her womb, where she created and nurtured him, and he's throwing it contemptuously in her face. He's fashioning a victory over her, and each time he kills, he will relive that victory. But this is his mother. Whatever the rage and fury he directs towards her, she is still his mother. He may have no wish to cause her pain, or he may not have the mental ability to inflict pain on her. Hence, the Ketamine. His purpose is to impose his power over her in the most primitive and rudimentary fashion.*

*The profile of the subject is as follows: Male. White European. Heterosexual. Probably an only child, probably raised chiefly by his mother, his father either being significantly absent or deceased. His circumstances are likely to be wealthy, certainly in his youth. The family fortunes may have changed for the worse during puberty.*

*The subject is likely to be aged 25-35, probably quiet, introspective, a reader of books, a studier of technology. He may have qualifications or employment in a field which requires a knowledge of electronics or security systems. He is likely to be employed in a subordinate role. He may have sought to be in the company of supervisory women. (a counter-intuitive response complex. An example would be choosing to be a male nurse, a role where he is more likely to be managed by women. It is NOT suggested that nursing is the role chosen by the subject but given merely as an example)*

*As stated, the subject is an organised offender. He is patient and has a high degree of self-discipline. He will be able to concentrate and monitor for long periods of time without being distracted. He will have the capacity to focus on his objective and wait patiently for the right moment to act. He is not impulsive. He is likely to have formulated plans and contingencies to deal with his identification and/or arrest. He may have organised for his escape, perhaps to leave the country or*

101

*assume a new identity.*

*Whatever his mental state, he is able to instill trust and confidence in his victims. This may be a simple matter of manipulating his personality for the circumstances, aided perhaps by his looks, demeanour and clothing, (people trust good-looking and well-dressed individuals). Or perhaps by the role he performs or claims to perform, such as a police officer, doctor, or a representative of some welfare agency. Whichever it is, he is able to make his late middle-age female victims trust him implicitly.*

*The subject will display organised traits in his non-criminal role as well as his murderous activities. It is hardly conceivable that this characteristic would not be apparent in his day to day living. In his domestic life, for example, his car will be clean, tidy and always serviced on time, his bills and credit cards will be cleared and never slip into arrears. He will be punctual and become irritated at other people's lack of personal discipline. If machinery or mechanical equipment is involved in his employment, it will be clean, well-maintained and up-to-date, for example the latest phone or the best computer. His obsession for control, no matter how hard he tries to disguise the fact, will inevitably bleed into other areas of his existence.*

*If he has a partner, or a wife, he will be controlling but self-disciplined enough for it to not seem unnaturally or unacceptably so. His overt need to project power will be satisfied for now by the murders he is committing but as the murderous process escalates, as the vast majority of these cases do, his need for total control may seep into his domestic life. I would expect his partner to eventually notice a difference in his behaviour and the most obvious area for that will be in his desire to dominate others.*

*There is no evidence of sadism. There is no reason to think he tortured or killed animals in his youth or engaged in arson attacks, as is common in subjects who develop into serial murderers. There is no reason to think he is overtly violent, either domestically or socially. The subject will have the ability to control his anger, even with serious provocation but should extreme violence be deemed necessary in his view, (to escape, to punish, to destroy a witness or evidence) he will not hesitate to resort to it.*

*The catalyst which prompted the start of this murder cycle was almost certainly the death of the offender's mother. This restraining force in his life was removed, like the curtain going up in a theatre, revealing all the exciting possibilities laid out on the stage behind it. Possibilities for him to explore and play amongst, the possibilities that were hitherto hidden from view, but were just behind the curtain, all along'.*

*In conclusion, the subject is unlikely to cease offending and will become a more proficient murderer as his experience increases.*

The report went on for several more pages, he would examine them later, he was all profiled out. Grant couldn't doubt the expertise and intuition that had been at work to produce the profile, but how much was accurate? It seemed the professor had summarised their quarry as a control freak with a mummy complex. Was that it? In his gut he felt, although some insights may be valid, some traits and actions accurate, this case wasn't as simplistic as that. He would talk with Paul and garner his opinion.

# Chapter Twenty-Four

Two days after the delivery of the offender profile, a document the investigating officers were still absorbing and assessing, shocking news arrived in a sudden and unexpected fashion. The door to the main office burst open to reveal the shape of DC Dirty Don Chamberlain.

"There's another one!" The proclamation was made in a loud, near-triumphant voice.

Rob Pagett instinctively hefted his camera to his shoulder in a smooth movement to focus on the herald. "Say that again," he commanded.

Dirty Don obliged. "There's another one, and you are *not* going to believe who it is!"

Pagett tweaked a control on his camera and zoomed in, the frame in his viewfinder filled with Don's smiling, reddened face as he excitedly announced the murder of a fellow human being.

"Got it!" said Pagett to himself. "Beautiful, that's going in!" He turned and saw Isla Baxter looking up from a screen bearing a crime report that DC Pat Kerrigan was explaining to her. She nodded her approval.

Grant and Heidi observed from the other side of the room. Dirty Don's dramatic entrance had disturbed their just concluded mutual agreement that Martine Walsingham's ex-husband was *not* involved in her murder. Their separation was as amicable as was possible in the circumstances, and Martine's substantial pay-off was hardly likely to dent the finances of Graham Walsingham, who seemed genuinely bereft at the death of his ex-wife.

As Dirty Don blurted out his news in as inappropriate a manner as it was possible to do, Grant wasn't sure which of his emotions was strongest. The shocking information of another murder or the horror at how a Met Detective managed to look so gleeful as he broadcast his terrible news, which, thanks to Pagett's quick-on-the-draw filming, could now appear in the forthcoming documentary.

* * *

With the discovery of the body of world-renowned, Oscar-nominated actress and Welsh National Treasure, Juno Jenkin, things moved very quickly. Within twenty-four hours, the investigative squad morphed into a cross-border Task Force, the nucleus being DCI Winter and the Met Police Squad dealing with the Paula Bingley case. Several Surrey Police Officers from the Martine Walsingham case, headed by DI Heidi Yorke, were seconded to the West London-based Task Force, and the CID main office adapted into a dedicated Incident Room. The officers dealing with the more mundane, day-to-day work were ejected and crammed into the Crime Squad Office, two floors up. Through jealous eyes, they watched their comrades ensconced down four flights of stairs about to exploit the career-enhancing, high-profile, and soaring overtime opportunities suddenly presented to them.

Several CID Officers from the division covering the hotel in Park Lane where Juno Jenkin was found had blended seamlessly into the team, which was already up and running. DCI Paul Winter found himself heading a large and diverse group of officers with varying skill sets, varying experience, and varying degrees of resentment at the roles to which they were assigned.

* * *

It was nearly two o'clock in the morning. "Fucking hell, Granty," wailed DCI Winter privately to his best DS. "I know it's high profile, I know that involvement in this case will loom large on all our C.V.s, but if I had a glass of Scotch for *every* twat that's knocked my door today moaning about the investigative action they've been assigned, I'd be lying on the floor under my desk singing *Bohemian Rhapsody*."

Grant frowned; he'd seen Paul Winter lying on the floor, under his desk, singing *Bohemian Rhapsody*, and it wasn't a good look, or indeed a good sound. The memory of Freddie Mercury deserved better.

There were still officers bent over glowing computer screens dotted about the Incident Room; one was in his chair, the backrest on full recline, eyes closed, dribbling mouth open. The guvnor had worked logistical miracles that day and was winding down to go home, satisfied that the team was housed, briefed, and directed. In the morning, the investigation, with the renewed impetus of probing three linked murders, would roll on like a juggernaut.

Grant smiled across the desk at his boss and responded. "Please, Paul, never inflict your version of that song on me again. Anyway, it's in the nature of coppers to bitch and moan. The only time they don't is when they're in that state." He nodded through the glass wall to the comatose DC, who'd been on duty nearly twenty hours. "You've said your piece; everyone knows what they're doing and what's expected of them. You did good today, boss."

"Thanks, Grant." The DCI paused. "It's bloody horrible, isn't it?" He shook his head slowly. "There's going to be hell to pay with this. It's one thing to butcher a helpless drug addict, or a has-been 'it girl', but when you carve up a national treasure in a Park Lane hotel, in the middle of the fucking day, well that's another thing entirely."

Grant had to agree. It *was* a different thing altogether. The pressure to make an arrest, to secure a conviction would be unprecedented. On top of all that was the presence of Isla Baxter and the ubiquitous Rob Pagett, who was running around like a dog with two dicks, filming grimaces, frowns, and bewilderment. God knows what the final cut of this episode of *Isla Investigates* would look like. Grant was glad that it was Paul Winter who had his back, had *all* their backs, so they could get on and do their job.

\* \* \*

June Jenkin was the daughter of a coal miner from the South Wales town of Aberdare and thus possessed impeccable working-class roots and credentials, a crucial element in the public's love affair with her.

June had first come to the eye of the public and transformed into the more enigmatic *Juno* with a bit-part in a daytime soap. She was pretty, had a twinkle in her eye, and the camera loved her. The director knew his stuff too, recognising these facets he developed her bit-part to become a much-loved character. By the time Juno Jenkin was twenty-one she was nationally known. In a public relations coup, she left her daytime soap show and walked onto the set of the most popular, evening, twice-weekly drama in a flurry of publicity, newspaper, and glossy magazine articles; her celebrity soared.

Her real-life marriage to her on-screen love, Huw Vaughan-Hughes, was the celebrity wedding of the year. Huw, as Welsh as Juno, was good-looking, ambitious, and, in the early years at least, an attentive and loving husband. Their union was blessed with a son, whom they christened Osian, an old and traditional Welsh name.

After nearly ten very profitable years as a jobbing actress in a popular soap, Juno took a leap of faith into the unknown. Hearing of a proposed prestigious, high-production-value television drama project, she obtained a copy of the script and gate-crashed the casting meeting. Juno made the astonishing offer to take the lead role for no pay. The rest was history. Juno's emotionally stirring and gritty portrayal of a struggling 1950s mother and victim of domestic violence who found the strength to leave her husband and strike out on her own was a revelation. Juno Jenkin, from the soaps, could act! More serious roles were offered, this time *with* pay. As her star climbed, her husband's waned, trapped in a twice-weekly parochial purgatory. Hollywood eventually beckoned, and Juno spent more time on the West Coast of the United States, starring in lucrative and lavish cinematic productions, hob-knobbing with the A-List elite, and earning a fortune. Huw, torn apart with resentment and jealousy, drank more heavily and blatantly played away from home, barely attempting to hide his indiscretions. Their son, Osian, was sent away to a boarding school. Both parents *did* love their son in their own way but he was an inconvenience for a mother based in Hollywood and for a father who was busy chasing skirt and downing Scotch.

The post-mortem on the body of Huw Vaughan-Hughes, which had been cut from the wreckage of his mangled Porsche 911, showed a blood-alcohol level five times the drink-drive limit, a fact not made public. The nation wept for Juno.

Juno Jenkin played the role of her life as she emotionally broke down in a news interview about the tragic loss of the love of her life. She exited the limousine at the funeral with the trained grace and demeanour of a star, stunning in the blackness of her dress, her pretty face shrouded in dark lace, a perfect picture of lamentation. Her son, nearly as tall as she was, held her arm, their mutual love supporting each other through their difficult loss. The nation wept with them.

When she'd first heard that the resentful, shagging, self-absorbed, drink-soaked wanker that was her husband had fatally wrapped his car and himself around a lamppost, Juno Jenkin *had* wept. Wept with joy. Finally free of the small-town man, in a small-time role in a small-time production, she grasped the opportunities of freedom with both hands, cementing her place amongst the A-Listers. Eschewing the attentions of the leading men of Hollywood, she concentrated her attentions on the older, balder, fatter producers and directors; they were not only richer and more powerful, they were also more grateful.

Several years after she'd buried her husband with a smile in her heart, if not on her lips, a *genuine* personal tragedy was visited upon the life of Juno Jenkin. The event took place on the day *before* the Academy Awards ceremony in which she was a nominee. Everyone was mortified, but not for the obvious reason. The votes were already in and counted, Juno had been in the running for the award but significantly *hadn't* been picked. The politics of Hollywood had decided the recipient of the Oscar for best actress long before. Of course, the personal calamity precluded Juno's presence at the award ceremony, she was already in first class, heading back to England, this time truly grieving. The members of The Academy were livid at the turn of events, if the disaster had occurred even one day earlier, they could've cooked the books and changed the name on the card, presenting her, in absentia of course, with the small golden statuette. How good *everyone* would have looked. What drama and high emotion that would've evoked. Someone could've made a movie about it. As it was, it was a chance missed.

Three years later, Juno married a Hollywood producer on a beach in Hawaii. He was short, fat, and covered in a mat of body hair, which made Juno gag just looking at it. Thankfully, her new husband was as gay as a box of Speedos and only interested in bedding their smooth-skinned Mexican pool cleaner. It was a perfect arrangement. On the back of two personal tragedies, two personal losses, Juno Jenkin's career went interstellar. She had become one of the world's best-known faces and highest-paid stars.

# Chapter Twenty-Five

J uno Jenkin was in London to publicise her latest film. The production company had provided an opulent suite at the astronomically expensive Park Lane London View Hotel. The setup was routine, a process of press junkets she'd previously endured with a dozen different film productions in a dozen different cities over the years. One room in her extensive suite was set aside for the interviews. The arrangement rarely varied, from city to city, hotel to hotel, two plush chairs faced each other at a slightly oblique angle, an occasional table in the background bearing an impressive floral display enhanced the framing of the shot. The room was provided with, and pre-set for, a swift turnaround of use, with softbox lighting, umbrella diffusers, sound kit, and lavalier lapel microphones resting on each chair, waiting to be clipped in place once bums had descended and were comfortably ensconced. The visitors needed merely to provide their own camera, crew, and interviewer, then plug in, do their thing, and toddle off to let in the next lot waiting outside to jump on the media-merry-go-round once more. The interviewers came from magazines, newspapers, national and local news channels, chat-show programmes and any other sycophantic organisation who may provide helpful publicity and raise the profile of the forthcoming movie release.

For Juno, as for any actor, the repetition of facing the same questions, with the same degree of fawning sincerity, over and over for hours at a time was a trial and a true test of acting skill. To sound fresh, interested, and exhibit surprise at the insightfulness of the interviewer, especially when half the questioners had already sought the same 'unique' angle, was part of the bread and butter of stardom and sadly unavoidable. These rounds of publicity-seeking splurges were an integral part of the pre-shoot contract with the production company. As much as Juno baulked at smiling sweetly at the peasants who fawned and pretended to be her intimate friends, as frequently as she had to simper and laugh at the knuckle-dragging Philistines who feigned knowledge and professed insight into the complexity of her role, as repeatedly as she had to endure a dab of powder here and a touch up there, Juno Jenkin knew that by 5pm they would all piss off and leave her to snort a line or two of top grade cocaine in peace.

It was 5.15 pm, and as required, Juno had been left completely alone in her suite. The advisers, the publicists, the production reps, the whole shebang all knew that as soon as Juno's contractual obligation was completed, she was to be left alone and unmolested until she, and she alone, decided to emerge from her suite to engage with the world once more. Woe betide anyone who failed to abide by this stipulation from the unpredictable and volatile star, infamous for her Welsh temper. The suite which took up half a floor of The View, was cleared of staff unless summoned, vacated by all associates of the production, empty of all souls but that of Juno Jenkin.

Juno was dabbing her nostrils with a tissue, she smiled to herself relishing the rituals and sensations of snorting the coke a few moments earlier. The familiar, mild petroleum smell of the drug as she slipped the opening of the clear plastic baggie, the tapping of the whitish powder onto her pocket mirror, the preparation of two lines, the search in her purse for the silver tube and the moment of expectation, before inhalation. As the cocaine soared and roared into her nasal passages the accustomed numbness of the back of her tongue, nose and throat was surpassed by the energising hit. Juno glided to the wide glass doors which opened out onto the balcony, she stared at the expanse of Hyde Park sprawling on the other side of Park Lane. The mass of trees appeared to be breathing, sending her feelings of goodwill. Juno span on the spot, revelling in her contented solitude. The door buzzer sounded.

Irritation overwhelmed her at the intrusion into her private time. She dabbed her nose once more with the tissue and answered the door.

"Oh!" was her first response, quickly followed by, "my God, is that really you?"

"It really is. How are you?"

Juno was taken aback, neither expecting any visitor and definitely not expecting this one. "I'm good, good. What can I do for you?" Juno shook her head. "Sorry, what am I thinking, come in, come in. I can order champagne if you like."

"That would be lovely, I'm sorry to arrive unannounced but I need to talk to you about something, it's important."

The door to the Presidential Suite closed. In the corridor outside, the three CCTV cameras scanning the passageway saw nothing, recorded nothing. Juno Jenkin, International Film Star, National Treasure and darling of the red-top reading public, hardly felt the needle stab the side of her neck, nor the impact of her body on the soft, deep pile of the carpet. Her world was a woozy fusion of cocaine and Ketamine, she smiled and laughed, amused at the goings on, trying to talk she found her numb tongue didn't want to play. When her clothes were pulled from her, she laughed even more, the possibility of some sexual contact wasn't an unpleasant or unwanted thought, the cocaine often made her horny, in the past several room-service boys had benefited from her drug-stoked libido.

"*Are you listening to me? Can you hear what I'm saying? I want you to know why. To understand? Can you hear me?*" The voice was shifting pitch from an impossibly deep bass to a ridiculous soprano; Juno laughed even harder. The stinging slap around the face *was* a surprise, the effect more so...hysterical laughter. The tone was very angry now; the voice was admonishing her in even measured tones, but definitely angry. Juno felt a tugging sensation which was difficult to assimilate in her addled world but she felt a chill, a coldness, it felt as if she was cold inside. The tugging sensation was now a ripping feeling, it didn't feel right at all. Juno finally stopped laughing and, with a force of will, tried to move her arms, which were leaden. Her only view was of the ceiling, it gave her no information so she closed her eyes and concentrated on her hands, walking them across the carpet, tip-toeing her fingers, dragging the weight of her arms as they progressed. The intruder was muttering, out of her sight, present but apart somehow.

Juno's hands reached the side of her hips and with determination crawled up the side of her body, it was when they fell inside the sodden, sticky cavity that she started to scream. The screams were silent. Her mouth opened and closed, emitting soundless shrieks and squeals of horror as her hands explored the deep, gaping hole in her abdomen.

*"Open your eyes!"*

Juno obeyed. The face appeared above her own, snarling.

*"Here, this is for you."*

An object from a horror film, a grisly, gristly, lump of something, dangled just above her eyes, warm drips fell to wet her face, salty liquid dribbled into her open, silently screeching mouth.

*"This, this is what did it!"*

The object was lost from view for a moment and then slammed with such an impact into Juno Jenkin's face that it took her breath.

Juno screamed and screamed silently as her heart pumped her life blood away.

\* \* \*

It was unusual for the star in the Presidential Suite to neither call for room service nor to make an appearance for her evening repast in the hotel restaurant of cuisine bad boy Michelin-starred chef Konstanz Bassa. Her standing orders for privacy were respected. The following morning found her production team and aides, each full of excellent coffee and nourishing breakfasts, rapping her door and repeatedly pressing the door buzzer with no response. The Duty Manager attended with a key card and gained entry to the suite.

When the open-mouthed huddle beheld the naked body of Juno Jenkin on her back, her bloodied hands buried deep into the abdominal cavity so brutally excavated into her body, with her womb lying across her face, the excellent coffee and nourishing breakfasts made a rapid reappearance, adding to the distastefulness of the crime scene tableau.

# Chapter Twenty-Six

"How can this be? I mean, *how* can this be?" Grant stood eight feet from the body, his back against the wall, DC Amber Bennett at his side.

It was a good question. This attack had been discovered a maximum of sixteen hours after it could have been perpetrated and committed in the heart of London, in one of its top hotels, on one of the most famous women in the world. Unlike the tiniest ripple caused by the death of Paula Bingley and the larger waves triggered by Martine Walsingham, the slaughter of Juno Jenkin would provoke an international media tsunami.

The crime scene was discovered by the hotel duty manager in company with four film production team members; there would be absolutely no controlling the details of this butchery. The evening television news bulletins would lead with Juno's death, the newspapers would be plastered with the story in the morning, and already social media was alive and fizzing with the news and numerous insane speculations.

"It's horrific. Do you think she knew? Do you think she realised what was happening to her, Skip?"

"If she was full of Ketamine like the others, perhaps she didn't; at the very least, hopefully, she didn't feel any pain. There's evidence she was taking cocaine, too. The post-mortem and tox reports will tell us. In the meantime we've an answer to the second biggest question of all, we finally have the link between the victims. Now we only need to find out *who* is doing this."

"Only? That's a *big* only." Grant had to agree, but more victims would reveal more information, and more information would take them a step closer to the suspect, and the death of Juno Jenkin had gifted them with a huge prize.

\* \* \*

"There's another one, and you are *not* going to believe who it is!" had been Dirty Don's excited proclamation.

DCI Winter had been sitting on the corner of a desk, chatting with a DS from the Area Drug Squad who was trying to identify the lazy-eyed, pony-tailed, drug-dealing frequenter of the Migliorè Coffee House. They'd just shared a joke, and Paul Winter's head was thrown back in amusement. As Dirty Don's words reverberated around the main office, the laconic cameraman, Rob Pagett, pressed the button to record the inauspicious moment. The DCI's reaction in the background of the shot was *not* one of amusement, but the camera lens had caught him in the frame, he'd be seen to be laughing heartily, the incorrect assumption would be obvious.

*"Get in my fucking office, now!"* The shock of the guvnor's words silenced every conversation more successfully than Don's news. It was a rare day indeed that Winter admonished anyone publicly, his bollockings when made, were always deserved and made in private, a matter between him, the bollock*er* and the offending bollock*ee*. For DC Dirty Don, broadcasting the murder of Juno Jenkin, he made an instant and instinctive exception.

DCI Winter stood at the entrance to the glass box office, holding the door, his face a barely contained image of human thunder. Don Chamberlain skulked through the door, his features displaying contrition and fear. He knew he'd done wrong, he'd been carried away, he knew he was going to cop it.

Grant looked at Heidi Yorke, glanced back to the guvnor's office, and stood up. Winter saw the movement, and it caught his eye. The DS assumed an expectant face and telegraphed it across the space between them. Winter nodded his assent. The message, 'Can I be in on this?' and the answer, 'Yes, get in here', communicated without words. Grant flicked his head sideways at the Surrey Police DI; 'come on then!'

The small space was crowded with the four officers, Paul Winter sat, he directed Grant and Heidi to do the same, leaving Dirty Don conspicuously standing.

"Right, Donald, we'll discuss the *manner* of delivering your news privately in more detail, but for now, what's happened?"

During the next few minutes, the Detective Constable relayed the information passed to him from the station control room relating to the grisly find in the Park Lane hotel. Don had used his initiative well enough to contact the originating station and establish the facts as known and the uniformity of the offences being dealt with. The CID attending the scene were suitably briefed to begin the proper processes but were aware that this was part of a much bigger picture. DCI Winter nodded. Dirty Don had done the right things, the right way in the right order, then screwed it all up with his camera-hugging need for attention on delivering his news. The sting had been pulled; Paul Winter decided to close the book with a few well-placed words.

"Thank you, Don. For the record, well done, also for the record, you're a twat. Think before you speak next time. Now go and capitalise on the links you've established, get to the scene, build some bridges but don't be pushy. We're going to be taking this from them, and they'll be pissed off, remember that. Be gentle. This is going to go sky high. Now, sod off." Don looked sheepishly from Paul to Grant to Heidi and back to Paul.

"Sorry, Guv. Twat is right. Won't happen again."

Grant had listened with mounting interest and realisation as Don's story was laid out before them. Pieces suddenly fell into place. Dare he believe it? As the door closed behind Don, Grant leant forward, his body language telling his colleagues he was about to speak, but he held off for a few seconds, gathering his thoughts, wanting to get it right.

"I think this is it Paul. The breakthrough." Grant hesitated again. Winter knew his man and held back. "Juno Jenkin. It's *Juno Jenkin*. What's she famous for? Jumping from a soap to Hollywood, *and* for losing her son the day before the Oscars. Her son, *remember* Paul? Do you remember? It was a huge story, one of the biggest of the year." Heidi was looking from one face to another, then she saw the moment the penny dropped written on DCI Winter's face.

"*Oh Fuck!*" Winter slapped his own forehead. "Her son was killed in a plane crash."

"Not *a* plane crash, Guv." answered Grant. "*The* plane crash."

"Would someone let me in on this?" Heidi asked, still looking back and forth from Maddox to Winter.

Grant twisted in his seat. "The Frankton Abbey rugby sevens crash, eighteen years ago. The sons of the rich and famous from Franks' Public School were on their way to Italy, one of their fathers had an executive jet, the team were flying to play in a tournament when the plane crashed in France. No survivors. We already know Paula Bingley's son, Chase Bingley was on the flight."

"And so was Juno Jenkin's," put in Winter.

Grant slammed his hand down on the desktop. "Martine Walsingham! Did she have a son? She was married before; what did we find out? What do we know? Oh God, please let it be she had a son killed on that plane." Grant realised what he'd said, how it had sounded, and blanched. He'd been spared the ubiquitous lens of Rob Pagett's camera, but at that moment, he felt as much a twat as Dirty Don.

# Chapter Twenty-Seven

D
C Amber Bennett held a sheet of paper in one hand, a whiteboard marker pen in the other. She wrote the list, the names, down one side of the board, her head moving back and forth from the paper to the board. It was an initial, internet-based compilation of the casualties of the Frankton Abbey rugby sevens air crash. Seven young men who'd been winners in life's lottery smashed into the claggy, clay soil of a French field.

At the top left, she wrote Chase Bingley, linked by a horizontal line to the name Paula Bingley. Next, she wrote Osian Vaughan-Hughes, a line leading to the name Juno Jenkin. There followed the other five names, Garson Thompson, the team captain, the twin brothers, Japhet and Jacob Gold, Lynton Fiennes, and the final name Gary Whittcock. Amber stood back and surveyed the roll of names, an inventory reminiscent of a memorial to the war dead. The answer to the horror of the murders was hidden amongst these names. Who were they? Why had two of their mothers been butchered? She was convinced Grant Maddox was absolutely correct, Martine Walsingham's name would soon been linked by a line to one of these boys.

\* \* \*

DCI Paul Winter replaced the receiver on the phone, scribbling a last few notes on the pad as he did so. "Okay, Granty, that's arranged. The school is e-mailing a contact list from their archives for the dead boys, along with the most basic information about them. Until next of kin gives permission, they are constrained by confidentiality. Which is fair enough. You're seeing the headmaster tomorrow at 10am, a nice day out, take Bennett with you. The confidential info we need may be cleared for us by then, I'll e-mail all the details for you to print a hard copy. Happy?"

Grant nodded. "Hmm, 'happy' isn't the word I'd reach for first Guv." He pushed at the newspaper sitting on the desktop as if it were a soiled nappy. Emblazoned across the front page above a photo of a radiant Juno Jenkin the single word, '**DISSECTED!**' "They've got their headline," he said.

Grant pushed at a second newspaper, resting by the first. Three pictures, the centre one of Juno twice the size of Martine's and Paula's graced the front page. In large type beneath, the question was posed, '*Who is the Dissection Killer?*' "Our Press Bureau haven't really helped us have they, Guv? They've thrown everything out there except the removal of the wombs."

Winter shrugged. "Out of my hands, they've access to the information and have the support of the Big House. I said my piece but was overruled. This is *Juno Jenkin,* for God's sake. It's seismic. At least no one's linked the victims to the Franks' School air disaster...yet. They think it's sensational now, with just these three women butchered; wait until someone notices what ties them together. It'll be a media nuclear bomb going off." The DCI shrugged again. "You keep doing your thing Granty, don't worry about all the politics and the media stuff, that's my job, God help me. Talking of media stuff, how are our embedded reporters doing? Hang on, talk of the Devil."

Rob Pagett strode towards the office door, bereft of the ubiquitous camera on his shoulder. He looked in through the glass wall, Winter beckoned.

"How can I help you, Rob?" Winter asked.

"I think I can help you, but I need to tell you something first."

"Okay."

"I was there the day before she was found." Pagett's voice, monotone as usual.

"Where were you?" Winter asked, puzzlement writ large on his face.

"At the hotel, at the Park Lane London View."

Paul Winter's mouth dropped open. *"What?!"*

"I freelance as a cameraman, several of the glossy magazines, the celebrity gossip and chat publications, they produce websites, blogs as well as the photos for the mags. They've no in-house cameramen, no capacity to film, edit and produce, so when a celeb does a junket like Juno was doing, they sub-contract it out to a freelancer like me."

"And you were there *with* Juno Jenkin?" Grant was incredulous.

"Yeh, me and a dozen or more others, throughout the day, in and out for different clients, doing the same stuff over and over but with a slant, depending on the brief. That's where I can help you, it's a small crowd, we all know each other, I've got names, mobile numbers and e-mail addresses. Wouldn't that be useful to know? Save you a mountain of time tracking everyone down?"

*"What the hell!* Why wait until *now* to announce this, you were here when Don burst in, you heard who the victim was at the same time as the rest of us and you wait a full twenty-four fucking hours to tell us?" Grant was furious, his unhappiness about the presence of the journalists finally bubbling to the surface with this casual revelation.

"Okay, calm down, Detective Sergeant." Winter was official now, the senior officer. "Rob, answer the question. Why wait until now?"

Pagett looked bewildered at the response from the officers. "Are you kidding me? I saw nothing, have no evidence to give you, and you lot have been running around like headless chickens since the Juno Jenkin news hit, sorting out offices, turfing a load of people out, dragging another lot in, pushing desks around, plugging stuff, unplugging stuff, carrying boxes, scribbling on wall charts. *My* job is to film and record all that and that's what I've been doing, *my* job. When a bit of peace descended, I came here, of my own free will, to help you and *him*..." Pagett jammed an aggressive thumb in Grant's direction, "...who's been looking at Isla and me as if there was an unpleasant smell under his nose since the day we arrived, and now he starts throwing the fucks at me. Well, I'll tell you what: You find all the cameramen and crews yourself." Pagett pushed back his chair and moved towards the door.

"*You!* Stay where you are." Winter's tone was authoritative and controlled, but his anger was barely concealed. It halted Pagett in his tracks. "*If* you want to carry on doing your job, *if* you and Ms. Baxter still want access to this investigation, you'll stop throwing your teddy out of the pram and pretending you've never had the word fuck directed at you before. You're supposed to be the tough guy reporter who's been to every trouble spot in the world, don't pretend to be upset by a swear word and frankly by sitting on this info for twenty four hours you deserve it and worse. Now *sit* down." Winter pointed to the vacant seat, like an angry headmaster directing an errant child to the naughty chair.

Pagett sat, a smile playing across his lips, but Winter wasn't finished. "This is the biggest news story of the year, and you and Isla Baxter are already here, on the inside. If you want to stay, you start by remembering this is a Police investigation, that's a *Police* investigation, first, last, and foremost. This documentary of yours is a very poor, very secondary side-line to us. So you, m'laddo," Winter jabbed an aggressive index finger towards Pagett, "need to know your place. I make one call," Winter tapped his telephone, "and you're gone, out of here. And remember, your contract with the Met relieves you of every second of recording you've made, every word of interview scribbled down, it comes back to us, *everything*, to be lost from the world forever. Now, if you feel like explaining why that's happened to Isla, then feel free to carry on with the attitude, Sonny. Is there *any* doubt now about where we both stand?"

The smirk which Pagett had been wearing had long since departed to pastures new. Now, his face was a picture of fury. He'd been put in his place by this besuited beanpole of a man and there was nothing he could do about it, the DCI had all the cards, *for now*. The ramifications of Winter's threats, if made real, were far too serious to contemplate.

Pagett back-pedalled. "Alright, alright. Sorry, okay. I should have told you earlier, but I've nothing to tell you. A bunch of freelancers and a bunch of TV crews turn up at the hotel, get a slap-up breakfast and then hang around for hours on end, drinking coffee and talking bollocks. Eventually, we get called to the suite, hook up our stuff to the pre-prepared kit that's been laid on, do a sound test and light test, and then wait around even longer for the prima donna to finally wander in and spout the stuff she's spouted a dozen times already. Twenty minutes later, thirty at the most, she wanders off, we unplug and set off to do our edits. There's nothing more than that, nothing. I was out of there by mid-afternoon, three at the latest. The down-to-earth woman of the people, Juno fucking Jenkin, can't stand the smell of us peasants for a second longer than she's contracted. Everyone must be finished, packed up, and out of the suite by 5pm. There were maybe four guys left, waiting to get something in the can when I left at 3-ish. I can give you their details. Okay?"

Winter smiled and opened his hands in a conciliatory gesture. "That's excellent information, Rob, brilliant. And yes, it'll help enormously to have those names, for witness statements, for elimination purposes, it'll save us time too, won't it Grant?" he asked pointedly.

Grant joined the face-saving playact. "Yes, Rob, that's good information, more than a bit naughty to wait so long, but I get it, we've all got jobs to do. For the record I do have reservations about your presence in this investigation, but I recognise fellow professionals and assure you that you're not an unpleasant smell under my nose, that'll be the guvnor's breath you're getting mixed up with."

There was a tinkling of light laughter before DCI Winter closed proceedings. "Granty, fuck off and get yourself a coffee; Rob's got some names for us. If I remember correctly, I can still write. Okay, Rob, my pen is ready."

Maddox was tight-lipped as he left the office and stalked to his desk. He did not like Pagett. Amber took a step back from the whiteboard, now crammed full of information. The phone rang. Grant lifted the receiver and heard Heidi's voice. She spoke briefly, Grant nodding as he listened. Amber saw the expression on his face and waited, Grant looked up and pointed towards the list of names, so recently recorded on the whiteboard.

"That was DI Yorke. It's been confirmed. Get your pen, Amber, and draw a line from the twins, Japhet and Jacob Gold. Martine's first husband was Samuel Gold. They were her boys. We've got our link."

# Chapter Twenty-Eight

I t was perhaps a quarter of an hour later that Rob Pagett departed DCI Winter's office and joined Isla Baxter, who was being entertained and courted by DI Dodds. It was common currency that Doddy had the raving hots for Isla Baxter. He was all over her like a rash, much to Detective Constable 'Dirty' Don Chamberlain's displeasure, a man who also held unrealistic ambitions in that area. As soon as Doddy vacated the scene, Don would descend like a Cheshire cat on speed, simpering and grinning lecherously over the documentary maker, imparting his knowledge and experience to a smiling and tolerant Baxter. It wasn't a pretty sight, but from Grant's point of view, and one he suspected was shared by DCI Winter, if Doddy was all over Isla, then he wasn't bothering the rest of the team with his petty and inept interfering. Don Chamberlain's behaviour was less tolerable.

Whereas Doddy had been cast as liaison between the Task Force and *Isla Investigates*, with the sole intention of getting him out of the way, Dirty Don had no such direction, consequently Doddy was quick to pull rank, thoroughly humiliate and kick Don into the long grass whenever he was spotted sniffing the spoor left by the object of his desire. The rivalry for Isla's attention was becoming an issue, and Paul Winter, snowed under with his responsibilities, hadn't spotted the matter yet. Grant resolved to speak with his guvnor about it.

Unknown to all, Dirty Don had a scheme in hand to stymie his rival's attentions. A scheme that would pass into police legend and as a curious by-product provide the breakthrough in the case.

\* \* \*

Grant's eyes wandered the Incident Room and landed on Isla Baxter who was sitting at her allocated desk. She was shifting restlessly in her seat, wincing as she did so. Muttering under her breath, she looked up to the ceiling, pulled a small, orange, plastic bottle from her pocket, and tipped several of the contents into her mouth, eschewing water to wash them down. Her eyes now wandered the room and met Grant's. The grimace left her face, and she smiled, rose, and headed towards the Detective Sergeant.

Isla smiled. "May I join you, Granty? I don't think we've ever exchanged more than a few words; I'd like to put that right. Do you have time?" Disarmed by the smile and reasonableness of the request, Grant felt he had little choice but to acquiesce.

"You're right, please, sit down." He waved a hand towards the chair normally occupied by Amber. "Are you alright? I couldn't help noticing…the pills."

Isla forced a laugh, "Oh, those." She shook her pocket, the pills within rattling. "Bad back, that's all, I took a tumble running from baddies a while back, and I've suffered since."

Grant nodded sympathetically. "We've just confirmed the suspicion regarding Martine Walsingham."

"Yes, I saw Amber amend the board. So that's it then. Three mothers to four of the Frankton Abbey air crash victims. What are your thoughts?"

Grant pondered on his answer, "We have lots of connections, some direct, others crossed, some go somewhere, some don't. At the moment, it's a bit like a bowl of spaghetti; unravel the strands, and we'll have our answers."

Isla laughed. "Well, I don't think I've ever heard it explained like that before; how are you going to unravel your spaghetti then?" She leant closer, her eyes locking on his, her body language reinforcing her interest in his answer. The woman beside him was a highly regarded and world-famous investigative reporter, her face known to millions. Now she was sitting next to *him*, hanging on *his* words, wanting to know *his* opinions, valuing *his* insights. He was beguiled and discomforted simultaneously.

"My first thoughts are for other potential victims. If three mothers have been murdered, then it's an obvious assumption that the others are in danger. We're tracing these women, and we'll provide protection for them. Next, we need to establish some facts about the boys who died. I'm going to see the Headmaster at Frankton Abbey tomorrow morning, maybe he can give me an insight into these boys, I'm sure they're the key."

"If they're the link, why the wait? It's been years. Are you sure it's connected to Frankton Abbey?"

"It has *something* to do with the boy's rugby team, it *must* do." His exasperation was obvious. "The boys who died, something happened, something the boys did together, something which stretches all this way, over time, reaching to their mothers."

"Why do you keep calling them *boys*?" There was a sudden edge to her voice. "You make them sound like children." Isla sat back in the chair, the intimate connection between the two broken by the movement.

"Weren't they?" Grant puzzled.

"When the tentative link was first suggested, I did some research, basic stuff, online. As I recall, three of these 'boys' were eighteen, and the other four were close to that. They *weren't* children. Back in 1940, eighteen-year-olds were flying Spitfires and saving the country by winning the Battle of Britain." Isla paused, thinking. "These Frankton Abbey 'boys' of yours were adults; they knew what they were doing." Isla twitched her fingers, air-quoting the word 'boys.'

Grant was rocked, "What do you mean, 'doing'? What do you think they knew they were doing?"

Isla rolled her head, frustrated with herself, trying to explain her view. "As far as I'm aware, nothing. *You* speculated they did something together. But whatever they did, they were as responsible as an adult is, responsible for their actions." Isla paused, seeking the words to make and press her point. "This isn't coming out right. My view is, think of them as adults, not children, that's all. I'm saying you shouldn't limit your thoughts, shouldn't think of them as innocent children, incapable of doing wrong. They were the spoilt brats of privileged parents who relinquished day-to-day responsibility for their upbringing by farming them out to a place like Frankton Abbey."

Grant was intrigued by this new interpretation of the boys as men; he raised his eyebrows in encouragement, prompting more from Isla.

"Look, I know what I'm talking about. I came from a very privileged background; my parents shipped me off to a girls school as soon as they could. You should have seen it, like a castle, turrets, towers, just missing a moat and a dungeon. It was absolute hell. The girls were hideous, and *they knew exactly* what they were doing. Bullying was endemic. Outwardly innocent but vicious harpies behind dormitory doors. Don't be fooled by outward appearances, Grant. Examine these so-called boys, see what they were really like, what they did, to each other and everyone else, don't you think it's a perspective you should consider?"

Grant raised his eyebrows again. "That's quite a speech about a group of boys who died horribly in an air crash eighteen years ago."

Isla held her hands up defensively. "Whoa! Don't misunderstand me, don't think I'm not sympathetic, it must have been awful, it's a long way down from thirty thousand feet, terrifying. But I know that class of people, they've a sense of entitlement, a superior attitude, they aren't automatically pleasant or humane, don't get misty-eyed because they were young and they're dead, that's all I'm saying."

"It's true, they *were* eighteen or close," Grant acknowledged, remembering *he'd* been in a war at that age. He was disturbed by Isla's words, she was right, he *had* felt misty-eyed as she'd put it. Her professional experience and worldly wisdom suddenly seemed more expert than his own. Speaking ill of the dead was a natural anathema in decent society but he was a criminal investigator, he shouldn't let convention sway his views and opinions, keeping an open mind was essential. The life of the international documentary maker, both her schooldays and her work, had taught her a lesson about making assumptions, which, regarding these 'boys,' Grant had let slip from his mind. He looked anew at Isla Baxter; she'd seen him making, or beginning to make, an error of judgment, and she'd steered him back to the right path, and he was grateful. It made his forthcoming visit to their old school and the personal details he hoped for all the more critical.

The two fell into thoughtful silence, eventually broken by Isla. "I hear Rob's attitude and big gob has been winning him friends." Isla laughed, jerking her head sideways to where Rob Pagett sat alone, his eye to the viewfinder of his camera, apparently reviewing some of his filming.

Grant laughed, too. "Nothing to worry about, just something he should've mentioned a bit earlier than he did. It pissed me off, I expressed an opinion more forcefully than I should have, he got into a strop and the guvnor told us *both* off. It's sorted."

"I'm relieved. This project's very important to me, and I honestly think it's important to the Met Police, too. We seem to have found ourselves in the middle of a significant national event, a horrific one granted, but of real importance. I think we've the chance to show the human side of investigating a series of murders like this, let the public see the calibre of the men and women who are keeping them safe."

Isla reached out and placed a warm hand above Grant's knee as she spoke. He felt her magnetism and charisma, and he couldn't help but be tempted to glow under her effusive praise, but Grant Maddox was one of the original seen-it-all, done-it-all men. He had a lifetime of experience, from the Falklands and Ulster as a Royal Marine and close to three decades as a copper. It all mounted up, it meant he recognised a bit of soft soaping when he saw it. He was seeing it now.

He patted the hand on his leg and smiled at Isla Baxter. "You're far too kind. Now if you'll excuse me, I need to be off." Grant Maddox was no DI Dodds or Dirty Don. He was grateful for a new insight and possibly a new approach, but he wouldn't be put into anyone's pocket and was impervious to calculated flirting.

He rose from his chair and called out to DC Bennett. "Amber, we're off on a road-trip first thing in the morning, sort out a pool car with a full tank, something nice please, not a clapped-out old banger. Meet me in the canteen at half six, tea, toast and then we're going back to school."

"Right, Skip!" Amber called back.

As an afterthought, he added, "Chuck a change of clothes in a bag, who knows what we'll learn or where it'll lead us. We might even get an away day out of it."

DS Maddox had no idea how prophetic his throw-away words were to be.

# Chapter Twenty-Nine

The house was quiet; he wondered if Connie had taken Saffy and gone to stay with a friend. She had in the past when Lydia's reaction to the day had been more emotional, more charged with anger, and directed recrimination. Last year Lydia had been quietly sullen, sobbing periodically but attempting to function. There was no guarantee what direction her emotions would take, only that there would be emotion.

It was the anniversary of the day Saleh Cesar rang the doorbell. To ignore it, or even suggest such a course of action to Lydia would be to deny the event and would seem a betrayal. As if he hadn't betrayed her enough.

"Lyddy, Lyddy, it's me, I'm home." He called out quietly from the hall as he kicked his shoes aside. He poked his head around the door into the sitting room, which was empty, and padded on stocking feet to the kitchen, which was also unoccupied.

The bedroom door was open, as it always was; Lydia didn't like closed doors. The room was in darkness, the curtains drawn. He saw her shape in the bed, lit from the landing; she was facing away, her dark hair on the cream pillow.

"Grant?" her voice was hushed.

"Yes, love."

"Come and cuddle me. Just hold me, nice and tight." Grant slipped out of his clothes and slid into the bed, spooning around his wife, who wriggled in towards him. She felt good.

"I'm alright." Her voice was soft and calm. It was neither trying to convince nor transmit a falsehood. It was a simple statement. Internally, Grant exhaled a sigh of relief, not for himself, but for his wife, deciding not to speak. "I've been thinking," she murmured. "Of course I have. I've been thinking, and I want you to know something." Grant pushed his face into her hair, it was soft, it smelled clean, it smelled of Lydia. "I know you'll never stop blaming yourself, never stop taking the responsibility, I know that. But I want you to know it wasn't your fault. It *wasn't* your fault. Whatever I've said in the past, in my pain, in my anger, in my desire to throw hurt out all around me. At you. You know what I'm talking about. Whatever I've said, it wasn't right; it wasn't real. Grant, it wasn't your fault. I don't think I can change how I am; the wax has set in the mould, and that's it, but I want you to stop punishing yourself. Can you do that? Grant? Can you do that for me?"

Grant Maddox couldn't speak. His breathing came in short gasps. In the enveloping darkness, he held his wife, and tears rolled silently down his cheeks.

# Chapter Thirty

"*Really?*" Grant stared at the fluorescent green, eight-year-old Ford Focus. "Tell me, did it go like this? 'I know just what the skipper needs: a day out driving around in a radio-active bogey.' That's what you thought, was it?"

Amber shrugged, looking helpless.

"Couldn't you have got one with more dents? Oh!... No, you couldn't. It's going to take an hour to go through the logbook and check off every mark and scratch before we search for the starting handle and get to crank this baby up. I'll tell you what, you do that while I go and get the bloke with the red fucking flag who'll walk in front of us."

"It's all they had." Amber smirked, looking from under her lashes.

"I bet it was." Grant opened the vehicle logbook to the page recording reported damage. It was a golden rule for the police driver to check every mark on the car corresponded to a mark made on a diagram in the logbook. If a mark didn't match and it wasn't reported before driving a single yard, the new driver would be culpable for the damage. Having 'damage found' against your police driving record was a bad thing and ultimately could lead to suspension from driving police vehicles altogether, a huge and inconvenient ball-ache. Grant began to circle the Focus like a bad-tempered Apache, muttering to himself as he did so. "I bet the pool-car wankers were pissing themselves, palming this off on us. What prick thought to buy a car *that* colour? What is it? An anti-theft device..."

Amber managed to stifle her laughter. Just.

\* \* \*

131

It was going to be at least a two-hour drive through the rush hour traffic. Grant's ill humour at the motorised heap he'd been allocated finally abated. "We're going to be a laughingstock when we roll up to the front door of Frankton Abbey in this fucking thing." There was laughter in his voice as he spoke. "We've an appointment with the Headmaster, a bloke called Henry Rose-Gummer, M.A. Ed, M.S Ed *and* OBE. Surely he can't be as stuck up as he sounds, can he?"

Amber caught the change in her sergeant's mood, laying a mischievous bet. "I dare you to shake his hand and say *'Mornin' 'Arry, 'ow's it 'anging'*, in your best cockney, I dare you. I'll buy lunch if you do."

Grant laughed again before suddenly hitting the brakes as the Westbound A40 traffic ground to a halt. "You do realise that'll be the only thing going through my mind when I meet him now."

"Yep!" Amber replied triumphantly.

\* \* \*

Having cleared the Hanger Lane gyratory at the North Circular Road, progress on the A40 out to the M40 motorway was clearer, the bulk of the traffic heading into the capital as the detectives headed west out of it. The Bogey, as it was now christened, although cosmetically a disaster, was subject to the usual police servicing and maintenance, consequently it purred comfortably along, nibbling at the miles towards Frankton Abbey. The bantering conversation bounced between speculation on the forthcoming school visit and theories regarding the case and the links between the boys, their mothers, and the killer. Even the rivalry between DI Dodds and DC Dirty Don Chamberlain for the attention of Isla Baxter was discussed with amusement and disdain in equal measure.

Leaving the motorway they made steady westward progress, conversation slowed, reduced to the giving and receiving of directions as they closed on their destination. The road sign-posted Frankton Village and nearby Swinbrook, followed minutes later by the turning they sought, Grant directed the car onto the long driveway which led to Frankton Abbey School.

"Like…Wow!" Amber was right. The view of the frontage of Frankton Abbey School was most definitely a 'Wow!' The manicured, cross-mowed patterned lawns that stretched away, left and right into the distance were the apron and wings of a green stage upon which the beautiful, imposing building stood. The driveway straightened and pointed arrow-like towards the arched entrance to a hidden inner courtyard beyond.

The Tudor red-brick wall, pierced by the arch, was flanked on each side by tall, three-story high, half-octagon turrets, each topped with a grey, leaded cupola, the tip of which bore a wrought iron, heraldic animal bearing a flag.

Beyond the broad block of Tudor frontage were a series of other buildings, modern but of local cream sandstone, in keeping with the environment. Boys could be seen milling about between the structures, small, distant figures in rich red blazers and dark trousers, others in white shirts and shorts were jogging towards a taller, glass sided hall, presumably the gym. This, then, was the fabled Frankton Abbey School, the most expensive private school in the country, perhaps the world, for the sons of the powerful, the influential, the rich, and the famous.

"I mean…Wow!" repeated Amber.

\* \* \*

Grant navigated The Bogey through the archway into a gravelled courtyard and parked between a Bentley and an Overfinch Range Rover. The Quad was surrounded on all four sides by lofty, looming internal faces, generously adorned with leaded windows. Ahead at the top of wide, worn steps were two soaring oak doors, one of which was open. If it was supposed to look inviting it was failing miserably, rarely had they seen anything so imposing. The sight on first viewing by very young boys, abandoned by their parents beneath this entranceway, must be terrifying. Amber's imagination saw fairy-tale Jack running out the towering open portal, the golden goose under his arm, chased by a bellowing giant.

The detectives ascended the steps and entered the imposing Tudor Great Hall, surprisingly bright, natural light from high windows was augmented by two crystal chandeliers. The walls were adorned with shields, brightly painted with coats of arms. In one corner stood a full suit of armour, the gauntleted hands gripping a broadsword, its point resting on the floor between the comically elongated points of metallic boots. A desk was placed, intimidatingly far away, across the full width of the hall, opposite the entrance. This piece of office furniture was incongruously modern and occupied by a plain-faced woman in her mid-thirties. Her blonde hair was tied back tightly in a ponytail, her clearly athletic body sheathed in a conservative grey suit. The hall echoed to the detective's footsteps on the ancient flagstones as they approached the receptionist whose glistening badge gave her name as Miss Isle. She smiled an artificial smile but remained silent until Grant and Amber stood immediately before her. The receptionist followed Ambers eyes as they fell to the badge, her expression a challenge to the young detective. Amber stifled an urge to laugh, surely 'Miss Isle' should rush into marriage if only to acquire a less ballistic combination of title and surname.

"Good morning, miss, good morning, sir. Welcome to Frankton Abbey School. How may I be of service to you?" Amber raised an eyebrow; thankful she was with Grant Maddox rather than Dirty Don Chamberlain. Such a worded greeting would have certainly provoked a toe-curling, embarrassing response involving a hand playing pocket billiards and a lascivious wink. Instead, Grant made the introductions, displayed his warrant card, and provided the information that they were expected by The Headmaster.

Grant and Amber, sporting bright yellow visitor badges, were guided through a maze of corridors and up a winding, spiral staircase by something called a 'duty-boy'. To Grant, he looked as if he'd spent the previous two hours in a dishwasher set to a high-temperature clean cycle. Duty-boy, perhaps twelve or thirteen years old, was in every respect from haircut to uniform to accent, immaculate. As they submissively followed, Grant and Amber exchanged wide-eyed expressions, both thrown out of kilter in the other-worldliness of the Frankton Abbey experience.

Duty-boy halted at a door bearing a brass plate engraved, 'Headmaster'. Duty-boy turned to examine his charges, implausibly, under the gaze of a mere child, Grant and Amber felt obliged to stand upright and straighten themselves, Grant pulling his sleeves down, adjusting his tie, while Amber tidied a loose strand of hair behind an ear. Why they both felt so compelled was baffling, each assumed a conditioned reflex was at work, emerging from a deeply buried school-days reaction to a door marked 'Headmaster'. The added surprise was duty-boy really was examining them, he gave a crisp, snappy nod of his head, satisfied the detectives were turned out to his satisfaction. For a fleeting second Grant considered carrying out Amber's dare, greeting Henry Rose-Gummer, *'Mornin' 'Arry, 'ow's it 'anging?'* He shook the thought from his mind.

# Chapter Thirty-One

D uty-boy rapped the door twice, stood back, and waited. A few seconds later, a deep voice called out, 'Come!'

The shining boy opened the door. "Good morning, Headmaster; your visitors are Detective Sergeant Maddox and Detective Constable Bennett."

"Thank you. You may wait outside."

"Yes, Headmaster." The boy gave another crisp, snappy bow of his head as the detectives entered the office of Henry Rose-Gummer, M.A. Ed, M.S Ed, *and* OBE.

The smell of old leather and furniture polish assailed Grant's nostrils as he surveyed the room. Grant wasn't taken aback to see the headmaster seated in a high-backed leather chair or that the chair was behind an extremely impressive antique desk. What did take him aback was the whole ensemble was situated on a raised plinth about twelve inches higher than the rest of the room. The headmaster was black-gowned, in his late sixties, pale-faced, with short, thinning, grey hair. He stood as they entered, nodding to Amber, an evident courtesy to the presence of a lady, he didn't acknowledge Grant, he re-took his seat and gifted his visitors with a tolerant smile.

To the headmaster's left, silhouetted against the large window, looking across the lawns, was another, black-robed figure. He stared through the ancient, distorted glass, his back to the room and its occupants, hands clasped at his rear like a Royal temporarily halted on a walkabout. He was tall and the robes failed to disguise his slimness, a pencil thin neck protruded from the dark collar upon which perched a narrow skull with close cropped dark hair. He made no effort to turn or acknowledge the visitors, gazing intently out the window.

"Good morning, Detectives. May I examine your credentials?" The officer's attention was turned to the headmaster's enquiry. It was not an unreasonable request, considering the confidentiality of the information they were hoping to obtain.

"Of course, sir." Grant offered his warrant card. "May I thank you for seeing us at such short notice?" Rose-Gummer nodded, apparently satisfied with Grant's I.D. before squinting at Amber's warrant card and handing it back.

"You may be seated." The headmaster waved majestically to the plain, wooden chairs positioned close to the wall opposite him. Grant and Amber, catching each other's bemused expressions, took a chair, positioned them closer to the headmaster's desk, and sat, feeling like naughty children, finding themselves looking upwards at a steep angle to the man opposite. The effect was similar to having a Range Rover pull up next to an MG at the traffic lights, its driver peering down. Height intimidated.

"What can I do for you? I'm a busy man." It was apparent the headmaster didn't wish to engage in small talk or discuss the weather, which was fine by Grant, who was feeling happier by the second that the hideously green, radio-active bogey was blighting the quadrangle of Frankton Abbey School.

"Firstly Sir, may my colleague take notes, this is merely to refresh our recollections of our conversation, the record would not be primary evidence but I need to inform you could be part of advance disclosable documentation to a defendants legal representative." The headmaster looked to his left. The slim figure before the window nodded his head almost imperceptibly. The headmaster turned his attention back to Maddox. "You may."

"Thank you, sir." Grant tipped his head toward the figure at the window. "My colleague needs to note those present in the room."

The headmaster sighed audibly, telegraphing the tiresomeness of the whole episode. "You may note the presence of Dr. Dominic Wagstaff, the Deputy Head of Frankton Abbey School. He is here as a witness and to give legal advice." Rose-Gummer made no effort to disguise his irritation.

Amber wrote the details in her notebook, her downturned face hiding her expression. Grant, without her advantage, failed to halt the hoisting of a surprised eyebrow at the unexpected direction and tone of what he'd hoped would be a simple and productive encounter.

Rose-Gummer noted the visual leak and continued. "I have the reputation of this institution, its students, and their parents to consider. That is my priority, Detective. A priority from which I will not be deflected."

Amber kept her face down in her notebook, happy it was Grant and not she facing this monstrous man. Maddox took a deep breath.

"Headmaster, I assure you that we're here to ask for help, not to point any fingers."

The headmaster frowned briefly. "I've said I'm a busy man. Ask your questions, Detective."

Grant resisted the urge to duel with the figure which loomed above him and moved on. "You spoke yesterday with Detective Chief Inspector Paul Winter; he is head of an investigation into the murder of three women."

"Yes, we spoke, and he acquainted me with the case at hand."

"Then, sir, you will be aware that the three victims were mothers to four of the Frankton Abbey students who tragically died eighteen years ago in the air crash in France."

"Your Mr Winter passed this information on to me, yes. I repeat, Sergeant, what can I do for you?"

Grant glanced to Amber, clearly this was going to be like pulling teeth with tweezers.

"We were hoping, Sir, that you may have records, any information at all, relating to the deceased boys and, as importantly, their families. We're seeking a link, anything that may help us to identify why their mothers, after all these years, are being killed. I'm not at liberty to give details, but I can tell you that these are extremely brutal killings."

"The newspapers have christened the perpetrator 'The Dissection Killer,' I understand." The headmaster did not disguise the revulsion in his voice on mentioning the press. "The media are ever eager to promote sensationalism and uproar in their contemptible rags. *This* establishment does not approve of sensationalism, nor of uproar. Frankton Abbey School is an educational institution, the parents of our boys, many of whom are subject to hostile and intrusive media attention themselves, expect decorum and propriety from this faculty. We do not like publicity, Detective Sergeant. The association of this school with the tawdry reporting of these events is something we are *very* keen to minimise. You understand?"

"I understand very well Sir. I can assure you that our sole intention is to identify and arrest the person responsible for these murders, and our intention is to do so in a manner which retains the dignity of all those concerned. As I speak, the link between the victims and the deceased students of this school has *not* been made public by the police, I assure you it is also our intention to minimise any such publicity."

"You use the word intention a great deal. Tell me, Detective, what if that intention, which is defined as merely a wish or goal after all, is not fulfilled. *What then,* Detective Sergeant?" It was an extremely pointed question. The conversation was not progressing as Maddox had envisaged at all. His police officer mind rejected *any* priority other than the apprehension of serious offenders; this man was obsessed with a very different priority altogether.

"Sir, I am a police officer; my job is to follow the evidence, to apprehend offenders, and bring them before a court. I took an oath twenty-eight years ago, a promise to do exactly that, to do it without fear or favour, without malice or ill will. The evidence has led me to the door of your school, sir, and to your office. I assure you that it is my *intention* to protect the reputation of the innocent and of victims of crime, but I *will not* be deflected from my duty merely to protect reputations. I think that is what you may have been asking me. If so, you have your answer...sir."

Henry Rose-Gummer stared down at the officers seated below him. He pushed a document wallet which had been resting unnoticed on the desktop forward to the edge.

"This is the information I am at liberty to pass on to you. Thank you for coming to see me. Good day to you both."

# Chapter Thirty-Two

G rant stood and took the folder. "I need to examine this information before I leave. We've come a long way today; if I have questions about this, I'll need to ask them now." The headmaster leant back in his chair, a picture of barely tolerant impatience as Grant examined the documents within. He scanned each in turn, moving swiftly through the bundle of papers, his expression changing, his features tightening.

"Mr Rose-Gummer, other than full names, date of birth, and attendance dates for this school, the only information we requested, which is here, are contact addresses for next of kin. There is no detail on the boy's associations, interests, or backgrounds. There are no assessments of personality, ambitions, strengths, weaknesses, or, importantly, any misdemeanours. Where is their background information? Their teacher's character assessments? Where are the annual reports? Where are the *stories* of these boys? I need to find out about any connections with their parents and the parents with each other. I want to know about the relationship the school had with the parents before and after the crash. What contact was there between the parties? Have any of the mothers, especially the victims, ever contacted this establishment? I think you know exactly what information you were being asked to provide, Sir." Grant waved a sheet of paper, "I don't need to know that Chase Bingley got a B in math's when he was twelve."

"Detectives, there is not a single member of the teaching staff at this school who personally knew the students who passed away eighteen years ago. Staff move on, retire, or expire. The records you hold in your hand are the ones we have. I have no more to give."

"Then I require the details of staff who *did* know the boys, their names and contact details." Grant slammed his hand down on Rose-Gummer's desk.

The headmaster's face began to turn purple; his voice shook with the effort of control. "Those details are confidential. I'm sure you are aware of the procedures that you will need to engage in to require me to furnish you with that information."

Grant opened his mouth, about to speak, but before the words formed, the figure at the window turned. Dr. Dominic Wagstaff's robe swirled dramatically as he span, the effect something like the appearance of Dracula in a Hammer Horror, it was a good comparison, a more Christopher Lee lookalike it would have been difficult to find.

"Detective Sergeant Maddox, the Headmaster is merely presenting a view of one side of the coin. You are presenting a view of the other. We need to remember what we're looking at is the same coin. Ultimately, what we want is the same thing, that we order those wants differently is surely the only thing which separates us?" Wagstaff's voice was deep, possessing a calming quality that demanded attention. Immediately, Grant identified the true authority in the room and, recognising the bone that was being thrown to him, responded in kind.

"Of course, this is a difficult and sensitive situation. I'd ask you to appreciate the bubble in which we operate, the focus, which is required of us, the detachment necessary to maintain our objectivity. If I've appeared indifferent to the quite correct consideration for the children in your care, I apologise. I reiterate I'm here to ask for help."

Wagstaff nodded slowly and deliberately. "The Headmaster understands and appreciates your situation and will help where it is appropriate and lawful to do so. I have your details Detective Sergeant Maddox, I'll see what can be done to assist you. May I ask you to consider something? This building has stood on this spot for over five hundred years. It has been a place of learning for nearly two hundred years and has been in its present form for over one hundred. We are caretakers, Detective Sergeant Maddox, mere curators of this institution. Each Headmaster hands our good name on to the next, each student is a carrier of our standards and traditions, to be passed on, baton-like, to the student who follows him. You understand Detective Sergeant Maddox?"

Grant understood perfectly; Rose-Gummer was on his last legs, ready to leave the stage, and Dr. Dominic Wagstaff was waiting in the wings, eager to take his place. The importance of continuity was personal for these men. When the well-feathered nest is beckoning you, there is a need to make sure it doesn't get blown out of the tree, Rose-Gummer and his deputy clearly suspected this case had that potential... but why?

Wagstaff had used the words 'appropriate and lawful' to qualify the help he'd give. It was apparent the two men's delivery was different, but the message was the same: Grant was convinced little or no cooperation would be forthcoming from Frankton Abbey School.

The headmaster's face was still traversing the colours of the spectrum as Grant turned his attention back to the elevated figure behind the desk. "I'll wait a short while for the help I have asked for Headmaster. People are dying, in comparison, tender sensibilities do not count for much in my book...sir."

The headmaster reached a new colour as he spluttered. "Our conversation is at an end. *Duty-boy!*"

The office door opened, and the shiny child stood in the doorway. "Yes, Headmaster."

"Show our guests out."

Grant stopped in the doorway and turned to face the Headmaster of Frankton Abbey School, noting Wagstaff was looking out the window once more. "I said, Sir, that the link between the murder victims and the deceased students has *not* been made public by The Police. Perhaps I should add the caveat *yet*. You should also know that the willingness or otherwise of this faculty, by which I mean you, Sir, you personally, to help the police in the investigation or not help, is also something that may become public. It is so *very* hard to keep the details of a high-profile, sensational story out of the public domain. Perhaps you should cogitate on that. Good day to you."

# Chapter Thirty-Three

Grant and Amber dropped their visitor badges on the receptionist's desktop, signed themselves out in a leather-bound visitor book, and wordlessly stalked, grim-faced, across the five-hundred-year-old flagstones.

Grant's face was taut, his expression dark, his teeth clenched, convinced the two men knew something important, and he was going to do his utmost to find out what it was. Their belligerence and obstructiveness were beyond what could reasonably be expected in the circumstances. If the good name of the school was merely threatened by the revelation that mothers of dead children were being killed, what reasonable person could hold the school to account for that? Unless the school was culpable in some way. There *had* to be more. Grant also knew his conclusion was not based on anything he could present to a court of law, none of this was fact based, hard evidence. This was the gut feeling of an old copper, and it wasn't permitted to submit gut feeling to a jury, under oath, from a witness box. 'It didn't look right, it didn't sound right, it didn't feel right' was not allowable evidence, but it should be.

Amber broke the silence as they descended the steps into the quad. "Skip, you were utterly brilliant in there with that stuck-up tosser and fucking Dracula. I was so proud of you. I'd have been intimidated into just nodding and smiling sickly."

Grant's expression eased an iota. "That whole set-up was meant to intimidate and demean us. *Pricks!* Perched on his platform, looking down his nose, making us sit on fucking naughty chairs and that smirking vampire!" Maddox picked up on Amber's accurate description. "He was the power, the real power, and there's more going on here, I can feel it! My spider sense is tingling! The trouble is," Grant waved the document wallet, "we haven't got anything like the information I was hoping for. I wanted insights, links, relationships, breaches of discipline, punishments, and even a scandal or hint of one. I'm looking for a bloody reason!"

"Do you really think they know something? Are they hiding something specifically or just slamming the door shut to protect their fee-paying parents?"

Grant halted. "This case is about connections. Find the connections, and we find the killer. We have seven students from Frankton Abbey killed in the crash eighteen years ago. We have three women, mothers to four of those dead pupils, butchered. In the middle is this school, and two men protesting far too much about us, asking a few simple questions to establish the background of the players in this drama. Yes, Amber. They know something."

Amber grinned, "your spider sense really is tingling, isn't it?"

Grant, too exasperated to respond, slapped his thigh with the document wallet in frustration, fumbling in his pocket for the green monstrosity's ignition keys as they reached the car. "We need a break," he snapped, "a bit of good luck and time is pressing. Three dead mothers." Grant counted the number off on his fingers. "That leaves three women who we *must* consider to be in danger. At least we have *their* details now," he said, waving the file again. He shook his head. "If we've got to go to court to force the school to pass on details from teachers who knew the boys…well, how long will that take?" Amber leaned over the bonnet of their car, reaching to the insect-splattered glass of the windscreen, the action snapping Grant out of his irritated musings. "What are you doing?"

Amber held up a small, folded piece of paper, which she opened. "Skipper," she called, "you asked for a bit of luck. This was under the windscreen wiper," she explained. "It says, '*Swan Inn, Swinbrook. 8pm*'. That's it. That's all."

# Chapter Thirty-Four

Although Grant had declined to address the headmaster as *'Arry'* nor enquire of him how some unspecified item on his person was hanging, Amber still insisted upon paying for lunch. It was a short drive from Frankton Abbey School to The Swan at Swinbrook, a sixteenth-century, picture postcard coaching inn built of cream Cotswold stone, nestled next to the River Windrush.

On arriving, Grant reported in with DCI Winter, passing on the recently obtained family details of the victims of the air crash contained in Rose-Gummer's documents. The priority was obvious, three mothers to victims of the air crash were still alive but potentially in terrible danger, they needed to be found and protected. 'Leave that with us at this end', Winter had said simply and decisively. Grant sighed with relief, if nothing else maybe the hideous slaughter would now be stopped in its tracks. On hearing of the note on The Bogey's windscreen and its tantalizing promise, Winter had been intrigued, "Curiouser and curiouser," he quoted, "Obviously, wait and see who turns up, dig and find out what you can. If you need to stay over, do so, I'll authorise it on expenses, just get receipts for *everything* and *don't* go over the top on food and drink, okay?" Grant thanked the instinct that had made him and Amber pack bags.

"Would I?" his words dripped irony.

*** 

Lunch was good, the glass of wine that washed it down even better. Amber

145

was happier still she'd be able to claim the expense back from The Job *and* retain the moral high ground by offering to pay out of her own pocket before that fact became known. Amber's suggestion to walk lunch off seemed loaded to Grant, but he accepted with alacrity.

The pair of detectives walked the few yards to the bridge and peered over the low wall, staring down at the water passing by below them.

"People love water, don't they?" Grant mused. "They like to live by the sea, a lake, or a river. Why is that?"

"Amniotic fluid?" suggested Amber. "We all spent the first nine months of our existence floating around in a sort of water. It offers a comfort, a reassurance of a time of which we have no memory but which is hard-wired into our sub-conscious. How's that for a theory?" The pair drifted back, past The Swan, and up the hill towards the church. It was a place she'd expressed a desire to visit, saying there was a surprise there.

"It's a good theory," he responded, "we're back to the womb again, aren't we? Something which differentiates the sexes, something which contains the water which warms and protects us when we're at our most helpless and vulnerable." Grant stopped walking and faced Amber. "Why does he rip out their wombs? *Why?*" He shook his head in exasperation. "I've read and re-read the offender profile and it all seems a bit glib, a bit simplistic. He's cutting up his mother, over and over again, because she wasn't nice and he's jealous she was able to give birth to him? He's smashing up the swimming pool he learned to swim in. *Is that it?*"

Amber nodded. "I know what you mean. The fact is," she continued, "we now know these attacks are targeted. We've seven dead boys, and between them, because two were twins, we have six mothers, three of them are dead. *That's* targeted. It kicks the Nutty Professor's theory into the long grass. Some basket case with a *Mommie Dearest* complex wouldn't target these victims specifically. Any wealthy woman in her fifties would do, surely? The trouble our bloke is going to get at them, the electronic surveillance to be overcome for a start, the time he's invested, and especially the chances he took to get at Juno Jenkin, that was risky and audacious in equal measure. He wants *these* women, no others, just these. *We need to know why.*"

146

"I know," mused Grant. "The more answers we get, the more questions pop up. It's like hitting the bloody moles with a mallet at a village fete. Infuriating."

They continued their walk up the hill to the church. Both minds whirring, processing speculations, *both* minds infuriated.

\* \* \*

"There." Amber pointed to three headstones, revealing her surprise to Grant. "Swinbrook was the home of the Mitford girls; they were famous in the years between the wars, the 'it-girls' of the age, beautiful, talented, and controversial. My mum loved everything about them and brought me here once, when I was a little girl, look," Amber pointed to the first headstone. *"Nancy Mitford, Authoress,"* Amber read out loud, then nodded to the resting place of her sister, *"Unity Valkyrie Mitford*, she was a devotee and close friend of Hitler; she shot herself when Britain went to war with the Nazis. She was the symbol of a whole class that was seduced by fascism in this country. Amber nodded to the third grave and read. *"Diana Mosley, née Mitford*. She was married to Oswald Mosley, the British fascist leader."

Amber wandered away, Grant trailed slowly behind, passing numerous headstones; each had a story, each the final physical representation on earth of a person who'd once lived. " Look, here's Pamela." Grant followed her gaze. "She was the quietest, most reserved of the sisters. The Poet Laureate, Sir John Betjeman was besotted with her but all she wanted was to farm and tend her animals, she turned him down."

Grant viewed the gravestone, reading the inscription out loud, *"A valiant heart*. Why is she alone, separated from her sisters?" Grant asked.

"I've no idea," Amber answered honestly. It's amazing that three of them are together at all, they'd such a contrary relationship in life. All the physical beauty, all the talent, the incredible wealth and privilege they were born into, it didn't guarantee they liked each other or got on, didn't guarantee long life or happiness."

"The boys on that plane," Grant mused aloud, "they had it all. Young, fit, healthy, hugely wealthy and privileged. The whole of life lay out before them, not as a trial or vale of woes. They were the golden boys denied. Denied by the stupidity of a poorly executed repair."

As Grant stood in the churchyard, surrounded by the evidence of so many lives lost, opportunities denied, and reflecting on the demise of seven young lives snuffed out in an undistinguished French field, he was overwhelmed by a sudden feeling of great sadness. The emotion showed, and Amber, perceptive to his moods, asked, "Are you alright, Skip?" her voice full of concern.

Grant shook himself and smiled. "Of course! I've had some things on my mind outside of this case, just between you and me." Lydia's words burrowed, unwanted, into his thoughts, '*I want you to stop punishing yourself. Can you do that?*' "Nothing to concern yourself about…but being here, in a place like this, and listening to you telling the story of the lives of others, well, you can't help but wonder about stuff, can you?"

The officers strolled on, finding a bridleway in the corner of the graveyard, which led to a grassy path and open fields beyond. Neither really spoke, satisfied to be alone with their thoughts and reflections.

Amber had come very close, in the graveyard, to telling Grant about Aston. It was the emotion of the location, and the moment, the talk of young life lost, the sadness and reality of standing at the resting place of her mother's heroes, of happy times shared with her. The feelings had welled up in her but not spilled out.

Grant never came close to telling about Lydia and *his* shame.

# Chapter Thirty-Five

They'd picked a shadowy, far corner of the dining area to wait on events. Having both enjoyed a hot meal with a glass of wine *and* obtained receipts, they waited, glancing periodically at wristwatches. The hands moved slowly towards eight o'clock. Each arrival to the bar seemed to be heading in their direction, eliciting expectation and a sudden rise in pulse rate, only to subside as the man in the red shirt sat with a single woman or the old boy with his collie dog slumped in a chair and nursed a pint of real ale.

It was fifteen minutes after the appointed time. Amber looked over her sergeant's shoulder as a short, fit-looking man began to zig-zag his way through the tables and chairs towards their corner.

"Maybe our man, Skip."

Grant controlled the urge to turn, listening to Amber's commentary.

"Definitely heading our way. Dark trousers, cream shirt, blue jacket." Grant saw Amber smile winningly at the unseen man behind him.

"May I join you?" The visitor sat at the table next to Maddox. "My apologies for being late." The man offered no explanation. Grant twisted in his seat to see the owner of the voice full on. He had steel grey hair, cut short, neat and tidy, and below average height, but despite his age, which Grant estimated to be his late sixties, his body appeared taut and athletic.

Grant offered his hand. "I'm Grant, this is Amber. We're Detectives with the Metropolitan Police, and you are?" The visitor's grip was strong, lengthy, and accompanied by a piercing look into Grant's eyes, the Detective Sergeant felt he was being assessed.

"You look ex-military to me. Am I right?" The visitor still held Grant's hand, vice-like. Grant felt a strength of personality, a no-nonsense quality that would brook zero bullshit.

"Four Two Commando, Royal Marines."

"William Watson, B Company, Two Para. Pleased to meet you." Watson released his grip, turned to Amber, and offered his hand. "Pleased to meet you, too." Amber's hand was gripped far more gently, and surrounded by macho military declarations, she resisted the rising urge to announce her previous military experience as both a Brownie *and* a Girl Guide.

"Can I get you a drink, Mr Watson?" asked Amber.

"A pint of *Hooky* would be very good, thank you. Please, call me Bill." Amber looked to Grant, who raised and waggled his near-empty wine glass and grinned. Heading to the bar she left the men to talk about whatever ex-soldiers talked about.

"Ulster?" asked Watson, "South Atlantic?"

Grant answered each enquiry with a slow nod of his head.

"Hmmm," continued Watson, "do you know anyone remotely interested?"

Grant gave a sardonic laugh. "Not even remotely."

It was Watson's turn to nod. "Makes you wonder, doesn't it? I needn't ask if you lost friends. If you were there, you did. We all did. I find as I get older I spend more and more time thinking about my mates and asking, what was the point? I still haven't found an answer."

"When you took the King's Shilling," said Grant, "did *you* ask the Recruiting Sergeant, 'as we go along, you *will* make it absolutely clear what the point of it all is, won't you?' I know I didn't. I was eighteen, I wanted some order in my life, I wanted some excitement and I wanted comrades. I got all three. We all have bits of baggage to carry, but trying to find a point in it all isn't one of them. You'd go mad."

Amber placed the glasses on the table. "Who's going mad then?"

"We all are." The two men spoke the words simultaneously and laughed.

Grant raised his glass and toasted. "Two Para."

Watson raised his in response. "Four Two Commando."

Bewildered but aware that male bonding was occurring, which may pay dividends, Amber raised her glass, again refraining from mentioning the Girl Guides *or* Brownies.

Grant reached into his pocket, took out the small piece of paper, unfolded it, and held it up to William Watson. "I think you want to get something off your chest. I want to listen."

\* \* \*

"I left the Para's as a Physical Training Instructor with a chest full of decorations, a lifetime of experience, and good references. A mate got me into bodyguarding, the money was good, the travel was nice, and you got to mix with all sorts, the rich and the famous. It was okay for a while. But I'd spent twenty-two years on the move in The Mob, with real men, and after three years of messing about with pampered boy-band members, self-absorbed actors, or corrupt financiers, I needed something more permanent, more fixed, and anyway, I'd met a special guy in a club in Oxford." Watson halted in his story. "You understand?" His last two words heavy with meaning.

Grant nodded. There was nothing new about gay soldiers. Grant had known several gay Royal Marines, their sexuality an open secret, despite its then illegality, in the services, few cared. When bullets were flying about, when your life hung by a thread, only a fool questioned the sexuality of the man who would willingly risk his life to help you.

"This man I met, he taught at Frankton Abbey, it was through him I took the post of P.E. teacher at the school. We were together a while but when he moved on, I stayed, I was happy, settled, I had a small apartment in the grounds which came with the job until I moved into my little house in Swinbrook last year." Watson paused. "Look," he glanced from Grant to Amber and back again, "I was there. Eighteen years ago. I was there."

Amber gasped. "You knew the boys? The boys who died in the crash?"

Watson turned to look at Amber. "I was the physical education teacher, they were the rugby seven team, *my* team. I was their coach. I knew them all."

Grant and Amber stared at each other, both managing to keep huge and highly inappropriate grins from their faces.

# Chapter Thirty-Six

A fresh pint of *Hooky* was placed on the table, its delivery acknowledged with a smile and a tilt of the glass towards Amber, as Bill Watson began his story.

"Obviously the murders are all over the press, but the penny didn't drop with me." Watson offered, sipping at his beer. "The twins, Japhet and Jacob's surname was Gold. The newspapers report of their mother's murder gave a different surname, one that meant nothing to me, Martine something-or-other. I didn't know she'd re-married or what her new name was. As for Chase Bingley's mother, well Bingley isn't that uncommon a name and I had no reason at all to link her name to Chase, it was only after Juno Jenkin's murder I even took notice of the papers. I mean, good grief, *'The Dissection Murders'* and *Juno Jenkin* a victim! I thought fleetingly, maybe, just maybe Juno could have been linked to the Bingley case by the surnames of two of the boys. It was a momentary thought, no more. But when your senior officer called to arrange for your meeting with the headmaster, *then* I realised there was a link. Nothing is secret at Franks, Detective; your visit was *the* hot topic I can tell you. I knew it had to be about the boys and their mothers. The headmaster gave you the bum's rush, threw you some scraps and dismissed you. That's what I heard." Watson placed his finger on the side of his nose.

Grant nodded, he wanted to keep his replies short and concise, to not disturb the flow of information from Watson. More detailed questioning could wait until the whole story had been spilled.

"What did you think of *Doctor* Dominic Wagstaff?" Bill continued, "he's always there, circling over the headmaster like a bloody vulture."

"Yes, he was there," Grant said.

"He looked like a vampire," Amber chipped in, Watson's obvious disdain for Wagstaff, freeing her to speak openly. "A smiling assassin, I thought," she continued. Grant raised a warning eyebrow which Amber caught, the message clear, 'watch what you say, stay neutral'.

"Circling like a vulture," said Grant, "what do you mean?"

Watson took a long pull at his drink. "The headmaster has been at Franks a long time, and the good Doctor, only of philosophy, mind you, is the heir apparent. He's been waiting a long time to get behind that elevated desk and wants the place to remain a going concern for himself. Any scandal, any adverse publicity, could threaten his inheritance." Grant nodded his understanding. "Old Rose-Gummer walks a tightrope; his clientele are very suspicious of the media at the best of times. *Any* publicity is frowned upon, the wrong sort could be extremely detrimental for the school."

Watson drained his glass.

"The boys?" prompted Grant, wanting to steer the conversation back.

"Ah, the boys! You're not supposed to speak ill of the dead, but I tell you, five of those seven were the nastiest, cruellest shits you could ever meet. I despised them, and they despised me. The funny thing is, that hatred saved my life. Any chance of another beer?"

\* \* \*

Watson took a large swallow of his fresh pint before continuing. "Garson Thompson and Osian Vaughan-Hughes were the core of the group. Garson was the team captain, Osian, Juno Jenkin's son, was his best friend. They were both fit, strong, fast, perfect for sevens rugby, highly intelligent, attractive, confident, and good company. The other boys at Franks were drawn to these two like iron filings to a magnet. But they were rotten to the core, bullies, sadistic, and without conscience. The younger boys at school lived in fear of them. They could, and did bad-mouth the staff, including me. Garson's family was wealthy beyond imagination, and Osian's mother was famous beyond imagination. They were a catch for the school, Franks poster boys. Rose-Gummer's predecessor, Dr. Braden Walker set the tone, he let them run amok. I think you can imagine what that was like for a man like me?"

Grant could. A seen it all, done it all, ex-Para who'd spent his life with real men having to bend before spoilt, arrogant, done-nothing brats. Unbearable.

"One example, on the practise field I caught Garson with a tackle, brought him down, winded him, made him wheeze like a wounded seal, it showed him up, the fit young buck, caught and felled by an old-fart, short-arse like me. He didn't like it, so got his own back. The other two close ones were Lynton Fiennes and Chase Bingley. Lynton was a giant, six and a half feet tall, and built like a brick shithouse. Outwardly, he was softly spoken and seemed different, more considerate, but he was as rotten and as entitled as the rest, just as nasty and like the others, willing to please Garson. He must've got the nod from Garson, he took me out, a high tackle and fell on me, all accidentally on purpose. Cracked two of my ribs. Bastard!" Watson took another gulp of his beer, the irritation of the memory evident.

"The Gold twins were chalk and cheese…under the skin. Jacob was the older by ten minutes, apparently, he was like the other boys: arrogant, rude, entitled. He loved the girls and loved to put it about. He was hung like a tyrannosaurus, always waving his cock around in the showers, a really horrible young man. His brother Japhet, seemed the same but was a play-actor. He was sensitive and intelligent but needed to survive in the world they inhabited. It was a weakness how he behaved sometimes, but I think he at least had a conscience. He… he had some private issues which because of who and what I am I recognised in him, so we became closer. I helped him, I think. He'd come to me sometimes, and we'd talk. You understand what I'm saying? Pastoral care from someone who understood. You must remember that this was back in the 90s, AIDS was still a *Gay Plague,* and the stigma associated with being homosexual was cruel and open. Japhet could never behave in a way that was visibly different from the rest, but when we talked alone, he was a changed boy. I think if he'd survived, lived longer, he would've come to terms with things and become a good man. He was devoted to his brother, loved him, I think they had that special bond peculiar to twins. He wouldn't ever do anything that could harm his brother. Remember that, understand that. It's important."

Grant turned his mouth downwards in a serious expression. "Forgive me for needing specifics. Can I clarify, you're saying that Japhet's private issues were in regard to his sexuality? He was gay?"

Watson nodded. "He *was* gay, and he knew his father would never accept him. He was terribly torn. You should know there was never, ever any impropriety between us. Ever. Or with any of the boys at the school."

Grant shook his head sadly. "I never thought there was, nor implied it. I'm saddened you feel the need to defend yourself."

Watson looked embarrassed but felt the need to explain. "Perhaps you can imagine the potential for allegations? Especially back then. There are many who think a gay man *must* be a paedophile and *some* who wouldn't think twice to make use of that bigoted opinion."

"Not at this table," Grant answered firmly but noted Watson's emphasis. It was apparent someone *had* used that prejudice.

Watson shrugged and nodded his acceptance. "I talked a great deal with Japhet, helped him understand and accept his situation. I think he was close to the point of liking himself." Watson halted, deep in thought, apparently making a decision. Grant looked to Amber who raised a questioning eyebrow, Grant shook his head almost imperceptibly, the message clear, 'wait'.

"The last boy on the team, he was the outsider. Gary, Gary Whittcock. His father threw him into the bear-pit at Franks. He was a huge lottery winner and thought he was doing Gary a favour, sending him to Franks. He was so, so out of his depth. The media had made his father a figure of ridicule and the boys turned on Gary, it was brutal. He was such a nice lad, he tried so hard to be strong, I found Gary crying once, how lonely he was. The other boys were merciless to him. The name-calling, the abuse...horrible. He'd some steel, though, that boy. He played the game, he *never* showed them the pain he felt, only to me and eventually to Japhet." Watson paused again, thoughtful. "They found each other. No one ever knew, no one has ever known, except Gary, Japhet, and me. And now you."

"Gary Whittcock and Japhet Gold were lovers?"

Watson nodded.

This was more information than Grant Maddox could have ever hoped for but the detective in him had to test the evidence. "The headmaster said there was no one at the school who knew the boys personally, but here you are. I find it hard to believe he'd let himself be caught in a deliberate lie."

Watson smiled. "I'm sure he was careful with his words. I no longer teach at the school. I'm heading towards seventy now. I'm carrying so many injuries it's a wonder I can walk. I'm a groundsman now, only part-time. I keep my eyes and ears open, I talk with the boys, I know all the staff. I'm sure old Rose-Gummer worded his assertion carefully."

Grant slammed the flat of his hand into his forehead. The headmaster's words came back, "The slimy bastard!" Grant exclaimed. "He said there were no longer any *teaching staff at this school* who knew the boys. You're right, he worded it *very* carefully."

Watson smiled resignedly. "You can take that another step if you like. The headmaster isn't part of the 'teaching staff' either.

Grant slammed his hand on the table. "He was at the school? He knew the boys too?"

Watson nodded. "Head of History. He knew them all *and* he was Franks Parent Liaison, he knew each boy's family. His job was to be the point of contact with the school. Schmooze them and pour oil on any troubled waters, keep them onside and onboard and most importantly paying not only their fees but additional donations, new gym, new swimming pool, new art facility etc. Obviously now, as The Head, he no longer teaches, nor do I. So he never told you a lie."

Grant was appalled at the duplicity to which he'd been subjected, every cell of his body wanted to challenge Rose-Gummer, in truth he wanted to subject the arrogant old man to the same treatment as a certain Capo Del Barista Supremo and drag him across his preposterous elevated desk to receive an extremely vigorous shaking.

Grant took a breath, controlling his fury. "Bill, we know someone is killing the mothers of your rugby team; we don't know *why*. You've given us so much more than we knew before, but there *must* be something, something must have happened which is connected to these murders, something which prompted this whole thing. Can you think of anything, anything at all, to answer that question?"

Bill Watson, ex-Para, ex-bodyguard, ex-P.E. teacher, gave the deepest sigh imaginable, and shook his head sadly. "I *was* told something, something that happened. I don't know how it could be linked, but that's not my job to work out, is it? That's yours."

Grant's voice was almost a whisper. "That is *my* job exactly, Bill. Will you tell me what happened?"

"I will."

# Chapter Thirty-Seven

Amber placed three fresh drinks on the table and rested back in her chair, notebook on her knee, leaving Grant wordlessly leaning towards Watson, who was deep in thought. Amber understood the pressure of silence, often the key that opened the door to the truth. Watson had a story to tell and had expressed a reluctant desire to tell it. He was carrying a secret he'd sworn to keep and was engaged in an internal moral dilemma. A single word out of place could slam that opening door shut and seal that secret back inside Watson's heart forever. They would wait in silence.

"It was Japhet Gold who told me." Watson finally broke the quiet. "Gary Whittcock was there too but didn't speak, not a word. They weren't asking for my advice on what to do. Japhet knew what I'd have said and that would have meant betraying his brother, something he'd *never* do. I told you to remember that. No, this was like a confession to a priest who was committed to a vow of silence. What Japhet told me was an unburdening. They call it un-loading nowadays, don't they? He wanted, was looking for, some sort of approval for his and Gary's actions in the circumstances." Watson looked from Grant to Amber. His expression must have mirrored that of Japhet and Gary eighteen years ago. An expression, pleading, 'don't think badly of me'.

"The Gold's parents had a large apartment in Covent Garden. It was empty practically all the time, just a place in central London, used once in a blue moon, worth millions! It was a few days before the team were due to fly out to Italy for the Seven's Tournament. Garson said they should go into

159

London, go clubbing, get pissed and coked up, screw some girls, and crash at the Gold's apartment. It would be a good way to get ready for the tour. Jacob Gold was all for it. Japhet went along with his brother, as he always did." Watson gulped at his beer, collecting his thoughts.

"I've no idea which club they went to but Japhet and Gary ended up somewhere else, I'm only guessing a gay pub or club. I don't know where the others went; it's not important. It was the early hours when the taxi dropped Japhet and Gary off outside the apartment building. They'd been drinking and taking drugs." Watson shrugged, his body language conveying the view it's what kids do.

"When they went into the apartment, the rest of the team, Garson, Osian, Jacob, Lynton, and Chase, were already there, but they weren't alone." Watson swallowed. The moment had arrived. Grant and Amber had to lean in to catch his words. "There was a young girl in the apartment. She was naked and very, very distressed. One of the boys was having sex with her, two others were holding her down, another had a hand over her mouth. The boys were laughing. Japhet and Gary watched open-mouthed as the others, all of them, raped the girl. Garson was the ring-leader, he was always the ring-leader, he called to Japhet to 'have a piece' and mocked Gary when he hid himself in the kitchen. They'd picked the girl up in a nightclub, got her drunk, got her high, and brought her back to be used. It's just the sort of thing they'd do. I told you, they were arrogant, selfish, and entitled. This girl only existed to entertain them." Watson drained his glass, clearly emotional.

Grant nodded wordlessly to Amber, who rose to replenish the drink. Watson gathered himself, avoiding eye contact with the detective, looking in the direction of the bar where Amber was handing over the cash for his drink. Looking back to Grant, his face transmitted his discomfort at uttering his next words; words Grant surmised he didn't want to say in front of Amber.

"They weren't satisfied with raping her, they sodomised her, all of them. *Animals!*" Watson shook his head slowly, looking to the bar once more. "They hurt her too, you know. Not content with playing out every fantasy they could think of, they hurt her, too. Japhet said she had bite marks on her breasts." Watson paused. "And she was bleeding. I don't know if that meant she was a virgin or if they'd caused a rupture somehow or both. But they hurt her. A lot."

Grant felt his pulse rise, his heart thump in his chest. He could feel anger rising in him. He wanted to say something to Watson, wanted to ask questions, wanted to encourage him, reassure him, communicating these facts didn't make you complicit in the crime. But he stayed silent. Waiting for the old Para to find his voice once more. Amber placed the beer on the table.

Watson looked up, a picture of misery. "Thanks, love."

"You're welcome."

Watson shook his head as if shaking off excess water. "Anyway," he said, trying to put a lightness in his voice to distance himself from the gruesomeness of the narrative. "Anyway, Japhet and Gary didn't do anything to help this girl. That was their shame; that's what they carried. You have to remember they were two against five and five complete bastards at that. Gary went to the kitchen and tried to shut out what he was hearing, while in the next room, it was playtime. Japhet, because of his brother, watched for a while, then joined Gary. Later they heard the sound of the boys on a computer game, laughing and joking, taking the piss out of each other. Japhet left the kitchen, he told me he saw the girl staggering slowly around the room, picking up items of clothing. She was crying, wiping her nose on the back of her hand. She moved slowly, in pain. No one was paying her the slightest bit of attention, busy playing, busy snorting cocaine. Japhet was ashamed. He told me that. He was ashamed about what happened, he was ashamed about what he did, or didn't do, to help her at the time. I believe him. He *was* ashamed. He told me that Gary pushed past him, put an arm around the girl, picked up an item of clothing she'd dropped, and helped her to the bathroom. The two helped her dress, they washed her face, did the equivalent of saying 'there, there, it's alright now.' But it wasn't. They walked to the lift and went with her to the street. Japhet hailed a cab, gave the driver a hundred pounds, and told him to take her wherever she wanted to go, then he pushed another hundred pounds into her pocket. They shut the taxi door, and she left."

Watson lowered his head, holding it with both hands, like a tired man. When he looked up, he tried to smile a smile of relief, the worst was over, he'd got it out, at last. He took another drink and continued. "I had a room at the hotel near the airport where we all stayed the night before the flight. That's when I saw Japhet and Gary, they came to my room. The words of that terrible story were the last thing they ever said to me. The next day, their jet slammed into the ground in France. In any other world I'd have been on the plane with them but Garson hated me so much I was made to travel independently, in cattle class on a scheduled flight. They thought that was so funny, them on the executive jet, me on a budget airline. I said to you earlier, their hatred saved my life. It did. Otherwise, I'd have been with them and as dead as they are."

Watson sat back, his beer glass in his hand. He took a long, deep drink. He looked as drained as his glass. *Now* was the time for Grant to speak, to pull more from the story.

"Who was the girl? Did they say who she was? It's *very* important."

Bill Watson shrugged. "It's eighteen years ago. I put it in a box, at the back of my mind. What they did to that girl was terrible, unforgivable. The inaction of Japhet and Gary was terrible too. Inexcusable but understandable. Japhet could *never* say anything, to do so would condemn his twin brother. Gary couldn't speak out either because to do so could risk exposing their relationship and would also condemn Japhet for his inaction. They decided to do nothing."

"Except tell you about it?" offered Grant.

"Except tell me about it," echoed Watson. "I told you, it was a form of confession, the best they could do. I'm not excusing them. I *would've* tried to persuade them to go to the police, eventually, after the tour, but events overtook us all."

"The girl. Did they say *anything* about the girl? Who was she?" Grant pressed.

"Japhet said her name was something like Cassie or Lassie. That's all I can tell you. I wish it was more. It's been a burden; a weight I wish I'd never been given to carry. You can't turn back time, can you?"

Grant wasn't listening. Something in his memory was stirring. '*Cassie or Lassie*,' he mouthed silently.

"Cassie?"

# Chapter Thirty-Eight

The three figures at the table sat in silence. Each stilled by their own differing thoughts. Bill Watson had told his story, betrayed a trust, and even if the true villains of the piece weren't the two boys he'd mentored and still held in affection, by telling the truth, he'd blackened their names and their memory too. He felt shame and guilt.

Amber Bennett, not yet aware of the full horror of the attack, was appalled at what she'd heard. She closed her eyes and considered those who'd stood by and done nothing and tried not to condemn them as much as the perpetrators of the horror. It was a difficult task, the police officer inside her struggling to understand the mentality of anyone who could find a reason to turn a blind eye when presented with someone in dire need of help.

Grant Maddox's thoughts were racing. Watson's revelations about the true nature of the Franks Seven's team were eerily similar to that expressed by Isla Baxter so recently. *'You shouldn't think of them as innocent children, incapable of doing wrong.'* She'd been right, but her prescient warning regarding their character was uncanny. Hot on the tail of that disclosure were the complications of the team's internal relationships. That two were engaged in a clandestine relationship with each other, that one of those was unable to break a bond with his twin, and, of course, overriding everything was the hideousness of the brutal rape and torture of a helpless girl. *'Cassie or Lassie',* he'd said. Grant counted the connections, the traumatised girl, drunk and drugged uttering her name to Japhet and Gary. Japhet, ashamed and secretive, passing it on, eighteen years ago to Watson. Then here, at this table, an old man carrying terrible knowledge, finally uttering the words to the detectives. That was three jumps, Chinese Whispers spread over nearly two decades, it could be enough to have changed the original. *'Cassie or Lassie'* or even something else that sounded similar. It was just out of reach. It was infuriating. He recalled Lydia's oft-spoken words at such moments. *'Forget what you're trying to remember, it'll just jump into your mind when you least expect it'*. It was good advice, that conundrum he'd struggle with later. For now he had a witness who was talking, he needed to draw out as much as he could.

It was Maddox who broke the silence and the solitary thoughts of the trio. "Bill." Watson seemed to jump at the sound of his name; his delving into a dark past and the combination of several pints of strong beer had induced a temporary trancelike state. "Bill, what did you do? What happened next?"

"They all died. And I lived. My plane landed in Milan an hour after theirs crashed into a field. I was at the hotel, sitting in the lobby, looking at my watch, waiting for them to turn up. I was convinced they were fucking about somewhere, that Garson had decided to explore the city or something, leaving me like a tit in a trance. It's the sort of thing that would amuse him. I was cursing them, but they were already dead." He hesitated, a catch in his voice. "It crossed my mind later that my loathing had caused the crash…the silly thoughts you have." He looked to the two faces at the table. "I wouldn't have wished them dead, not really." Grant was torn between interrupting the flow of his witness or trying to guide him back to the relevant path. His decision was taken from him. Amber reached across the table, laying her hand softly on top of Watson's, she stroked it gently for a moment then squeezed, holding him.

"Not silly, just human." The contact and soft words from the young woman affected Watson profoundly as with eyes welled, he turned to Amber.

"You're very kind." Amber smiled gently and gave an encouraging nod; it was enough to spur him on. Grant watched in admiration.

"I flew home to a media frenzy, it was all over the television and papers. The Headmaster then, Braden-Walker, was a nervous wreck, seeing doom and disaster for the school at every turn; that's when the current headmaster,

Rose-Gummer, stepped up to the plate. Give him credit, he handled it like a pro, giving interviews to press and TV, looking solemn enough but positively Churchillian in the need to support the pupils and carry on. He liaised with the parents of the dead boys, arranged for a memorial to them at the crash site, and set up the brass plaque in the Great Hall bearing their names. He pulled a public relations triumph from the wreckage of that jet and secured the Headmastership for himself when Braden-Walker retired." Watson paused, wriggling his empty glass on the table, the message clear.

"Let me top that up for you." Amber was out of her chair as she spoke, taking the empty glass with her. Watson twisted to face Maddox, his movement betraying the effects of the alcohol he'd consumed. Grant presumed it to be the necessary lubrication to tease the story from his lips.

"Do you see anyone from back then? Attend any re-unions. Are you in the FVF?" Watson asked a sad note of nostalgia in his tone.

Grant shook his head. He was aware of the good work of the Falklands Veterans Foundation but his experiences were tucked away, he neither needed nor wanted to unlock the horrors by being reminded.

Watson seemed to understand. "I get it, I do. It took me years, but I went back to visit my mates, you know, those still on patrol. I re-walked the hills and mountains, in the wind, you remember the constant wind? It blew away some demons."

Grant said nothing but acknowledged what Watson had said with another slow nod. As Amber placed the drink on the table, Watson closed the subject. "Well, it's not for everyone." He raised the glass in a silent salute.

"You were back at school?" Grant prompted.

"Yes. Back at school." Watson took a generous swallow of the beer, wiped his lips, and held his fist to his mouth, thinking deeply once more. "I did tell. I went to the headmaster, Braden-Walker. I told him about the rape, told him everything."

"*Everything?*" Amber asked.

"No. Not everything. I didn't reveal the nature of the relationship between Japhet and Gary. I kept my word, kept their secret. Until today."

"What happened?" Maddox asked the question.

"What do you think? I was silenced. Rose-Gummer was at the headmaster's side. They listened until I finished. I don't know what I thought they'd do, but I should've guessed. The headmaster deferred to Rose-Gummer. I think the whole thing had broken him. Rose-Gummer said, 'Mr Watson, there's nothing to be gained from this information. Even if it's true, and we have no proof of that, what's to be gained? The boys are dead.' I said, 'The victim, the girl is out there, shouldn't we find her? There's been a terrible crime.'" Watson's agitation at the memory was clear.

Watson took another drink, lifting his glass too high, some of the contents spilling down his chin. Seemingly unaware, he grimaced and spat his next words with bitterness and loathing. "Rose-Gummer stood directly in front of me, blocking my view of the headmaster, 'Mr Watson, ' he said, 'you are employed by the school, and your home on our grounds is provided by the school. If you wish to keep both, you will forget this preposterous accusation against the good name of our recently deceased pupils. Furthermore, you should know that your sexual predilections are well known to us, should it be necessary for your employment at Frankton Abbey to be terminated it would take very little to ensure you were *never* employed again. Mr Watson, we don't even need to officially accuse you of anything; suspicion of your activities at a boys-only school would be enough. I trust you see the position in which you find yourself?' That was it. They had all the cards. I shut up."

"Until now," Amber said softly.

"Until now," Watson answered.

"I must ask this. Will you provide a statement? Would you give evidence if necessary?" Grant asked the question, knowing full well the evidential value was zero. Practically everything Watson had told was hearsay. Japhet Gold's description of the attack on the girl was not known to Watson from his personal experience. It was inadmissible in a court of law.

Watson hesitated, when he spoke it was with a grim certainty. "Yes."

Evidential or not, Watson's information had to be the breakthrough Maddox had been desperate for. It could be used as a lever in questioning and was another piece in the connective jigsaw of the case. Most importantly there was a victim to find, a witness who *could* give evidence, the name was still irking Grant. '*Cassie*', where had he heard that name before?

# Chapter Thirty-Nine

Grant and Amber had taken rooms at The Swan Inn. It was on expenses; it was justifiable, it was needed. They were tired, mentally and physically, *and* they'd had a glass or three of wine. It had been near to eleven when Bill Watson had taken his leave, more than a little worse for wear, full of the local brew paid for by the Met Police Commissioner. After reporting back to Paul Winter, the detectives had discussed the new information but had skirted around detailed study, they needed rest, it had been a long and eventful day.

* * *

Perhaps it was the unsettling unfamiliarity of a bed other than his own, next to Lydia, that prompted the thoughts to come charging back. More likely, it was the conversation with a former comrade that evening. The mention of shared experiences.

It was two words and a question mark that linked them and thousands of their comrades in a terrible shared experience. *'South Atlantic?'* Watson had asked. Grant had been unable to verbalise an answer.

It was such a little war. The Falklands were such little islands.

In the darkness of his room, memories flooded. *'South Atlantic?'* Yes, he was there, little more than a boy. A boy, but old enough to be responsible for his actions. Like the boys from Franks. Some of them were the same age as he was in the South Atlantic. Just boys? They'd done a terrible thing. *Just* boys? Boys could do terrible things; Grant knew that. Terrible things.

\* \* \*

And he was back … *Tension grew as the light began to fade. The men were scattered, hunkered down in hastily dug foxholes. Groundsheets were pulled over the scrapings in the claggy soil, camouflaging their positions from possible air, artillery, or mortar attack. As the shadows, already long, lengthened further and finally disappeared, the earth seemed to move and convulse as the Marines began to move. All around, the terrain undulated, like a stop-motion film of seedlings pushing their first green shoots upwards into the fresh air, as the men of 42 Commando, Royal Marines, emerging from their hiding places, stretching cramped limbs, evacuating bowels and bladders, filling stomachs with energy giving food, preparing to advance up the dark shadow of the hill two short miles away.*

*Marine Maddox was posted to a position in the centre section, looking left and right, squinting in the darkness to see the order in which his friends were placed relative to him. Even plastered with blackening cam-cream Grant recognised the huge nose and goofy, snaggle-toothed grin of 'Beak' Bodley a few feet away.*

*"Don't fucking smile anywhere near me Beak!" Grant called in a hushed voice. "The Argies will see those teeth from a thousand metres and zero in on all of us." There was a ripple of laughter from the shadowy figures all around.*

*"Don't you worry about me Granty, me and the lads are all taking cover behind your fat fucking arse." More laughter.*

*Grant had to respond. "Forget my arse, if you don't keep moving the Intel Unit will mark your nose on the map as a topographical fucking feature." Much more laughter, even from Beak Bodley this time. Unnoticed the platoon sergeant prowled through the gloom towards the men.*

*"Glad to see you're all having such a good time. We'll see who's still fucking laughing in the morning, shall we? Now shut the fuck up and advance to the jump-off point... MOVE!" As the Marines shuffled eastwards, whispered banter continued, as did the giggles. What men these were, Grant thought, what comrades to have at your side, what couldn't they overcome together? He looked up and saw the dark, menacing, humped shape of their objective in the distance and felt surprisingly safe.*

# CHAPTER THIRTY-NINE

*For Marine Maddox, as he advanced up the hillside, the noise was felt as much as heard. The air itself seemed to have acquired a thick density, heavy with the throat-scorching taste of cordite and draped with smoke from landscape-illuminating star-shells. Everywhere was rent with the concussive, explosive sounds of war. Automatic small-arms fire, the whoosh of mortar bombs passing, seemingly so slowly overhead, and the deep, stomach-churning thuds of heavy artillery shells plunging into the earth before detonating in the soft soil overwhelmed mere human senses.*

*He heard screams, saw bodies, some still, some dismembered, some the enemy, some not. He would make sense of all that later, when there was time, when the objective was secured, when his mates were safe. Every soldier worshiped at the altar of 'it'll never happen to me', Marine Maddox was no different.*

*He actually saw the mortar round enter the earth in front of him, several yards away, accompanied by a soggy thwack sound. The slim, metallic tube plunged into the spongy, rain-sodden soil, travelling at one hundred and ten metres per second. It was over a metre under the earth when it exploded.*

*His world was confused and spinning. Flat on his back and numbed with shock Grant was still trying to make sense of what had happened when he felt strong, urgent hands patting over his body, along his arms and legs, he was rocked to one side, hands feeling along his back. He heard frantic, repeated, reassuring words, 'you're alright, hold on Granty, hold on, you're alright, you're alright', as he was rocked over again, to the other side, the feverish patting continuing, searching for a hole, for blood, for an injury, before being allowed to slump back, to his flat-out, prone position. The immensely ugly face of Beak Bodley appeared, inches above his own.*

*"There's fuck all wrong with you Granty, get off your huge, fat arse and stop fucking about. Last one to the top's a sissy." The urgent care and compassion for his friend moments earlier now concealed in abusive banter. Beak slapped the side of Grant's face, Eric Morecambe style, grinned a huge grin and hissed the word, 'Pussy!' before disappearing from view. He never saw Beak alive again.*

*Grant shook his head from side to side, re-orientating himself. He still had one hand on his SLR which he pulled across his chest, hugging the rifle like a comfort blanket. In front of him was a crater a metre across and of indeterminate depth, a sudden far off explosion momentarily lit the scene and he saw a wisp of smoke was still curling upwards from the hole. Taking Beak's swift physical examination as gospel, Grant dragged himself to his wobbling feet and continued his advance, the intensity of small-arms fire ahead of him calling like a clarion, he advanced up the hill.*

*A long, buzz-saw brrrrrrrr of a machine gun emitted from the weapon pit thirty metres to his left. Grant's crouching posture contracted further, he brought his weapon tighter into his shoulder into an off-aim ready, both eyes open along the side of the long barrel. He fitted a fresh thirty round magazine into the rifle, set the selector to automatic and advanced rapidly towards the left flank of the gunpit. As the enemy fired again, muzzle flashes revealed two dark clad men in the fox-hole. They never saw him. One burst of fifteen rounds had a devastating effect on his targets, who crumpled, lost from view below the lip of the dugout. Grant advanced cautiously; weapon ready to dispatch its remaining fifteen rounds.*

*The two outstretched hands appeared from the inky-blackness of the hole first, followed by a man's face. 'Manos arriba, manos arriba!' Grant shouted; it was a superfluous command straight from the small handbook issued on route from Ascension Island a few short weeks ago. The Argentinian's hands were already as 'up' as they were ever going to be. Grant was five metres away. There was enough ambient light from the constant pyrotechnics in the immediate vicinity to show the man's features. He was no teenage conscript, perhaps thirty years old, his face was weathered, hard and alert. Considering the circumstances he seemed remarkably unafraid. Grant recognised a professional soldier.*

*"No dispares. No dispares." His enemy's request to not shoot was stated flatly, without an element of pleading or begging. A simple, straightforward request, man to man, soldier to soldier.*

*Grant, still woozy from the concussive effects of the mortar explosion, stared at his adversary along the top of his rifle. For a moment in time, the world was reduced to this: a frozen tableau of procrastination, a hole in the ground containing a man who was dead and another who was helpless, and a man nearby with the power to preserve a life or take it.*

*The whole of the hillside was illuminated by the explosion, followed by intense small-arms fire from many sources. A scream cut through it all, an English voice*

172

*cursing, calling out to God, calling for help, followed by a chorus of shrieking, desperate voices, knifing through the cacophony of battle. 'Medic! Medic!' The words chased by an equally frantic series of shouts. 'Support! Support!' The spell was shattered, the tableau broken. A shadow ran by, rushing towards the sounds of combat, 'Come on! Come on! They need us.' Imploring, appealing to the static man with the raised rifle, then he was gone.*

*Grant's first loyalty, his only loyalty, was to his comrades. He was needed further up the slope. His presence could make the difference between victory and defeat. Between his friends living, or his friends dying. He looked with fresh, ice-cold eyes at the soldier in the hole, his hands above his head, waiting for Grant's reaction. The light machine gun, so recently used to cut down his fellows, was still functional, within inches of the Argentinian. The choice was clear. Take this man prisoner and remove yourself from the battle. Or don't....*

*Grant pulled his rifle tighter into his body, leaning forward into the weapon, his finger curling around the trigger. The Argentinian soldier understood exactly what Grant was thinking, understood the choice he was facing, and knew how far down his enemy's list of priorities his life was placed.*

*Grant never knew if he would've pulled the trigger on the unarmed, surrendering man. He never knew if he would have, could have, killed a prisoner in cold blood. It was in his mind; he could concede that but a thought is different from a deed. Grant was forever grateful to his enemy for his sudden lunge towards the weapon so close to him, indebted for the decision made for him. The Devil's Cup was on the table, but he didn't need to drink from it. The situation had become one of kill or be killed, so he killed. The rifle jerked in his hands, and the rounds impacted the body of his enemy, who fell from sight into the darkness to rest with his comrade. Grant replaced the magazine and ran up the hill towards his hard-pressed friends.*

* * *

The stoic face of the man he killed, just one of many, haunted him from that day onwards. Would he have shot the man if he hadn't reached for a weapon? Did he deliberately provoke his enemy in order to justify his slaughter? In his mind, he could see the man watching Grant preparing to shoot. How could he possibly know whether the trigger would have been pulled or not? The Argentinian had to react as he did, take the chance to try and save his life.

As he lay safely in the comfort of a strange bed, in a country pub, many miles from home, the choices he'd faced swirled about in Grant's head, as they had for many years. He searched but couldn't find an answer to a simple question.

'Am I a murderer?'

# Chapter Forty

Amber Bennett watched in fascination as her sergeant demolished his full English breakfast, washed down with copious amounts of tea and fresh orange juice. It wasn't as if she'd never seen him demolish a fry-up in the morning before; a cholesterol-packed, artery-blocking start to the day was a Met Police tradition. What held her in rapt attention was this was his *second* plate of sausage, eggs, bacon and beans.

"Peckish then, Skip?" Risking the loss of a piece of Cumberland and accompanying baked beans, Grant gave his best Homer Simpson reply.

"Can't talk. Eating." Amber laughed, sipping her apple juice and pushing aside her plate, now empty of toast, avocado and poached egg. She stretched back in the chair, contemplating the last twenty-four hours. In her service to date, she'd never had a day like yesterday, with its see-saw of emotions and experiences. The drive to Oxfordshire with her mentor, full of banter and humour, followed by the interview with Frankton Abbey's headmaster and his undead sidekick, which took her close to previously unexplored levels of irritation only to be swept away by the excitement of the note secreted on the radio-active bogey and the staggering revelations made by Bill Watson during the evening.

The lateness of the hour and the consumption of alcohol had precluded much discussion between Detective Sergeant and Detective Constable the previous night. Now, at the breakfast table, Grant seemed intent on initiating a coronary in front of her.

"I can actually *hear* your arteries starting to clog up," she offered. "I've checked if they have a defibrillator here and you'll be pleased to know they do, it's in reception." Amber grinned and gave a mocking double thumbs up as Grant wiped the last fusion of baked beans, egg yolk, and H.P. sauce from his plate with a piece of toast saved for that very purpose.

Grant Maddox leaned back in his chair, mirroring his colleague's posture, and rubbed his stomach with one hand while downing the contents of his teacup, held in the other.

"I'm so happy," he declared.

"I hope you took out group insurance with the Federation Skipper; your missus will be collecting any time soon, I reckon."

"Can I tell you something, Constable Bennett?" Grant placed the empty teacup in its saucer. "In twenty-eight years as an officer of the Metropolitan Police, I have never, repeat *never,* had my bed and breakfast paid for by our illustrious Commissioner. Never. On that basis, I think it's a fair assumption that it will never happen again. Now the old adage taught to me by a long-dead copper was, never scratch your arse when you can tear great big lumps out of it."

"Skipper, that's a pretty disgusting saying that doesn't make any sense, and I assume that this Confucian Officer died of a heart attack, the same as you're going to do."

"It means to make the most of something while you have the chance, and for your information, you heartless bastard, my friend did die of a heart attack." Grant planted a plainly mock expression of deep sadness on his face, prompting more laughter from Amber.

Grant had put aside his dark recollections of the previous night, of the horror on the slopes of a mountain eight thousand miles away. They were re-buried, back where they belonged, only to resurface if a few select words, a picture, a sound, or a smell dug into the recesses of his mind and disinterred them. He'd forced himself into a good place, and the hearty breakfast and the presence of his young friend held him there.

"Okay, Amber, what do we make of Mr William Watson?"

"Well, the first question is, do we believe him?"

"And do we?"

"It rang true to me. Why would he lie?" Amber paused. "Could we be dealing with proxy killings? What your new best friend gave us is the motive for such a scenario, vengeance not on the guilty party but on an association, their proxy."

Grant nodded. "I'd been thinking of that. An association proxy killing theory makes some sort of sense. We *need* to find the girl from the apartment. She's the key. Watson said she'd been hurt, *really* hurt during the attack, you were at the bar when he gave me more details. They anally raped her, bit her breasts, and she was bleeding from the vagina. I think Watson was embarrassed about describing that in front of you."

Amber nodded her understanding. "It keeps getting worse, doesn't it? Have we reached the bottom yet, Skip?"

"I don't know. But we're faced with trying to find the victim of an eighteen-year-old rape."

"Trawling hospital records?"

"It's where we'll start. Okay, come on, the Bogey awaits. Let's get back to London."

\* \* \*

Grant dropped his bag next to Amber's and slammed the car boot shut. He jumped at the apparition standing before him, previously hidden by the open tailgate.

"Bill!"

\* \* \*

The garden was empty, a few wooden tables with benches were dotted about the grassed area at the rear of the pub, several chickens ran freely, clucking happily, sometimes passing under the legs of the trio huddled together. William Watson's face was a portrait of unhappiness.

"There's more." Watson's words hung between them. As Amber reached for her notebook her thoughts immediately flew to her comment such a short while earlier. 'Have we reached the bottom yet?'

"We're listening, Bill," Grant replied.

"This is something I heard by a roundabout route. I don't know how you can use it, but it might give you a lead to follow." Bill Watson paused; Grant stayed silent but nodded encouragement. "So you can't hold me to the reliability of it." Grant maintained the pressure of silence, nodding reassuringly.

Watson sighed deeply, clearly reaching a decision. "Rose-Gummer and Wagstaff had an unexpected visitor. A woman, a middle-aged woman. She was honoured with an audience immediately, without a prior appointment, and she wasn't happy. She was talking about the rugby sevens and the air crash. She told them a diary had been found. She said she could finish the school, and she wasn't alone." Watson looked from Grant to Amber and back again. "That's it. I know it's vague, but…" His voice trailed off. "…but I lay awake all night in a dilemma, not sure if I should say anything or not. Whether it means anything or not. I decided that was a decision for you to make." Watson seemed to slump. For the first time, the ex-Para looked old and frail, depleted somehow. It was Grant who broke the silence.

"How did you get this information, Bill?"

Watson laughed a short, mocking laugh. "The same way as everyone in the school, including me, knows what was said between you two, The Head and The Vampire yesterday. Whoever is duty-boy is honor bound to listen at the headmaster's door and report on what is said on the other side. By that means and some others, everyone gets to know everything. I told you, nothing much happens at this school which stays a secret." Grant shook his head wishing sincerely that was the whole truth.

"Who was the woman?" Watson turned to Amber who'd asked the question.

"I don't know. She asked for Rose-Gummer on arrival, was picked up by the duty boy, and taken straight to his office."

"What did she look like, anything about her at all?" Amber's voice betrayed a hint of frustration. Watson merely shrugged.

"When did this happen, Bill? How long ago?" Grant's voice was flat and unemotional even though inside he was shaking at this new line of inquiry.

"Two months back. Just before Martine Gold was killed." Watson referred to the name he knew the first victim by.

"Just *before* the first killing? Could it have been Martine Walsingham?" Amber echoed, unable to hide the excitement in her voice. "What did this woman want from Rose-Gummer? What was she demanding, to presumably not finish the school? Who were the others? Whose diary was it?"

Watson shut his eyes, shook his head from side to side, and held both hands in the air, a signal he was overwhelmed, a sign to 'stop!' Amber realised she'd said too much, pushed too hard, and looked to Grant, contrition on her face.

"I *knew* it would be like this." Watson's voice was a mixture of irritation and resignation. "I *don't know* who it was. That's as much as was passed on. I've come here, and I've told you what I know. You can make what you wish of it." Watson stood, using the table edge to help him stand, groaning as he did so. "Fucked knees." He offered by way of an explanation, the conversation was clearly at an end.

Grant and Amber stood up, too. Watson held out his hand to Grant, his eyes downcast, not making contact with the detective, apparently embarrassed at his minor outburst.

"It's always an honour to shake the hand of a Royal Marine." Watson finally looked up into Grant's eyes. Maddox gripped Watson's hand firmly.

"The honour is mine, Para." Grant's voice shook slightly. He wasn't sure why.

# Chapter Forty-One

"Well, that opens a *whole* can of worms." Amber held her hands in front of her face and waggled all her fingers. "If we fill in the gaps Watson's presenting us with, there's a blindingly obvious conclusion."

Maddox looked across the table to his colleague and smiled. "Okay, fill in the gaps."

Amber, garnering her thoughts, glancing at her notebook, written as Watson had told his story. "Okay, there's a lot missing but the implication he's making is a middle-aged woman contacts the headmaster, she's one of the mothers of the rugby seven, maybe even Martine? Her age and the subject she wants to discuss points to her or another victim."

Grant nodded.

Amber continued. "Okay, *who* she is grabs Rose-Gummer's immediate attention, and she's ushered in immediately. She's very unhappy about something and that something must be whatever she's found recorded in a diary she's recently found, the assumption has to be it's a diary from one of the dead boys." Amber looked up at Grant, seeking approbation, finding a smiling DS with a nod attached.

"The information she'd found was clearly explosive from the school's point of view. If it could finish Frankton Abbey, it must have been. A pupil's conduct can reflect badly on any school, but ultimately, a school cannot be held responsible for that behaviour. It must be something *more* to threaten a school like Franks. It *must* be involved or seriously culpable, something it did or should have done or not done, and then, and this is the clincher,

covered it up. Now, that *is* something that could finish an institution."
Amber paused, this time to be rewarded with words from her sergeant.

"Keep going."

Amber re-read her notes. "Then there's the icing on the cake. She
tells Rose-Gummer and The Vampire she wasn't alone. She's passed this
information on to another person or persons, other victims, maybe? From
what we found out last night, this information could relate to the rape
and assault of the girl and the school's inaction when informed by Watson.
What this woman wanted, we can only guess at, but...what if removing this
woman from the scene and anyone associated with her was the only way
the school could be saved? According to Watson, the first murder happened
maybe a month after this meeting."

"It's a very interesting theory, Amber. You're suggesting the school is
murdering the rugby seven mothers, drugging them, and cutting out their
wombs. It seems a little extreme, doesn't it?" Grant raised an eyebrow, but
neither his tone nor his expression was dismissive.

"It does put that way." Amber thought deeply. "Okay, consider this: the
school is famous, almost infamous, for accepting the sons of anyone who can
afford to attend. It's well known that some unsavoury characters from the
world of foreign politics, let's call them what they are, dictators, send their
sons to Franks, and it's long been suspected that Crime Lords from here
and abroad do the same. Is it such a long stretch to imagine that someone
at the school could know someone from the underworld, someone who, for
the right amount, could do this and have the knowledge to disable alarms
and cameras? A professional."

"Why not a simple bullet in the back of the head? Why go to all the trouble
of dissecting the victims? Why throw a womb in her face?"

"Didn't DI Yorke say something about hiding the true motive of a crime
with an extreme M.O.? Like the case in America where the husband wanted
to kill his wife. You have to admit, once the police have a modus operandi,
a pattern of offending, we get fixated, and investigators automatically go
down a certain road and make certain assumptions. Perhaps that accounts
for the savagery of the killings, it's just a set up to make us think only of

looking for a nutter or a man with the professor's 'Mummy Complex'.

"It might seem far-fetched," Grant shook his head, "but it's got to be considered. We need to revisit Frankton Abbey before we head back to London.

"There is one other thing, Skip." Grant turned to Amber as he struggled to extricate himself from the bench/seat combination, raising a questioning eyebrow. "I don't want to trample on this man-to-man, warrior-to-warrior thing you've got going with Watson, but *all* this depends on us accepting every word of his story as true."

# Chapter Forty-Two

A call to update DCI Winter on developments was followed by a call from Winter to Headmaster Rose-Gummer to fix an immediate appointment to speak, once again, to the detectives.

Maddox parked the Bogey in the courtyard of the Tudor Hall with more satisfaction than the previous day. The arrival process was a duplication of the previous visit, the same grey-suited and grim-faced Miss Isle noting their names and issuing their visitor badges. This day's duty boy was a different child but clearly from the same immaculate, polished mould. As Maddox and Bennett entered the headmaster's office, they were greeted with the looming form of Dr. Dominic Wagstaff standing at the left shoulder of a seated Henry Rose-Gummer. The Headmaster opened his mouth to dismiss duty boy, but Maddox got in first, addressing the shining child directly.

"We're familiar with the route. Please return to the hall or the box you're kept in during the day. *Do not* wait outside. Thank you." Grant closed the door.

Inside her head, Amber Bennet was whooping like an American cheerleader, while Rose-Gummer's jaw nearly hit his desktop. She noted that the vampiric deputy head observed proceedings without expression, a standing statue with his hands clamped behind his back.

Grant advanced to the desk before him, declining the chairs the detectives had used the day before. He remained standing, looking down on the seated headmaster whose space Maddox deliberately invaded by placing both hands on the polished wooden surface and leaning forward.

"Headmaster, Dr Wagstaff." Grant nodded a curt greeting to each man in turn. "Let's acknowledge something, shall we? I want to find out some facts which, for your own reasons, you do not wish to divulge. You do not want us here, and I don't really wish to be here either. So shall we dispense with the pleasantries and the sparring and get down to it?"

"Very well, Detective Sergeant." It was Wagstaff who responded. Neither detective was surprised.

"What do you know of an alleged serious sexual assault on a girl in London two days before your pupils died in the crash? You should be aware, Headmaster, that we know you were a member of the teaching staff at the time and so have personal knowledge of the dead boys."

"Ah." An expression of recognition spread swiftly across Wagstaff's face, accompanying his verbal reaction. Rose-Gummer was silent, his only reaction a miniscule twitch of an eyelid.

"I see that you are both familiar with the allegation. At this stage, I'm not going to go into why you felt it necessary to withhold this evidence from a murder enquiry." Grant wanted their omission to sound as serious as possible, a threat hanging in the air. Wagstaff recovered from the revelation before Grant could say more.

"It appears that you have been speaking with our former head of physical education and, as of this moment, our *former* groundsman, Mr William Watson. It *is* correct that he approached Mr Braden-Walker, who was headmaster here at Frankton Abbey a short time after the tragedy, it *is* correct that our current headmaster, Mr Rose-Gummer was privy to that information."

"Have you lost your tongue, Headmaster? Are you unable to speak for yourself?" Grant targeted the question directly at the seated man. The headmaster coloured at the unaccustomed discourtesy but left it to Wagstaff to respond.

"I shall take the lack of contradiction as confirmation that your source is indeed Mr Watson." Wagstaff raised a *Mr Spock* eyebrow that Maddox ignored. The Deputy Head, satisfied, continued. "As I'm legally qualified, Detective Sergeant, we've decided I shall be the school's mouthpiece." Grant recognised his attempted goading of Rose-Gummer as a cul de sac and turned his attention back to Wagstaff.

"Very well. Perhaps *you* can explain the school's response to this information?"

"Of course, Sergeant." Wagstaff smiled a coffin-lid smile. "I suspect you were informed that the school rejected Mr Watson's story out of hand, that he was threatened should he divulge the story with all sorts of retribution. Dismissal, eviction from his school accommodation, even the exposure of his sexuality." Wagstaff paused. "I fear your informant has been, to use a modern idiom, economical with the truth. Upon hearing Mr Watson's story, the school consulted our solicitor for legal advice. That advice was that no formal allegation of a crime had been made. Mr Watson, for his own reasons, declined to approach the police on his own account, leaving that decision to the school. The school was not legally obliged to make a formal report, in reality lacking the information and authority to do so." Grant was beginning to feel uncomfortable.

"However, this establishment is not one to simply hide behind the law and an obligation to do the right thing. Mr Rose-Gummer was very active in handling the aftermath of the tragedy, Mr Braden-Walker having had something of a breakdown. Mr Rose-Gummer had the feelings of the victim's families to consider, imagine your recently dead child's reputation being blackened by such an unsubstantiated hearsay, drink, drugs and rape, without the ability of the accused to defend themselves? Nevertheless, Mr Rose-Gummer instituted a search to find the victim of the alleged assault."

Grant's eyebrows shot up in astonishment . This was news.

"I see you're surprised, Detective. There are records held in the school to substantiate the employment of a private detective firm, tasked with tracing the alleged victim. Remember we only have Mr Watson's word that Master Japhet Gold relayed the story at all. It is possible the whole narrative is a fantasy. The detective company traced the nightclub the boys attended and indeed, it is true, our students did not cover themselves in glory, evidence of excessive alcohol consumption and use of drugs was shown, as was the boys showering attention on a number of young ladies. No one at the club could provide any substantive proof that the boys left with a girl, never mind one who was drunk and drugged. Our investigators gained access to the Covent Garden apartment where the 'crime' was alleged to have taken place. Again, it is regretful to tell that evidence of a profusion of drinking and drug-taking was found, but no trace of, or anything to support, the presence of a girl or of an assault was discovered. No discarded clothing, no blood, no other bodily secretions. Nothing. You didn't expect any of this, Detective? No. I'd have thought a man of your experience would be long acquainted with the expression, there are two sides to every story."

Wagstaff was correct. Grant hadn't expected this. Further the deputy head was *doubly* correct, he'd taken Watson at his word, reliant on his fellow-feeling for a man with a similar background and experiences to his own. Could he be wrong about Watson? Was it all a tissue of lies? Wagstaff's arrogant revelations recalled to mind Grant's feelings induced by Isla Baxter when she'd correctly pointed out his preconceptions of the rugby seven 'boys' to him. He felt a sudden lack of confidence in himself. Was he losing his touch?

Grant pushed back. "My experience, Dr Wagstaff, as you are calling it into question, is that there are *three* sides to every story. That provided by the two protagonists and the third, the truth, which lies somewhere in between." Grant felt it was a good repost and some of the high ground had returned to him. "I shall need the report which was compiled." A red A4-sized bound booklet, which Wagstaff was holding behind his back landed on the desktop with a thwack.

"The private investigators report Detective Sergeant. You will find it is most complete. The company searched hospital records for a victim with the described injuries without success, and questioned staff at the club the boys attended and examined CCTV. They searched and examined the Covent Garden apartment and traced dozens of taxi drivers operating in the area to find one who may have taken the victim from Covent Garden. None was found. The investigation company were most thorough, they should have been, the report will also show the extortionate invoice presented to the school. In the circumstances, with reference to the feelings of the parents of the deceased to be considered, with reference to the school's legal responsibilities, and after the costly investigation instigated by this establishment, we concluded that no further action was required or justifiable. I should add that Mr Watson was informed of the school's actions every step of the way by Mr Rose-Gummer and in conclusion concurred with our response. May I surmise he didn't tell you *that* either?"

Grant picked up the report, glancing briefly at its cover before handing it to Amber. "I understand that two months ago a middle-aged lady visited, she spoke about the air crash and mentioned a diary. Who was she, and what did she want?" Grant noticed Rose-Gummer furrow his brows, whether from guilt-ridden surprise at Grant's knowledge of the meeting or from bewilderment he couldn't tell. It was Wagstaff who reacted.

"I have no idea what you're talking about, Detective. I have no knowledge of any such meeting." Grant looked directly at Rose-Gummer.

"I'd like to hear from your lips, sir, that no such meeting ever took place." The headmaster looked up at his deputy who gave the slightest of nods.

"No such meeting as you've described took place."

It was a brick wall, and Grant had just run straight into it.

* * *

The choreography had been planned as they took the circuitous route back to the Great Hall reception area. As Miss Isle turned the heavy leather-bound visitor book to face the detectives and sign out, Grant leant over the desk, looked left and right, indicating his next words were secret and confidential. "Miss Isle," he said, it was difficult, but he managed it, "my colleague and I are investigating a series of murders." Grant looked left and right again. "Particularly *brutal* murders of women."

"Brutal?" the receptionist echoed, her eyes wide.

"Very," offered Grant, his face grim. "I need to ask you some questions. You may have very important information which could help us. Do you have a moment or two to spare?" Grant looked left and right once again. The Great Hall contained only the three persons at the desk, a suit of armour, and an unspecified number of spectres who hung unseen in the ether.

"Yes, of course, but you understand I'm not at liberty to breech anything which can be classified as confidential, not without reference to Mr Rose-Gummer."

"Of course not," Grant reassured her smoothly. During this distraction, Amber, holding the visitor's book ostensibly to sign out, quickly searched through the earlier dated pages. "Do you recall a visitor, perhaps two months ago? A middle-aged lady, possibly the mother of a former student, met with The Head and Deputy Head. She was unaccompanied, possibly upset or angry. Do you recall such a visitor?" Grant slipped sideways a fraction, blocking the receptionists' view of Amber as she rifled through the pages.

"No, no, I can't recall anyone like that, not at all. You don't have her name?"

"If only I did, miss. But you're sure? Is there anyone else who may have been at reception?" Miss Isle shook her head as Amber slid the book back onto the desktop.

"I'm the only receptionist at this establishment. To my knowledge, there was no visitor as you've described."

As the detectives took their leave, Amber gave a tiny shake of her head. William Watson's angry woman remained elusive.

# Chapter Forty-Three

Grant and Amber had just finished recounting to Paul Winter the details of the visits to Frankton Abbey School and William Watson's revelations. The red-covered private investigators report supplied by Deputy Head, Dr Dominic Wagstaff, lay on the desktop where the DCI had dropped it after speed-reading its contents and conclusions. Grant and Amber looked on in silence as their guvnor placed his hands behind the back of his overburdened head.

"We're going to need a bigger boat," he said at last. Amber turned to Grant, a look of utter bewilderment on her face.

"We're going to need more people," Grant deciphered.

"Lots more people." The Juno Jenkin case is expanding dramatically, as you'd expect. The more we look, the more we find and have to clear before we move on. With the new lines of enquiry you've found opening up, we need more people. The Press are baying for blood and upstairs want some progress reported."

The door to his office opened, and DI Heidi Yorke entered. "Not disturbing anything, am I? I heard you two had an eventful away day." She smiled at Grant and Amber. Winter nodded her towards a vacant chair. "What's that?" Heidi leant forward and pulled the red-covered file on the desk towards her. *"AirTight Private Investigations?"* She read from the front cover, "Why are they involved?"

"You know this company?" Grant couldn't hide the surprise in his voice.

*"Do I?"* The sarcasm and disapproval dripped from her tone. She began to flick through the pages, explaining as she did so. "Martine Walsingham

engaged the services of AirTight to spy on one of Bernard Campion's infamous parties. But she didn't know it was a Campion company run by his younger brother, Clifford. Campion must've pissed himself laughing when he found out his troublesome neighbour was his latest customer because he had his brother set up a ridiculing hoax report and added insult to injury by invoicing Martine for the job. According to the housekeeper, Mary-Mary, it was the final, humiliating straw, after that as far as Martine was concerned it was all-out war. She was willing to do *anything* to ruin Campion. It led to the ransom strip dispute, which was still unresolved at the time of her murder." The office fell into silence as the ramifications of the DI's words sank in.

It was Grant who coalesced those thoughts into ordered words. "So, William Watson tells the old headmaster, Braden-Walker, that the boys have raped, and worse, an unknown girl whilst off their heads on drink and drugs. He leaves out the relationship between Japhet Gold and Gary Whittcock. Remember, what's left of the school's rugby seven team are still smouldering in a crater, The Press are all over the story, not least because Oscar nominee and national treasure, Juno Jenkin's son is one of the dead. The rest are the sons of the rich and nearly as famous. Headmaster Braden-Walker goes into a mental melt-down, and the current headmaster, Rose-Gummer, steps forward to deal with the families, The Press, and everything in between."

Amber Bennett smiled and nodded enthusiastically as Grant verbalised the narrative. "That's right, Skip," she said, "Rose-Gummer must have seen an opportunity rather than a crisis, a chance to set himself up as the successor to Braden-Walker as headmaster. He was looking long term, heading off anything that might rear its ugly head in the far future, so he commissioned AirTight to investigate. Is it beyond our imagination to think that their brief was to look but not too hard? To produce a report which at a future date would cover the school and the staff, to fob off any criticism?"

"Well, it worked," Grant offered. "When Wagstaff slapped that report down on the desk, all the wind was taken out of my sails. He'd just bomb-proofed himself and the school."

"*Wagstaff?*" Heidi interjected. "Did you say Wagstaff?"

"Yes. Dominic Wagstaff, the Deputy Head at Frankton Abbey. He's the up and coming man, the mouthpiece and the person calling the shots. I think Rose-Gummer is a spent force. Why do you ask?"

"What does he look like?"

"Like a fucking vampire!" Amber couldn't stop herself. "Sorry, but he does."

"Hold on, I'll look him up." The DCI was tapping furiously on his computer keyboard. "The staff are pictured on the school website. There you go. Deputy Headmaster, Dr. Dominic Wagstaff, Ph. D. LLB. M.A.Ed. You're right, Amber," smiled the DCI, "he *does* look like a fucking vampire." Winter turned the screen to face Heidi. "Any good?"

Detective Inspector Heidi Yorke's eyes couldn't have opened any wider as she looked at the face before her. "Oh my God!" She exclaimed, putting her hand to her mouth. "I'd interviewed Bernard Campion, obtained his statement, you remember the one where he described his relationship with Martine Walsingham in less than glowing terms. As I left his office there was a man seated outside, waiting. I recall him because he was so unusual looking, tall, slim, gaunt. As I passed the secretary she said to him, 'Mr Campion will see you now, Dr. Wagstaff.' It's him." Heidi pointed to the face on the computer screen. "That's the Dr Wagstaff who walked in to see Campion as I walked out."

# Chapter Forty-Four

D I Heidi Yorke and DC Amber Bennett sank into plush armchairs as the secretary placed two cups of coffee before them. Fanned across the marble-topped table in an inch-perfect presentation were several glossy magazines promoting the various enterprises of Bernard Campion. Each cover bore the beaming face of the man a few yards away on the other side of polished mahogany double doors, which the detectives were waiting patiently to pass through.

The secretary evidently received some signal on the chromium panel which sat on her desk, she rose from her seat, and as she opened one of the dark-wood doors she smiled broadly, "Mr Campion will see you now."

\* \* \*

Bernard Campion was a fit-looking fifty-five-year-old, tall, athletic, and tanned. His hair was a suspiciously uniform dark brown without a hint of grey. His perfectly straight and proportioned teeth dazzled the observer, a triumph of the porcelain implanters craft, while the skin of his face was stretched taut, Botox oozing from his pores. Despite the tear hazard, he beamed a broad, welcoming smile and rose from behind his desk to greet the detectives, shaking hands and directing them to be seated.

"Detective Inspector, how lovely to see you again. I'm sorry you were kept waiting."

Heidi gave a non-committal smile. "Not at all Mr Campion, it was short notice so thank you for your time. This is Detective Constable Amber

Bennett."

Bernard Campion beamed a winning smile. "Miss Bennett, I'm charmed. Ladies, how may I help you?"

Heidi's expression was fixed now but non-threatening. "Please, Mr Campion, can you describe your association with AirTight Investigations?"

The smile on Bernard Campion's face disappeared for a second but returned very quickly. He was good, used to thinking on his feet, practised in the art of recovery. "AirTight Investigations? That's a company established about twenty years ago, properly registered and accounted for and headed by my younger brother Clifford. May I ask why the interest?"

Evincing a benign, non-threatening curiosity and evading an answer, Heidi replied. "Yes, of course. When we last met, as I left this office, you were about to see Dr Dominic Wagstaff, the Deputy Head of Frankton Abbey School. What is your connection to him and the school, Mr Campion?"

This time, the smile left his face a little longer before reasserting its presence. "I have three sons, each has been a student at Franks."

"And Dr Wagstaff?" Heidi pressed.

"It's a private matter, a confidential matter."

Heidi remained silent, waiting. Banking on silence. It took a few seconds.

"I suppose it would do no harm to tell you, this conversation isn't in the public domain?"

Heidi shook her head slowly.

"Very well. As an expression of my gratitude to the school for their good work in educating my sons, I've offered to provide a new sports hall. I'm personally bearing the cost of the demolition of the existing facility and the rebuilding and equipping of a new one. It will be the envy of every school in the world. Dr Wagstaff was attending on the day of your visit to inform me that the Board of Governors had decided to name the new building 'Bernard Campion Hall'. He wished to seek my permission and approval to do so."

"Were your sons attending the school at the time of the rugby sevens tragedy?" Heidi Yorke's jump from one line of questioning to another a dissembling and deliberate act.

"Err. Yes, let me see, my two younger sons were attending the school at that time. My eldest had just left for university, he knew some of the boys who died, from the years below him. My other boys were much younger. Can I ask you where this is going, Inspector?"

Heidi smiled innocently. "Yes, of course. Can you tell me how AirTight Investigations came to be engaged by Frankton Abbey School to discover the identity of a young woman, the alleged victim of a serious indecent assault? You obviously knew of such an investigation. You are the link between the school and AirTight, after all."

"A serious indecent assault? That's police speak for a rape, isn't it?"

The two detectives' faces were expressionless, Campion looked from one to the other before replying.

"Mr Rose-Gummer, in conversation, mentioned an allegation, more of a rumour really, that was threatening to blacken the names of the recently dead boys and by association the good name of the school. He felt it was without foundation, the tittle-tattle of someone with an axe to grind. *But,* and this must be to Rose-Gummer's credit, he wanted to be sure. He must've known of AirTight Investigations to have had such a conversation with me. I made the introductions and stepped back to allow the process to take place. That was the beginning and end of my involvement. Am I under suspicion for anything, Inspector?"

"Are you aware of the result of the investigation?"

"Yes. No trace of the alleged victim was ever found; however, it *was* apparent that the boys concerned had been taking drugs. The allegations were spiteful, and as the boys were all dead, nothing was to be gained but embarrassment to reveal their drug-taking. The case was closed."

"Mr Campion, is there any possibility that anyone directed the investigation to fail? That it wasn't really an investigation at all? Merely an exercise in smoke and mirrors?"

"Ladies," Campion rose from his seat, the smile gone from his face, "I'm sure I have something urgent to be doing right now. It's been a pleasure." The interview was apparently over.

Bernard Campion opened the office door, keeping his right hand pointedly in his pocket as the detectives left.

# Chapter Forty-Five

"You're kidding?" DCI Winter couldn't hide the surprise and pleasure in his voice. "Really?"

"Really!" Grant was beaming back at his boss. "Pat Kerrigan was at Hendon Training School with him." Grant jabbed a thumb over his shoulder in the direction of the Detective Constable who was sitting at his desk, phone pressed to his ear and smiling at the guvnor who peered around Grant's broad shoulders. Kerrigan pointed to the handset with his free hand, quickly followed by an 'okay' gesture. "He's on the phone to him now," concluded Grant.

"Well fuck me." Paul Winter couldn't believe their luck.

\* \* \*

As Grant discussed the Airtight Investigation report with Amber, he named its author; by chance, DC Pat Kerrigan was passing their desks. "Did you just mention Morgan Lovelace? *Sergeant* Morgan Lovelace?" Kerrigan asked. Grant and Amber looked at each other in astonishment.

The AirTight Investigation report was compiled and signed off by a person described as a 'Senior Investigator' named Morgan Lovelace. It wasn't a common name, and on hearing it, DC Pat Kerrigan's ears had pricked up. 'Morgan the Organ' was an old friend from Training School days he divulged, when asked how he'd earned his nickname Kerrigan replied, 'Don't ask', and winked. Morgan the Organ was now Sergeant Lovelace of the Metropolitan Police, serving at an East-End Station. It was a fortuitous stroke of good fortune that Grant felt the investigation deserved.

* * *

Winter and Maddox plonked themselves down unceremoniously on the opposite corners of Kerrigan's desk as he rang off with a promise to 'hook up for a bevvy soon'. Pat grinned, the long scar that he'd never explained and which ran down his left cheek and through both lips contorted his smile but granted him a piratical roguishness.

"Well?" Winter pressed urgently.

"Well," Kerrigan replied, his wonky grin spreading wider in his joy. "Morgan had dropped out of university, he'd been accepted by the Met and while waiting for a start date applied for a job with AirTight Investigations, he figured it would help with his career. He was sadly mistaken, only staying a week. The 'training' consisted of a morning pep talk, he did some filing, answered a few phones, and then a couple of days in was given his own missing person case." Kerrigan referred to notes he had taken during his conversation with Morgan. "In his words, he was told to call a few hospitals and ask if any girls had been admitted, no times or dates, though. It was very vague and meant to be. The point was to get some genuine and verifiable names as proof of contact, to show he'd made the enquiries if anyone ever checked up. Likewise, he was to call Cab Office and get a contact name, asking for taxi drivers who may have picked up a girl, again no details given. Even as an inexperienced twenty-year-old he could see it was a sham. It was obviously laying the groundwork to show that something had been properly done when it hadn't. The report, such as it was, was compiled by someone else, presented to him to sign and then it disappeared. The only thing he recalls about it was the name of the client, Frankton Abbey School."

"Hardly a 'Senior Investigator' then," Winter commented.

"No guv. He said it was a pants job, he quit after a week and went to a supermarket to stack shelves until he started in The Job."

Winter patted Kerrigan on the shoulder. "Good work, Patrick. Well done. Granty, why doesn't any bastard tell the truth, the whole truth, and nothing but the truth anymore? This has deniability built into it. The school can say it employed AirTight in good faith to find the truth of the allegation and paid good money to do so. They're in the clear. As far as AirTight is concerned, they can present a document with names, places, dates, and times as evidence of an investigation. If pressed they can either contradict our friend Morgan the Organ or say he compiled a false report or just did a bad job, which he signed for. We can't prove that's not the case. So they're in the clear as well."

Grant nodded in frustrated agreement. Someone, somewhere, was lying, but who and why?

# Chapter Forty-Six

In the few days since Grant and Amber had returned from Oxfordshire with new information and lines of enquiry, the pace of the Task Force's investigation had accelerated and taken on a fresh pro-active form. 'Upstairs' had given DCI Winter three more DCs, a DS, and a civilian Crime Analysist, Charlie Buller. The latter's specialised skill would free up two detectives who were struggling with the mountains of data which needed linking, cross-referencing, and collating. The analyst, proficient in operating HOLMES, the Home Office Large Major Incident Enquiry System, could only improve the efficiency of the task force.

With the information grudgingly provided by Frankton Abbey School, the surviving rugby seven mothers now had names. Helena MacDonald, whose son was the gigantic Lynton Fiennes, now like so many of the mothers, divorced, remarried, and re-divorced, had been located living comfortably in a Kensington Mews house, entertained by the frequent presence of a twenty-something gardener.

National Lottery winners Vernon and Sandra Whittcock were still together, happily married, but forever mourning the loss of their only son Gary. The couple spent most of their time in a large Georgian house in the centre of an estate in Kent. They kept to themselves, forever grappling with the question of whether their massive lottery win had been a gift or a curse.

The privacy and freedom of Helena MacDonald and the Whittcock's was seriously impacted by the information they may be targets for the so-called *Dissection Killer.* This startling revelation was followed by the arrival of a detachment of armed officers to provide protection until the issue was resolved. The answer to their obvious question, 'How long will this go on,' an unsatisfactory, 'We don't know.'

Tracing the mother and father of team captain Garson Thompson was more problematic. The super-rich couple had fallen off the radar, socially and economically. The investigative team found and followed the wake left behind Jeffrey Thompson's activities but not the vessel which left it. A hugely successful financier, he'd sold all his business interests on the death of his only child, Garson, and, along with his wife, disappeared.

\* \* \*

There was a lightness and uninhibited atmosphere prevalent in the Incident Room. The reason was obvious to all. The absence of Isla Baxter and her cameraman Rob Pagett, along with the incompetent, egotistical Detective Inspector 'Doddy' Dodds, was being relished by all, all that is, except DC 'Dirty' Don Chamberlain. If anything, his distress, sense of effrontery, and misery were adding to the Task Force's sense of well-being and cheerfulness. Dirty Don was complaining to anyone who would listen, and to several who wouldn't. The crux of his grievance was the theft of his utterly brilliant idea.

Dirty Don had been researching the crash of the executive jet. The possibility it wasn't an accident at all *had* to be considered and Don was tasked with trawling through reports from the British side of the enquiry, the Air Accident Investigation Branch, and its French equivalent. When he wasn't deluding himself into believing he was God's gift to women, Don Chamberlain was a pretty useful detective. This fact was recognised by Paul Winter, who countered his unfortunate habit of sniffing around the ladies by deploying him to tasks which would bury him under piles of detail. It was mid-morning when Don surfaced from his pile of detail with his utterly brilliant idea.

Don hadn't found the merest hint that the crash of the British Aerospace 125 had been caused by anything other than a poor repair several years before its final plunge into a French field. It was when he saw the picture, on-line, of the crash-site he had his idea.

Isla Baxter was enjoying a mid-morning cuppa in the canteen with Rob Pagett when Dirty Don stuck his head around the door and spotted the object of his desire. It was with deep satisfaction he saw the ubiquitous Doddy was temporarily absent from Isla Baxter's side. Don saw his opportunity and pounced.

Don had discovered a large commemorative stone had been placed at the spot where the jet had plummeted into the French clay. The stone bore sad and reflective words in French and English and listed the names of the casualties.

"Now that we've linked the murders to the crash, don't you think you need to film the scene, document the memorial? Maybe talk to some locals who witnessed the accident. I've several names and addresses from the French air accident investigators. Don't you think that would be a cool angle, Isla?" Don was practically purring. Isla's response almost made him roll over to allow her to tickle his tummy.

"I think that's a *brilliant* idea, Don. Absolutely wonderful. It would certainly be a chance to change the scenery from the office and the drudgery of the investigation."

Don then hit her with his crowning glory. "I also thought it would be a nice touch, you know, to show the humanity and respect the investigators hold for the poor boys if I came with you and laid a wreath at the memorial from the officers of the Task Force."

Isla thought for a few seconds and glanced at Rob Pagett, who shrugged. "I like it, Don. I really like it. Will you get me the details of the location of the crash, something about the memorial, the reports of the accident, and the witnesses? Also, a nice hotel nearby would be good, and maybe you could look into travel arrangements and car hire. I like to plan things like this properly so we get all we need in one visit. Well done, Don. I'm so, *so* grateful." Don scampered away like a loyal Labrador to do his mistress's bidding.

Detective Constable Don Chamberlain was in heaven.

\* \* \*

Detective *Constable* Don Chamberlain was in hell.

Detective *Inspector* Dodds was in heaven.

Doddy also thought a visit to the crash site and the placing of a wreath in memory of the dead was an utterly brilliant idea. An idea made even *more* utterly brilliant by the officer accompanying Isla Baxter being one of senior rank, as befitted the solemn occasion. A rank of Detective *Inspector* seemed appropriate.

Detective Chief Inspector Paul Winter thought the placing of a wreath at the memorial was crass, virtue signalling at best and bordering on disrespect at worst. The obvious intention for the act being self-publicity rather than a sincere undertaking. Having said that, the operation would mean the office would be devoid of the *Isla Investigates* team and the idiot Doddy for a few days. It was too good an opportunity to miss. He blessed the scheme. Don Chamberlain's incessant complaining was a small price to pay.

# Chapter Forty-Seven

Grant was at his desk reviewing the forensic evidence gathered from the three crime scenes. For this day and age, for the ghoulish, blood-spattered nature of the crimes and considering the electronic attacks on alarm and surveillance systems, it was a pitifully thin file. He'd decided on a course of action when Detective Inspector Heidi Yorke entered the Incident Room, grim-faced. She headed purposefully towards DCI Paul Winter's office, catching Grant's eye, she jerked her head slightly.

Grant dropped into the chair next to Heidi as Paul Winter stretched his long legs under his desk and flexed his arms behind his head. Grant had arrived at the Incident Room before 6am, Winter was already behind his desk and Grant knew that when he left that evening, the DCI would still be there.

"Heidi, you look grim. What have you got?"

Heidi nodded in acknowledgment of the observation. "Grim is right, Boss." She opened a buff file she'd carried with her. "I've located Margo and Jeffrey Thompson, Garson Thompson's parents, and it ain't good."

Grant saw Winter slump in his chair. "Go on."

Heidi took a breath and looked down at the closely typed and apparently e-mailed reports contained in the file. Grant saw the edge of a colour photograph sticking out from under the top sheet of paper. He couldn't discern the full picture, but a bare human leg was visible…spattered with blood.

"They're both dead, Boss. Margo *and* Jeffrey. They were murdered *seven* months ago." She paused to let that fact sink in. "That pre-dates what we thought was our *first* victim by six months." Heidi paused again before revealing the shocker. "They were killed in their villa overlooking the sea in the Bahamas."

*"The Bahamas!"* Winter couldn't disguise his surprise. "The bloody Bahamas?"

"Bloody is right, Boss. I'll precis the report, which was compiled by the Homicide Squad of the Royal Bahamas Police Force. They have a lot of British ex-Old Bill; they know their stuff, and they've been as good as gold, very open, very helpful, they've e-mailed everything they have on the case. Margo Thompson was the victim of an attack in her home on a Saturday afternoon. Her household staff were released for a traditional siesta-style afternoon break; she was alone. There were no signs of forced entry. Mrs Thompson was found naked on the kitchen floor; her abdomen had been slashed repeatedly. Her husband, Jeffrey Thompson, is believed to have returned home during the attack, disturbing the killer or killers. He was found in the hall of the villa with his throat cut. Both victims died as a result of massive blood loss. The report concludes that although nothing was taken from the villa, a fact confirmed by the housekeeper, it's believed the incident began as a burglary/home invasion. This escalated into an attempted but uncompleted rape of Margo, evidenced by her nakedness. It's thought she resisted and was rendered insensible by a blow to the side of her head by a heavy blunt object. A bloodied ornament was nearby. Before the attacker or attackers were able to complete the rape of the victim, they were disturbed by the return of her husband. He seems to have been ambushed in the hall, and his throat cut with a very sharp blade. This intrusion by the husband must have spooked the attacker, who fled the scene. No arrests have been made. No significant forensic evidence has been found, no witnesses forthcoming. There were no security systems or CCTV at the villa."

Heidi paused to let the information sink in and continued. "The investigation seems more than adequate, considering the information and evidence they had to go on. The differences between our cases are interesting, though. Tox reports show no drugs in Margo's system. No Ketamine or anything else other than prescribed HRT. Whoever did this seems to have relied on a good old-fashioned whack to the head to subdue the victim. The abdomen was cut and slashed; there's a picture here." Heidi pulled the e-mailed photograph showing the white marble of the kitchen floor awash with bright, red, fresh blood. "Margo was discovered in the late afternoon, only hours after she'd been slaughtered. You can see the attacker has started to open her up, but her womb, ovaries, everything, in fact, are still there. If he was after her womb, he failed. The unexpected return of Jeffrey Thompson probably stopped that process in its tracks."

Grant rubbed his chin as he spoke. "This points to a messy, amateurish, unplanned, and unprepared assault. After this the killer *must* have sat down and thought about the process more deeply and honed his skills. He could've been caught; what if Jeffrey had company with him, someone young and strong? Or had got away and raised the alarm? This must have really shaken our attacker."

"But this is definitely our man." Paul Winter observed. "The focus of the assault is the woman's abdomen; he was after her womb, and the fact she was the mother of Garson, I'd say, clinches it."

"She was the *first* victim. Garson's mother was picked first." Grant said thoughtfully. "Watson said that Garson was always the ring-leader, he said that going to the club, getting a girl was his idea, it was Garson who led the rape on the girl, encouraged the others and mocked Japhet for not joining in. Don't you think that's significant? Our man went after Margo first and all the way to the Bahamas." A thought stirred. A memory that was just out of reach, like trying to remember the name of an old school friend, you should know, but it was a curl of morning mist at that moment.

*The Bahamas?*

For the second time in such a recent period, Grant was stymied by his memory. For the second time, he considered Lyddy's teasing words, '*Forget what you're trying to remember, it'll just jump into your mind when you least expect it*'. She was right, it always came back but they were starting to stack up, he shook his head, he was getting too old for this game.

But another realisation *did* hit him with sudden clarity. His brain did start working. However, the abrupt and unexpected comprehension had nothing to do with a sun-soaked paradise four and a half thousand miles away and everything to do with a small village a few miles off the A40 in Oxfordshire.

"Guvnor." Grant's face was taut, his voice betraying his tension. "We need to contact Thames Valley Police, ask them to send a car to Swinbrook and arrest William Watson."

# Chapter Forty-Eight

D CI Winter directed new investigative actions resulting from the revelation of two more murders to lay at the feet of the *Dissection Killer*. Flight details and cruise ship manifests to and from The Bahamas were downloaded to be searched and sifted in the hope a name may jump out; it would be a long and laborious job. The disgruntled Dirty Don was the obvious choice. Isla Baxter, her cameraman Rob Pagett and DI Dodds return from France was imminent, it seemed a good idea to keep Dirty Don well away.

The disclosures made by William Watson, had exposed a possible motive for the crimes, as a matter of the highest priority, officers were tasked with finding 'Cassie' or 'Lassie', the victim of a hideous and prolonged assault. Despite the assertions of the offender profile and the initial thoughts of the Bahamian Police, it had to be considered possible the *Dissection Killer* was a woman, the missing Covent Garden rape victim, intent on committing what Amber Bennett had called proxy murders. Cassie or Lassie *had* to be found.

* * *

It was time for the course of action Grant had been considering. "Right you," ordered Maddox, "redeem yourself, sort out a pool car, something which doesn't look like a piece of snot. We're going for a ride."

"Okay, Skip. What are we up to?" Grant slapped his hands together and rubbed them with relish.

"Back to basics." He pressed a few buttons on his mobile and held it to his ear.

"Hello, Heidi? Grant here. There's something I think we should do. You, me, and Amber."

\* \* \*

The three officers squeezed into the Bogey for the journey from West London to the leafy lanes of Surrey. When Grant had seen the re-appearance of the bright green pool car, he'd scowled at his DC.

"It's all they had," she shrugged, grinning.

\* \* \*

As they drove, DI Yorke thumbed through papers relating to the crime scene of Martine Walsingham's murder. Grant had said back to basics, and he meant it. He wanted to visit each scene, view them with new eyes, with the new knowledge they'd acquired in recent weeks. Maybe something had been missed. The hedge-lined, narrow country lane widened to reveal a curved, concave wall with high, dark wood gates between two tall stone pillars.

"This is it." Heidi Yorke exited the car and entered the code held in the case file into the keypad. The gates juddered, slowly opening to reveal the long drive up to the house.

The three detectives leant on the open doors of their day-glow car. A CCTV camera was mounted atop each stone pillar. The keypad had another camera built into its panel. The day the killer arrived, they'd seen and recorded nothing.

"The cameras weren't interfered with in any way?" Grant mused.

"No. Nothing so simple as spraying paint over the lenses or cutting a wire that'd be noticed immediately *and* alert the occupant. Besides, the system was state-of-the-art enough to detect any change in the flow of electricity, such as caused by a cut wire. In that case, a tamper alarm is activated at the monitoring central station, and a message is relayed to the police control room to respond." Grant nodded with approval. Heidi knew her stuff. "The control box *inside* the house was sabotaged. The alarm engineer we consulted was impressed, he said, 'It's what I'd have done.'"

Grant shrugged. "The box in the house, was it swabbed for DNA and dusted for prints?"

"Yep. About the first thing I ordered. There were so many sharp edges and bits of wire and stuff sticking out, it seemed a good chance our man could have pricked or scratched himself, but it was clean. Nothing."

"So, how did our guy get inside the house? How did he get at the box?" asked Amber.

Heidi shrugged, "The fact is, not a *single* crime-scene has shown a *single* sign of forced entry. Not here, not in London, not in the Bahamas."

\* \* \*

At the front door, Heidi opened a clear plastic bag, removed a key card, and swiped the entry lock to gain access.

"The place was cleared up and sealed after the forensic examination, but I've got pictures in the file here that tell the story."

The marble floor had been cleaned, Heidi held the photo in front of the group, superimposed over the actual scene, the image showing what had once lay before them, the contrast was shocking. Martine Walsingham's naked, defiled body was spread-eagled and surrounded by a pool of darkened, dried blood. The obscenity of her severed womb lay across her face.

Grant closed his eyes and imagined the process which had been played out here. Dismissing the horror, thinking of the practicalities, how to physically do this, what happened next, how to get away with it? A thought fluttered across his mind, he reached for it, screwed his eyes as he tried to remember something, from the distant past, something he'd seen on television.

"Lizzie Borden," he blurted out, meeting only quizzical silence from both Amber and Heidi. "You know the rhyme, 'Lizzie Borden took an axe, gave her mother forty whacks. When she saw what she had done, she gave her father forty-one.'"

"*What* are you talking about, Grant?" asked Heidi.

Grant was suddenly animated; he'd had an idea. "It was a real case, a famous double murder in America in the late 1800s. Lizzie Borden was tried for killing her father and stepmother with an axe. Their heads hacked to pieces; it was a slaughterhouse. Lizzie was a respectable teacher but didn't get on with the victims and was arrested. There was a film made about the case with Elizabeth Montgomery as Lizzie Borden, you'd know her, the woman from the TV comedy *Bewitched*."

"I know that; I watched it as a child, the woman with the nose wriggle," put in Amber, attempting to wriggle her nose and failing as her eyes crossed.

"Lizzie Borden was acquitted of the murders, though a lot of the evidence against her was compelling. But…" Grant held up a warning finger. "…no one could explain how she'd butchered these two people in a limited time frame in a hugely messy and bloody fashion *and* didn't have a *single* drop of blood on her clothing. Those were the days of long dresses, corsets and stays, frills, stockings, and so on. At the murder sites, there was blood everywhere: up the walls, across the ceiling, and spattered all over the floor. The killer must have been dripping with blood, it was reasoned, but witnesses immediately after the attacks saw Lizzie was spotless, and so was every item of her clothing in the house, each of which was accounted for. No time for washing it, and none burned or disposed of. She was acquitted."

"And?" pressed Heidi.

"The film offered a solution; it was so simple but at the time, in the 1890s, so shocking and utterly appalling an idea that no one even considered it."

"*And?*" demanded Heidi.

"Lizzie Borden *did* kill the couple but was bollock naked when she did so. She washed the blood off herself *after* the killings and dressed in clean, spotless clothes." Grant looked to Heidi and Amber, eyebrows raised, looking for understanding as he continued excitedly. "Whoever did this to Martine," he jabbed a finger at the photo Heidi was holding, "and gutted Paula and Juno *must* have been covered in blood, but would *you* want to make your escape with all that evidence on you?"

Amber beamed. "The victims, incapacitated with Ketamine, electronic surveillance disabled, planning, and preparation so he knew he wasn't going to be disturbed, stripped off, did the deed, and washed afterward. Brilliant Skip!"

Grant turned to the DI, "Heidi, the shower room. Has it been cleaned or disturbed in any way since the murder?" Grant hardly dared to hear the answer.

"It's untouched, Granty. Untouched."

Grant clapped his hands together so hard that the two women jumped. "Right! Let's get forensics back here and spray Luminol all over the shower; we need to know if there's evidence of blood. We'll get the waste pipe and shower trap removed, if the killer used it maybe his head or body hair is in there. We could get a DNA match. This could be it, guys."

Heidi was on her mobile before Grant had finished speaking.

* * *

The next destination was the hotel suite overlooking Park Lane in central London, which had witnessed the dissection murder of Juno Jenkin. It had been deep-cleaned, re-painted, re-carpeted, and was about to be made available once more for the use of guests. The shower cubicle had been washed and polished to gleaming, but Grant requested a test for the presence of blood anyway and for the waste pipes to be inspected. Should a hair be found, just one, should DNA be recovered and should it match that which might be found at the other scenes, it would be compelling evidence. A check of the file showed the initial investigators had swabbed and dusted the sabotaged hotel alarm and CCTV camera box with negative results. Grant shared an approving nod with Heidi. Everything which should have been done had been done.

* * *

The detectives' final destination was Charleroi Mansions. The shower at Paula Bingley's much neglected apartment had clearly been untouched since the death of the occupant, Grant was on his phone and ordered the same tests and examination as the country house of Martine Walsingham and Juno Jenkin's hotel suite. He turned to his young partner, Amber Bennett, asking, "Can you look through the papers in the file there? What was the result of the fingerprint dusting and DNA swabbing of the alarm and CCTV control box, which was nobbled here?"

Amber flicked through the sheets, turning pages back and forth several times. "Fingerprint section came back as a zilch on dabs Skip. Regarding the DNA swabs, the examination was requested, Sarge, er... hang on, yes, there's the completed proforma with the docket reference. *Triplicate* forms were sent to the pedants up at the lab as usual, sent off the day after the scene examination, and marked urgent, but this file hasn't been updated with a result. No result at all, yay or nay. That seems really wrong." Amber flicked back and forth through the file, running a finger down line after line of text, checking her facts. "Sorry, Skip. No result is updated on this file. No results. So obviously, no comparative search has even started yet either."

Grant rubbed his chin, perplexed. After a few moments, a light seemed to come on. "Amber, can you look to see who oversaw the requests? Who receives the Lab results, updates the file, and initiates the comparative searches?" He suspected he knew the answer even before Amber turned to the relevant page.

"Oh." Amber looked up, straight into Grant's eyes. "It's Detective Inspector Dodds."

Grant's body sagged, and he slammed his forehead with the palm of his hand. *"Bollocks!"*

# Chapter Forty-Nine

Grant Maddox's ability to take DI Dodds to task regarding the forensics report at Charleroi Mansions and what it may or may not contain was severely curtailed by events in the Incident Room, which had unfolded as the three detectives were driving towards Central London and the scene of Juno Jenkin's murder.

Isla was holding court with several officers and civilian support staff at her desk, regaling them with the events of the previous two-day visit to France. Rob Pagett sat nearby, scanning paperwork listings and notes of shots, recordings, interviews, and scene setters.

The door to the Incident Room swung open with such force that it hit the stops, sending a loud bang echoing through the expansive room. All conversation halted, and every head turned to view the intruder. If jaws could make a sound as they dropped open, the noise would have been deafening, as it was utter silence descended, a silence of shock and amazement. In the doorway stood Detective Inspector Brian 'Doddy' Dodds. He was smiling broadly, swaying slightly from side to side. He held a police officer's flat cap at his front, over his groin. This was a blessing because everyone present couldn't help but notice that the Detective Inspector was stark naked.

"*ISLA!*" Doddy boomed. "*ISLA!*" The Detective Inspector staggered forward, grinning an insane grin, one hand reaching out before him, like a one-armed Frankenstein's monster, clawing at the air in the direction of a properly astounded Isla Baxter. His other hand, thankfully, still held the flat cap, what was hidden beneath the focus of attention for the whole room.

*"ISLA!"* Doddy called again, still loud but this time with a hint of forlornness, a trace of sadness. *"ISLA!"* Everyone was frozen to the spot, but Rob Pagett, seeing a once-in-a-lifetime opportunity, grabbed his camera, hefted it to his shoulder, and aimed the lens at the approaching, stumbling figure.

Then it happened. Deep down, everyone knew it would. Detective Inspector Dodds let go of the cap and, with both arms stretched out, imploringly, towards Isla Baxter cried piteously, "It's all for you."

It was with mounting horror that the witnesses to the event observed that the hat hung in place in front of Doddy's gentleman's area. As if more attention needed to be drawn to this fact, Doddy began to laugh hysterically, looked down, and declared, "Look! No Hands!"

As Doddy lifted his head, his eyeballs rolled backward, disappearing into his skull, leaving only the whites visible, the smile left his face, and with arms still reaching out before him, he fell backward with a nauseating slam. The hat span around amusingly for a few moments on Doddy's erection like a spinning plate on a cane before coming to a halt, hanging sadly off the gift DI Dodds wished to give to his beloved, Isla Baxter.

\* \* \*

As Grant, Heidi, and Amber entered the Incident Room, every face swivelled to greet them; each seemed to be fitted with the broadest grin they'd ever enjoyed. It was obvious something had happened.

From the DCI's office came the muffled noise of shouted accusations. "I *KNOW* it was you, Don. I *know* it was you. Who else would do it? What was it? Ecstasy? LSD? Heroin? What did you give him, you stupid fuck?"

Grant looked from face to face. "What's happened? What's going on?"

Detective Constable Pat Kerrigan gave the answer.

"You've missed a real treat Skip, someone slipped something into Doddy's tea, he marched in here bollock naked, with a hard-on hidden under a patrol cap, he made some declaration to Isla Baxter then collapsed. It was the greatest thing ever. The best bit is Rob Pagett got it all on film. This is legendary, Skipper. *Legendary.*"

It seemed the whole room was of one accord; there was certainly no love lost between the rank and file and Doddy Dodds. Grant's face twitched slightly; a laugh was forming, but he was a supervisory officer, and this was a serious crime committed against a colleague. He turned to face Heidi and Amber. It was a mistake. Their faces were further advanced than his in the crumble towards uncontrolled hilarity. It was no good; the dam burst, and the room echoed to their raucous laughter, which set everyone else off once more. Their noise even drowned out a near hysterical DCI Winter who was screaming at his prime suspect, Dirty Don Chamberlain, who denied it all.

# Chapter Fifty

Lyddy had prepared lasagna and a dish piled high with piping hot slices of garlic bread.

"No, Monza?" asked Grant. "Wasn't she due here?"

"Yes, Daddy, she called," answered Connie. "She arrested a juvenile shoplifter who doesn't speak English; she's going to be off late."

Lydia couldn't hide her disappointment; there was nothing better in the world than having her family at her table eating her food. Grant nodded in silent understanding.

"Funny thing happened today at the office," Grant began, hoping to lift the mood. "A very unpopular DI who had the hots for our Isla Baxter got his tea spiked with some unspecified hallucinogen. He stripped off naked and pranced into the Incident Room with a massive hard-on, declared his love for Ms. Baxter, then collapsed."

"Oh, the poor man." The embodiment of kindness, Lydia Maddox's first reaction was always going to be sympathy for the victim, no matter how unpopular he was or deserving of the treatment. "Is he alright?"

Grant stifled his laughter, "Carted off in an ambulance to hospital, drivelling on about his beloved Isla. The PC posted to stay with him called in and said he's doing okay, but…and this is brilliant, he still has his massive hard-on. The bed sheets are sticking up like a pyramid! No sign of deflation at all." Connie put her hand to her mouth as she laughed, knowing it was wrong. "Half the team wants to know what he was given, so they can get some," Grant added.

This time, all at the table burst into laughter. Grant grinned at his wife and buried his elbow in his groin, holding his hand up, balled into a fist, an obscene phallic gesture. "Imagine if it *never* goes away! It might make weddings, Christenings, and funerals a bit awkward." He swivelled his phallic arm around comically, bumping into the edge of the table and knocking the side of his wife. "Don't mind me everyone, I've just got this permanent boner, carry on vicar, nothing to see here!" Grant's antics halted the meal consumption as laughter turned to near hysteria. "As if all that isn't bad enough, Isla's cameraman was in the office and filmed the lot! I mean, Oh My God! Can you imagine!"

It took several minutes for calm to return to the Maddox dining table. It was not the moment Grant expected his breakthrough to come, but it was exactly as Lydia had often said, *'Forget what you're trying to remember, it'll just jump into your mind when you least expect it'.*

He'd trawled his mind at the time, trying to find the memory, to mentally download the image. *'The Bahamas, The Bahamas'.* He'd been in Paul Winter's office with Heidi, hearing the shocking news that Martine Walsingham wasn't the first victim at all, that it was Margo Thompson and her husband in the bloody Bahamas. Then, his processing had been overtaken by William Watson, his role, and Grant's order for his arrest. The former memory he'd been grasping for had slipped away. As he tucked into lasagna and garlic bread, surrounded by his family and not even thinking about it, the memory returned in clear, bright Technicolor. *The Bahamas!* The tattooed arm of Rob Pagett. Mali, Mexico, The Congo, and finally, The Bahamas. Each tattooed image with a bite taken out. *Rob Pagett* had been in The Bahamas.

Grant's thoughts rushed in a torrent. Pagett was a cameraman, an expert in electronics, would alarms and CCTV hold any mysteries or challenges to him? *And* Pagett had been at the hotel, the Park Lane London View Hotel, he was one of the cameramen for Juno's series of promotional interviews, *'They sub-contract it out to a freelancer like me'.* He'd been there, the very day Juno Jenkin had been dissected alive, *and* he'd been so reticent to come forward immediately and admit it.

The next thought hit Grant like an express train. The tattoo on Pagett's *other* arm was different, it had images that were personal, sad and tragic, not the representations of triumphal, professional assignments with a Rob Pagett bite taken out of them. The picture was of an angel, a beautiful girl in loose robes and a forlorn expression, and two names beneath the figure. He remembered now. Grant Maddox was thinking fast and as clear as crystal. The tattooed names were *Robbie* and *Cassandra*. The pieces were falling into place. Frankton Abbey's P.E. teacher, Bill Watson, asserting it was the truth, had repeated the words told him by Japhet Gold, eighteen years previously, a day before his death. The girl, the girl who'd been so brutally and heartlessly assaulted and raped, her name was *'Something like Cassie or Lassie'*. It wasn't Lassie, it was *Cassie.* He'd said Cassie. The girl was *Cassandra!* 'Robbie and Cassandra!'

# Chapter Fifty-One

The turmoil of Grant's thoughts was interrupted by the sound of his mobile's ring-tone; the intro of Black Sabbath's "Thrill of it All" caused his wife and daughter's heads to turn and for Connie to shake her head sadly at her highly conservative and traditionalist father's love of heavy metal music.

*"Really? Tomorrow?"* There was exasperation and irritation in Grant's voice. He rang off, excusing himself from clearing up after the meal. He had a call to make.

* * *

"Amber, it's Grant. Yes, I'm fine. No, nothing's wrong." Grant was sitting in the small room designated The Den, where he'd retreated to call Amber Bennett. "Look, I've just been warned for Crown Court, 10am tomorrow, the Melvin O'Hara case. Yes, I know I was listed for the end of the week, yes it's shit timing, just wait and listen for a second." Grant rolled his eyes. "Listen, I need you to do something and do it very, *very* discreetly."

Grant waited a moment, his pause and silence calculated to stress the importance of the task he was giving her.

"I want you to look into Rob Pagett for me...yes, Rob Pagett, the cameraman. I want you find out when he and Isla were in the Bahamas, they made a documentary about tax exiles and tax dodgers soaking up the sun there...yes, I'm sure, he told me so himself. He has tattoos down one arm with the locations of all his exposés, and The Bahamas is one of them.

219

Find out when he was there, find out if it matches the date of the Thompson murders." Grant jerked the phone away from his ear as Amber shouted, '*Fuck me!*' at the top of her voice.

"Very kind of you to offer Amber, but I'm happily married. Look keep this to yourself, and there's more." Grant laughed. "Yes, you're right that is enough but listen, on Pagett's other arm is a tattoo of an angel, a girl, a very sad looking girl, it looks like a tribute. Under the angel are two names, Robbie and Cassandra."

Amber understood immediately.

"It's possible Bill Watson's Cassie could be the same girl as Rob Pagett's Cassandra. Dig around, Amber, look into his Facebook account and all his social network stuff, and find out who Cassandra is: a girlfriend, a wife, a relative, a friend? I want the link. I want her found. Pagett was at the Park Lane London View Hotel the day Juno Jenkin was killed, and we know he was in the Bahamas and he has someone who means something to him called Cassandra or Cassie. There are too many coincidences for me. Another thing, look into his qualifications and employment history, try *LinkedIn*, or his production company. We know he has expertise with electronics and cameras; Isla Baxter said so, so see if he has the skill to nobble alarm systems. Have you got all that? I won't be able to take calls at court, so I'll have the ringtone on silent so text me, keep me updated. I'll be out of the office at court for a day, maybe two, so I'm depending on you, Amber. Be *very* careful and don't tell anyone, not even Winter, not yet. Pagett's too close to us and embedded in the investigation, so we can't risk him knowing he's being looked at. The last two mothers are protected and safe. We need evidence before we can do anything."

He was about to ring off when another thought jumped into his mind. "When you get a spare moment..." He jerked the phone away again at the sarcastic laugh assaulting his ears, "...chase up the lab results on the DNA swabs from Paula Bingley's apartment. Oh and Amber...get an early night won't you, it could be a long day tomorrow." Grant rang off as the abuse began to assault his ears.

# Chapter Fifty-Two

Grant had spent day one of O'Hara's trial kicking his heels and drinking coffee in the police room. He was called to the witness box on the morning of day two. He'd been giving evidence for two hours when the court broke for lunch. He hurried to the police room, examining his phone on the way, anxious for news from Amber or from Thames Valley Police and the arrest request made for Watson. The previous day Amber had been conspicuously silent, he hadn't chased her, he was giving her space to work. TVP had sent a vague update about ongoing enquiries to trace William Watson, who wasn't to be found at his Swinbrook home. It was all very frustrating.

Today Amber at least didn't disappoint, he felt a bloom of pride for his young colleague, she'd certainly been busy, her text indicated success in her search for information on Rob Pagett *and* she'd found a Lab Report manila file, *unopened* at the bottom of the in-tray on DI Dodds desk. She urged Grant to call her, being unwilling to commit detail to the texting medium.

\* \* \*

"Amber, it's Grant. What you got?" His sentences were short and clipped; he wanted news.

"I'm fine, Skip; everyone around me here wants to know how's the trial going?" Grant understood immediately that Amber wasn't free to talk.

"I'm two hours in, still telling our side of the story; the defense will be tearing into me this afternoon. The other matter, *have you got anything good*?" Grant was desperate for information.

At the other end of the connection, Amber nodded calmly at Grant's urgent question. "That sounds promising, so we may only be a day or two from a result then? And yes, I've some really interesting stuff at this end, I think you may be definitely onto something Skip." Grant punched the air, silently mouthing, 'Yes! Yes! Yes!' as he did so.

"Look, Amber, whatever happens here, I'll be released by about four-thirty or five clock, I'll swing by the Incident Room, and we can catch up, okay."

To Grant's immense joy, she answered, "I think you should. Good luck this afternoon. Laters."

The glass door to the police room opened, and it went dark. The light was blocked by the enormous presence at the entrance of his ex-firearms colleague and friend, Sergeant Babatunde Okafor.

"Granty!" the deep, booming voice of his friend echoed around the sparsely furnished space.

"Babs!" responded the DS, jumping to his feet. "How the hell are you, you great, big, 'orrible bastard?" The pleasure at seeing his friend was undisguised. The tall, stocky Grant Maddox was swamped and thoroughly engulfed by the bear hug from Babs, whose huge hands, slapping his back in good-natured camaraderie, nearly drove the breath from his lungs.

"Good Man, really good. Tho' I wasn't expecting to be called on the O'Hara job this week, scheduling fuck up, I'm guessing."

Grant nodded sympathetically. "It couldn't be timed worse for me, stuck in the middle of this *dissection* job."

Babs smiled, "Me and my boys are making a fortune in overtime looking after your two ladies." Babs rubbed his hands together in a universal display of avarice. "I've got eight lads on a round-robin out in Kent with the Whittcocks. The locals haven't the firearm resources for twenty-four-hour cover, so we're on aid there…shame!" He rubbed his hands greedily again. "And I'm with a few boys at the Mews house in Kensington, looking after Helena MacDonald." The two officers slumped onto the hard polyprop chairs, leaning forward into each other.

"What's Helena like?" Grant enquired. "I haven't had time to see her yet.

We sent a liaison officer who says she's not the most cooperative of people."

Babs laughed, throwing his head back. "She's not so bad; she just insists on living her life her way; we're cramping her style. And a really big part of that style is her toyboy. My God, Granty, she gets him to perform so often it's a fire risk. I've been outside her front door in the middle of the night, on time and a half, you understand?"

Grant nodded appreciably, remembering the all-nighters he'd pulled for the love of money.

"You can hear them, Man. Hear her anyway. She screams, wails, and yells. She makes more noise than a howler monkey. There's more bandicooting, hibbety-dibbing and gland to gland combat in that house than in a Bangkok boom-boom joint on payday."

Grant roared with laughter. "Fuck it, Babs, I really miss you, mate. You slaughter me." Babs joined in with the laughter.

\* \* \*

It was gone six-thirty by the time Grant Maddox staggered into the Incident Room, physically exhausted and even more mentally drained after three and a half hours of verbal duelling with O'Hara's Defense Counsel. Amber had been waiting expectantly; she was out of her chair and crossing the room before the door shut behind her sergeant.

"Let's walk, Skip, maybe get a drink." Amber winked at him. Grant did an exaggerated about-turn and caught the door before it shut.

\* \* \*

In a dark corner of the nearest pub, with a glass of wine before each of them, so reminiscent of the furtive assignation they'd engaged in at Swinbrook's Swan Inn so recently, the two detectives huddled forward conspiratorially.

"Well?" It was all Grant could say.

Amber grinned broadly. "This'll seem like a list, Skip. First off Pagett is an electronic whiz-kid. I found him on LinkedIn, he's available, like he said, for all sorts of freelance work and he's up to the eyeballs in all things electronic, cameras, sound set up, everything. His qualifications confused the hell out of me, but I asked someone in the know what it all meant, and the bottom line is that Pagett could wire, unwire, route, re-route, configure, and re-configure anything that was at any of our crime scenes."

"So that is one *big* tick!" enthused Grant in a whisper. "Well done, Amber, good work. What else?"

Amber chuckled. "You don't want much, do you? Okay. I found the Lab Report from Charleroi Mansions. Actually on DI Dodds desk, in his in-tray, Doddy had just ignored it, too busy sniffing around Isla I suppose."

"*And!?*" Grant could barely hold his impatience in check.

"There's a blood trace. Whoever was working on that system scratched themselves ever-so slightly on a protruding wire. But it was enough; we had a DNA sample of whoever was in that box. It's being profiled and will be run through the system looking for a match as a priority."

Grant rubbed his chin, thinking out loud. "We need elimination samples from every possible legitimate alarm engineer who's ever been near that box. If the trace is none of them, we have our suspect. If we get some hair from any of the showers, and the DNA matches the blood from the box, we definitely have our suspect. We can't get too excited, the blood may yet be from an alarm company man but I just feel it isn't. I'm shaking inside Amber. My spider sense is tingling."

Amber grinned at her sergeant. "Well, Spidey, you'll be pleased to know that only seven employees have ever been in that control box since its installation; six are still with the company, and I've arranged for elimination samples to be taken in the next two days. The seventh moved to a rival who I've called, and they're getting back to me."

Grant beamed at his colleague. "Oh, you're good. You're very good. You're such a credit to whoever mentored you. What a guy he must be."

Amber beamed back. "Oh, he was alright, I suppose." Amber held up her hand for a high five, and Grant obliged before asking,

"What else?"

Amber laughed again. "You think there should be more, do you?" Grant nodded enthusiastically. Amber laughed, caught up in the excitement; after so many dead-ends, after struggling for so long to find links and connections, for things to be falling and then slotting so mechanically into place was thrilling. "Okay, there *is* more. Isla Baxter and Pagett flew into Nassau in The Bahamas ten days before the Thompson murders. They door-stepped half a dozen ex-pats who they asserted owed millions in tax or who were corrupt or both. But Skipper, they *were* there when Margo and Jeffrey Thompson were killed. Isla flew from Nassau to Miami on the Saturday afternoon of the attacks but Pagett stayed on, he was alone, unseen, unsupervised. He was there for two more days filming backgrounds, scene setters, posh hotels, country clubs, and private beaches, all the stuff which links the meat of the documentary together."

Grant could only shake his head, his mind filled with what needed to be done.

"There's one more thing Skip. I've scoured Pagett's social network," she paused. "He had a sister."

"Had?" breathed Grant, his voice little more than an exhalation. "Past tense?"

"*Had*. Past tense. A twin sister." Amber's voice was a whisper. "Her name was Cassandra Pagett....and she's dead."

# Chapter Fifty-Three

"Thank you." Grant nodded his appreciation to the officer who opened the interview room door for him, hindered as he was holding two mugs of tea. The officer pulled the door shut behind Grant, who took three steps to the table and placed the drinks on its surface. He pushed one mug towards the seated man. "Thought you might like a wet. The custody sergeant said you take it with milk and two sugars, NATO style."

"Thanks, yeh, old habits die hard."

Grant took the seat on the opposite side of the table and wriggled into the chair, making himself comfortable. "Well, Bill, I didn't expect to continue our conversation in these circumstances." Grant waved a hand around at the battleship grey, windowless walls that surrounded them. "We were looking for you, but you weren't to be found. I understand you went on a bit of a bender in Oxford, got so pissed you woke up in a cell wondering who you were and what had happened."

William Watson smiled ruefully. "You need to be careful of the words you use Detective Sergeant, do you really want to accuse an openly gay man of going on a bender?" Watson sipped at his tea and laughed sardonically. "Lovely brew, by the way."

Grant returned the smile. "How's your head? You're rested and well now?"

"Am I fit to be interviewed, you mean? The doctor says I'm okay, and so do I."

"You understand this is serious, Bill; this has to be formal? I've no choice."

Watson winced. "I apologise for putting you in this position, Grant. I'm ashamed."

The two men looked at each other for a few seconds. Grant broke the moment and pressed the record button on the tape recorder, and read Watson his rights from the laminated sheet of text fixed to the desk. He paused and emphasised one section. "You have the right to have legal representation with you, Mr Watson. We can stop right now or at any time if you change your mind. Do you understand?"

"I have no intention of doing anything but tell you the truth and I know you won't try and trick me, I trust you. I don't need representation."

"I hope that's the case, Mr Watson, you understand what harm you've caused and what further harm may have come to pass. Will you tell me the truth now?"

Watson nodded slowly, took a deep drink of his tea, and began. "Everything I told you and the lady officer in the pub at Swinbrook was true. Everything about the boys, about Japhet and Gary, about me. It was all true. The night before the crash which killed them all, Japhet Gold told me about the attack on the girl."

"Called Cassie or Lassie?"

"Yes, something like that."

"Could it have been Cassandra, Mr Watson?"

"Yes, it could have been. What happened to her, what they did, I told you everything, I couldn't make up something like that."

"Very well, but the next morning you met up with myself and DC Bennett in the carpark of The Swan at Swinbrook and gave us more information. Tell me about that."

Watson shifted uncomfortably in his seat. He cupped the tea mug nervously, drumming his fingers on its rim. "I'd had more than a few with you and the lady the night before; I'm not blaming the drink; I take responsibility, but I got home and started thinking. That bastard Rose-Gummer and the old headmaster, they treated me like dirt, let the sevens treat me like dirt, made threats, threats to dismiss me, blacken my name. They demoted me, brought in a new head of department, I ended up just an assistant but I was stuck. It was demeaning."

"Have you heard of AirTight Investigations? Were you made aware of a search for 'Cassie' being made by the school?" Grant leant forward, giving his question extra weight.

"No. Never. I've never heard of them, and a search? That's news to me." Watson's face was a picture of bewilderment.

"Alright. The meeting with us in the morning. You made some very serious allegations. You said that a middle-aged woman had visited Rose-Gummer, that she stated she'd found a diary, that she could finish the school and she wasn't alone, do you remember that?"

"Yes"

"Do you remember saying when that conversation had taken place?"

"Yes."

"How long ago, Mr Watson?"

"About two months."

"Was that statement true?" Watson held his head in his hands.

"No. It was a lie."

"Was any part of what you said that morning true?"

"No. It was all a lie."

"What was your intention when you told that lie, Mr Watson?"

Watson looked up, a picture of misery. "I wanted to hurt Rose-Gummer and Wagstaff. They're both bastards. I wanted it to seem they were involved somehow in the murders. I wanted them to sweat, to feel what it's like to have someone more powerful calling the shots, bearing down on you. I wanted them to suffer."

Grant felt miserable, too. This man, whom he'd admired and with whom he had so many shared experiences, had reduced himself to a petty creature, willing to misdirect a murder investigation merely to exact spiteful revenge. It was unworthy, and it saddened him deeply.

"Did you intend that the police would think the middle-aged woman was one of the rugby seven mothers?"

Watson's reply was a whisper. "Yes."

"The fabrication of a secret diary, apparently recently discovered, and the implication that its contents could finish the school, was this intended to

228

be a false pointer towards the truth of the assault on the girl we are calling Cassie?"

"Yes."

"This invented woman's assertion she was not alone in possessing this knowledge, was that meant to imply that other mothers of the sevens were involved?"

"Yes."

"And the whole point of this fiction was to imply that a member of the school or an agent acting on behalf of the school was killing the mothers to hide a terrible secret. Is that it?"

"Yes. That's it."

"You've caused a great deal of trouble. Huge numbers of man-hours have been wasted because of you, and more would have been wasted, but for a mistake you made. You gave the timing of your story, the event that kick-started the killings, as being two months ago."

"Yes. Before Martine Gold, Japhet and Jacob's mother, was killed. Before it started."

"We found out recently, Mr Watson, that there was another murder, one which preceded that of Martine Walsingham by half a year. We didn't know about it, and nor did you. It showed up your story as a lie."

Ex-Para, William Watson sighed and nodded, smiling at Grant. "I'm glad. It was the worst thing I've ever done, and I regretted it immediately. Besides the trouble I've caused you and your colleagues I've brought trouble on myself. On the afternoon of your second visit to Frank's, I was sacked and forbidden to ever step foot on their property. I've been hitting the bottle since. Now it's out, now it's over, I can regain control, get back to an even keel."

"It may not be over yet." Grant stood. "It's not my decision, but there's a very real possibility you'll be charged with an offence. It may be just wasting police time, but it could be perverting the course of justice. Bill, you could end up inside."

Watson smiled weakly. "I suspect you may put a word in for me."

Grant smiled back, just as weakly, the fatigue was overwhelming. "Interview concluded." He pressed the black button on the recorder.

# Chapter Fifty-Four

Dirty Don Chamberlain wasn't having any of it but *everyone* knew he had *everything* to do with it. However, knowing and proving were two entirely different things. Don had weathered the cacophony of furious accusations levelled at him by DCI Winter, who, although not a fan of DI Dodds, wouldn't and couldn't countenance the drugging of a senior officer…no matter how riotously funny he thought it was privately.

Consequently, Winter banished Don to a dark corner of the basement of the Police Station, condemned to sift through towering piles of old documents to identify irrelevant paperwork for shredding. A mind-numbing process known as 'weeding.' This task would almost certainly take three or four days of solid scrutinising.

"Guvnor!" pleaded Don, "please Guv, what's the point of that? It's a non-job. You're punishing me for something I didn't do."

DCI Winter pulled himself to his full height and pointed a long bony finger menacingly towards the door like the Ghost of Christmas-Yet-to-Come, and with a shaking voice, ordered Don to "Get out of my fucking sight and weed, be grateful you have a job weeding, and if I ever get proof you spiked Doddy's drink I'll flop you lower than whale shit, slam you lower than a rattlesnakes ballbag! Now, *get out!*"

Unwilling to be flopped lower than whale shit or slammed lower than a snakes ballbag, Dirty Don had scampered away to sift and weed, content at least that he'd evened the score with Doddy, got away with it, *and* entered the hallowed pages of Police Legend.

The DI Dodds episode persuaded Isla Baxter to find another area to concentrate her efforts until the aftershocks of the incident had subsided. She had, of course, encouraged Doddy's attentions and the detective they called Dirty Don as well. Her experience was that if a man could be employed as an on-side play-thing with a sweet smile, a breathy expression of gratitude, a gentle touch of a hand to a shoulder, or even better, a manly chest, then all sorts of doors could be opened, all manner of information could be elicited. Isla knew she wasn't beautiful but she knew she wasn't unattractive, she had charm, charisma and of course, best of all, fame. A person, even mildly star-struck, could become a means to an end, and Isla Baxter was all about the ends. She'd built a reputation as *'Isla the Brave,'* the action girl. It was Isla Baxter who'd be where the tear gas was densest or the danger most manifest. Her name had passed into common usage as a measure of the seriousness of any situation. 'It can't be that bad, Isla Baxter hasn't turned up yet', being a single, oft repeated, example.

Isla concluded it may benefit her if she and Rob Pagett absented themselves from the Incident Room for a day or two. If her presence was deemed to be unconducive to the efficacy of the investigation, her wide-ranging and unique access contract could be terminated, and all her film material would be surrendered. She couldn't risk that. Therefore, Isla Baxter sought and was granted permission from the Borough Commander to approach and interview Helena MacDonald, mother of Lynton Fiennes, currently residing under armed police protection in a quiet Kensington property in Lousten Mews. Ms. MacDonald was a woman of some means who possessed a formidable strength of character and, for now anyway, also possessed her womb, ovaries, and fallopian tubes.

# Chapter Fifty-Five

DCI Winter was intrigued when Grant phoned, asking to meet him regarding a matter of some urgency and delicacy. "Perhaps we could use the Chief Super's office. He's out on a jolly for the day," Grant suggested.

As he entered the vacated office, Grant and Amber jumped up.

"My God! What is this? Is it a coup?" Paul joked.

"Sorry, Boss, you'll understand in a few moments."

"Okay, guys," Paul said, "tell me."

\* \* \*

Twenty-three minutes later, Paul Winter slumped back in the chair, put his hands behind his head, and exhaled a breath that just kept on exhaling.

"First and foremost, good work. No! Great work, both of you. Second, Holy Shit! The guano is going to hit the fan with this one. Not content with having one of the world's most famous people gutted in a central London Hotel, it seems possible her killer is here, living and working at the heart of the investigation...and making a fucking documentary about it. Thank God I'm on record as opposing their presence and was overruled!"

"Guv, although it looks pretty damning, we still need to tie this all up." Grant wanted to row back a little. "We haven't enough evidence to arrest. The Luminol tests on the first two showers came back as positive for blood, we're waiting for DNA on those traces, but it's likely to only be the victims blood. The third shower cubicle, at the hotel, had been thoroughly cleaned, so zip! What I'm hoping for is even a single hair left by the killer stuck in the shower trap or waste pipe. If we get a DNA hit there, any defense barrister would struggle to find a reasonable excuse for its presence."

"We're also waiting for a profile for the blood in the control box at Paula Bingley's." Put in Amber. "It may belong to an alarm engineer. We're waiting for elimination samples from them."

"But we are putting a picture together now," Paul observed. "Remember The Holy Words of criminal investigation…Means, Motive, and Opportunity. Pagett has the means. You've found he's skilled enough to attack the alarm and camera systems at all the crime scenes. That's something only a few people could do. Regarding the motive, if the girl the PE teacher named as Cassie is Pagett's twin sister, Cassandra, we must speculate there's a connective motive. Do we have more on when and how Cassandra died?"

Amber frowned, giving a one-word answer. "Ongoing."

"In fairness, we have to tread really carefully," offered Grant, jumping to his colleague's assistance. "We can't risk alerting Pagett that we're looking into her."

The DCI nodded in understanding. "And we've the whole truth from the P.E. teacher? We're accepting Campion is building a sports hall, there's no secret diary and the school's in the clear?"

Grant nodded. "We're content the first part of his story is true; the rest, from the second day, was pure spite. A file is off to the CPS on whether to charge Watson or not and, if so, for what offence."

"What's your feeling, Granty?" Winter asked.

"What's to be gained from a charge? It was his evidence about Cassie which gave us this line of enquiry after all. A formal caution and a bollocking seems appropriate to me."

Winter deduced Grant's desire. "I'll put in a word with the CPS, push them in that direction, okay?" Grant smiled and nodded.

"Okay!" Winter clapped his hands. "We have means and motive; how about opportunity? Pagett arrived in the Bahamas ten days before the killings, time enough for a recce on Thompson's villa, and Isla Baxter fucks off on the day of the murder? He's free and unaccountable, so opportunity is a big tick 'yes' for that one. Okay?" He looked left and right for agreement and met with nods of affirmation.

"Martine Walsingham and Paula Bingley? We know Pagett was in the country, so he's available in both cases. The CCTVs have been attacked in advance, he'd the opportunity there too, so more ticks. Yes?" It was accord from all present.

"But the big one for me is Juno Jenkin. I mean, Jesus! He was there! On the day, in the building, he was there! Add to that his reticence in coming forward to tell us. It's damning in my eyes. He says he was out of the hotel at 3pm-ish, but he was one a crowd of tech guys, all mixing about. We have their statements, yes?" Winter looked to Amber.

"Yes, Boss. None give Pagett a concrete alibi after 5pm when Juno shut up shop and was last seen alive. A couple of guys *suggest* he was there or there about, but it's all a bit vague. I suspect a lot of these chaps toot the snow when they shut down for the day, it throws doubt on the veracity of the statements and crucially the timings."

"Christ, is there *anyone* who isn't shovelling cocaine up their fucking nose?" Winter lamented. "Well, that's another huge tick for opportunity as far as I'm concerned. Anything else we can put in the plus box?"

"Two things," put in Maddox. "First, Mary-Mary, Martine Walsingham's housekeeper, remembered a call from the alarm company a week before the murder. It was a heads up for a routine service, no specific appointment, she informed Martine to expect a visit. It's all a bit vague, we're checking and tracing calls received at the house but if it *was* Pagett who called, he may have been able to get in the house before the killing to sabotage the alarm, returning later to carry out the attack."

"That's good, Grant." Winter beamed, "As I recall, the concierge desk at Paula's was unmanned at weekends, so there'd be no problem with access to sabotage the alarm there."

"That's right, Guv, and of course, we know Pagett admitted being in the hotel before Juno Jenkin was killed." Grant paused to let these facts settle, then opened a file he was holding. "The second thing is I think we can still consider elements of this." He waved a bundle of papers as he spoke. "As much as I'm sceptical about offender profiling, and frankly, there's a lot wrong with Professor Cassilis's report if we're right about Pagett. But there are some intriguing aspects to consider."

"Go on," encouraged Paul.

Grant opened the report, scanning the pages of words and blocks highlighted with a fluorescent yellow pen. Running a finger down the sheets, he spoke almost absentmindedly. "Okay, suspect is likely to be '25-35 years old'. Pagett is 34. It goes on the suspect is likely to have, 'a knowledge of electronics, security systems or cameras.' Well, that's true of Pagett. 'If there is machinery or equipment involved in his employment, it will be clean, well-maintained and up-to-date', and 'he may have sought to be in the company of supervisory women'," Grant raised his eyebrows tellingly. "And we should note this: the suspect is, 'likely to have formulated plans and contingencies to deal with his identification and/or arrest. He may have organised for his escape, perhaps to leave the country or assume a new identity.' That's the good stuff, Boss, what I think could be accurate if our man is Pagett. You'll remember the profile went off into one with his mother-complex theory, which I think we can de-bunk with what we now know of our victims and what connects them, but what if we transpose Pagett's *sister* into the equation? If *she* is the motive and the trigger."

"Winter leant forward, leaning on the desk. "Go on."

Grant took a deep breath. "We still need to nail down the motive and explain the perversity of the attacks, the professor said, 'the womb is a most powerful symbol of femininity, of feminine fertility, it's the source of a woman's ability to create a human being'. If Cassandra is 'Cassie', if Pagett's twin sister was raped and abused by the boys from Franks, if it turns out her death is linked to the attack, isn't a desire for revenge the most natural thing in the world? But, the air crash killed all the boys, they were put beyond the reach of any act of vengeance. It must have been maddening, perhaps literally."

"But..." continued Amber, "... what if you direct your fury at the person who was responsible for creating the object of your wrath, the mother of each rapist. What if you take it a step further, focussing on the very organ, inside that mother, that held and nurtured the monster to whom you direct so much hatred, '*the source of a woman's ability to create a human being.*' Her womb."

Winter slowly shook his head. "This is the maddest logic ever. But it *does* have a logic, perverted for sure, but it makes some sort of sense." The DCI slammed his hand down on the desk decisively. "Okay, we turn all our resources onto Rob Pagett. This is what I want. Chase up the search on the DNA hit from the Paula Bingley Control Box, it's a top priority, on my authority. Likewise, the elimination samples from the alarm company. Find an excuse to get a DNA sample from Pagett. Say we need it for elimination reasons, get one from Isla Baxter too, all our officer's DNA is on the system for that reason, say it was overlooked but should have been done on Day One. Once we have his sample, we can compare it to anything else that crops up and specifically the hit we already have on the alarm box. Get that done ASAP, okay?"

Amber nodded.

"Next, we need to find out about his sister. You found social media references to her death, find out when, how, why? We need to link her to the Franks boys and that night in Covent Garden. Grant, get Heidi in on this and ask her to look into that for us."

Grant nodded in agreement.

"Now, Granty, this is your area of expertise," Winter acknowledged the eight years of Grant's service as a Specialist Firearms Officer, "the armed protection of the other mothers, MacDonald and Whittcock. How do we stand with that?"

Grant sat back in his chair, "Babs Okafor is overseeing protection. I know him really well. He's the best there is. However, the problem with all protection is the Principal, the person being protected. Ironically, when you're dealing with people, it's a variable you could do without. I saw Babs yesterday at Crown Court, he's happy enough that the Whittcocks are on board with the programme, but Helena MacDonald in Kensington has a young-stud gardener, she's mad for his cock, and she wants her privacy. Consequently, her armed protection consists of a couple of our guys outside, all hours, all weathers, covering front and rear. If she would just let one of our guys sit in the utility room, or the hall, actually *in* the house, it would make all the difference. She'd be all sown up nice and tight."

"*Shit!*" DCI Winter swore. "Isla asked for and was given authority by the boss to visit and interview Helena MacDonald. Pagett's with her. We're letting him case the bloody joint."

"When are they attending?" asked Grant.

"Today…" Winter looked down at his watch, "…right now."

# Chapter Fifty-Six

Grant stuck his head in the canteen, scanned the tables, and saw Alex Surtees, the relief area car driver, "Alex," Grant called.

"Morning Skip, keeping busy, how's the bank balance?" Everyone knew the Task Force was putting in the hours, caning the overtime budget. It was a gentle tease.

"Good, thanks, Alex," responded Maddox, "I need a quick favour, actually. Can you get me to Lousten Mews in Kensington, the place that's plotted up with the firearms section? Any time about five minutes ago would be fine."

Surtees was already rising from his seat. "As luck would have it, Skip, I've just completed my rostered refreshment break and am now available for police work. Your carriage awaits. Mind you, if we get a shout, you'll have to come along for the ride." Grant smiled following Alex and his young colleague, the car's radio operator, downstairs to the station yard.

\* \* \*

As the patrol car travelled London's streets, the driver and operator's heads swivelled left and right continuously, constantly on the lookout, while personal radios chirped and the vehicle's main set squawked, despatching calls, giving circulations, and passing messages.

Not for the first time, Grant felt a sentimental longing for the uniform response days of his earlier career. The CID was a wonderful role, no question, and the team with which he was surrounded was second to none, but the role enjoyed by Alex Surtees and his operator had an immediacy, a simplicity to it, a much more cut-and-dry world. An incident unfolded, you responded, you dealt with it. You made a report, and it was over. Weeks, sometimes months later, you may end up in a court case, but the grinding, repetitive desk-bound toil of a major investigation wasn't known. Grant's reflections were disturbed as the car halted, and Alex's broad Geordie accent declared, "There you go, Sir, nine and a half bob on the meter, I hope you enjoyed the journey, all tips accepted."

The Detective Sergeant laughed, "Here's a tip for you, Alex, never eat yellow snow." Grant noted mild chuckles at his terrible joke as he exited. "Thanks, chaps, appreciate it. I don't suppose..." Grant never finished.

"Yesssss, give us a shout on your personal radio when you need a taxi ride back. Glad to be of service." Alex gunned the powerful engine, the rear wheels span, and the area car sped away.

* * *

Lousten Mews was an eighteenth-century, narrow cul-de-sac, perhaps seventy yards long, its cobbled road surface lined with bright, well-maintained, white-washed houses, most of which sported a large potted plant outside its front door. There were no cars parked along its length, no bustling pedestrian traffic, no suicidal weaving cyclists or zooming, high-revving courier motorbikes. None of the normal noises of The Capital intruded into the mews. Grant looked along the roadway, hidden, tidy, and clean, yet it was in the heart of a city of nearly ten million souls. He shook his head slowly as he progressed into Lousten Mews, gazing at the privilege only real money could buy.

He saw the painfully young looking officer ahead on the right, by the front door to number eight, he was partially hidden by a miniature tree in a bright blue pot. His G36 carbine, which was phasing out the MP5 of Grant's era, was slung across his chest in a low-ready position, right index finger stretched across the trigger guard in the approved manner. Grant smiled as he approached very slowly, pulling his warrant card from his pocket, holding it up for inspection.

"Detective Sergeant Maddox, how's it going? On time and a half, I hope?" Maddox greeted him.

The officer examined the warrant card, not immediately responding to Grant's good humour. Once satisfied, his face broke into a smile. "Maddox? Are you Sergeant Okafor's old buddy by any chance?"

Grant nodded, "I'm afraid so. We go so far back you weren't even a glimmer in your old man's ball bag. When we were on firearms together we were issued with flintlocks."

The armed officer laughed at the joke. "What can I do for you, Skip?"

Unaware if he was being observed or overheard by Pagett, Grant remained as casual as he could. "I'm on the Investigating Task Force. I haven't had a chance until today to visit Ms MacDonald, I wanted to meet her and check out the lie of the land. What's she like? Do you get cups of tea and the odd biscuit?"

The officer laughed, leaning forward, looking left and right conspiratorially, lowering his voice to answer. "I can tell you there's a damn sight more on offer if you want it," he winked. "There's a young guy, Shane, mid-twenties, good-looking-and-knows-it type; he's in and out of here pumping up the old lady's tires on a regular basis but as soon as he hops it, she's at the door here, all smiles, huge cleavage, and heavy breathing. It's on a plate for the taking, I'd say."

"Is Shane in there at the moment?" asked Grant, wanting to move away from discussing Helena MacDonald's sexual predilections.

"No, Skip...but guess who is? Only Isla bloody Baxter and her camera bloke. Doing an interview, went in about ten, maybe fifteen minutes ago."

"Okay, thanks for that. I'll ring the bell and introduce myself."

The young officer, still smiling, pressed his radio transmit button and spoke. "Two oh eight, two oh eight from six seven one, receiving?" A crackle of white noise came from the handset. "Two oh eight, two oh eight. Are you there, Matt?" The officer looked to Grant, an expression of grim annoyance on his face. "Radio black spot, Sarge. We're stuck in a narrow, dead end road, surrounded by high, solid, brick buildings, it affects the signal." He tried again. "Two oh eight, two oh eight, say something, Matt." He shook his head once more.

The officer's handset crackled. "Are you calling me Tosh? You're signal strength is R1 with loadsa background, go ahead, go ahead." Years of experience with radio traffic allowed Grant to discern the words amongst the distortion a civilian would have no chance to understand.

The young officer, now identified as Tosh, smiled, "There we go, we get there in the end." He pressed the transmit button once more, "I'm receiving Matt, usual radio issues. I've got a DS from the Task Force with me. He's entering the premises at the front door, received?"

The radio crackled; the feint distorted reply was given. "Just about received. Let me know when he leaves. Are the others still inside?"

"Yes, yes. Still inside."

"Received. Thanks, Tosh."

Tosh smiled once more. "Bloke at the back is in the know now, we don't want you getting slotted by accident, do we?"

"No, we bloody don't." Grant extracted his warrant card once more and rang the doorbell to number eight.

# Chapter Fifty-Seven

To Grant's disapproval, Helena MacDonald answered the door in person. True, the outside Protection Officer was present and had checked his identity and reason for attending, but it wasn't beyond imagining that the lone officer could be approached and dealt with very quickly and very quietly, by knife or silenced firearm unknown to his comrade at the rear. A knock at the door, and the Principal was there to be despatched with ease. Grant wished wholeheartedly that Helena would consent to an officer being posted inside her property.

"Ms. MacDonald?" Grant held up his warrant card, "Detective Sergeant Grant Maddox, I'm one of the Task Force officers involved in the…" he paused, wishing he hadn't been about to use the media's headline.

Helena finished his sentence, eliciting an internal wince in the Detective Sergeant. "Dissection Murders?"

Grant shrugged; how could the power of The Press be countered? "I'd really rather not use such an emotive expression."

Helena MacDonald smiled sympathetically, making Grant smile back. In her mid-fifties and without doubt an attractive, mature woman, the front of Helena's skin-tight top plummeted to reveal a cleavage that an Acapulco cliff diver would happily plunge into, while her short skirt, stretched a fraction too-tightly across her hips, exhibited a pair of long and shapely legs.

"Please excuse the intrusion. I understand you have visitors, but may I come in and speak with you?" Helena stood aside in the doorway, requiring him to twist sideways through the threshold, his chest brushing hers.

"Please come in, straight through to the sun-room at the rear, that's where we are." The walls were plastered with photographs, almost exclusively of Helena's dead son, Lynton Fiennes.

The sunroom was well named, wide, high, and bright, containing armchairs, sofas, occasional tables, and the swivelling heads of Isla Baxter and Rob Pagett.

"Hi, guys!" called Grant, fixing his stare on Pagett and looking for an expression that may tell the detective something. "Sorry to interrupt, I've been wanting to meet Ms. MacDonald but struggled to find a minute, it turns out this was the minute."

"Granty!" Isla's face was all smiles, "good to see you. I was starting to think you were avoiding me."

Grant tore his look away from Pagett, who'd maintained a neutral expression and addressed Isla. "Not at all, been doing lots and there's lots to do," he offered, with a non-committal shrug.

"Good, you all know each other. May I offer you a refreshment, Sergeant?" Helena asked, following Grant into the room.

"No thank you Ms. MacDonald, if I may I'll just sit here, quietly and wait while you continue with Ms. Baxter, pretend I'm not here."

"Please, call me Helena. Very well. Where were we, Isla?"

Pagett shouldered his camera as Helena took her seat opposite Isla Baxter. The two women leant in towards each other. Helena straightened her skirt, pulled at her top and shook her hair, satisfied she was composed, she nodded to her interviewer.

"Helena," began Isla Baxter, her voice gentle and encouraging, "tell me about your son, Lynton. What sort of a boy was he?"

The conversation continued for thirty minutes, covering the tragedy of Lynton's death in the crash. She recounted the moment she'd heard the news of the loss, not just of her only child but of all the future potential he'd promised, now gone forever. A viewer would have a heart of stone to not be moved.

Grant watched Pagett carefully, his features visible, the camera seated on the shoulder away from the side Grant was sitting. As Lynton Fiennes, the mild-mannered giant, the soft-spoken gentleman, the sportsman, the super-intelligent, humane, near-adult who was considering a career in life-saving medicine, was described by his mother, Maddox scrutinised Rob Pagett. Was that a twitch of a facial muscle, a sign of contempt unconsciously leaking? Was that a curl of the lip into a sneer, an indication of disdain? Could that flicker of the eyelids signify Pagett's contained and controlled fury at this adulating elegy for the brutal rapist of his twin sister? Grant watched and listened.

"Well, thank you, Helena, thank you so much. I think everyone can see how difficult it's been to speak about Lynton and may I say how much I admire your strength and resolve at this difficult time. Somewhere out there is a madman, he's killed already, you know you may be his target, can you think of any reason at all why that may be so?"

Helena shook her head sadly. "I've wracked my brain, Isla. I've thought of little else since the news about dear Juno broke. I knew her, you know. From our involvement at Franks. I can't imagine why this is happening. Jealousy perhaps? Is someone full of envy and resentment at the perceived privilege of the boys? Is that anger being directed at the boy's mothers for some reason? I don't know. What I do know, Isla, is I'll continue to live my life. As we've discussed, I'm a survivor. I survived the loss of my son; I survived the loss of my husband and I've survived cancer. I have life; I am full of life; I grasp at life. No twisted maggot is going to force me to hide in a corner. That's my attitude. I can be no other way. I can only be me."

"Helena MacDonald, I think that's as good a way as any to conclude. I thank you sincerely." Isla froze for a few seconds and announced. "And cut! Okay, that was great. Thank you so much, Helena."

"Thank *you*. Thank you for the opportunity to speak about my son."

Isla Baxter reached out and lay a hand on Helena's knee. "It was my pleasure. Now you understand that we'll need to edit and cut this interview. The finished documentary couldn't carry every minute. Secondly, the contract we have, which granted such intimate access to the investigation, only permits the transmission of our programme *after* the conclusion of this case and is subject to scrutiny and censorship by the Met Police. You understand all that?"

"Yes, I understand." Helena patted the hand still resting on her knee. "You've been very kind, very understanding."

Grant watched as Pagett, who'd remained silent since the moment Maddox arrived, unplugged leads from the camera and placed it in a rigid, protective carry-case.

Pagett wasn't looking at anyone, intent on his work as Grant spoke, watching for a reaction. "I must say I'm grateful to have been here. I also want to express my sorrow for the passing of your son. He sounds like a wonderful young man, kind, thoughtful and a genuine loss to the world. Any man would be proud to have him as a son, isn't that right, Rob?"

Pagett lifted his head and looked Grant in the eye. "Yes," he answered. "Very proud."

Grant was used to the sneering aspect Pagett saved for him and his colleagues. The detective had long ago assessed Pagett as a man who disliked, even hated police officers, but the expression on the cameraman's face at that moment, the moment he was required to express the sense of pride he'd feel if Lynton Fiennes was *his* son, was of a different magnitude. 'Yes', he'd said, 'very proud'.

Pagett looked as if something very unpleasant you might find on your shoe had been held under his nose. It was there for the blink of an eye before he continued to pack away his equipment. It was enough. Grant knew he'd found his man.

# Chapter Fifty-Eight

H elena MacDonald waved farewell to Isla and Pagett as they settled into their Uber, which was to return them to the Central London office of their production company. Grant stood behind her, watching the car reverse out of the mews. Tosh, still on duty outside, raised a salacious eyebrow in Grant's direction as Helena began to close the door, trapping them alone in the house.

It was with some gratitude for the safety of his career and his marriage that less than five minutes later, the doorbell rang, and the fake-tanned, snake-hipped form of Shane the gardener bounded into the house. Whether Helena was considering jumping on Grant's bones or not, her attention was now wholly directed at the vacuous stud-muffin, thirty years her junior, who insisted on calling Helena 'Kitten.' Even if the will had been there, and it wasn't, Grant couldn't compete.

Helena's back story explained much: a life of wealth and privilege peppered with tragedy and loss. The final straw: her survival from a diagnosis of cancer, which should have carried her away within twelve months. Now, she was enjoying her third year of remission, and how she was enjoying it! Who'd condemn her? She was doing no harm to anyone, and Grant judged her as a kind and charming woman. If she was deluded as to the real nature of her long-dead son, was there anything more understandable than that?

Grant attempted to convince her to allow a Protection Officer to be in the house without success. Helena was helplessly fatalistic, another symptom of her life story. Whatever was going to happen was going to happen, no matter what.

Grant left the mews house with mixed feelings, convinced, if he wasn't before, that Rob Pagett was the so-called Dissection Killer. Grant's arrival must have limited the cameraman's ability to obtain information about the house, Helena's routine, and the armed police protection. That this may have been achieved had to be weighed against the possibility that Pagett, ultra-sensitive to any possible threat, may have perceived Grant's suspicions. Was the testing question of expressing pride in Lynton's life a step too far? Time would tell.

\* \* \*

That evening, Grant, Heidi, Amber, and Paul Winter met in the vacated Borough Commander Office. "Where are we guys?" Winter asked as he poured measures of the golden liquid into polystyrene cups and passed them around.

"It's Pagett," Grant stated with finality before describing the events at Lousten Mews earlier in the day.

Winter nodded, acknowledging his friend's insight. "Okay, it's Pagett. What about *actual* evidence we can present to a court?"

Amber spoke up. "We've a DNA result on the blood trace from the alarm box at Paula Bingley's building, there's no record held on the database, it's a new trace and it doesn't match the six current employees of the alarm company. The seventh, who'd moved on, was located by Sussex Police who took a saliva specimen, we'll get the result in twenty-four hours. If that doesn't match our sample, we can confidently say the DNA in the box is from whoever disabled the system."

"Now *that's* evidence. Well done, Amber," Winter enthused.

Amber, glowing under the DCI's praise, continued. "The company which installed and services Martine Walsingham's alarms has no knowledge of phoning about a service visit, so we can conclude it was prep for the killing."

Winter shrugged. "It makes sense. Phone records?"

Amber nodded. "We're still waiting, but I'm expecting the bogus call was a one-off from a burner phone, which is in a lake somewhere."

"And where are we on getting a DNA sample from Pagett?"

Amber brightened up. "Isla and Pagett are attending the Progress Briefing in the morning. I'll hit them with the old 'whoops, sorry, but I should've taken samples for DNA elimination at the start of the investigation, so I'll take a sample now, please.' insert girly grin here, scenario." There was a smattering of laughter. "Once we get that, and if it matches the alarm box, we have him!"

"We'll have enough to arrest and hold him," cautioned Winter. Putting him forensically at the scene of one nobbled surveillance system is a different thing entirely from proof he scattered dissected bodies from the sunny Bahamas to leafy Surrey to smoky old London."

"I've got something to help there." DI Heidi Yorke, who'd sat in silence so far, opened a folder that sat on her lap.

Winter took another sip of the good stuff, "The floor's yours, Heidi."

"On the forensic front, we had hits for blood in the showers at the Walsingham and Bingley residences. The Juno Jenkin scene had been thoroughly cleaned, the hotel management was keen to get the suite back on the market, likewise the Thompson Villa in the Bahamas has been deep-cleaned and marketed for sale by the executor of their estate. As suspected, the blood at both showers was from the victim...*but* we have found several hairs, short, light brown hairs, from a person who was not Martine Walsingham in her shower trap." Heidi paused to fully enjoy the growing smiles of those around her, everyone picturing Rob Pagett's short brown hair. "This is really significant because unlike the shower in the Bingley apartment, which has a contaminated provenance, we have a statement from housekeeper Mary-Mary Murphy that the *only* person who ever used that shower, from the day it was installed to the day we examined it, was Martine Walsingham herself. The DNA trace of the hair can *only* be from the person who showered there to wash off the blood and bits of the victim."

"Fucking hell!" Grant couldn't hide his excitement. "We're so close now."

Heidi smiled broadly, "We're waiting for the hair samples to be DNA tested, and compared to the alarm box blood hit we already have from Amber's good work, if they're identical, we have the killer's DNA profile."

Winter's voice was insistent. "We *need* Pagett's DNA sample in the morning, Amber, as a matter of urgency."

Amber shrugged. "We can't compel him, Boss, you know that, but I'll do my best."

"I know you will," Winter smiled reassuringly.

"I found Cassandra," said Heidi, the words landing like a hand grenade in their midst. "I found her school," her tone was subdued, "it was a challenge to dig without the risk of alerting Pagett, but I found her school. A very nice, private school for girls only, out in High Wycombe. Dunstan Grange School for Girls has to be seen and believed. It's like a castle; it has turrets!" Grant thought back to the long drive to the Tudor frontage of Frankton Abbey. What was it with schools with turrets?

"Cassandra was a boarding pupil, very bright, IQ in the top 1% of the population. She played piano and violin to concert standard, she was slim, pretty and painfully shy. I spoke with the Head Mistress who was the newly appointed Head of House when Cassandra was there, she knew her. I had to press her, but she admitted it was possible that she might have been bullied. Then I had to hear all about the strict policy the school had regarding bullying and all the safeguards that were in place. It seemed a sensitive issue. Anyway, whatever was happening in Cassandra's life, it came to a head just before her seventeenth birthday. Eighteen years ago, she took her own life."

The room was hushed. "I see." Winter eventually whispered, a flash of pain crossed his face on hearing of the death of so young a girl, it was too close to home and the terrible loss of his own daughter. "I see," he repeated. "There was an investigation?"

Heidi nodded. "The Coroner was being generous, I think, as they do sometimes, an act of kindness to the family, he returned a verdict of misadventure rather than suicide. I have the Coroners Court report here." Heidi took a piece of paper from her file and read slowly, her voice hushed. "The Coroner, Dr. Beechcroft-Jones, said after the verdict, '*There is no doubt that this young lady deliberately ingested the cocktail of alcohol and paracetamol which led to her tragic death. However, a conclusion of suicide can only be reached where there is clear, compelling, and irrefutable evidence that a person has made a voluntary act for the deliberate and conscious purpose of killing themselves. An alternative narrative provides for a verdict of misadventure. Misadventure is the judgement in a case where someone dies as an unintended result of actions which were themselves deliberate. I can find no clear, compelling and irrefutable evidence that it was Cassandra Pagett's intention to die that day. Her actions rather speak of what is colloquially referred to as a cry for help. This court has heard rumours and inferences regarding this young lady's experiences at school. Rumours and inferences do not amount to evidence, however the old adage, where there is smoke, there is fire, presses me to urge the staff at Dunstan Grange Court School to look to their procedures for identifying troubled youngsters and for providing the necessary support for those thus identified. The conclusion of this court is that Cassandra Pagett died as the result of an accident, that there was no real or deliberate intent to end her life. The judgement of this court is therefore one of Misadventure.'* That was about as damning of the school as he could get, given the lack of evidence. The result was her death was a cry for help. Obviously there's no mention of the rape, it was a secret she kept to her grave. It's heartbreaking." Heidi laid the sheet of paper on the desk.

Grant slowly shook his head. "How does Cassandra's suicide, after being bullied at a girls' school and then suffering the attack in Covent Garden. lead to her twin brother butchering the mothers of boys from another school who were killed in an air crash *eighteen years* later? Where's the catalyst, the initiating spark?" He shook his head again. "What's the link? How soon after the assault did Cassandra die?"

"A month after the air crash."

"What school did Rob Pagett attend? Was it Franks?" Amber enquired, hopeful heads turned to Heidi.

"Sorry, no. It would have been a fantastic link, but no. Robert Pagett attended a private boarding school in Dorset, again, no links to Franks in any way."

The detectives fell into silence. Satisfied as to *who*, they still wanted to know *why*. The case was building. They each hoped the answers would be revealed when Pagett was questioned. But first, they needed enough evidence to arrest.

"Right!" DCI Winter announced. "This is where we are then. Firstly, the evidence we have we keep in this room between us. The Task Force of over thirty officers and support staff is now effectively you three working and me watching." There was a round of light laughter. "We keep the DNA hit on the alarm box blood to ourselves, likewise the existence of the hair from Martine Walsingham's shower. I want those samples compared double quick. Grant, can you chase up the final sample from Sussex police of the last alarm engineer? Let's clear the decks. Heidi, see if we can get more on Cassandra. Amber, sort out the cheek swabs from Pagett and Isla Baxter in the morning and Heidi get the analysis prioritised. Grant, are you happy we have our women properly protected?"

Grant nodded. "I can only reiterate that Babs Okafor is the best there is."

"Okay, people," Winter concluded. "We know what we're doing. It's the endgame. Let's get him."

# Chapter Fifty-Nine

The Incident Room was slowly filling for DCI Winter's 9am Progress Briefing. Detectives and support staff drifted through the doors clutching cups of tea and coffee while others crammed bacon sandwiches into eager mouths, ketchup dribbling down greasy chins.

Rob Pagett and Isla Baxter entered the Incident room in good time for the briefing, as usual, Isla seemed in good humour, smiling at the Task Force staff, greeting many by their first names, to the recipients, obvious joy. As usual, Rob Pagett seemed morose and occupied, nodding to several who greeted him but saying nothing. The couple had barely arrived at their table, the camera case barely touching the surface before a smiling, jolly Detective Constable Amber Bennett pounced.

"Morning Isla, morning Rob." Amber dropped a bulging polythene bag down on the table and began opening a second identical one which was in her hand. Giving neither Baxter nor Pagett time to respond, Amber dived into her spiel. "I'm in a world of shit and need you two to dig me out. I was tasked with obtaining cheek swabs from you both at the start of your attachment here. It's something we all have to do, like taking elimination fingerprints well, I got side-tracked, and I thought, as DI Dodds was your liaison officer, he'd done it, and it turns out he hadn't big surprise, uh?" Amber snapped on a rubber glove. "Well, anyway, the DCI asked me yesterday to confirm it had been done, and I had to say no. He wasn't impressed." Amber took the cotton bud sample stick from its sterile container. "I just need two swipes from inside your cheeks and I'm off, it'll be done before the briefing starts, thank you soooo much." Amber gave her best pre-planned girly grin and advanced on Pagett. "Say ah…" Amber stood smiling cheerfully before the cameraman, surrounded by Task Force officers, the cotton-bud a few inches from his face.

Rob Pagett glanced around, looking to Isla and back to Amber, still smiling innocently, and repeated, "Say ah. It doesn't hurt, open wide." Pagett opened his mouth. Amber's insides were water. This was it, the hinge point of the case.

Pagett closed his mouth. "I'm not sure I agree to this. What happens to the record of my sample? This all seems a bit *Big Brother* to me."

Amber kept the smile on her face. "S'ok. At the end of the investigation, if you want your record removed from the database that's your right, *and* if you want you get to go to see the record destroyed in your presence. Bring friends and family, have a picnic, make a day of it if you like. The fact is, Rob, you and Isla have been given access to crime scenes, and we must have a record of your DNA, or the scene could be considered compromised and contaminated when it comes to court." Amber shrugged. "A defense counsel would tear us up for arse paper and *far* more to the point you'll be digging me out of a hole, so pleeese, Rob, help me out." Amber moved the swab-stick closer still to Pagett's mouth, still smiling.

"For God's sake, Rob!" Isla interrupted. "I'll do it first. I never thought you'd be such a pussy."

Pagett grimaced. "It's the principle." His words sounded weak and weaselly; nearby faces were turning to see what the problem was.

"It's to help us catch a multiple murderer, isn't that principle enough?" was Amber's simple reply to Pagett's protestation; she still smiled and again, encouragingly offered up, "Open wide and say ah…" Cornered physically and morally, Pagett opened his mouth. Amber lunged before he could change his mind, swiping the swab repeatedly across the inside of Pagett's cheek.

From a far corner of the Incident Room Grant Maddox was watching inconspicuously, his expression of bored impatience as he waited for the briefing to start never changed. Inside, he was cheering wildly, like a football fan whose team was ahead by a goal as the whistle blew in the F.A. Cup final.

# Chapter Sixty

The Progress Meeting of the previous morning had passed with little incident and apparently little progress, all recent developments known only to the few. Winter had watched with relief as Amber obtained first Pagett's sample, followed by Isla's. Pagett's samples had been fast-tracked for analysis and would be available for comparison in eighteen to twenty-four hours.

Dirty Don Chamberlain cut a forlorn figure at the meeting, desk-less, seat-less, aimless; he'd stood amongst the crowd, and when the obligatory final words were uttered by Winter, 'any questions?' he'd raised a hand and bemoaned his fate, still sifting in the dungeon of the station basement. The room was filled with barely suppressed laughter as Winter had growled, 'keep sifting', and ended the proceedings.

The drama of the DNA swabs and Dirty Don's misery was yesterday's news, today was a new day and Paul Winter was sipping at a mug of hot tea in his office, awaiting the arrival of the Isla Investigates team. A wad of papers was before him listing Isla Baxter's proposed filming and interviewing schedule for the coming days, to be discussed that morning. Following DI Dodds's dramatic departure, DCI Winter took on the role of liaison with Isla Baxter personally. The list contained nothing controversial that could interfere with the ongoing investigative actions, with one glaring, notable exception. Having interviewed Helena MacDonald, Isla Baxter now wished to visit Sandra and Vernon Whittcock at their estate in rural Kent. The Whittcocks, their life turned upside down by the threat of murder and the presence of armed police protection, simply did not wish the further disruption of documentary makers in their world. Winter was delighted; they'd made his refusal to Isla easy; he was not about to hand Pagett the opportunity to engage in a reconnaissance of another potential victim's environment.

\* \* \*

DCI Winter glanced at his watch as he saw Isla Baxter, through the glass wall of his office, she was forty minutes late. He waved her in, Isla settling opposite him as she had done many times.

"On your own today, Isla?" asked Winter.

Isla shrugged, a worried and mystified expression on her face. "It seems that way. Rob was a no-show at the office today."

Winter felt a shudder of concern advance up his spine. "Really? Not well? Hangover, maybe?"

Isla shrugged again. "I phoned him, but the number cut to voicemail straight away, and the Find My Friends App located the phone at his flat. I went there before coming here. I've his spare keys. It's why I'm so late."

"And?" Winter was feeling worse by the second.

"He wasn't there." Isla grimaced, her face a picture of deep concern. "His iPhone was on the hall table; he goes nowhere without it; I'm really worried. It's something that's always been in the back of our minds. Rob and I have spent years upsetting, unmasking, exposing, humiliating, and helping convict dangerous and powerful people all over the world. We've taken precautions, obviously, but it's always been a possibility that someone, somewhere, at some time, may strike at us as vengeance or to stop us from investigating. Paul, I want to report Rob as missing."

\* \* \*

The disappearance of Rob Pagett, publicly at least, had to be taken at face value and with due deference to Isla Baxter's valid concerns. The possibility existed that Pagett, recognising their suspicions, had fled. The fear was fuelled by a few, brief words of warning expressed in the offender profile. *'He may have organised for his escape, perhaps to leave the country or assume a new identity'.*

Paul Winter was riven with self-recriminations. Should he have predicted Pagett's flight when he was pressed to supply a DNA sample? Should he have arrested Pagett on the skinny, circumstantial evidence and then subsequently taken DNA samples? They were still awaiting elimination DNA from one alarm engineer, what if it was *his* blood, not Pagett's that was found? In such circumstances, he'd be immediately released and free to destroy any physical evidence he'd have access to. Robert Pagett could have been lost from prosecution forever.

"Guvnor," Grant said on hearing the news after Isla's departure, "we can beat ourselves up all we like, but the fact is we're constrained by the reality of our limited resources, the demands of evidential procedure, and the law. We haven't got the officers for a surveillance op, not even close, and we don't yet have the evidence to make an arrest. A few tattoos and a few co-incidences. It's not enough. It's that simple."

Paul Winter accepted the words of comfort but could see the case disappearing down a drain only slightly more quickly than his career. "Find the fucker Granty," Paul rallied, "find out where he is *and* increase the protection on MacDonald and the Whittcocks. And I don't care if having plod with a gun interrupts Madam's sex life. I want a bloke *inside* her house. Standing at the bottom of the bed, watching and giving marks out of ten if need be. Got it?"

Grant had huge sympathy for his friend. They'd taken a risk with Pagett. There was often a balance to be struck between striking too soon and risk losing evidence or waiting too long and losing a suspect. It seemed the latter was the case.

\* \* \*

The officers met late on the night of Isla's report of Pagett's disappearance, the day after he had last been seen. Grant had found the vacant office of

258

the Borough Crime Prevention Officer in a far-off corner of the station, and they squeezed into the small space. Winter, Grant, and Amber rubbed knees and shoulders as they waited for Heidi Yorke to join them and cram in. When she did, her expression was a mixture none could read.

"News," she announced. "I had departures checked at local airports. Pagett flew to Schiphol, Amsterdam, just over twenty-four hours ago, last night at 8.45pm from London City Airport with KLM. His car is at the carpark, collecting tickets."

"Shit!" Grant couldn't stop himself. "He was *so* switched on. It seems obvious now, but he gave me a look when I made the comment about having pride in Lynton Fiennes, it just felt like he knew that *I* knew."

"That's not possible, Granty. He doesn't have second sight. We don't know what triggered this, it's more likely being cornered into giving a DNA sample, we had to do that, now we have to carry on, do the analysis and prove he's our man. When we've done that, then we find him, extradite him, we try him and convict him. Okay?" Paul Winters's words were practical and pragmatic.

"Could he still be here?" Amber asked. Three faces turned to her. "If he was so organised, so prepared, so clever, couldn't he have falsified his escape? Is it possible?"

Winter sighed, unsure whether an alerted and elusive Pagett, still moving amongst them, intent on murder, was better or worse than having him disappearing out of the country. "Obviously, we'll check that up rather than just trust a manifest, but we may have to accept he's gone."

The gathered officers left, deflated, to head home and get some sleep, the spectre of failure hanging heavily above them.

# Chapter Sixty-One

Overnight, things had changed. The status of Rob Pagett as prime suspect had been evidentially confirmed. A very bitter, football-sized pill, sweetened by a few granules of sugar.

DCI Winter gathered the Task Force for a mid-morning Special Briefing. To Grants relief Isla Baxter had phoned, leaving a message, apologising for her non-appearance, stating her intention to set up a camp-bed at her production company office and trawl through the numerous files containing the multitude of threats of death and worse which had been directed at her and Pagett over the years, searching for an answer to his disappearance. Her absence made everything easier.

Paul Winter had been briefed by Heidi, Grant, and Amber with developments at 6am that morning. Between them they'd prepared and collated the briefing pack which was about to be circulated to the Task Force, it was time for all Investigating Officers to unite and sing from the same hymn sheet for the remaining duration of the case.

At ten o'clock, Detective Chief Inspector Winter stood before his team. "Ladies and Gents, the first part of the briefing today will be given by DS Grant Maddox, for those who don't know him, he's a *very* famous detective." The audience burst out laughing. "Granty, over to you."

"Ladies and Gents, for reasons which will become abundantly clear, there has been ongoing an investigation within the investigation. This has centred on forensic evidence, which I'm now able to share with you. The exclusion of most of you from that process was unavoidable and absolutely did not reflect in any way upon your abilities or trustworthiness." Grant looked around him. The tired faces, lined from working long hours and unrewarded effort, looked at him, daubed with confusion.

"We've recovered and identified a DNA trace which was found inside the disabled control box for CCTV and alarm systems at Charleroi Mansions, the venue of Paula Bingley's murder. I can now inform you the DNA came from Robert Pagett, Isla Baxter's cameraman." Grant halted. It felt as if all the oxygen in the room had been removed by the sharp intake of breath from all present. Then the office went crazy.

Grant let the throng quieten naturally, perhaps a minute later Grant raised his hand to still the last of the astonished Task Force members. "That's pretty much the only good news, I'm afraid, people, but it is good news: we finally have a very real suspect for these murders. The bad news is that Pagett has flown the nest. Two nights ago he flew from London City Airport to Schiphol, Amsterdam, he travelled on his own passport, a trace on that document shows he took an onward flight yesterday morning to Bogota, the capital of Colombia. The good news is that we have an extradition treaty with Colombia; the bad news is that Pagett has probably planned his escape and may have a false identity to fall back on."

The room was silent. Some took it as a slap to the face, most as a kick in the balls. It was unbelievable. The killer had been so close all along.

"I know, I know, we all know that we deserve better, our victims deserve better, but we deal with what we have. We build our case; we prepare for the day when we get our hands on him. So listen in, this is what we've got."

For the next thirty-five minutes, Grant told the whole story. The reported sexual assault and subsequent suicide of Pagett's twin sister, the tattooed names, the presence of Isla and Pagett in the Bahamas when the Thompsons were murdered. The expertise of Pagett in electronics and sabotage of surveillance and alarm systems. The false alarm company call to Martine's house. Pagett's availability for the crimes committed in Surrey and West London, his presence at Juno Jenkin's suite on the day of her murder. It was all laid out. Finally, Grant waved the briefing notes, which were about to be distributed.

"In the trap of the shower at Martine Walsingham's house, a cubicle spattered with her blood, we have recovered hair samples which did not belong to Martine Walsingham; thanks to information from the housekeeper, we know it can only belong to her killer. We are still waiting on the lab for the results of the DNA sample, which we can then offer for a comparison and match. The sample we recovered is unfortunately forensically problematic due to its location, the presence of water, detergents, etcetera. We fully expect it to confirm Rob Pagett as our *Dissection Killer*. In the meantime, we carry on, and we build our case. DCI Winter has prepared a file for Interpol; when Pagett is found, our evidence needs to be watertight. The appendix of the briefing document lists the actions and the officers assigned. Thank you. DCI Winter wishes to speak with you."

The atmosphere of the room had crashed to earth, the officers shoulders had slumped. Each reflected on their own relationship with Rob Pagett. None had become close to him; he wasn't that sort of a person, but there had been interaction, there had been banter, there had been exchanges of views and experiences. To now discover there had been a viper in their bosom all along was crushing. To a greater or lesser degree each member of the Task Force suffered an overwhelming feeling of humiliation. Paul Winter felt it, too, and it was this he wished to address.

"Ladies and Gentlemen." Winter looked about the Incident Room and tried to catch the eye of many of his team. "Ladies and Gents of this Task Force. I don't know about you, but I'm full of many very strong emotions at this moment. I'm angry, oh boy, am I angry! I would get into some very serious shit with the pink and fluffy brigade if I told you what I wanted to do to Rob fucking Pagett at this moment. However, as angry as I am, I have another feeling, an over-riding sense of betrayal and foolishness. We welcomed that man into our fold, into our club if you like. We shared our thoughts, hopes, and fears with him. We told him our jokes, told him about our families, opened up to him, and he betrayed us. I feel foolish." Winter scanned the room slowly once more. He saw faces fixed on him, some nodding slowly in agreement. "Now I want to say this to you. Do... Not...Feel...Foolish. Absolutely none of what has transpired reflects upon a single person in this room other than me. Every one of you is at the top of your game, you are the best there is and remember the embedding of Isla Baxter and Rob Pagett was something outside of our control, people way above our pay grade made those decisions. So, feel angry, yes. Feel betrayed; yes, we all were. But none of you, and this is an order; none of you is to reproach yourselves in any way or feel foolish about what has transpired. There'll be a media shitstorm for sure, it's inevitable, but that's my job to deal with. You, my team, you carry on with your job. This case still needs to be won in a court, and it's your job to win it. The task to bring that suspect before the court passes out of our hands...for now. I want to thank you all. I'm proud of you all. Please examine the briefing notes; as Granty said, your assignments and actions are listed at the end. Thank you. Carry on."

To DCI Paul Winter's utter astonishment, the gathered officers and support staff slowly began to clap their hands, and the sound increased in volume until the Incident Room walls seemed to vibrate with the volume of applause. Winter smiled an embarrassed smile and rushed to get behind the closed door of his office, desperate to hide his emotional response.

Fifteen minutes later, the Task Force had wearily returned to work. Some continued to seek witnesses, some searching for the source of the Ketamine. Some to CCTV near to or at the approaches of the crime scenes, others cross-referencing statements and known movements of victims and witnesses. A hundred minor tasks, the toil and grind of criminal detection.

\* \* \*

Paul Winter took the lift to brief those upstairs, the faceless ones; he was too tired to take the stairs. He explained everything. To his surprise, the response was not as critical as he'd expected. He recognised it was these senior ranked men and women who'd parachuted Isla Baxter and Rob Pagett into the investigation in the first place. When Heidi had first revealed the escape of their suspect, Paul Winter had sighed and declared, sadly, with no hint of triumphalism, "I can't tell you how relieved I am that my deep reservations about allowing such access are written down are on the record, as was the fact I was over-ruled."

When Winter returned to his office, it was with the framework of an operational stand-down in the planning stage. The suspect had been identified and fled the country, but nothing had been found to the contrary. The necessity for the ongoing and monumentally expensive Task Force needed to be addressed. All overtime was cancelled with immediate effect. Winter had been directed to draw up a staff reduction plan, half the Task Force was to be returned to their home stations, the rest to build a case in preparation for Pagett's discovery and extradition. The crippling expense of twenty-four armed protection of Helena MacDonald and the Whittcocks was to cease, that protection withdrawn and replaced with frequent drive-by visits from local uniformed officers. 'Flying the flag', they called it. DCI Winter could only take the speed with which the senior ranks wished to contract the operation as a vote of no-confidence in how he had managed it. In truth, he was full of self-doubt. Was it possible to describe the hunt for the *Dissection Killer* as anything other than a shambolic failure?

\* \* \*

Grant patted the seated Amber Bennett on the shoulder as she stared at the computer screen. "Okay, Heidi and I are off to see Isla bloody Baxter at her offices. She needs to answer a few questions about her dear friend Rob Pagett. Please, tell me, Amber, please tell me that sitting in the yard is something other than the bright green bogey for us to drive?"

DC Bennett shrugged and smiled. "Sorry, Skip, it's all they had."

# Chapter Sixty-Two

The journey to the *Isla Investigates* offices in the dreadful green car was made mostly in silence. The failures of the case hung heavily over both officers. Grant drew some positives from the experience, the happy and productive relationship with the Surrey Police Detective Inspector who sat beside him for one. The blossoming of Amber Bennett both as a detective and as a friend was another and certainly, something to be relished and prized. The truth was, however, that so much of the case was shrouded in a Satanic darkness. The revelation of the brutal rape and assaults on Cassandra Pagett and her subsequent suicide was heartbreaking. It was no excuse for Rob Pagett's blood-soaked reaction, but that there was a reaction was within human understanding.

The fully conscious dreadfulness of the victims' final minutes and the horrific sight of the dead women's bodies would remain with Grant. The appalling images all police officers sometimes see remain for all time, only requiring the closing of the eyes for the gruesome tableaux of man's inhumanity to flash up, like a photographic slide projected onto a screen. The sight of Juno Jenkin, talented, beautiful, rich, and famous, leaped at him. Small, naked, vulnerable, and desecrated. The expression of terror and shock revealed on her face at the moment of death when her womb, cruelly cut from her body, had been lifted from her features. Her searching hands buried deep into the carved hole of her abdomen as she sought to understand what was happening to her. It was an overused word, but truly, this was horror.

"I guess I'll soon be booted back to leafy Surrey?" Heidi interrupted

Grant's thoughts. "My lot are paying my wages and your lot are reaping the enormous benefits of my presence, they can't let that go on for long can they?"

Grant chuckled. "I guess you're right; money rules, as they say. You'll be a loss to the Task Force. It'll be a shame to lose you." Grant paused. "I'll miss you."

Heidi swallowed hard, she felt it too. "Truth be told," she continued, "I've felt right at home in London, felt at home with the Task Force. The truth is..." she hesitated, "I'd really like to stay."

Grant was surprised, pleasantly so. "Well, talk to Paul." The hope and gladness in his voice undisguised. "Later, of course, when some of the dust has settled. I mean, how difficult could it be to transfer?"

The discussion was interrupted by their arrival at a modern, low-rise office block which proudly displayed the signage *TransWorldMediaProducti ons Ltd,* emblazoned above the entrance. Grant parked The Bogey in the only vacant visitors bay and a minute later he and Heidi were showing their warrant cards to the pretty receptionist, a sign on her desk declared her to be Chardonnay.

"We're here to see Isla Baxter," Grant stated bluntly.

Chardonnay smiled sweetly, "The *Isla Investigates* office is on the second floor, but neither she nor Mr Pagett is in at the moment."

Heidi Yorke leant forward. "When was she last here?"

The receptionist ran a finger along a page of a book, talking to herself as she did so. "Let's see; this is the in/out book, and...she...was...last here ... three days ago."

"Three days!" Grant couldn't hide his surprise.

"That's right. She's in and out a great deal, often abroad, as you'll understand if you know her work. The management team of *TWMP* manage several production companies based here. Tamsin Greystoke oversees Isla Baxter, but she's away on holiday at the moment."

Grant pressed. "Ms. Baxter left a message saying she was going to stay in her office, she was trying to find a reason for Rob Pagett's sudden disappearance." The receptionist's face was as blank as a blank thing on

National Blank Day; she looked from Grant to Heidi and back to Grant, huge false eyelashes fluttering like fruit bats in flight. The lights were definitely on, but no one was in.

"Can we see her office, please?" Heidi interjected. "Now, please."

Ten minutes later, the building maintenance man unlocked the door marked *Isla Investigates.* It was neat, it was tidy, it was empty. The two detectives stood on the threshold, neither entering the room. In the absence of a warrant and fearful that any evidence which lay within could become inadmissible should they enter, they contented themselves with the knowledge that the office contained neither Isla Baxter, with or without a camp bed, nor any sign of Rob Pagett. The maintenance man witnessed their probity.

"We need to turn this place upside down and inside out, but first, we need to find bloody Isla Baxter." Grant shook his head, stymied and irritated, thanking the maintenance man who re-locked the door.

Heidi was already on her phone, calling Isla. "Her phone cuts to voicemail after three rings, Grant. This isn't right at all." Her concern was obvious. They waited at the lift door as the man with the office key descended the staircase. Satisfied they were alone, Heidi voiced a fear and a theory, "Grant, what if we've got the right person, Rob Pagett, but we've made the wrong inference regarding his disappearance? It is possible that our case could overlap something sinister from Isla's past investigations. What if someone or some group has lifted Pagett or worse? What if someone is travelling on his passport, leaving a trail, like breadcrumbs through the forest for us to follow, while Rob Pagett is at the bottom of a lake somewhere. I mean, Bogota…Colombia, only a slight connection to the world's most powerful and violent drug lords." Her voice was full of irony. "And now Isla has disappeared. She left a message saying she was staying in her office, that's all, she could've been coerced, under duress to say that. Rob's disappearance as we closed in on him could have been a coincidence. It is possible, coincidences do happen." Heidi let her words hang.

Grant rubbed his chin at this new idea, this new complication. For a moment, the clean, swift, and clinical nature of uniformed response policing sounded very appealing.

"Oh fuck!" Was all Grant could say, reverting to the Met Police's time-honoured response to everything. "Let's get back to the Incident Room. We need to reassess this."

# Chapter Sixty-Three

Grant needed fuel before he could do anything else, so he decamped to the canteen, leaving Heidi to report to the DCI their findings from the offices of *TransWorldMediaProductions Ltd*. Adding a very liberal portion of HP sauce to his beans on cheese on toast and armed with a knife and fork he was poised to attack his meal when the figure of Dirty Don Chamberlain loomed above him.

"Got a minute, Skip?" he asked, slumping into the chair opposite before Grant could answer.

"Sure," Grant replied, "I'm not doing anything." He stared at the cooling food before him and raised his eyebrows sarcastically.

"Good!" offered Don, seemingly oblivious. "I've got something for you." Grant gave up, lowered his cutlery, and turned his attention to the detective. "You know I've been tasked with weeding timed-out documents."

"Sifting in the dungeon," Grant corrected, "a punishment for drugging a Detective Inspector and inducing a hard-on which lasted three days."

"*Allegedly*, Skip, allegedly." Don delivered his words earnestly.

"Oh, there's no criticism intended, Don, honestly. It's just at my age, I'm really interested in what could give *me* a boner for three days. Any suggestions?"

Don shook his head, intent on delivering his news. "I've found something, Skip, I really have." Grant had to admit that for all his faults and personality defects, Dirty Don was capable of flashes of investigative competence, it was what had saved him several times from Winter's Wrath. Grant relented.

"Okay, I'm sorry. What have you got?"

Don dropped an index card on the tabletop. "We still keep a lot of card files on subjects coming to notice, anything which may be considered significant, of interest, or of potential future use. The cards, as paper records aren't subject to the Data Protection Act, not yet anyway, it's a loophole that'll be closed eventually, anyway a lot of stuff is kept and labelled, *'Do Not Weed'*. It's a way for us to keep records which perhaps should be available on a Freedom of Information request but aren't."

"I get all that. What's this then?" asked Grant, nodding to the card, which had an old black and white photo in the corner and had been amended with several hand-written notes down the side. Each dated, each note in a different hand, with a different pen.

"Look at the picture, Skipper. It's a youngster who came to light for a minor theft, shoplifting sweets, there's some notes about him from the Arresting Officer and some more from the Cautioning Officer. It's exactly the sort of record we're weeding out for shredding. Actually it should've gone years ago but slipped through, someone not sifting meticulously, not like *I've* been doing." Don couldn't resist a bit of self-aggrandisement. "Anyway, one minor offence, no repeats. I was about to bin it when I saw the picture and remembered the bloke you chased and lost."

More interested now, Grant turned the card towards him and stared down at the face on the photo. He was very young, a tiny boy, a South Asian. The top half of the picture was the back wall, the subject was really small, his face appearing to peak up from the bottom edge of the photo, it was apparent the officer taking the picture had neglected to wind the stool seat up to a suitable height. Grant stared intently at the dark-skinned face, short, neatly cut hair. His eyes stared fearfully forward to the camera. His eyes! *His eyes!* Looking at Grant from the index card was the cross-eyed face of Anil Butt.

"I thought it might help." Don shrugged. "So I brought him in."

"*You brought him in!*" Grant was open-mouthed. "You brought him in? He's here?" Maddox was incredulous.

"Well, yeah. In the interview room." Don shrugged again. "He was still living at the address shown on the card with his parents. Anyway, I thought, strike while the iron's hot, so I went to his house for a chat." Dirty Don chuckled, shaking his head at the memory. "He's such a pussy, Skip, easy meat, he readily admitted to being Paula's dealer, so I suggested I could arrest him for her murder, but perhaps we should have a talk first, nice and friendly like. I thought he was going to shit himself inside out but he can't wait to talk, he *wants* to talk all about it. I know it's slightly under The Ways and Means Act, but I thought, what the hell! I did right, didn't I Skip?"

"Don, if you weren't so ugly and perverted, I'd kiss you." Grant paused, the baked beans forgotten, "In fact, I may kiss you anyway," rising from the table and advancing towards Don, his lips puckered.

# Chapter Sixty-Four

It had been the day Anil Butt had dreaded. The knock on his bedroom door, his father staring malevolently around its edge, the words, 'A policeman is here to speak to you.' Spoken with undisguised disgust, dripping with shame and embarrassment, the son who brought nothing but disgrace on the family name. Anil rapidly surveyed his bedroom. There was nothing untoward on view, but opening a few desk drawers, lifting his mattress, and unlocking the under-the-eaves cupboard would easily add up to several years in the small room with a heavy metal door, unsanitary toilet arrangements and bars on the windows. The place he'd spent so much time in fear of.

Anil found the plain-clothed officer seated in the lounge, at least the neighbours wouldn't know the visitor was a policeman. He was self-consciously sipping at a cup of tea while his mother and father sat opposite him in silence. Rarely had a scene screamed of so much discomfort and awkwardness. As he entered the room, the officer carefully placed the best china on the coffee table and stood.

"Anil? Good morning, I'm Detective Donald Chamberlain." Dirty Don offered his warrant card. Anil didn't even glance at it. His heart was trying to get out of his chest, his lungs were close to exploding. The two faces of his parents were scowling at him, their looks as injurious as knives being thrust into his body.

"Yes," was all he could stutter in reply.

Don turned his attention to Mr and Mrs Butt. "I'd really appreciate a few private moments with Anil, please."

Butt Senior scowled some more. "I think my son would prefer us to stay, Officer." Don could see that Anil would prefer having a large pineapple inserted where the sun didn't shine rather than share the next few minutes with his parents.

"I understand Sir, of course I do, however Anil is an adult and I need to speak confidentially. I can probably conclude our business here and now, or if you'd prefer, I can arrange a police van so we can speak privately at the station?" Don had read his audience and played his trump card. The thought of a marked police van pulling up outside their house, in their quiet and respectable street, into which their son would be placed and taken away was beyond comprehension. The officer had thrown them a bone; they snapped it up.

* * *

Anil sat opposite Dirty Don, his knees clamped together, his hands on his lap, a naughty schoolboy, caught with his hands in the tuck-shop till. A picture of misery.

"We know you knew Paula Bingley. Are you going to deny that?" Anil shook his head, his mouth so dry he couldn't speak.

"Good. We also know you supplied her with drugs."

So there it was; it was over. Anil Butt closed his eyes, he could hear the metal door slamming shut, he could smell the disgusting toilet in the corner of his cell. He could picture the gloating eyes of the inmates relishing his skinny, unviolated body and the abuse they were planning to inflict upon it. It was over.

"That's right, isn't it?" Don pressed. Anil nodded slowly once more. Don couldn't believe it, this was easy. Spurred on, he pushed his luck. "If I searched your room, I'd find lots of drugs, wouldn't I?" Anil nodded once more. "Is that a yes, Anil?"

"Yes, sir."

Don had to remind himself of why he was there; this was his best chance to rehabilitate himself into the good graces of the Task Force generally and

273

his hero, Paul Winter, in particular. The sole objective was the solving of a series of gruesome murders, one of which was of a world-famous actress, it was not to knock off a two-bit, back-bedroom drugs supplier.

"You know that Paula Bingley was murdered, don't you?"

"Yes, sir. It wasn't me. I liked Paula. It wasn't me." The next words Anil Butt heard almost made him cry.

"We don't think it was you, Anil. But you understand if I need to do it, I can arrest you in connection with her murder. But Anil, I'm not here about the drugs. I don't care about the drugs. I need your help to catch the man who killed your friend. Can you do that?"

Anil was as bewildered as Don wanted him to be. The policeman said he didn't think he'd killed Paula Bingley but *was* willing to arrest him for doing so. He knew he was a supplier of drugs and even possessed drugs upstairs in his room but expressed a disinterest in pursuing him for that crime. Now, he was asking for help.

"I want to help, sir," seemed to be as good a reply as any.

Don leant forward. "Tell me about Paula Bingley." Anil mirrored the detective's posture and softly told his story. Softly because he was certain, his parents were behind the door, ears pressed to the wood, straining to hear.

Behind the door, ears pressed to the wood, straining to hear, were Mr and Mrs Butt, desperate to catch the details of the activities of their son, which had led to a policeman sipping tea from the best china in their lounge. In the lounge, Don's eyes grew wider and wider as the significance of Anil's story became evident. It was unbelievable.

Ten minutes later, the story finished, Don slumped back in the chair, aghast. "Anil, I want you to come with me; I want you to talk to someone; he's a very famous detective." Don grinned broadly. *He was back in the room!* "I want you to tell him what you've told me. I think we can find a way to forget about the drugs. Will you come voluntarily?" Don stood, his next words uttered a little louder. "I don't want to have to arrest you for murder."

Anil and Don turned suddenly to stare at the door, disturbed by the banging sound coming from behind it. Mr Butt had tried to catch his wife as she'd fainted but had been unable to stop her head from hitting the door handle as she collapsed. Faced with the prospect of explaining to his parents the last sentence uttered by the detective, which they'd both heard loud and clear, Anil Butt jumped at the chance to get away from the house and escape to the safety of the police station.

* * *

Grant sat opposite Anil Butt in silence. He let the silence last an uncomfortable time. It must have seemed an age to the young man when, in fact, it was less than a minute. A minute is a long time to sit looking at someone without communication. The truth was Grant also felt uncomfortable, it was a natural human reticence to stare at a person who through no fault of his own, when he returned the stare, was looking at two places simultaneously. Anil's lazy eye was decidedly pronounced; he felt a wave of pity for the abuse he must have been subjected to during his life.

"Anil, I'm Detective Sergeant Grant Maddox, I'm investigating a series of murders, one of the victims was an associate of yours I believe. A lady who lived at 3F Charleroi Mansions, her name was Paula Bingley. Do you remember her?"

Anil nodded. "Yes. She was a nice lady."

"I'd heard that too. A nice lady. How did you know her?" Grant leant forward. "I want you to know I'm investigating murders; I'm not interested in arresting you for supplying drugs. Do you understand?"

Anil nodded again. "Yes. I sold her drugs."

"Okay, tell me about the last time you saw her." Grant leant forward just a little more, pushing, exerting pressure.

"I knew where she lived. The block of flats. I'd walked her back there once when she felt ill. She was a nice lady; I felt sorry for her. She'd told me some really sad things about her. Her son was killed, she said."

Grant nodded. "That's true, he was."

"In an air crash?" asked Anil.

Grant nodded slowly. "Yes. An air crash."

"Hmmm," responded Anil, deep in thought. He hadn't been sure about such an incredible story and felt a wave of guilt for doubting her. "She always paid me, never asked for credit, always paid top dollar, she was nice. I felt sorry for her."

"I understand. Tell me about the last time you saw her." Grant spoke gently but still pushing, teasing the words from Anil.

"We met at the coffee shop, the Migliorè; she bought a few wraps off me. She didn't look well, worse than normal. When she left, I followed her. From a distance. I just wanted to make sure she got home okay."

"That was kind of you." Grant encouraged. "What day was this? Can you remember?"

"It was Saturday. I remember she's the only person I ever saw at the weekend."

"Carry on. You wanted to see her home safely?"

"Yeh. There's lots of steps up to the flats…lots of steps. That other time, when I helped her home, she needed to hold my arm to get up them. I thought I needed to help her again, but I didn't. I was watching her, and she met someone who helped her. She knew the lady."

"The *lady*?" Grant emphasised the word. "She met a *lady* she knew. Are you sure? A lady?"

Anil nodded. "Yes, I'm sure. She looked a bit like that lady off the television, the one who does the reports."

"What lady off the television, Anil?"

"The investigation lady."

"Do you mean Isla Baxter, the *Isla Investigates* lady? Is that what she looked like?"

Anil nodded. "Yeh. She looked just like her."

# Chapter Sixty-Five

Grant ran out of the room, calling out over his shoulder to Don Chamberlain. "Get it all down in a statement." He bounded up the stairs two, sometimes three, at a time, his mind racing with a barrage of thoughts.

Each victim had let their killer in. Never a sign of forced entry, never a hint of anything other than an open door, a welcome. Isla Baxter was famous, her face known to everyone, who would have refused her approach, her interest? It explained a fundamental issue in the investigation. But why she'd teamed up with Rob Pagett remained a mystery. What *was* apparent was that with her colleague's specialist knowledge, any surveillance equipment could be disabled, leaving Isla a clear run at the victim. The *why* screamed at Grant. Why? The Frank's boys had raped Rob Pagett's twin sister. How or why did he persuade Isla to engage in his warped revenge on the mothers? Why would she agree to that? After all, what was Cassandra Pagett to her?

Grant's mind raced back to his conversation with Isla about the boys from Franks. *'These boys of yours were adults; they knew what they were doing.'* At the time, it was a pointed comment that jarred. *'What do you think they knew they were doing exactly?'* he'd asked. Isla had put his mind at ease, the invective of her words dissipated by generalisation, by the description of an entitled, arrogant class. She'd made a good point, a point which he'd embraced with thanks. *'Don't get misty-eyed about them because they were young and they're dead'.* Isla was right; the natural human foible to think well of the dead was a trap it was easy to fall into, especially if the subjects under consideration were young. There was more, though; what was the link, the connection between Isla, Cassandra, and her brother Rob Pagett? It hit him instantly, exactly as his wife so often said, out of the blue. The single word. *Turrets!*

He swung around on the handrail on the landing, speed walking almost to a jogging point, thoughts surging through his brain. Isla Baxter had evidenced her opinions about privileged boys with her own experience of a single-sex school for the rich and advantaged. *'My parents shipped me off to girls' school as soon as they were able. You should have seen it, like a castle, turrets, towers, just missing a moat and a dungeon.'* It was a throwaway line, a little bit of self-disclosure to prove her point but it was close, so close to something Heidi Yorke had said, *'I found Cassandra'*, she'd said, *'I found her school'*, her words returned. *'Dunstan Grange School for Girls has to be seen to be believed; like a castle, it has turrets!'*

As Grant pushed open the door to the Incident Room, the links fell neatly into place. Isla Baxter *knew* Cassandra Pagett; they were school friends. The connective triangle was complete.

* * *

No one had seen such an expression on Grant Maddox's face before. Every muscle was taut, his jaw set, his eyes staring somewhere into the distance, a picture of concentration and resolve. As he speed-marched towards Paul Winter's office, people practically jumped out of his way; failure to do so ran the risk of being trampled underfoot. Grant pushed open the door and beheld Sergeant Babatunde Okafor seated opposite DCI Paul Winter.

"Granty. What's happened?" The DCI saw from his DS's expression something momentous had occurred.

Babs twisted on his seat, equally concerned, "Are you okay, mate? You look totally stressed out."

"Sit down," Winter invited, "what's happened?" he asked again.

"There's no time Guv. She's out there. It was Isla. Isla did the cutting, did the killing. Pagett cleared the way but it was her, *it was her!*"

The DCI took control. "Sit down, Sergeant." Then, more calmly. "Grant, sit down, please, invest a minute to tell us what's happened; it'll save time in the long run. What are you talking about?"

\* \* \*

Grant sat silently in the front seat of the Armed Response Vehicle, which Babs was directing towards Lousten Mews. Babs was talking as much to calm and distract his friend as anything else. He'd never seen Grant so agitated or resolved.

"I came in to see you, to grab a coffee and a bun. I'd been ordered to pull the armed protection off Helena MacDonald and thought I'd nip in to see you on the way." Grant rewarded Babs with a smile but kept his counsel, too much was hurtling through his mind for small talk, he was somewhere else.

"So it was Isla all the time then?" Babs asked, trying to pull his friend back from wherever it was his thoughts had taken him.

Grant seemed to jerk, a sleeper awakened. "Yes, sorry, Babs, a hundred miles away. Anil Butt, the drug dealer, was the key. I missed him by a flea's bollock the day Paula Bingley was found. That much!" Grant held up his finger and thumb a millimetre apart. "That close! It's infuriating. I can't find the words to describe how mad I am. If I'd spotted him in the coffee shop sooner, if I'd grabbed him before he made it to the taxicab, maybe, just maybe Juno Jenkin would be alive." Grant shook his head.

"Man, you'll go craaaazeeeey if you spend your life full of what if's. You did your best, no one can ask more."

"Anil saw her Babs; he saw Isla bloody Baxter walk into the apartment block to be butchered. *Argh!* Okay, you're right, you're right. Let that go." Grant shook his head as if he was shaking off excessive water, shedding the guilt, casting off the hamstringing effect of self-reproach. "Right, so where are we with the protection, Babs?"

Babs Okafor smiled again, recognising Grant was back.

"That DCI of yours is a pretty decisive guy. He's countermanded the cancellation of protection on his own authority, didn't even make a phone call for approval. I like that in a guvnor."

"He's a good one." agreed Grant.

"So I've got two more guys on route to Kent for the Whittcocks, and I'm going to back up the Mews guys myself, right now, until we organize a proper rota."

"Is everyone updated with the new intel?" asked Maddox.

"That's yes at the Whittcocks, no at Helena's. We've had radio issues at Lousten Mews."

Grant remembered the difficulties young Tosh had previously suffered. "Yes, a radio black spot."

Babs shook his head with frustration. "In this day and age! I tried to call, but they've their personal mobiles turned off when on the post; it's standing orders. I called the house phone at number eight, no reply. Helena is probably getting her ashes hauled by young Shane."

Grant laughed. "Well shagging Shane or not, Helena bloody MacDonald needs to be convinced the threat to her is real; she's got to have an officer inside the house 24/7, no arguments."

"Agreed." Babs turned into the Mews, slowing to allow the black taxi cab to pass, exiting the narrow street, before parking the ARV.

The two sergeants walked toward number eight, spotting the officer half-hidden behind the tree by the door. Grant recognised Tosh from his previous visit.

"Hiya Skipper. Looking bloody awesome as usual." Tosh offered as he beheld the gigantic Babs Okafor.

Babs smiled at the informality, it was something he'd learned at the feet of his mentor, Grant Maddox. As long as everyone knew their place and role, informality didn't weaken a team; it bonded it.

"Sergeant Maddox, isn't it? Hi again." Tosh continued. Grant smiled and nodded.

"Righto Tosh, we've got a change of circumstances; I've been calling you on the radio; did you hear anything at all?" asked Babs.

"Nothing Skip, same old, same old, radios are screwed. What's happened?"

"We're upgrading the protection, there's been developments, it's hard to believe, but the suspect for the 'Dissection Killings' is Isla Baxter, so we're…"

"*Sarge!*" Tosh interrupted, his face blanching. "She's here. Isla Baxter is here. She went through that door less than a minute ago."

Three faces turned simultaneously to look at the door to number eight.

# Chapter Sixty-Six

Grant Maddox took charge and control; Babs Okafor deferred without a thought.

"Babs, you're going to use those size fourteen boots of yours to put that door in, then get on the car radio, get support here. Make the junction there the RVP, I want everyone, especially an ambulance, here ten minutes ago. You, Tosh, this is now an armed containment, let the guy at the rear know, if you have to shout, tie a message to a brick and chuck it over the roof, I don't care. *Tell him!* No one in, no one out. Babs, when we know the cavalry are on the way cover this mews somehow, contain it." Babs nodded. "*Whatever* happens in there, Isla Baxter only leaves here in cuffs, got it?"

The two uniformed armed officers nodded their understanding.

"And a last thing, you've got the G36," Grant pointed to the carbine, hanging from a sling about Tosh's body, "so you can spare me the Glock." Grant moved his finger to point at the automatic pistol holstered at his side. Grant turned his face to Babs, "I'm still authorised, I've kept my blue ticket. You've the authority to issue me that weapon."

Babs Okafor nodded and looked to Tosh. "It's issued, give him the Glock."

Tosh, his head spinning at the course of events, unclipped the retentions on the holster, drew the weapon, and, holding the muzzle, passed it, handgrip first, to Grant. "It's in condition one. A round in the spout racked and ready to go."

Grant accepted the weapon, and years of usage and training conditioned his response. "Condition one, racked and ready. Understood," he echoed, pushing the Glock into the back of his trouser belt. "Babs, kick that door in."

From the moment Tosh had uttered the words 'Sarge!... she's here', to the moment the door to number 8 Lousten Mews, flew into the hall, the woodwork around its lock shattered and broken, seventy-eight seconds had elapsed.

\* \* \*

Grant stepped over the ruptured door, shattered by the brute force of the man-mountain, Babs Okafor. One thing was certain, this wouldn't be a covert search to contact operation, most of Kensington must have heard Babs' 'universal key' in operation.

"Isla! Isla Baxter! This is Grant Maddox. Speak to me, Isla." He called out as he advanced into the house.

His mind flew to the last man to have disturbed Isla at her 'work.' Jeffrey Thompson, returning to his Bahamian villa, interrupting the murder of his wife, Margo. He'd had his throat cut for his trouble. The image was enough, Grant reached behind, took the Glock 17 from his belt, gripping it two handed, level with his chin, the barrel pointing vertically upwards in a high ready position.

Ahead, to the left, was the corner of an open door, he moved away from it to the right, creating distance, edging forward slowly, looking into the widening space, opening the angle, slicing the cake as the tactical manoeuvre was called. As he drew level with the open door, he saw the expanse of the room revealed, bit by bit. He held his breath as he saw the figures a few yards away.

\* \* \*

Helena MacDonald was seated in a high-backed chair facing Grant, her arms slumped in her lap, her eyes wide open, staring at Grant as he edged forward, filling the doorway. On the floor, beside the chair, was a syringe, the plunger pushed to its furthest extent. Helena's posture, expression and the hypodermic on the floor told the story, she was pumped full of Ketamine, conscious and aware but unable to move or even speak.

"Helena, I know you're very frightened," he addressed the immobilised figure in the chair, "but it's going to be alright, it's going to be okay. I'm here to help you." Grant's words were met with a snort of derision from Isla Baxter.

She stood behind the high-backed, floral pattern chair, her left hand reaching over its top, grasping Helena's hair in a fierce, vice-like grip, holding her victim's head up, pulling it backwards into the chair's upholstery, exposing the neck. Isla's right hand, reaching around, was holding the scalpel, the tip of its blade pressing into the flesh two inches below Helena's left ear. The threat was obvious; a simple sweep of the hand would slice open Helena MacDonald's throat.

Grant's view of Isla Baxter was obscured by her victim and the chair, his antagonists face peeking out from behind Helena's head, only one eye and part of her face visible. The distance from Grant to Isla was perhaps fourteen feet, far too risky to take a shot at so small a visible target that was so close to a non-combatant. That would be a last resort; talking was always the first.

"Isla, it's over. It's all over. Put the knife down, please, put it down, there's nothing to be gained, this woman has done nothing to you."

Isla glared, her voice tight with emotion. "What do you know, Detective Sergeant Maddox? Nothing, you know nothing. And it's only over when I say so."

Grant took the opportunity to buy time, to buy time for support to arrive, for medical assistance to arrive, to buy time for Helena MacDonald. The more time they talked, the more time there was for a solution to present itself.

"Okay, Isla, you're right; I know nothing, so tell me. Tell me everything."

Isla snorted a laugh once more. "Get me talking. That's the tactic, is it? My dear Granty, don't take me as ignorant or inexperienced. I know a bit about you, what you've seen and done but I'd put my experiences in this world up against yours in a heartbeat. Don't play me like a novice." Isla wriggled the blade at Helena's throat, drawing a bead of blood at its tip. Helena stared ahead, oblivious to the tiny cut, her eyes wide, fear written in them.

"Don't hurt her. She really hasn't done anything to you. Show mercy; you have the power to show mercy. You've all the cards, Isla. Drop the knife, and we'll walk out together."

"I don't think so, Granty. I don't think so." Isla looked away towards a net-covered window as the noise of two-tone sirens penetrated the room. "All your friends are here, Sergeant, but it's just us three at this party."

The sirens cut out, silence returning. He could imagine the Biblical bollocking Babs was giving to whoever had ignored the silent approach order, which would certainly have been mandated for what was now a siege situation.

A deep, booming voice penetrated the room from the direction of the shattered door.

"Grant, you okay? Can you give a sitrep?" Babs Okafor was out of sight but only a few yards away.

Grant didn't take his gaze away from Isla. He spoke softly. "I'm going to answer that officer. I'm going to tell him I'm alright, I'm going to give a sitrep, that's a situation report, is that okay?"

"Go ahead."

Grant took a deep breath and called out to his friend, keeping his eyes on the tableau in front of him. "Babs, I'm good. I'm with Isla Baxter and Helena MacDonald; they're both good too. Miss Baxter is in a position to seriously injure Helena with an edged weapon; I am not, repeat not, in an immediate position to stop her. We're talking about it. Do not enter or disturb us Babs, except on my say so. Understood?"

"That's understood," Babs called back. "Everything you asked for is in place; I'm at the door." Babs's tone changed; his deep, resonating voice softened. "Grant, if you need me, I'm two seconds away."

"Thanks, Babs," Grant called back, stifling the emotion he felt. He nodded towards Isla, his voice calm and quiet once more. "Okay? You understand,

Isla, there's no escaping this."

Isla's answer chilled him.

"You're quite wrong, Grant. I have my escape very well planned."

# Chapter Sixty-Seven

Y ou were going to tell me Isla. Tell me everything I didn't understand. Talk to me; you're a storyteller, that's your job, it's what you do, and you do it better than anyone. So, tell me." Grant kept his voice calm, his tone even; he was pleading but didn't want it to sound that way. He was appealing to Isla's vanity to buy time, but he also needed to know the story that only Isla Baxter or Rob Pagett could ever tell. Pagett was probably a continent away, maybe lost forever; only Isla could ease the burning need shared by every copper, the desperate need to know.

"I know about Cassandra; she was Rob's twin sister; I know she was at school with you, a friend?" Grant paused but received no response. "I know Isla, I know what those bastards did to her in the apartment in Covent Garden, Japhet Gold told his P.E. teacher, who told me. I know what they did, I know that Japhet and Gary Whittcock helped her, and I know she took her own life. Tell me about Cassandra, she was your friend, wasn't she, Isla?"

Grant waited.

It seemed an age before Isla replied; perhaps it was twenty seconds. When she spoke, Grant sighed with relief.

"You're right. I am a storyteller, so I'll tell you the story. I'll tell you for two reasons. The first is so this piece of shit here knows the truth about her precious son. The *'wonderful young man,'* the *'genuine loss to the world.'* Do you remember her saying that, Grant? Do you remember making Rob express the pride he'd feel if Lynton Fiennes was his son? You nearly made him choke. That was clever, you suspected him by then of course and

287

wanted to see a reaction." Isla shook Helena's head violently by her hair as she spat the words. "Well, Mummy, you're going to hear the truth about your wonderful son. That's the first reason I'll talk, and the second, Grant, is so you can tell the truth. Those lovely boys from Frank's, the tragic loss of their young, unfulfilled lives. *Bullshit!* I'll tell you, Grant, if you promise to tell the truth about *them*. Do you promise?" Isla's voice was shaking with barely contained rage, the hand holding the knife at Helena's throat quivering, the bead of blood rolled down the skin, leaving a thin red line on the flesh. "Do you promise?"

"I promise." What else could he say? "Tell me the story, Isla; I'm listening."

\* \* \*

"You've done well. You've learned a lot, so here's the rest."

Grant leant back on the door frame, taking some of the weight off his body, he rested the slide of the automatic pistol against his chin, the muzzle pointing upwards. If he needed to react quickly, he wanted to be as rested as possible for that moment, the better able to respond. He'd no idea how long he'd be here, the uncomfortable truth was, the longer, the better.

"Yes, I knew Cassandra Pagett. A kinder, sweeter, lovelier human being you would struggle to find. She was clever, I mean *genius* clever, and incredibly talented musically. Cassandra played Debussy at a school concert once. It was so beautiful it made me cry. She wasn't finished, she walked away from the piano, picked up the violin and was equally sublime."

"I was told she was brilliant."

"*Much* more than brilliant, but even as I was listening, utterly entranced, I could hear girls around me, sneering and scoffing, planning to 'get her.' That's the reality of the upper classes for you." Isla shook Helena by the hair once more. "It's true, isn't Madam?" Helena stared out, helpless, trapped in a horror movie.

"I befriended Cassandra. I was in the year above, and I tried to protect her from the bullies. I succeeded to a degree, but Cassandra was sensitive and susceptible to the drip, drip, drip of constant, undermining criticism. I spent a week with her at her family holiday cottage during summer term, and that's when I met her twin, Rob. He was totally different from his sister, just as clever, but science and technology were his talents; he was full of surly self-confidence, moody, and brooding. A natural rebel, instinctively anti-authoritarian, I should've really disliked him, but I didn't. Rob Pagett adored his sister, he loved her deeply and purely, he saw all the good in her which he didn't see in himself, and he saw I cared for her and wanted to protect her. He was grateful to me for that. There was never any physical attraction or relationship between Rob and me; there may have been eventually, I'll never know, that was taken away." Isla paused meaningfully. "Rob and I became friends, linked by our love for Cassandra. I need you to remember this, Grant Maddox. This whole story is about Cassandra. You need to understand that."

"I'll remember that," Grant replied. "I'm paying attention. I want to know."

"The school granted an exeat, a free Friday, Saturday, Sunday and Monday. My eighteenth birthday fell on the Saturday, I was about to be an adult, about to legally enjoy all the so-far forbidden fruits. I wanted the day, *my* day, to be a party, to be fun, to be memorable. My parents, as usual, were nowhere to be seen, so I invited Cassandra to join me in my plans. The allowance from my parents back then would make your eyes water even today, so I could afford a room in a good hotel in London, I packed a party dress and killer heels and Cassandra did the same. She was nearly seventeen, innocent and inexperienced, I decided I was old enough and wise enough to show her a good time, take her mind away from the hell visited on her on a daily basis. Do you know the expression, Grant, the road to hell is…"

"…paved with good intentions." Grant interrupted, "It's true, far too often."

"Yes, it is. Far too often. We looked wonderful, Grant, and felt even better. Young, pretty, and glamourous. We enjoyed lots of cocktails in the hotel bar and, at midnight, climbed into a taxi, both already wobbly, and asked the driver to take us to a club, any club, a great club, a happening club. We'd no idea you see, we were young and foolish and vulnerable but didn't know it. *I* didn't know it." Isla paused. "When you're young, you think you know everything, you think that…" her voice trailed away.

Grant tried to see her face, so much of it still obscured by Helena. Isla was remembering, wishing she could have made other decisions, wishing things had turned out differently.

Isla re-gathered herself. "In the club we danced, we drank more cocktails, we flirted with boys. It was huge fun. A good looking guy hooked up with us, he bought us some drinks and brought his friend over too. The first was called Garson, his friend was Osian. They were with a group, they said. They had a private booth, they said. Why don't you join us? they said. Why wouldn't we? We were whisked off our feet. There were three other boys in the booth, Chase, Jacob, and a huge, muscle-bound giant of a young man..."

Isla shook Helena's hair violently again, "...and that was your very own monster wasn't it, Helena? Your Lynton! The five boys were fit, good-looking, obviously wealthy, well-spoken, attentive, and good company. We drank more cocktails, not paying a penny, we danced, and we laughed. I looked across and saw Cassandra kissing Jacob; she was enjoying it. Garson started to kiss me, and I enjoyed it too. I felt a little bit woozy soon after. I thought it was the drink; we weren't used to it."

Isla paused again. "It wasn't."

"The drinks were spiked." A statement from Grant, not a question.

"Yes. They'd spiked our drinks." Isla shook Helena violently once more. "Are you listening? This is for you, too. That wasn't very nice of them, was it?" Isla spat the words close to Helena's ear. "Drugging young girls drinks! Not nice!"

Grant needed to distract Isla, her fury was rising and falling like a sudden tide, the scalpel, so close to the skin, a slip and Helena's life blood would jet from her carotid artery like a red fountain.

"It's a despicable thing to do, Isla. The act of a maggot. I understand your anger and the hatred you feel for them. I really do. I have daughters." It was a disclosure, an act of empathy. "Please, tell me the rest."

For the first time, Isla seemed hesitant. She moved slightly; perhaps her position behind the chair was getting uncomfortable.

"This is difficult. I know you think I'm insane. I know you think I'm a monster. I'm neither, I want you to understand." Isla's voice broke. "This is difficult." Grant looked carefully; Isla was crying.

"Isla," he said gently, "are you alright? Isla, put the knife down and come here; please come here, come here to me."

"I think you're a nice man, Grant. Everyone says so, and all my experience with you confirms it." Isla hesitated. "I couldn't have known it would be you, I thought it would be the young one, the one outside." Isla was sobbing by now. "It's difficult. Very difficult. You see, it's all my fault. Cassandra. My fault."

"Isla…"

She cut him off, sniffing loudly, regaining control of herself. The story needed to be told.

"I'm not sure how we got there. To the apartment. I didn't know where we were. There were sofas, there were drinks, there was music playing. I saw the guys snorting cocaine; there was lots of cocaine. I think Cassandra snorted some, I didn't." Isla paused. "It's difficult," she repeated. Her voice became disembodied. "I saw Cassandra start to struggle, her hands were thrashing about, I didn't understand what was going on. The drink, the drugs. I didn't understand. Then I felt the hands on me, over me…in me. Then I understood."

# Chapter Sixty-Eight

Grant was appalled. He'd understood the attack in the Covent Garden apartment had been on Cassandra alone. Here was the missing piece from the jigsaw. Isla Baxter was a victim, too.

"I'm going to tell you now. I'm going to tell you as dispassionately as I can, like a reporter. I think as a good man, a husband, and a father to daughters, you can fill in the horror, the breach of trust, the brutality, the theft of innocence, all on your own."

Grant felt the need to say something, to build a bridge of compassion, but also because, as a man, he felt the need to apologise for the actions of his gender. "I didn't know, Isla. I didn't know you were there too. I'm so sorry, I didn't know."

Isla seemed to not hear. She'd put herself into another place to tell her story. She talked, her tone flat, relating the facts without an emotion that might enhance the detail.

"There were three on me. Garson, Osian and Lynton. They stripped me naked. Their hands were all over me, they pushed fingers inside me. You should know, Grant, I was a virgin, a good girl. They slapped me, they slapped my face, they slapped my breasts, they twisted my nipples, they said things like, *'she's loving it. She wants it, look she's gagging for it'*. They made me suck them, they slapped me when I protested. Osian pulled my arms up, straight above my head, and Garson was the first to rape me. He ejaculated on my face. *'There's the money shot'*, he said. He stuck his penis in my mouth. *'Clean it up you bitch'*. The others were laughing, making whooping noises. The room seemed to be spinning, I felt disembodied. Osian raped me next,

292

Garson kept his penis in my mouth, laughing. *'Like a good porno movie,'* he said. Osian bit my breasts as he raped me, chewed my nipple, he made it bleed. It was agonising." Isla stopped.

"You don't have to tell me all the details, Isla. You don't have to torture yourself; you don't have to re-live this," Grant whispered.

"I do," Isla whispered back. "To understand, you need to know it all." Grant recognised it was her right. He remained silent.

"Lynton wanted to try something different, Helena's wonderful boy. He took his turn, he raped me, vaginally, then he sodomised me. Someone, I don't know who, held their hands over my mouth as I screamed. I thought I was being ripped apart. I heard Garson's voice. *'DP her, DP her.'* Do you know what that is, Grant?"

He knew. DP, double penetration. Simultaneous vaginal and anal penetration. "Yes. I know." Grant's quivering voice was barely a whisper.

"I don't even know what they used. Perhaps a bottle, more likely from the injuries, caused some sort of ornament. But as the wonderful young man, the genuine loss to the world that this lady birthed, was ripping my anus apart, someone rammed something deep into my vagina. I thought the world was about to end; the pain was indescribable. I couldn't even scream."

Isla paused again. Her head lowered for a moment.

"Anyway, whatever it was, it brought the fun and games with me to an end."

Isla's voice was, matter of fact, disembodied from the repugnant brutality visited on her. "The blood was pouring out of me, bright red and lots of it. Jacob, who was raping Cassandra along with Chase, shouted that the blood was making a mess in his flat and to get rid of me. Somehow, I dressed. I ended up with a hand towel from somewhere, which I held between my legs. I was marched down some stairs, pushed into the street, and the door closed behind me. I was drunk, I was drugged, I was in terrible pain and I'd left my friend behind with those animals, she was on her own. I didn't know where I was. I thought I was in terrible trouble; I was terrified. I crossed the road, slumped on a step, and hid in the shadow of a doorway." Isla paused. "Do you understand? *I left my friend behind.*"

He *did* understand. As an ex-marine, he understood very well the sacred pact made between friends and comrades: no one gets left behind, you'd die first. He understood her anguish very well.

"I don't know how much later it was, a few seconds, a few minutes perhaps, the drugs and drink distorted time. Jacob's twin, Japhet, with Gary Whittcock, appeared and went to the apartment block door. They stood together in the shadow, they hugged, they kissed each other. I saw them laugh. Japhet opened the door, and they went inside. Later they came out with Cassandra, Gary had his arm around her shoulder, she was crying. Japhet was shaking his head all the while, looking left and right, pacing back and forth, I could hear him, he kept saying, *'fuck! fuck! fuck!'* over and over. I wanted to move; I wanted to call out. I couldn't. I don't know what it was they gave me, what drugs to spike our drinks. I was immobile. A taxi stopped and Cassandra got in, they paid the driver and it left." Isla rested. The telling was exhausting. Grant resisted the urge to speak, fearful of impeding the flow of words.

"I can't remember the exact details, the exact words. Gary and Japhet argued. They got really angry with each other. Gary wanted to call the police I think. Japhet wouldn't allow his brother to get in trouble. Japhet won. No one did anything." Isla sounded exhausted, and she sighed deeply. "Ooooh, that was difficult." A new, deliberate lightness in her voice.

"Thank you for telling me. It took courage." Grant had never been more sincere. "It's horrific."

"*That* horror ended. *The* horror didn't, Granty." Isla's tone was now almost chirpy, matter of fact. "I ended up in hospital of course but said nothing, I couldn't, the shame you see. I'd extensive internal injuries, so extensive I had to undergo a hysterectomy. Sadly, as can happen sometimes, that didn't go as well as hoped. It was a combination of the original injury, the hysterectomy, and plain bad luck. I was eighteen and condemned to a life with CRPS. That's Complex Regional Pain Syndrome or Chronic Pain Syndrome. The bottom line is, I'm in constant, excruciating pain. Right now, Granty, even as I stand here, talking with you, I'm in terrible pain. I've been unable to enjoy any sort of sex life, I've been denied the possibility of ever having children. I have no relief from my condition except for the one thing I discovered by accident. Ketamine, Grant! I found that an injection of Ketamine takes the pain away, unfortunately it leaves me paralysed for the duration of its effect. It's some choice, isn't it, paralysis or agony? What would you choose, Granty?"

A memory leapt to his mind. "I saw you once, saw you taking pills. For the pain? You blamed back ache, but it was this syndrome, wasn't it?" Isla shrugged dismissively. "I don't know what to say to you, Isla. I'm disgusted by what happened to you."

"Oh, it's worse, my friend, much worse. Do you think the pain inside me, in here, the physical pain, is the worst? No, that's nothing. *Nothing!* I once had a friend Grant, Cassandra Pagett. A beautiful, kind human being. She trusted me, and I led her into a snake pit. She relied on me, and I betrayed her. I abandoned her. I left her with five wild animals. They raped her, they sodomised her, they beat her, violated her in every way, they even pissed on her. Can you believe that? They showed their contempt for a beautiful human being by urinating on her like a dog cocking its leg up a lamppost. They wanted to live a porn film, like the ones they watched on their under-the-counter videos and whacked off to every day. They wanted to live a fantasy, and, in their arrogance, their sense of entitlement turned Cassandra and me into objects to be used to fulfill that. They de-humanised us."

Maddox saw the truth of it, every single word. The Franks rugby sevens were a disgrace to mankind. He hated them, too.

# Chapter Sixty-Nine

"I only saw her once more, between my trips to hospital. She told me everything that happened to her as if she was talking about someone else; they broke her mind, you see. Cassandra took her own life. I carry that. I think eventually, together, we could've been strong enough to tell the police. But looking back, from this adult perspective, I think it would've been a waste of time. Their families were too wealthy, too influential; they'd have made Cassandra and me look like tramps, like whores, who wanted what happened to us. You, of all people, know how a good lawyer can twist and distort the truth." Isla paused once more, thoughtful. "I'll tell you something strange, shall I?"

"I'll listen to anything you have to say, Isla."

"I sat in the dark doorway opposite the apartment that night. Looking at their door, Cassandra had left by then in the taxi. The street was empty. It was so quiet, otherworldly. Then, a couple walked by, hand in hand, laughing. I wanted to scream at them, *'How can you laugh? Don't you know what happened here?'* I remember pushing the towel hard against myself, between my legs. The step was wet with my blood, and I wished Grant, I wished really, really hard for retribution, for vengeance. My head was woozy, I felt sick, my body was full of cocktails, drugs, and pain, and I wished them dead. I decided to find a way to kill them. Right there and then, I promised myself, and I promised Cassandra, to kill them. Can you imagine what went through my mind later when the plane crashed? Their pictures were all over the papers. I recognised them immediately. It felt like I'd performed witchcraft. It felt as if the power of my thoughts, the righteousness of my cause, had manifested itself into reality." Maddox recalled similar words and wishes confessed to by Watson, sitting in an Italian hotel, waiting for his team to arrive.

"I would've done it, Grant. Especially after Cassandra died. Especially after losing my womb, especially after discovering my whole life would be filled with terrible physical pain. I had nothing, absolutely nothing to lose by finding them, by killing them. The crash saved them from me. It stole some time from their lives, but they were already doomed. Strangely enough, the desire to kill them didn't fade even though they were already dead."

Grant's voice was soft, gentle, as if he was talking to his own child. "I understand. Other people will understand. Come with me, Isla, take the few steps and come to me. You can tell your story so much better than I can. Come with me…please. Let me help you, spare this woman. Show your compassion, your humanity. The humanity that was denied you."

Isla continued without emotion in her voice. "Anyway, that's that. It all became academic, didn't it? The plane span into the ground, and the Frank's Rugby Sevens died in the French dirt. We visited the memorial to them."

"Yes, with DI Dodds."

"That's right. Your poor old Doddy. He didn't see me spit on the memorial stone or Rob creep back to piss on it, childish acts, but a joy nonetheless."

"I get that. Don't think I'm without understanding; what I don't understand is why you're holding a scalpel to the throat of this terrified woman. *You've* been terrified Isla, you've been drugged and helpless, you've been victimised, how can anything worthwhile come from her death, how can the memory of Cassandra be honoured with more blood, an innocent life destroyed? Is that what Cassandra would have wanted?"

"Granty, please don't hit me with the 'what would Jesus do?' angle. The logic that I use is warped and totally unreasonable. Do you think I'm so stupid or so deranged that I don't see that? What you're missing is the word logic *does* apply. No matter how warped and unreasonable, there is a logic. The Frank's sevens were out of reach, but someone had to pay. It started by accident. In the Bahamas." Grant saw Isla adjust her position, she was getting uncomfortable, the need to win time, for delay was uppermost in his thoughts. He looked hard to imagine and pinpoint Isla's outline behind the chair, could he take a disabling shot through it? Would that prevent the sweep of the scalpel or induce its destructive arc? It was an option, but not yet, not while Isla was still talking.

"Rob and I had been successfully working together for years when we went to Nassau to expose corrupt tax exiles; it was by pure chance I found Garson Thompson's parents lived nearby. I went to see his mother, she recognised me of course and welcomed me in. I told her about her son, what a monster he really was, what he did to Cassandra and me. She called me a liar and a whore. *Me! A whore!* I was filled with fury. I *became* fury. I grabbed something in my rage, I don't even know what it was and hit her head. She was on the floor, helpless. It came to me in a flash, the beauty of it, the pure symmetry. I found a good, sharp kitchen knife, stripped her naked, just like her son and his monstrous friends had done to me, and I began to cut and slice. I wanted her womb, wanted her to be as empty and hollow as I was. I wanted the thing which created and protected the animal *she made,* in my hand and I wanted to throw it in her face, to show my revulsion at what she'd done, bringing her foul, vile offspring into the world. Her husband came home before I'd finished. I had no choice. I cut his throat and ran."

Grant saw Isla was breathless, the memory of that watershed moment manifesting itself in a physical reaction.

"I told Rob what I'd done. I was lucky, there was a plane out that afternoon, in less than forty minutes he'd put me on it, I was gone before happy hour. He stayed and finished up the shoot before coming back. I decided I'd enjoyed the experience far too much." Isla chuckled. "It seemed logical to me, someone has to pay for sin, even The Bible tells us that."

Grant was aghast. "Are you really using *The Bible* to justify what you've done? Is that your vindication? *Really?*"

Isla laughed. "No, not really. I'm just teasing. I told you I'd enjoyed the experience far too much to stop. It was liberating in a way no one can ever understand. For the record, Rob Pagett was horrified, totally against it. He wouldn't have anything to do with the killing, but once he realised I wouldn't, *couldn't*, be stopped, he agreed to deal with the alarms and CCTV. He couldn't let me be caught, even though he disapproved. He's a loyal man."

"Is he really in South America? Do you know where he is?" Grant asked with zero expectation of an honest reply.

"Yes. No. Don't know. He has contacts all over the world, as you'd expect, and access to all sorts of travel documentation, as you'd expect. I suspect he's gone forever. So now my work is complete. Nearly." Once more, Helena's head rocked as Isla tugged violently at her hair.

Grant wanted Isla to think rather than act, to be distracted rather than focussed, he reached out, clutching for straws. "You killed Martine Walsingham even though her son Japhet had nothing to do with the attacks, he helped Cassandra get away, and Gary did nothing to anyone. Where's your logic there, Isla?" Grant could feel the climax was at hand, he was desperate, the curtain slipped slightly, enough to let his condemnation show.

Isla snarled, "Japhet may not have raped anyone but his brother did, besides, Japhet put his brother's welfare way above the monstrous crime being committed. *That* condemned Martine." A calm returned to Isla's voice, "As for Gary Whittcock, he was weak, he was afraid, and he was influenced, but he wasn't culpable, I know that. His mother was never on my list."

Grant shook his head, appalled at the cold, clinical assessment he was witnessing. He pleaded, "this has to end, it's enough Isla, it's enough."

"Not quite enough."

Isla Baxter drew the scalpel across Helena's throat, leaving a narrow red line as the blade slit deep into the flesh.

# Chapter Seventy

I t was a perfect *'Condor Moment.'* The expression stolen from a famous old pipe tobacco advertisement where the smoker's mind is momentarily divorced from reality. For the emergency services, the Condor Moment was that instant when *everyone* freezes with shock at the suddenness or enormity of something playing out before them, an unpreventable human reaction. On the police firearms course, it was talked of often.

*"It's going to happen to you; we all freeze with shock; the difference is training makes that moment shorter. We're going to train you, so when it happens, your Condor Moment is less than a heartbeat, we're going to train you to react and react fast, no matter what's happening in front of you."*

Isla Baxter stood aside from the chair, positioned now in full, exposed view. She stood open armed as if inviting a child to be hugged. The scalpel, red and dripping with blood, still gripped tightly in the fingers of her blood-spattered right hand, the policeman's Glock pistol levelled, in an automatic, trained reflex.

Her voice was soft, almost tender. "I won't move if you don't move Grant. I'm no danger to you; as long as you don't move, I won't move." The hint of a tired smile played across her lips.

Grant's brain raced; he'd never thought so quickly or clearly in his life. His assessment of the scene was instant. Helena MacDonald had suffered a catastrophic injury, and her life expectancy without emergency attention was measured in minutes, maybe even seconds. Isla Baxter was still armed and a deadly threat but was making no hostile move either toward Grant or towards Helena, she had even issued a challenge, a threat. Her intent was clear: to prevent medical assistance from reaching Helena in time to save her life.

In the briefest of moments, the tired smile changed, progressing through relief and resignation before finally reaching tranquillity. "Now, do you see my escape plan?"

Grant pulled the trigger, the 9mm bullet entering Isla Baxter as it was aimed, centre body mass.

# Chapter Seventy-One

"*SUPPORT! SUPPORT!*" Grant screamed at the top of his voice. "*MEDIC! MEDIC!*"

Babs Okafor was by him in an instant, weapon drawn, positioned at his friend's shoulder. Isla Baxter was lying on her back, about twelve feet away, her arms spread wide, her head twisting slowly from side to side, a soft groaning sound coming from her mouth. Grant Maddox was fixed in his firing stance, a twist of smoke curled from the barrel of the handgun aimed towards the prostrate woman. The course of events obvious to any observer.

Grant didn't move but explained. "She cut her throat."

In a smooth movement, Babs holstered his pistol, turned towards the hallway, and shouted, his booming voice shaking the ornaments. "*CLEAR! CLEAR! PARAMEDICS ON ME, PARAMEDICS ON ME,*" before rushing towards the seated casualty and clamping a huge hand across the slashed throat of Helena MacDonald.

Grant lowered his arms and moved towards Isla as green-overalled paramedics rushed past him to administer to Helena MacDonald. Isla Baxter's right hand was empty, the scalpel lying on the carpet six feet away. Grant knelt beside her, he saw the small dark hole in the centre of her blouse, the white fabric stained with a tiny smear of blood, the catastrophic damage the bullet had wrought on her internal organs hidden from view.

Isla was aware of Grant's presence, although her eyes looked straight up at the ceiling, as all her victims had done. Her voice was a whisper, the word forced out as part of her last exhalation.

"Sorry."

The room was filling with people now. Paramedics pushed him aside to get at the body on the floor, beginning the futile process of trying to revive Isla Baxter. Grant stood and moved away, standing against the wall, a member of the audience watching the drama. An airway was forced into her throat, her blouse pulled apart, buttons popping and flying around the room, the plastic, manual resuscitation bag squeezed by desperate hands, pushing air into unresponsive lungs, chest compressions, pushing blood through a ruptured heart. Dressings and paper wrappings were scattered about the floor. All the accoutrements to demonstrate the efforts made to save the life of the taker of life.

# Chapter Seventy-Two

Grant sat alone at the table in the canteen, sipping a mug of hot tea. He considered her last word, delivered with such difficulty, her final conscious act. It must carry some significance. *'Sorry.'* Was she sorry for her crimes? He thought not. He reflected on the life of Isla Baxter. Blighted on the cusp of adulthood, twice victimised. Firstly, the victim of the cruel, selfish desires of others, and secondly, victimised by herself, taking personal responsibility for the terrible fate of her friend. It was a brutal and pitiless stroke of fate to smite one so young. Was Isla, as she felt her life ebb away, expressing her regret one last time for what had befallen Cassandra Pagett? He didn't think that was it either.

Isla Baxter had been stricken with the loss of the normal pleasures and hopes of a woman, deprived of the joy of physical love, denied the chance to bear children, permanently blighted with pain and mental anguish. Was it any wonder she sought out the most hazardous places in the world, jabbing at cobras with a stick, provoking the most powerful and the most dangerous? It had been commonplace for Isla Baxter to be accused of having a death wish. On reflection, it seemed likely true.

By chance, Isla's path had crossed with the mother of the instigator of the terrible events in Covent Garden. She'd claimed her initial intention was to reveal the true nature of Garson Thompson to his mother, Grant believed that, why would she lie? That the situation had the potential to spiral out of control was obvious and her life's path was determined on that afternoon.

Isla Baxter did have a plan. There was a logic, however warped and twisted it may seem to those who hadn't suffered as she had. The mothers of the

Frank's rugby sevens couldn't have known what the seeds planted in their wombs would one day become and the price they'd pay for the incubation and delivery of such wickedness.

Isla Baxter had come so close to completing her plan, crossing off each name from her list. Grant clung to the cold comfort of the medics words as Helena MacDonald was wheeled away. 'She'll be okay; we got to her in time.' It should've eased his guilt, affirmed his decision to pull the trigger. It still felt like a failure.

The ripped bodies lay before him, a row of accusations. Couldn't it have been possible to shorten that ghastly lineup? Hadn't the Task Force failed? Hadn't *he* failed? It was a sad truth, but the nature of policing was often to fail. Real life wasn't like Hollywood, where fat, middle-aged officers always caught skinny, young criminals in a foot chase. Where the copper is wounded and gasps in manly pain but still manages to take the shot one-handed and put down the bad guy who is running full pelt fifty feet away, surrounded by innocent people who are never hit. It was bullshit! The books, the television shows, and the movies, where in a flash of inspiration, the detective solves the case and saves the girl and never writes a report, never goes to court or suffers the aftermath of a decision made in a split second, or endures self-doubt and self-recrimination. In fiction, the cop succeeds, smiles, and flashes his perfect teeth.

Grant took another sip of tea. He contemplated a paradox as he glanced down at the DNA report lying on the tabletop. It had been old fashioned 'coppering' which had pointed the finger, arrow straight, at Isla Baxter. It was detectives who questioned, listened, and searched meticulously, people who remembered obscure and minuscule details and who then followed the evidence. Police Officers led Grant Maddox to 8 Lousten Mews. The irony was not lost on him that the forensic report in front of him, linking the DNA from the hair in the shower pipe not to Rob Pagett but to Isla Baxter, had arrived at the Incident Room as her corpse was being zipped into a body bag and carried away. Scientific confirmation of human endeavour and intuition.

Grant was overwhelmingly tired; the adrenalin dump the confrontation with Isla Baxter had initiated had long since gone, leaving only fatigue. As he'd looked down on the dying woman, his bullet robbing her of life and ending her story, he couldn't help but remember another face from long ago, in a different place. The soldier in the trench had seen and recognised Grant's dilemma and was helpless in the face of a decision out of his hands. That un-named, foreign mother's son had a choice: to wait on Grant's verdict, good or bad, or to try and save himself. Grant was thankful to that unknown man, long dead and buried in the cold earth of a bleak island far to the south. Grant had reacted as his enemy had reached for a weapon, in doing so he'd erased the options and decided his own fate. The result, a forgone conclusion but leaving the question Grant had been unable to answer for thirty-three years. *'Am I a murderer?'*

Grant deliberated on how perverse and capricious Fate was. Isla had spoken of the beauty and symmetry of the acts she'd visited on others, mirroring the atrocity and consequences of the acts visited upon her. Fate had inflicted a symmetry of sorts on Grant Maddox. A lifetime ago, on a forgotten, windswept hillside in the Falklands, Grant had deliberately provoked his victim into an act which he could use to justify *his* slaughter. In Lousten Mews, Isla Baxter had provoked her victim into an act that would justify her *own* slaughter.

When Isla Baxter gasped her final word, when she'd said 'sorry', it was for him, an apology to him, for making Grant Maddox her final victim.

* * *

A very young, very fresh-faced uniformed constable entered the canteen, he looked about twelve years old. He saw Grant sitting contemplatively at the table, nursing his tea.

"Heard the news, Sarge?"

Grant shook his head, unwilling to make the effort to speak.

"Just heard the news, the jury came back with a guilty."

Grant was bewildered and looked it.

"Melvin O'Hara, Sarge. Guilty of murder, life imprisonment with a minimum tariff of thirty years to serve. Well done, Sarge." The image of Grace O'Hara's smashed skull flashed into his mind; the wife kicked to death by her husband.

The young officer lifted his elbows and made some strange, twisted shapes with the fingers of his hands, a parody of a gangsta rapper, calling out as he did so, *"You da man!"*

Grant Maddox didn't feel like 'da man'; he felt tired. He would be spending the next six hours at least writing a report, and he now faced an investigation by the Independent Police Complaints Commission, which was likely to last months, deciding whether he was justified in killing Isla Baxter. He wanted to go home. To the arms of his wife. He suddenly remembered, it was a family meal that night, his wife and both daughters at the dinner table, to share lasagna, his favourite. He sighed, reached into his pocket for his phone, and pressed the speed dial.

"Hi, Lyddy. Look, I'm really sorry. Something came up...no, no, nothing serious but I'm going to be late."

# Chapter Seventy-Three

## Three Months Later

D CI Paul Winter was on the telephone, Grant could see him through the glass wall of his office. He seemed to be stressed by something that was being discussed and was gesticulating to emphasise his words even though whoever he was talking to would never know. Detective Inspector Heidi Yorke, recently transferred from Surrey Police to the Met, was at her desk twelve feet away, squinting in concentration at something on her computer screen. Dirty Don Chamberlain was standing at her side, bent over, looking at the screen too. Grant noticed his sideways glance as he looked down, taking a peak as Heidi's blouse gaped slightly, allowing Don a glimpse of cleavage. Detective Constable Amber Bennett was weaving through the other members of the recently and permanently constituted Major Investigation Task Force, heading towards Grant with two cups of coffee in her hands.

Grant glanced down at the e-mail on his screen. The tech boys had been at it and given up trying to trace the convoluted path its originator had chosen to send it along before it pinged up in front of Grant Maddox.

He read it again.

*Hello, Grant. You will understand, of course, why I found it necessary to make a hasty departure from our green and pleasant land. I monitored the news with interest following the closing of the case in which we were so inextricably linked. I wanted to tell you something. As I think you know, I have no great love of authority and minimal respect for the police. Also, as I have nothing to gain and there is no necessity for me to contact you or tell you anything, you may conclude that what I am saying is true.*

*Isla Baxter had a deep regard and respect for you as a man and as an officer of the law. She saw that you were putting the pieces together, that it was only a matter of time before you closed the net. I wonder how much she managed to tell you in the moments before you put a bullet through her heart? Isla was in constant and excruciating pain; she was tired of living that way. It was her intention to end her life when she ended her work. As fate would have it, it was you who fulfilled that final wish for her. So, I say this to you, Sergeant Maddox: it was not your fault; you were simply carried along by the life force, which was Isla Baxter. We were used by her. The difference was I knew it was happening. You did not. Not until the end.*

*I cannot and do not wish you well; it's not in my nature to do so, and although you were trapped into committing the act, it was still you who killed my friend. As for myself, I am well and far, far from your reach. Look, if you wish, you won't find me. The case is closed.*

*Rob Pagett.*

Amber placed the cups on the desk. "Alright, Skip, I've arranged for us to attend the post-mortem in the Spencer case this afternoon at half past two. That okay?"

Grant glanced up and smiled wearily at his partner. "That's fine." He sighed deeply, "It never ends, does it?"

"No, Skip. Never."

# About the Author

Steve Packwood grew up in the industrial Midlands of England, moving south to London to become an officer of the Metropolitan Police in 1984.

He served in many departments and in many capacities until specialising as one of the British Police's very few firearms officers, ultimately qualifying as an Armed Protection Officer. There followed several exciting years safeguarding Prime Ministers, including Margaret Thatcher and Tony Blair, as well as visiting Heads of State.

Steve was invited to join the Royalty Protection Group, initially on Prince Charles's team (now King Charles III) and ultimately with H.M. Queen Elizabeth II at Buckingham Palace, Windsor Castle, and in Scotland, at Balmoral Castle. In 2014, Steve retired from the police relatively sane and reasonably intact after providing *"thirty years of exemplary service."*

Steve has been very happily married to Sue since 2012 and has two daughters from a previous relationship. It was Sue who encouraged him to start writing when he retired, mainly as a creative outlet after so many years of living a disciplined and regimented life but also, he suspects, to keep him from getting under her feet.

Steve and Sue are passionate about the theatre and love to travel, having so far ticked off the Far East and the Indian sub-continent as well as most of Europe. But they take special joy in crossing the pond to visit the USA, which they adore. The couple have relatives in Florida and good friends in New York, so these are the most frequent destinations, but they have plans to explore the rest of the country.

Steve has an adventurous spirit. As a qualified scuba diver, he has a passion for swimming with sharks, much misunderstood creatures he adores. He has also sky-dived, para-glided, abseiled and bungee jumped. Sue keeps a substantial life insurance policy in her back pocket. Steve considers himself amongst the luckiest of people and loves his life, often exclaiming with a satisfied sigh to anyone who will listen, *"Where did it all go so...right!"*

AUTHOR WEBSITE:
  https://www.levelbestbooks.us/steven-packwood.html

www.ingramcontent.com/pod-product-compliance
Lightning Source LLC
Chambersburg PA
CBHW050525110726
47899CB00005B/1599